in a rush

kate canterbary

copyright

This is a work of fiction. Names, characters, places, and incidents are the product of the author's imagination or are used fictitiously, and any resemblance to actual persons, living or dead, business establishments, events, or locales is entirely coincidental.

Copyright © 2025 by Kate Canterbary
All rights reserved. No part of this book may be reproduced, stored in a retrieval system, or transmitted in any forms, or by any means, electronic, mechanical, photocopying, recording or otherwise, without prior written permission of the author.

Trademarked names appear throughout this book. Rather than use a trademark symbol with every occurrence of a trademarked name, names are used in an editorial fashion, with no intention of infringement of the respective owner's trademark(s).

Editing provided by Julia Ganis of Julia Edits.
Editing provided by Erica Russikoff of Erica Edits.
Additional editing provided by Como la Flor Reads and Hawk Eyes Proofing.

For soft girls.

about in a rush

What's better than a revenge date?
A revenge *husband.*

Pro quarterback Ryan Ralston has always known two things. First, he's desperately in love with his best friend Emme Ahlborg. Second–and most importantly–he still has no idea how to tell her.

The marriage pact they made in their senior yearbook was the closest he ever came. Years passed and Emme forgot about their promise. Ryan never did, especially not on his thirtieth birthday.

Emme can't catch a break. Always unlucky in love, her cheating ex is a groomsman in her best friend's wedding—and there's no way she's showing up alone.

Ryan offers her the one thing better than a wedding date: a revenge husband. And he's not just any fake husband but the NFL's brightest star…and in need of serious reputation rehab.

Playing the part of the happy couple comes easy and soon enough, the lines between real and fake blur. They disappear altogether when there's just one bed.

All Ryan has to do is save Emme from her ex, find her step-sister an internship, and get his wife to fall in love with him—or fumble the one thing he's ever wanted:
her heart.

Content notes: incidences and discussion of infidelity, incidence of body shaming, parental estrangement, parental divorce, brief mention of parental death (ALS), chronic illness (main character-- endometriosis).

chapter one
Emme

Today's Learning Objective:
Students will make a splashy exit.

I SHOULD'VE KNOWN WE WOULDN'T HAVE A HAPPY ENDING THE FIRST time he tried to kill me.

I'd laughed it off as an honest mistake while I clutched an oxygen mask to my face with thick, swollen fingers and a tongue that lolled out of my mouth. Laughed as much as anyone held hostage by their immune system could. Yes, he failed to mention his famous corn chowder was loaded with crab. It was an easy mistake when you didn't grow up with an outrageously sensitive shellfish allergy.

Anyway, Teddy Lazarone was a firefighter. He knew what to do when my throat closed and he knew the EMTs who carted me to the hospital well enough to compare fantasy football stats while I wheezed. So I spent the night in the ER with docs marveling at the extent of my allergic response and pulling in every med student in the building to get a look at the way my tongue turned into a gag. Wasn't the first time.

Except it happened two more times in a year, and now—now, standing outside his apartment, a bag of shellfish-free food heavy on my wrist and my key a second from slipping into the lock—I heard "Harder. *Harder.*"

That voice, it belonged to a woman.

I knew without question there was someone on the other side of this door with Teddy. That wasn't TV or porn or anything else. Teddy was inside his open-plan loft apartment and he was in there with a woman. Who wanted it *harder*.

I'd always hated that he positioned the bed so close to the entryway. Everyone who visited was immediately in his bedroom. Seemed like a mistake.

God, so many mistakes.

"Baby, I'll give it to you as hard as you want," he ground out, the thin walls doing nothing to muffle the sounds of mattress springs and slapping skin, "but you're not gonna be able to walk tomorrow."

My cheeks burned like his palm had cracked across either side of my face. He'd said those *exact* words to me, that *exact* way, not four nights ago. He'd called me baby and I'd *loved* it.

I'd felt so special, so chosen. So precious. I'd felt like we had something real. Like the ring I'd found in his drawer last month was meant for me.

But I wasn't special. I'd never been special, not to anyone.

Now I was hot, boiling over with shame and anger, but also cold —*so cold*—and empty. All of this was made worse, if that was even possible, when the bag digging grooves into my wrist broke and my precarious pyramid of foil-covered dishes crashed to the floor. A mess of fried chicken, macaroni and cheese, baked beans, and coleslaw spilled all over my winter boots.

Teddy loved a home-cooked meal after a long stretch at the firehouse. I'd planned to surprise him. An early Valentine's Day since he was scheduled to work this weekend and we wouldn't be together for the holiday. I'd grated all that cheese for the macaroni by hand. I'd spent the whole afternoon telling myself he'd love it. Maybe he'd love it enough to finally propose.

I'd even made a fresh, dill-y chicken soup for myself. The last time I'd cooked a whole meal for him, he'd made a point of telling me I didn't need the same amount of calories he did. He wanted me to start eating a little lighter. My scratch-made popovers and scalloped potatoes were out of this world, but I didn't need that kind of fat and carbs.

And I'd listened to that bullshit. I'd *believed* it.

I couldn't believe how stupid I was.

The snap of his rusty old bedframe against the wall slowed. He grumbled something that I couldn't make out before she asked, "Did you hear that?"

"Neighbors. Don't worry about it." He slapped her ass. It was a sound I'd know anywhere. Up until five minutes ago, I'd believed him when he said he had never once wanted to leave his handprint anywhere until he got ahold of my ass. "Be quiet and let me finish."

Uh, yeah. I was familiar with that one too.

A hard, bitter laugh ripped its way up my throat. I stared down at the beans and macaroni clinging to my boots, the chicken buried under a heap of coleslaw around me. And I couldn't stop laughing.

There were more sounds from inside the apartment and then stomped footsteps. The door banged open, revealing Teddy with a towel clutched to his waist. I saw the snarl coming before he roared, "What the fuck?" His jaw went slack as he blinked at me. He blinked to the side. Toward the bed. Then, much less of a roar. "Oh. Hey. What's up?"

My laughter died as I shook my head. My eyes burned, but I wouldn't let that happen. No crying tonight. Not here. Not in front of him.

But Teddy and I weren't the only ones here.

A pretty face peeked around the doorframe. Dark, sex-tousled hair spilled over her shoulders as she pinned the hem of Teddy's t-shirt to her thighs. "Is everything okay?"

I leveled my coldest, most brutal, most detached stare at Teddy. "Great," I drawled. Panic filled his eyes as I went on severing every emotional tie I had to him with that glare. "But I wouldn't expect Teddy to explain it. He seems to have trouble remembering important details."

I kicked the chicken and beans away from my boots and strolled down the stairs like I couldn't care less.

I was good at acting like I didn't care.

chapter two

Emme

Today's Learning Objective:
Students will weigh the lesser of two terrible options.

MY BEST FRIEND PACED IN FRONT OF ME. "I'M GOING TO KILL HIM."

"Not if I kill him first," Ben, her fiancé, muttered.

I shifted the hot mug in my hands and stared at the marshmallows bobbing on the surface. Cocoa and Kahlúa, Grace's wintertime cure-all. In the summer, it was vodka with cherries and pineapple juice. In more than a decade of friendship, these remedies had never failed. Even in the worst of cases, they always took the edge off just enough to get us through.

But a nasty voice in the back of my head said that much sugar wouldn't do me any favors.

I'd never let myself care what anyone thought about my body before. Not in any significant way. I was short and round. Not plus-sized but *soft*. Depending on the clothes, curvy. I'd always drawn a lot of confidence from my full hips and generous bust. I was built a little different from everyone else and I'd convinced myself that made me special.

I had an exquisite rack and I knew it. I loved the way I looked in V-neck sweaters and wrap dresses. I liked being short and I liked being soft, and I liked that I was more Renaissance cherub than anything else.

Yet somewhere in the past year, I'd chosen to accept Teddy's pointless comments and started hiding in oversized button-downs and loose jeans. I'd allowed him to poke a finger into the squish of my belly and say, "A little less bread, babe."

He'd snatched up every piece of that confidence and replaced it with…soup.

I groaned to myself. I didn't think I could find my way through this one. I couldn't even give myself permission to lift the mug to my mouth.

I didn't remember driving here. Didn't remember much after walking away from Teddy. All I could think about was hearing him through the wall, hearing him break me with every squeak of his bedsprings.

And her face. I couldn't stop seeing her face.

I bet he'd lied to her about me. Called me an unhinged ex. Maybe I was just someone who couldn't take a hint. He wouldn't bother to tell her the truth, just like he hadn't bothered to stop hiding shellfish in everything.

But it wasn't a one-night thing. It wasn't an accident. He'd had the ring in his drawer all this time and—how long had it been going on?

"Did you know?" Grace asked Ben. "Because if you knew, I'm going to kill you too."

He stepped in the path of her pacing, his hands settling on her upper arms. "I know that's not a serious question, but I want to hear you tell me it's not a serious question."

She met his gaze, her chin tipped up in the defiant way Grace met every demand that landed before her. "You never heard anything? No chatter around the firehouse? None of that locker room talk you boys are so fond of?"

His fingers flexed on her arms. "I would've told you and you fuckin' know that, Grace."

I went back to the mug, the dull heat of it warming my fingers and the shape of the bottom digging into my palm. I didn't have the stomach to watch them know each other like this.

Once upon a very delusional time, I'd imagined the four of us together forever. Grace would marry Ben this summer, and Teddy and I would eventually get there too. We'd go on couples trips and take turns hosting parties and holidays. We'd find a place in the little suburban neighborhood where they lived and then Grace and I would get pregnant at the same time. Our kids would be friends and our husbands would argue over sports and everything would be good. We'd be good.

I stopped hearing their conversation and I drifted into a mental abyss where the only thing that existed was the mug, the cocoa, the marshmallows. I was alone here. Alone in this dark, deep nothing. And this was where I'd stay because any minute now, Grace would remember—

"You're going to have to find a new best man."

There it was. The kink my hollow little hope of forever would put in her big day.

"I know he's your friend, but—" She pushed her fingers through her long, dark hair. "He can't be in the wedding."

Ben dropped his hands to his hips. "Grace."

The trouble with being alone was that it often happened when I was with people, right in the thick of things. I was here, I was part of something—but I also wasn't. And right now, with Ben staring at Grace with *you can't be serious* eyes, I wasn't part of this. Not anymore. Not since stumbling in here with my cheese all over my boots and a hiccupy story about a pretty girl with sex hair.

Was the ring for her? It had to be.

Unless there were other women.

If there was one, there could be more than one.

If I let myself think about that, I'd never stop.

Grace mirrored his stance. "There's no way I'm forcing my maid of honor to walk up the aisle with the guy who cheated on her."

"Then they don't walk together. We have plenty of time to figure out the logistics. There's no reason to make any decisions tonight."

She resumed her pacing, tossing out a quickly grumbled, "It's not like we *need* to get married anyway."

"Excuse me? You want to run that by me one more time, sweetheart?"

As Ben stepped into her path once again, I turned my attention back to the cocoa. The marshmallows were surrendering to the heat and giving up their shape. I understood that in a strange, poorly translated way. I just knew something was happening to me right now, likely something I'd caused because I was the only common denominator in these shit shows, and I didn't know who I'd be when it was all over.

Grace said something but I wasn't listening. Ben sighed like he'd been punched in the stomach. I didn't really need to know what she'd said. It was sure to be ridiculous and dramatic, and probably featured an ultimatum or two. She drew a lot of inspiration from evil queens.

That was Grace's style. She fashioned herself as something of a villain, and though that vibe suited her, she was hardly villainous. She just knew who the fuck she was and couldn't be bothered to care whether anyone had a problem with that.

My style wasn't so clear-cut.

If I knew Grace at all—and I did—I knew she'd burn her entire wedding down if I didn't stop her. She'd do it, she'd have no shred of remorse, and it wouldn't fix a damn thing. I'd still dissolve until I barely recognized myself. I'd still break until all those spots formed thick, leathery scars. But there was no way I was letting her cancel this wedding.

I could pull it together. I could do that. I'd find a way to deal with Teddy over the next few months. I'd put on a smile and get through it for Grace, and—

No—*no*.

The pure wrongness shuddered through me. *I* wasn't the one who had to shrink into the shadows with my scars. *I* didn't have to hide behind my smeared mascara and broken heart. *He* was the one who'd done this. Let him stew in the discomfort he'd created. Let him see me wasting not a minute of my life mourning him, mourning *us*. Let him realize what he'd had and what he'd thrown away. Let *him* suffer.

"Grace, it's fine," I said, my voice dry, splintering over every syllable. "He's a dick. There's no reason to call off your wedding because a guy was a dick. I'm too tired to argue this with you so you just need to agree with me before Ben has a stroke."

She crossed her arms as she studied me. After a moment, she turned to her fiancé and asked, "Why are you friends with a dick?"

Ben, with his brows high and his eyes hopeful for a smooth landing, shrugged. "I don't know. He's saved my life a couple of times, but that's obviously unimportant to this situation."

"Very unimportant," Grace replied.

"Good, good," he murmured, a hand rubbing the back of his neck. "Glad we're clear on that."

She stared at him for a moment, her lips pursed as she weighed the options. I knew she didn't want to call off the wedding. She secretly looked at pics from the day she found her dress all the time. Our friend Shay had offered her family's tulip farm as their wedding venue and Grace wouldn't stop telling people about the farm's weirdly cute features. And she loved Ben a whole lot. Even if it didn't sound like it.

"What are you going to do about this?" Grace asked him.

"I was gonna call him and rip his head off for a few minutes, but I can tell him to stop having my back in burning buildings if you want." Ben held out his hands, shrugged. "I'm good either way."

These two. If I could've laughed, I would've. They needed to get married. They needed their big party and their special day.

And I needed to figure out how to put on a happy face while I melted into nothing, just like one of these marshmallows.

chapter three
Emme

Today's Learning Objective:
Students will take a walk down (naked, oiled) memory lane.

I STAMPED MY BOOTS ON THE MAT, DISLODGING WET SLABS OF SNOW AS I watched the last bus pull away from the school. Bus duty was far superior to putting up with the carpool loop. Even if some of the buses always ran late, I'd never find myself fighting with a minivan's sliding doors or directing traffic out in the middle of the street just to get the line moving.

Still, bus duty days when the cold, damp winter wind seemed to cut right through my coat and drive all the way down into my bones were rough.

Or maybe I was overly sensitive to everything right now. Every chilly day, every traffic jam, every paper cut, every last minor inconvenience made it hard to breathe. Hard to stop myself from pulling the blankets over my head and hiding from the world until it learned to treat me a little better.

It was probably a bit of both.

With frozen fingers, I pulled out my phone and fired off a quick birthday text to my best friend from back home. High school home, as it was. I had a lot of homes. Asking me where I was from was a ride most people didn't survive.

I returned to my classroom but headed straight to the adjoining door leading to Jamie Rouselle's first-grade room. The heat really cranked in there and she always had top-shelf snacks. Another bonus: I didn't have to pretend to be a functional human with her.

I was all right because I had to be all right.

Because it was frowned upon to be an unwashed hermit who ate dry cereal by the handful and watched rom-coms only to sob-scream "Lies!" at the happy endings.

Because I had a job that required me to keep twenty-six second graders entertained for seven hours a day.

Because Grace was never more than one feisty mood away from calling off the wedding. And it didn't matter what kind of emotional shitstorm I was living through, I wasn't about to let her do that or throw away the money I'd spent on that bridesmaid dress.

So, I was all right. I was okay. I was capable of functioning—but only when necessary.

I found Jamie pressing a can of Diet Coke to her forehead. "How long until April break?" she asked, her eyes closed.

"Fifteen school days." I dropped into a seat across from her at the small group reading table and dug into the bag of popcorn waiting there. "Assuming we make it that far."

She opened the Diet Coke with a sigh. "We'll make it."

"Speak for yourself," I said, shoving a fistful of popcorn into my mouth. The manners on me were A-plus. "Your class doesn't try to stage a coup every other day."

"I survived them," she said, "and you will too."

My second graders had been her first graders last year, and they were a handful. I didn't have enough paraprofessionals to support all the learning and developmental needs in my classroom, and the one I did have split her time with another class. The school had been trying to hire more staff all year, but now it was almost the end of March and I'd resigned myself to the situation.

Jamie tipped her chin toward the hall as she ate some popcorn. "Has Grace already left?"

Now that I'd staved off hypothermia, I shook out of my coat. "She's meeting with the photographer before her shift."

"You know," Jamie started, frowning at her Diet Coke, "I want to support this side hustle of hers, but I'm worried things would change between us if I did."

"Do you know what's involved in a full bikini wax? I do—because I used to live with her and listen to her stories." I shook my head. "Don't do it. And not simply because you'd need to hold your butt cheeks open for her to get all the way in there."

"I mean, I've been in stranger positions and with stranger people."

I choked down a laugh. "You don't need to get waxed. Moral support is enough."

Grace had worked as an esthetician all through college. She still picked up shifts after school and over the summers, and she'd added more in the past few months to chip away at the wedding costs. From what I'd gathered, she was very good at her work—always in demand—though I wasn't sure I wanted her ripping hair from my skin. I knew her evil side too well.

My phone buzzed several times on the table. I glanced at the screen while stuffing more popcorn into my mouth.

> Wildcat: thanks
>
> Wildcat: it's good to hear from you
>
> Wildcat: I was thinking about you the other day
>
> Wildcat: any chance you're free for dinner sometime soon?
>
> Wildcat: I'm around this weekend

"If that's Teddy hitting you up again, I'm gonna knock some sense into that boy with my—" Jamie leaned over to look at my screen. "Emmeline, my sweet, my heart, my love, who the hell is *Wildcat*?"

"A friend from high school," I said, laughing. "It's his birthday today."

"And his name is Wildcat?" She laced her fingers together under her chin. "How have you never mentioned this to me?"

I kept laughing. It felt strange. Rusty. Like my body had to teach those muscles how to move again. I guess I hadn't laughed much recently. "He played football at the University of Arizona. They're the Wildcats. I had opinions about him going to Arizona so I passive-aggressively called him Wildcat. That's how he's stored in my phone. His real name is Ryan."

"I'll be honest, I was expecting a more amusing story. Something about growing up in a survivalist cult's wilderness compound. Or maybe shape-shifting. That would've been a lot of fun." She returned to her Diet Coke with a hearty purr. "Tell me about this Ryan fellow."

I grinned at my screen as I shot back a quick response. "He plays football. Quarterback. For the Boston team. Or, New England. Whatever it is."

"You're on a birthday-text basis with a high school friend who went pro?"

I propped my feet up on the small chair beside me. I was *exhausted*. And I was wearing pants with an aggressive waistband-and-button situation that dug into my belly since I was painfully bloated. I should've remembered I was heading into the half of the month that necessitated soft, forgiving fabrics. "Yeah."

"Again, I have to ask—you've never mentioned this to me?"

I motioned to my phone. "This is the most I've heard from him in the past few months. Usually we send birthday texts and maybe a random thing about back home. He has a million things going on. These days, I barely see him once a year."

"But he's been thinking about you."

That could mean anything. He could've heard one of the songs we used to listen to on repeat while sharing earbuds or a line from a movie we'd quoted to death. He could've spotted some tangerines in the grocery store—if he even went to the grocery store for himself anymore. He probably had people for that. Most likely, he could've crossed paths with my current stepdad. Or any of the previous ones.

I reread the messages. I knew Ryan. It meant nothing.

"Is he a friend from high school or a *boy*friend from high school? Are we talking about some kind of first love situation?" she asked.

"Friend," I said. "We were always friends."

Friendship had always been a fragile, fleeting thing for me. Moving a lot as a kid meant I didn't have many lasting connections. Just as soon as I'd get settled and find my place in a social ecosystem, we'd pick up and leave. For a long time, Ryan was my only friend. Only true friend. And the only one who'd lasted after we'd finished high school and moved away from home. There were people I knew, people I'd hang out with, but no one else like Ryan. Not until I met Grace in college. Jamie and a few other teacher friends came along later.

Jamie gave me an assessing glance. "Are you going to meet up with him?"

"Yeah," I said, automatically. I'd really wanted to rot in bed all weekend, but I'd always make time for Ryan. Putting real clothes on and acting like a human for one night wouldn't kill me. "Even in the off-season, his schedule is go-go-go."

"In that case, I'm going to need to conduct a background check." She reached for her phone. "For your well-being but also mine, you're not allowed to mix and mingle with anyone who hasn't been preapproved. This is part of my research-based post-breakup rehabilitation plan so I'll accept no back talk about it. What's this Wildcat's last name?"

"Ralston," I said, going back for the popcorn.

"Ryan...Ralston? Why does that sound familiar?" Her brow wrinkled as she typed. "No, no, no. That can't be—*no*. You didn't casually go to high school with one of the most famous players in pro football, Emme."

She showed me a headline about Ryan's contract extension making him the highest-paid player in the League. I nodded. "Yeah. He's done well for himself."

"I'm never not fascinated by your life, Miss Ahlborg." Jamie huffed out an incredulous laugh before turning back to her screen. "There's also the matter of this."

She enlarged a photo of Ryan, completely naked save for the football loosely held over the juncture between his legs. He'd been part of a special feature in a sports magazine where all the athletes were tastefully nude. When it came out, he'd texted with a link and asked how much shit everyone from high school would give him about it. A lot, we'd agreed.

The hometown loved him, of course, but at their core, they were ballbusters.

"Someone's entire job was rubbing oil on him for this photo," she said. "They went to work one day, were handed a jug of the finest oil in the land, and sent in the direction of this naked, hulking man-beast. And they got paid for it." She shook her head. "I'm in the wrong line of work."

"Honey, they would've fired you the second you dropped to your knees and said, *Yes, Daddy*."

She thrust the screen toward me. "Can you blame me?"

I held a hand up to shield my eyes from the dark whorls of tattoos running over his glistening shoulders, down his arms, over his chest. The impossible indents of his abs and the cuts that bracketed the football. "I don't need the close-up."

"Well, I do." She tipped her head to either side as if she'd be able to sneak a peek behind the football. "Emme, he's *beautiful*. He's like a statue. Michelangelo could not have imagined anything like this. And his hair, my god."

I couldn't argue with any of these points but especially the last. It was unfair that Ryan's dark chestnut hair spent so much time trapped inside a helmet because it was *glorious*. Thick, lustrous, and always falling back into its proper shape no matter how many times he ran his fingers through it. Natural, sun-kissed highlights that a stylist could only dream of replicating.

I'd always teased him about having a secret hair care routine but the annoying truth was that he didn't need to put in any effort. He could wash his hair with bar soap and leave it to air-dry, and he'd still look like he belonged in shampoo commercials.

These days, he had a huge endorsement deal with a high-end hair care brand.

"He did not look like this in high school," she said. "Nature requires balance. Swear to me that he was gangly and awkward."

I opened my photo app and scrolled way, way back in time. "This," I started, "was from junior year. I will accept no criticism of my highlights or the amount of war-paint bronzer caked on my face. I was a child."

I handed her my phone. She lifted her fingers to her lips, tapping lightly as she swiped. "Nature must be getting its balance from somewhere else because it took nothing from him." She paused to *awww* at the screen and then reached over to pinch my cheek. "Weren't you the cutest thing ever? Look at that little face!"

I swatted her away. "You're embarrassing me, Mom!"

Laughing, Jamie said, "Now explain why you're holding two oranges in front of your eyes."

"Probably because my frontal cortex wasn't fully developed and I did ridiculous things just like everyone else at that time in their life?" I shrugged. "I don't know. I was really into those little tangerines. I'd have a whole bag of them in my locker, shove a few in my pockets, and eat them throughout the day. My nails were always orange from the rind."

Jamie hummed to herself. "I'm sure I did weird shit like that in high school too but I can't think of anything other than conducting séances in the bathroom. But that's pretty ordinary." She pointed to the screen and a photo from the sidelines after a game. Ryan had his helmet tucked under one arm, me under the other. A serious, scowling set to his jaw like always. "You two were awfully cozy. Just look at this arm around your shoulder. See the way his forearm is braced high across your chest? It's like he wants to paw at your neck. It's possessive."

It'd never been like that between us. We'd always been close but we were friends, the best of friends. We shared everything. Even sandwiches. There were no secrets between us. Our other friends joked that we spoke a different language when we were together and, all these years later, I thought that was right. We shared a mother tongue spoken in lands where everything was fucked up beyond reason and you just had to survive, to get *through* it, and that was why we fit together so well.

But there was no heat, no romance.

We both dated other people throughout high school. There was never a moment when it seemed like there could be more for us. If I had to choose, I didn't think I would've chosen more. He was the only person I had and I couldn't lose him. It wasn't the sort of thing I'd gamble on.

"And let's not forget about the fact he's soaked in sweat," she went on, "and you don't seem to have any problem with that. You're right up in there. It's like you're letting him mark you with his scent. It's very primal."

"He was not *marking* me," I said. "Where do you come up with this stuff?"

"I'm merely telling you what I'm seeing, love."

"Trust me, we're just friends. That's all it's ever been. I'm sure you'll uncover plenty of red carpet photos of him with supermodels and pop stars getting even cozier. He's made the rounds since being in the League."

"Oh, tell me more." She handed back my phone and returned to her own. "I'm in the mood to decode some more body language but I'm betting there are zero supermodels jumping into his arms while he was dripping with sweat, unlike some people."

I turned all of my attention to picking at my nails. I shouldn't have shown Jamie that photo. It was too hard to explain how it was with me and Ryan. We'd always been…close. You had to be there to understand it. "I'm sure there's something from after a playoff game, down on the field."

"Hmm. Nope. Not seeing any of that. Just your boy squeaky clean with a bunch of copy-and-paste blondes. Can we talk about all this pouting though? Never a smile from this one. Are those the only muscles he doesn't have?"

I shrugged. "He's intense."

She dragged her gaze away from the screen to eye me for a second. "You two must've been peas in a very dark and broody pod."

"We were not." And I wasn't. Moody, perhaps. Serious for no specific reason, yes. Completely unimpressed with the world and everyone in it, always.

"What was high school Emme into? Did you have a subversive Tumblr? Did you fall down the *Star Wars* fandom hole? I bet you could write some top-shelf Reylo filth. Or were you a Paramore girlie who couldn't pull back on the eyeliner to save your life?"

I blew out a breath. "I was a *Les Mis* girlie."

"Well, fuck."

I nodded. "My fanfic handle was Eponine1817."

"Mhmm. Yep. That checks out."

"That's how I met Grace, actually," I said. "We were both wearing *Anne Hathaway Theater Camp* t-shirts at freshman orientation. Spotted each other across the student union. Love at first sight."

Jamie's brow quirked. "I thought you two were roommates."

"We were. Once we convinced our assigned roommates to switch." After a moment, I added, "We played that soundtrack to death that first year. The RA on our floor was so sick of us. I ended up with a minor in French."

She took another sip. "But you weren't broody."

"Nope. Never *broody*."

She gave me a thumbs-up that said she'd let me believe my lies before slapping a hand on the table. "Wait! Wait. Now I remember why his name is so familiar."

When Jamie turned the screen toward me this time, it showed a photo of Ryan on the sidelines of a pro game, sweat pouring down his face. His jaw a hard, severe line. His eyes dark with that ruthless focus of his I knew so well.

But none of that concerned Jamie. No, she enlarged the image and jabbed her finger at the noticeable bulge in his game pants. "I remember when the internet was on fire over this last year."

I plucked the phone from her hand and set it facedown. "I don't think that's what you think it is. There're all kinds of padding and protective thingies in there. It's very complicated. Think about it—they wouldn't be slamming into each other without making sure their downstairs affairs were protected."

"It's like a topographical map."

She tried to grab her phone, but I beat her to it and held it close to my chest. I didn't need another eyeful.

Despite being there to watch Ryan win it all in high school, I didn't like football anymore. I wanted all the best things for my old friend, but I went out of my way to avoid Boston sports talk. But I knew a lot about the game. The players, the positions, the rules. And the equipment. And I knew Jamie's assessment of that topography was probably accurate.

Not that I'd ever tell her. We needed some shred of boundaries around here.

"Honey, I get it," I said. "I'm just saying I don't need to be involved in the *Where's Waldo?* search of Ryan's pants."

She sipped the last of her Diet Coke, her eyes narrowed. Eventually, she set the can down and folded her arms on the table. She tipped her head toward my phone, asking, "Did you tell him you're available?"

I reached for my phone and glanced at his response.

> Wildcat: Saturday? 7? 8?
>
> Wildcat: I'll handle the reservations
>
> Emme: Saturday at 7 works for me
>
> Wildcat: I'll shoot you the details when I have them
>
> Wildcat: can I send a car to pick you up?
>
> Emme: no, I'm good. thanks though

"I did and—"

"Let me see." She snatched my phone away and scanned the messages. After a moment, she handed it back to me. "You're legally required to tell me everything that occurs."

I laughed again and this one didn't feel like such a strain. It felt better. "I already knew that."

"As the coordinator of your post-breakup rehabilitation, I could always come along with you. For support and supervisory purposes. I'd be completely silent. No talk of body oiling or topography. You wouldn't even notice me."

"I think we'd notice a third person at the table, James."

"I'd say nothing. Unless you tried to do something stupid," she added.

I stared at her. "I don't think there's any stupid thing I could do with Ryan. He doesn't function that way."

"Let's just wait and see, shall we?"

chapter four

Emme

Today's Learning Objective:
Students will drown their sorrows in melted cheese.

I wasn't obsessive about being on time though I turned into a vicious little gremlin when I was late. Even worse if I would've been on time if not for other people getting in my way.

Case in point: half the sidewalks in this city being closed for construction or clogged with groups of people trying to figure out their Saturday night plans in the middle of Boylston Street.

By the time I reached the Newbury Street restaurant, I was fifteen minutes late and hot from darting in and out of traffic and elbowing anyone who got in my way.

I could feel the red in my cheeks. It was never pink with me, never a rosy blush, but always beet red like I was a sickly Victorian child with scarlet fever.

I stopped outside the restaurant to fix my hair and fan some cool air under my wintery layers. It was not the most elegant position—hunched over with my coat gaping open while I flapped the front of my sweater like I'd lost a cookie in there—though with my luck, it wasn't surprising to hear a car door slam and then, "Everything okay over there, Muggsy?"

"Shit," I sighed to myself. Straightening, I smoothed a hand down my sweater and over my hair. Still red-faced like I'd lost a slap contest, I turned to find all six feet, three and a half inches of Ryan Ralston staring at me. I barreled toward him, arms wide open. "It's so damn good to see you."

His arms lashed around me and my feet came off the ground, and a light, silly laugh loosed from my chest. It felt good to be with my friend again. It felt like coming home. Even if we were turning into the same people taking up the whole of the sidewalk that I was cursing and elbowing five minutes ago.

"Do I even want to know what you were doing over there?" he asked, his voice deep and quiet in my ear.

"Try to assume the best and ask no questions. The fewer details I disclose, the safer you'll be."

He set me down, his hands pausing on my hips as I regained my footing. He ran a cool, steady glance over me, lingering on my flushed face, and then motioned to the restaurant. "Does this work for you?"

I went back to fanning myself. "I'm good with anything."

"We both know that's rarely the case with you. Did you look at the menu?"

"If it's all the same to you, I'm in the mood to turn my blood volume into pure vodka, so the food is incidental to me."

A low laugh rumbled out of him. He had the best laughs. He wasn't much for smiling, but I could always count on him for a laugh that would fill all the nicks and cuts on my soul.

"I take it we have some catching up to do."

I headed toward the restaurant. "You won't believe the half of it."

He held open the door for me. "Try me."

I LEANED BACK IN THE SUMPTUOUS VELVET CIRCULAR BOOTH AND folded my legs in front of me because my feet didn't reach the floor, saying, "Give me your updates first so I don't feel bad about monopolizing the next hour with my pointless crises and personal dramas."

He stared across the table at me, his dark coffee eyes lighting with amusement. "*Only* the next hour?"

The server returned with our drinks—a beer for Ryan, something with muddled blackberries and herbs and quite a lot of liquor for me—and I held up my glass for a toast. "Happy birthday, old man. Enjoy the time while you have it. I hear it's all downhill after thirty."

A fraction of a smile pulled at the corner of his mouth as our glasses clinked together. His smiles reminded me of torn construction paper, jagged and unpredictable. Even his widest, truest smiles were uneven like that. And so, so rare. "Yeah, well, you'll find out for yourself when we're back here drinking to you in three months."

I took a long sip and returned my glass to the crisp white tablecloth. I was trying to take it slow though the fruit in this drink told my brain I was drinking juice and should chug it. But I didn't want to get sloppy or weepy. We hardly ever got to see each other and I didn't want to blow it by drinking myself silly. And this was a *very* nice place. That was probably why I'd never heard of it until Ryan sent a link to the menu.

"How's the family?" I asked.

Ryan fired a glance at me and then down at the table. Loosely translated: *Everyone is good, things are still hard, it's fine, let's not talk about it.* "Claudia moved home after graduation. She's managing social media content for that outdoor clothing company in Maine. She's very proud of a series of videos she made from the point of view of a moose shopping for winter gear."

"Oh, that's fun," I said, though even in my sorry state, the thought of returning to the coastal New Hampshire town we'd left felt like an unspeakable low. "Ruthie finished law school last spring, right? She's local now?"

He hooked a finger inside the neck of his navy blue sweater, nodding. It looked soft and silky, definitely a cashmere blend. I doubted he knew that. Certainly didn't care what his sweater was made of or that it probably cost more than my monthly rent. "She's a junior associate at a corporate law firm in the Financial District. The hours are rough but she loves it."

"And everyone else? All good?"

There were five Ralston kids. Ryan was right in the middle, surrounded on all sides by sisters. I knew the younger two, Ruthie and Claudia, much better than I did Chloe and Amber.

"Mom's doing well. She's cut back on her midwifery patients but still going strong." He shoved a hand through his hair. "It helps to have Claudia home. Gives her a place to focus her energy since my grandmother doesn't put up with all the hovering. Gramma CeCe calls me every week to read awful things that people have said about me on the internet, so she's great."

"Yes, I would like to be conferenced in for next week's reading, thank you for asking."

"She'd love that." He reached for his menu, cleared his throat. "She asks about you."

He didn't add anything about her asking when I might visit next or why I didn't come home when I only lived about an hour away. He knew the rules the same as I did.

I turned my attention to the menu. It differed slightly from the website, which drove a certain corner of my brain a little bonkers, but there were a few additions that made it worth the inconvenience. "Oh, what do you think about artichoke dip? My friend Grace—you remember Grace—she's from an artichoke family and she got me hooked—"

"What the fuck is an artichoke family?" he asked with a laugh, his brows pinched tight like I was really, really testing his patience.

It was so easy to test his patience.

"You know what I mean." I laced my fingers together on the table and leaned in. "There are certain families that know how to buy and cook and eat artichokes. They do it all the time. It's part of their lifestyle. I am not from an artichoke family and neither are you. I had to be introduced to artichoke culture."

He rested back against the booth, crossed his arms over his broad chest. He stared at me for a moment, his scruffy chin tipped up like he was trying to figure something out. He pushed his sleeves up, exposing the tattoos on his forearms. I'd always wanted to get a closer look, to figure out what all those designs came together to mean. A chunky watch sat on his wrist, the gemstones signifying each hour sparkling back at me.

"Are you fucking with me?" he asked.

"Why would I fuck with you about artichokes?"

"You've fucked with me over less."

"Name one thing," I said.

He held up a fist, unfolded his thumb. "You said you have to pay your rent in cash and deliver it to a bodega in Charlestown."

"That's all true," I said. "And I am ninety-two percent certain the market is the headquarters of the local mob."

"Mmhm." His index finger came next. "The last time I saw you, you told me one of your teacher friends moved to Rhode Island to marry a guy so she could inherit a tulip farm."

"Also true," I cried.

"Tulips bloom for like three weeks a year. You can't run a farm on tulips."

"That's the part you don't believe? That it's a *tulip* farm?"

"The whole thing is a classic Emme fuck-around but the economics of a *tulip* farm puts it over the top. Just like the mafia boss who owns your apartment building."

"You have so little faith in me," I mused.

His middle finger joined the other two. "What about the time you and Grace got arrested in Montreal but you talked your way out of it by playing an old voicemail from one of your stepdads and telling them you had diplomatic immunity?"

I jabbed a finger at him. "That happened! It was the year Jim's team won the Stanley Cup and everyone loved him for the first time in his sad little life."

"But diplomatic immunity?"

"The diplomacy of hockey," I said, full of feigned reverence. "I was an ambassador."

"You were a drunk college kid," he said, laughing.

"And I sorted out the situation. Diplomatically."

Adding his ring finger to the others, he said, "You told me you were anemic and that was why you couldn't stay warm and needed to borrow"—he leveled a pointed stare at me—"*steal* my sweatshirts."

"I *was* anemic." I rubbed my hands together. Ice cold as always. "Probably still am." When he went on staring, I shrugged. "I promise I'm not fucking with you about the artichokes."

"Admit that you like fucking with me."

"Only if you admit that you like it when I do."

"Maybe," he muttered, dropping his hand to his lap. "Get the dip."

"So, I'm already having the worst year of teaching in the history of public education and then Grace moves out in January to live with her fiancé," I said, shoveling a chip through the dip. "And I'm happy for her. I'm happy and I'm not jealous, and I'm not saying these things to sell myself the lie. But I wasn't even alone in the apartment for a week before Ines texts me to say she needs a place to live."

"What happened to the dorms at MIT?"

"Her dad 'forgot' to pay for the spring semester and she lost her room." I pointed another chip at him. "Honestly, I'm shocked she got through three and a half years of college without Gary going broke again."

"It's probably better if you don't ask any questions about where Gary got the money in the first place," he said under his breath. "It might implicate you in a RICO investigation."

"Oh, Gary," I murmured. "When will he ever learn?"

Gary was my first stepfather and my favorite of the bunch. My mom left him when our house in Miami was seized by the federal government and we were escorted off the property. But he was a *really* sweet guy. Far better than the two stepfathers that followed.

"I take it you invited Ines to move in," Ryan said.

"What was I supposed to do? I had an empty room and she's family...ish."

He arched a brow at that but went back to the dip without comment.

"Her schedule is packed with classes and labs and a whole bunch of other stuff, so I never see her. I think I saw her once last week and that was it." I took a sip. "But when she's there—in the middle of the night, I guess—she takes things apart. Microwave, hair dryer, blender. Doorknobs—everything, anything. I'll wake up in the morning and find the appliances in a million pieces on the kitchen floor but Ines is long gone. I demanded she return my hair dryer but I haven't had a smoothie since February. I'm back on Pop-Tarts."

He nudged a few chips toward my side of the platter. "No good deed unpunished."

"Yeah, well, I must've done a whole lot of good because the punishment just keeps coming."

I nodded toward the back of the booth, and Ryan immediately understood as he shuffled around to the bend. We were in the restaurant's most private booth but there was no hiding that my companion was a superstar in this town. The whole place was straining for a glimpse of him, for any clip of conversation they could steal away to tell their friends and coworkers that they'd seen Ryan Ralston out to dinner with some overheated girl who hated her job and had a cheating ex.

When we were at the back of the booth, I continued. "I was seeing this guy and I thought things were going well."

His knee brushed my thigh as he shifted. He glanced down and then back up at me, crossing his arms again. "The firefighter?"

I bobbed my head. The best thing about Ryan was that I could tell him all of my awful and ugly things like this, but they were never awful or ugly to him. They were simply the facts of a story. I couldn't remember a single thing he'd ever held against me. "Yeah, but I went to his place one night thinking we'd be getting engaged soon and found him in bed with someone else."

He winced. "Muggsy."

"My life is a slow-moving tragic comedy."

He shook his head. "How do you do it? How are you able to locate the most worthless guys in every town?"

"It's a gift." I rolled my eyes but Ryan only grimaced like I was missing the point. "But here's the really sad part. He's the best man in Grace's wedding and I'm supposed to be putting everything into making this special for her, but I'm out here white-knuckling it through every damn minute of wedding planning. I'm barely cutting it as a maid of honor and it's because of this trash-bucket boy who had a ring in his drawer that wasn't for me and I can't get away from him for the next few months."

I reached across the table for a glass of water. It was more to keep my hands busy than anything. Ryan's knee pressed into my thigh while he drummed his fingers on his elbow. Again, my attention snagged on the ink peeking out from under his sweater. All of it came after high school. Some toward the end of his college years but mostly since turning pro. If we ever had more time to talk, I'd want to hear about every piece.

"Obviously, I need a revenge date for this wedding," I said, laughing to fend off the bitterness, the hurt that still lingered right beneath the surface. The desire to scream until I lost my voice and the urgent, fiery need to make Teddy regret every single minute of it. I needed him to know how wrong he'd been—about all of it. "I've been working that angle hard, but do you have any idea how difficult it is to find a decent, tolerable human man who is actually, *literally* single and not just a creep on the internet? It's next to impossible. I have been looking and looking for years, Ryan. *Years*. I'm so tired of dating. I'm so tired of putting myself out there and talking and getting to know people, and then watching it come crashing down. It's one dead end after another."

I traced the rim of my glass while Ryan drew in a deep breath. He went on tapping his elbow. It probably hurt. I still didn't understand how he didn't dissolve into a blob of aches and pains after every game and practice. I knew I would.

"Then why are you doing it?" His words were low, like he wasn't sure he wanted me to hear.

"What am I supposed to do? Wait for my future husband to appear on the fire escape outside my kitchen window? I want to stop, but what is that going to get me? I know it's not cool to say it because I'm supposed to love my independence and not need anyone to complete my life—and don't even get me started on my parents and their marriages—but I want to be married, I want to be settled, and I want to stop feeling like I'm living in the in-between. I want to stop looking for someone to love me."

When I was finished heaving my sob story into his lap, he met my eyes with a dark, even gaze and said, "You can."

"What?" I turned the water glass, letting the condensation slick my palms. "What do you mean?"

"Stop looking. Marry me."

chapter five

Emme

Today's Learning Objective:
Students will explore new and exciting opportunities.

I couldn't stop laughing. Tears filled my eyes and my ribs ached. My face was burning hot again but I couldn't help it.

"Oh, you're precious," I said, patting his rock-solid biceps. "Oh my god. I haven't laughed like that in ages."

I mopped my face with a napkin. Half my makeup came away in the process. When I looked up, I found Ryan staring at me, no hint of humor in his expression. If anything, the crinkle of his eyes looked…pained.

I shifted in the booth to face him and folded my legs in front of me. Places like this probably frowned on criss-cross applesauce, but I was taking all the liberties that having the city's golden boy of football beside me afforded. "The next time I'm in my feelings, I'm going to call you and you're going to say something unhinged like you want me to carry your big-headed babies."

His brow quirked up. "I don't have a big head."

I wagged a finger at his long, rangy limbs and shoulders that barely fit through standard doorways. "Just look at yourself. They'd be huge, beastly children."

He stared at me then, that distress still pulling at his features. He started to say something, but the server arrived with our meals and that interruption seemed to shelve the big beastly babies.

But Ryan didn't move when the server left, didn't touch his food. His gaze seemed unfocused and far away, and I only managed a few bites before asking, "Do you want to swap?"

We always ended up trading plates. Even when he ordered something far outside my taste, I ended up eating half of it. Or pushing our dishes together and sharing.

I slid my plate toward him but he held up a hand. "Do you remember how we promised to marry each other if we weren't married by thirty?"

"I—" I gulped my water before saying something I'd regret because yes, *of course* I remembered. But I remembered it the same way I remembered the pepper spray I kept in my bag: It was nice knowing it was there but I didn't think I'd ever need it, and even if I did, the odds were high that I'd fuck it up and injure myself in the process. "What made you think of that?"

He crossed his arms over his chest again. It was his default position. He'd always drawn some joy in coming across as foreboding. He strived to be unapproachable. The truth was, he just didn't want anyone getting close enough to poke at his secrets and sore spots because they were right there at the surface, lurking just behind the cool glares and intimidating postures. And the big head, obviously.

"I think we could help each other," he said.

"By...getting...married?" I drained the rest of my cocktail.

Fuck it, drunk wasn't the worst thing to be tonight.

"Yeah," he said with a defiant chin lift that had me choking out a manic laugh. "You said you needed a revenge date. How about a revenge husband?"

This time, I was too stunned to laugh. All I could do was stare at him, my mouth hanging open and my fingers clutching at pearls I wasn't wearing. Small pulses of electricity lit up my body like someone was dragging their nails over my skin. We stared at each other for the longest moment. I wasn't sure I was breathing.

He looked so serious, and with more than his usual grim intensity. This left me no other choice than to drop a hand to his head and give it a rattle. "How many concussions did you get last season?"

"Just one."

I pulled away from him before I did something truly mortifying like running my fingers through his hair. This conversation was a damn minefield. One wrong move and fifteen years of friendship would blow up in my face.

"One too many," I said. "I'm worried about you, Wildcat. You're not making sense."

"What if I am?"

What? What does that even mean? What is this about?

I motioned to his plate. "Don't you need to eat like every forty-five minutes to maintain the whole two hundred and thirty pounds of hurricane-force muscle thing?"

The corner of his mouth twitched. "Two twenty-five."

"Well, then, you're wasting away." I gave him an admonishing head shake. "And I'm sure you worked out today."

He shrugged this off. "Only two hours. Off-season."

"Have some of this," I said, pushing my plate toward him. "It would be great for me if you did because I've been eyeing that cheesy veggie gratin thing."

We traded plates and I went straight for the small cast-iron crock topped with blistered cheese. I still heard Teddy's voice in my head when I ate anything that wasn't strictly *light,* but I was getting a lot of practice at flipping that voice off.

Ryan polished off my fish in about three bites, but something changed when he set his fork on the edge of the plate and glanced at me.

It was as if the energy between us switched to a higher frequency. I felt his gaze heating my skin. I didn't know what was happening right now or how to get us back to the way we always were, but I knew I needed to.

"Em, I was serious about—"

"Not until you tell me why," I said. I closed my hand around his wrist, my fingers flat on his pulse. It seemed quick, a hard and steady beat against my fingertips. "Either you tell me what's really going on or I'm dragging you to the nearest hospital to get your head checked."

He stared down at my hand for a long moment, a million thoughts whirling behind those eyes. "I think we can help each other," he said carefully. "All this stress you're feeling about the wedding, I can take it off your shoulders. I'll go to Grace's wedding with you and any of the other parties, and I'll keep that sonofabitch far away from you. You know I don't invite myself to fights but if that kid even looks at you the wrong way, I'll sack his ass so hard he'll be coughing up grass for days."

I couldn't ignore the immediate surge of relief that pulsed through me. The tension that had cemented itself in my body since the night I found out about Teddy faded a bit and my shoulders sagged. A deep, weary breath slipped past my lips and I fought hard to keep tears from filling my eyes.

It didn't matter that Ryan was plucking me out of the water by the scruff of my neck. Any port in a storm.

Just for a minute, I wasn't fighting to stay afloat. I wasn't in this all by myself.

When I was positive my voice wouldn't crack, I asked, "What's in it for you?"

He made a face like he already hated the taste of the words to come. "My image needs some work. I'm making some moves for life after the League, and if I want things to go my way, I need to acquire something resembling a family values vibe."

When he drowned those comments with the last of his beer, I

released his wrist and went back to the cheesy vegetables. But just as quickly, I jabbed my fork in his direction. A bit of broccoli flew across the table. "I don't buy that."

He rubbed his brows. "I wouldn't lie to you."

"Okay, but the League and the rest of pro sports is full of abusers, predators, bigots, and fools who invent their own trouble. They still have endorsement deals and cushy post-retirement gigs waiting for them."

"You're not wrong about that," he said, picking up the stray broccoli and depositing it on the edge of his plate. "But it's not true for my current circumstances."

"What do you need to work on? Even if you've earned yourself a reputation for heartlessly plowing your way through every new supermodel and rising pop star in the past five years, I really don't see how that's bad enough to warrant a fake marriage."

A muscle high in his jaw ticked as he signaled for another round of drinks. Eventually, he said, "Heartlessly?"

I jabbed the fork again. Some breadcrumbs went flying this time. "Didn't that British singer with the lavender hair release a brutal breakup song about you last summer? Poppy Whatshername?"

He blinked up at the ceiling. "It's not about me."

"It's widely accepted that it's about you."

"It's not about me."

"She slices and dices you, my friend," I said. "It basically charges you with leaving her in a pile of emotional dirty laundry without a backward glance."

"It's not about me," he said, biting off each word, thoroughly exasperated now.

It wasn't that I didn't believe him. I did. Or, rather, I wanted to, but when that song came out, the citizens of the internet had gathered the evidence and made a very compelling case as to his guilt in the matter. We'd talked back then, but he hadn't been too chatty. I hadn't pushed.

Was it possible that I hadn't pushed because I couldn't wrap my mind around the idea of him with a very young, very emotive singer who made waves everywhere she went? Sure. Or that the media had breathlessly documented every minute of their relationship, and for the first time in my life I had to look away when I saw my friend's face in my newsfeed? Also yes.

It'd felt disloyal to resent his girlfriend for no other reason than I *knew* she drove him up the wall, so I'd said nothing about it. No texts teasing him about landing on the cover of magazines with his hand in her back pocket. No long voice notes reading unhinged social posts about whether he was riding her coattails (impossible) or she was taking his focus away from football (also impossible). And no comments about the song that seemed to imply he cared little for a woman who wanted to give him her entire world.

I'd kept it all to myself. That was how it'd always been with us. We didn't talk too much about the people we dated. It was fine for the most part. I learned long ago how to play nice with the girls he hung out with, and he didn't even notice the guys in my life. It was *fine*.

"For what I'm working on," he said, still exasperated, "I need to turn the page from all of that."

I went back to the vegetables. "And you think getting married will do the trick?"

"Emme." He plucked the fork from my fingers before I could launch the cauliflower.

I lifted my brows in question, but he ignored that. He shifted closer to me and pressed my hand between both of his. I swallowed hard.

"I think marrying my best friend—the girl from back home, the one the media called my high school sweetheart in all of the Heisman packages because there are so damn many photos of us together after my games, the one who waited all this time for me to find my way back to her—will do the fucking trick."

Before I could stop myself to think through the implications, the grenade blast this would blow in our friendship, in my entire life, I said, "Okay."

We exited the restaurant into the bracing night air, but even that wasn't enough to snap me out of the fog of *what just happened?*

My head felt disconnected from my body, like I was in the deep of a bad sinus infection. My thoughts were glossy bubbles, drifting away and popping into nothing before I knew what they were. Could I blame liquor for this? Probably not.

It took a minute to realize there was a group of people—men, mostly younger, early twenties—gathered on the sidewalk. They were all talking at once, some doing their best impression of Ryan's passing stance while others simply bounced on the balls of their feet, vibrating with the pleasure of seeing Ryan Ralston in the flesh.

Sometimes I forgot that this was his life. That, to the rest of the world, he was a football phenomenon.

To me, he'd always be Ryan, the moody kid who secretly loved math and kept me tangerine rich.

The group lurched closer and I took a large step back. Ryan's arm circled my shoulders and he held a hand out to them, saying, "Give my girl some room, fellas."

The bubbles in my head all simmered and popped.

The men immediately backed up, showering me in a drunken chorus of "Miss, we're so sorry" and "Ma'am, we're at your service" and "Dammit, Doug, stop ruining everything!"

It must've been obvious that I didn't know what to do because Ryan leaned in close, whispering, "Relax. I'll handle this."

I tried to wriggle out of the photos—because why did anyone need me in a photo with Ryan and his fans?—but he kept that arm locked around my shoulders. I smiled through it all, even when Ryan growled and snapped "Don't even fucking think about it" when one guy went in for a side hug I hadn't requested.

It was fun to see his fangs come out. He didn't do that too often, instead choosing to let his glacial stares do all the talking.

Everyone got a photo, including Doug, who really did have a knack for ruining things, and Ryan ended it with a crisp wave and "Thanks for the support, boys."

Ryan led me toward the SUV I hadn't noticed waiting at the curb while the guys continued talking at him and shouting advice for the next season. One day, if I worked hard enough, maybe I'd develop the confidence necessary to tell professionals how to do a job that I'd merely observed.

"Oh, no, that's okay," I said as he opened the door. "I'll walk."

"If you think I'm leaving you here right now, you're out of your fucking mind." His hands settled on my hips, gripping tight. "It's ten thirty at night, freezing cold, and there are seven drunk guys over there who would think nothing of following you all the way home. Get in the fucking car, Emmeline."

Still suffering from too much emotional sinus pressure to process anything quickly, I bobbed my head but made no other move. A low, rumbly noise sounded in his throat and then Ryan picked me up and deposited me in the back seat without so much as a grunt. The last time anyone tried to pick me up, I was half dead from anaphylactic shock and Teddy had made it seem like *a lot* of work.

Ryan followed me into the back seat, shooting a frigid glare through the tinted window at the men still shouting at him. The car pulled into traffic without wasting a second.

"Bowen, we're going to the North End," Ryan called to the driver.

Bowen nodded and hung a hard right turn. I glanced over to find Ryan staring at me, his gaze steely. He remained silent while my too-full head spun.

Did I just get engaged?

Or was it fake-engaged?

How had this happened?

How would I explain it to my friends? To my mother?

And was this any better than what I'd had before? This solved some of my problems, but none of the big ones. None of the sad, tragic, lonely ones that would linger long after Ryan's deal went through. And wouldn't it be so much worse when it was over?

"Are you all right?" he asked.

"I don't know," was the only thing I could say.

I let him watch me while Bowen wove through the streets of Boston. Though I never gave him my address, he pulled up in front of my building like he'd been coming to this craggy little corner of Salem Street for years.

I reached for the door handle, but Ryan stopped me, saying, "Wait. I'll come around."

He gripped my elbow as I climbed down from the SUV, his other hand hovering near my hip. I'd love to say I didn't need that much help, but I was just a hair over five feet tall and couldn't dismount a vehicle this size without a firm grip on at least one handle.

"Thanks," I said as I crossed to the narrow sidewalk in front of my building. I didn't know what I was supposed to do or say now, but I knew I had to do something, anything. We couldn't leave it like this. "Um, so—"

"I'll walk you up," he said, flattening a hand beside my door.

His driver took off toward Charter Street. I watched as the taillights flashed before disappearing from sight. He was probably looping back up through Prince Street and not leaving Ryan here.

Because why would he leave Ryan here?

That wouldn't happen.

We weren't *that* kind of engaged.

Or...were we?

That would be something to think about.

I dug my keys out of my bag and Ryan watched while I struggled with the old, sticky lock. Once we were inside, he settled a hand low on my back. He kept it there as we wound our way up five flights of narrow, twisting stairs. We didn't say a word.

I turned to face him when I reached the small landing outside my door. He stopped a step below though that still didn't bring him down to my eye level.

He slipped his hands into his pockets only to immediately pull them out again. "Tell me you're all right," he said.

"I'm—I'm not sure. I'm fine," I hurried to add. "But I need some time to think. About everything. That you said."

A muscle twitched in his jaw. "And after you've had that time?"

"We'll talk," I said.

He pressed his tongue into his cheek, nodded once. "I have to be in LA tomorrow night, but I'll be back on Wednesday. Can we meet up later this week? I have some events coming up and it would go a long way to have you with me for them." He glanced over my shoulder at the off-kilter brass 5 and the hot pink skeleton wreath left over from last Halloween. "Or I could stay and watch while you think. Just like I used to."

There was no reason in the entire world for those words to warm my blood all the way down to my toes, and there was certainly no reason to feel a twist of anticipation low in my belly. None at all.

"You'd get bored without some calculus homework to entertain you," I said.

"Unlikely."

Before I could respond to that, a crash sounded from the other side of the door. "Don't worry," Ines called. "It's not broken." After a weighty pause, she added, "And I wasn't listening."

I met Ryan's gaze with a tired grin. "Later this week," I said. "We'll talk then."

He lifted a hand like he meant to reach for me but let it drop. "I'll text you my schedule," he said, though each word sounded waterlogged with reluctance.

I didn't like this. I didn't like the sense that I couldn't tell up from down. And I didn't like that I couldn't read his thoughts with one quick glance.

I beckoned him closer, my arms open. "Come here," I said, fisting my hand in his sweater and pulling him to me when he didn't move. "You're not allowed to leave me without a hug."

I held him close and, after a pause I didn't understand at all, he wrapped his arms around me. The scruff of his beard scraped at my neck, and for once I didn't wiggle away from it.

"I love you, you know," I said, my words muffled against his shoulder.

"I know. I love you too." Ryan drew in a deep breath and said, "Figure out what you need from me to make this work. Anything you want, anything at all. I don't care what it is, I'll get it done. If I can't, I have people who can find a way." He ran his hands down my arms. "We're in this together. Okay?"

I bobbed my head, humming in agreement while I was confused and conflicted as hell. "We always are."

chapter six

Emme

Today's Learning Objective:
Students will collaboratively hatch revenge schemes.

I OBSESSED ON SUNDAY AND THEN CRAMMED ALL MY QUESTIONS AND doubts and strange, sticky hopes in a box, and mentally shoved it into the depths of my closet. I was supposed to be thinking and processing and making sense of the weirdest marriage proposal of all time, but I didn't do any of those things. I didn't really want to think about it because I knew I'd run too far, too fast in all the wrong directions. I couldn't let myself do that again. Not when the last wound was barely scabbed over.

So, I left the obsession box in my mental closet all week, pretending it didn't exist while Ryan was out of town.

Even if I wanted to tell anyone about this, what would I say? Where does one start with these stories? *Hey, I might be fake-engaged. Is it too soon to register for a waffle iron?*

And more to the point, was I allowed to tell anyone about it? I had to assume the value of a fake relationship declined with every person who knew it was fake.

While I was very curious about the waffle iron and related topics, this week gave me no time to get lost in those details. My class required every ounce of me, every single day, and more than once I went home without visiting Jamie and stared at the wall for an hour just to decompress. I was late on my lesson plans for next week and hadn't even started the book I was supposed to be reading for the upcoming professional learning community meeting. Planning the school's June field day had always been my pet project, the one thing that got me through the final chaotic months of the year, but I hadn't even come up with a theme yet.

And then there was Ines. From what I could piece together, her degree program had a practical experience requirement she hadn't met. She'd been offered many interviews for summer internships, but that was where it fell apart for her. Ines had a tough time in artificial social situations like that. She was intensely literal and came across as abrupt when she was trying to be specific or concise. She didn't know how to play ball with opaque questions and struggled to notice when her responses were turning into sermons.

If I'd known how critical it was to get her a gig for the summer, we would've been working on interview prep from the minute she moved in. But here we were in early April with no internship, no upcoming recruiting events on the university's calendar, and the threat of her not graduating or being able to start her grad program hanging heavy over the apartment.

Ines now existed in the type of eternal panic that I referred to as bouncy ball anxiety—every time she thought about the internship requirement, her worries fed off each other until they doubled and tripled, every scenario in her mind worse than the one before, and she couldn't bear to be still because her body was buzzing. Just like a rubber bouncy ball thrown down an empty hallway.

Easy to spot. Not as easy to de-escalate.

Especially since I had no idea how to find a job in engineering.

And I was also a bouncy ball because I'd never actually stopped obsessing over what it would mean to marry Ryan Ralston.

RYAN STOOD IN THE MIDDLE OF MY KITCHEN AND MADE A SOLID attempt at pretending he didn't hate everything about the apartment. It was small and narrow, with a sharply slanted ceiling that forced him to stay on one side of the room at all times, and it always smelled like pastrami. We'd never been able to figure out where that feature came from.

He'd noticed the array of water spots on the ceiling, what with being so close to it and all, and the odd, rust-colored stain in the middle of the worn hardwood floors that Grace used to refer to as the scene of the crime.

There was also the matter of the disemboweled oven and all the other projects Ines had left in states of incomplete.

The place didn't show well.

"I have a condo," he said, peering at a window with dish towels tucked around it to ward off the draft. "I hardly ever use it. It's new. And"—his mouth hung open as the corner of the window casing came off in his hand—"clean. It's very clean."

"We're fine," I said, prying open the baby-proof latch on the refrigerator. The door had a tendency to pop open. That, or we had a ghost who enjoyed a midnight snack and often left it ajar. "I love this neighborhood, and if you climb out that window"—I pointed to the one he was trying to piece back together but making worse by the minute—"and onto the roof, the view is amazing. I spend every sunny day out there."

"I have a roof garden designed by an award-winning landscape architect," he replied. "And you don't have to climb out any windows to get there."

"I'm sure it's lovely," I said. "But this is my place, flaws and all."

"But—" He stared at the oven.

"It's okay. I don't really cook anymore."

"Anymore?"

I carried the drinks and snacks to the small table shoved up against the wall and ignored his question. No need to get into all of that. "You said you had a dinner meeting tonight." I tipped my head toward the empty seat across from me. "I don't want to make you late."

He cast a disapproving frown at the window and crossed to the table in one step. This really was a narrow apartment, even by Boston standards. The chair creaked under his weight and he gave me a wary glance before reaching for the glass of water I'd set out for him.

He seemed restless, and not simply because of the junkyard chic vibe we had going here. His shoulders were tight, his jaw ticking with every breath. His clothes—another round of jeans and a dark sweater—were perfect, though the way he kept shoving up his sleeves bordered on frenetic. Even his hair looked a bit wild.

Then there was the darkness under his eyes, like the early stain of a bruise. It was probably from jet lag. Understandable. I'd be a constant zombie with his schedule.

"Have you had a chance to give it some thought?" he asked.

Instead of responding, I fussed with the pretzels that'd slid into the cheese section of the plate. I didn't know what to say and I hated that because it was always easy with Ryan. There was never pretense or expectation or any kind of awkwardness. Nothing was off-limits. We'd always understood each other implicitly, and now—now, I didn't understand anything.

"You know I hate to pry into your situation with all of this," I started.

"Shut up. You love to pry," he said.

I looked up to find his eyes bright and a grin pulling at the corner of his mouth. And just like that, I pushed away all the tentativeness that had coiled itself around my neck since last weekend. That was all it took to get back to *us*. "Then you'll have no problem explaining to me what this is all about and why the hell anyone would care enough about your personal life that you'd need to invent a bride."

"Invent a bride," he said to himself, his eyes flashing wide like I was the one being ridiculous here. "I have two more seasons on my contract. I won't be shopping for a renewal after that." He ran his palms down his denim-clad thighs, his brows pinched tight like he was waiting for me to protest. He should've known that wasn't going to happen. "I'm working with a partner to buy a few pro soccer franchises in the US. One family currently owns most of the undeveloped men's and women's franchises and they have no intention of building those teams. They're holding out for the biggest payday possible."

"And you're telling me these bidders have to be *married*? Why complicate the money-grubbing mission with that kind of requirement? Seems weird."

"The Wallaces are ultraconservative," he said. "The vetting process has been unreal—and complete bullshit. They've narrowed it down to a small pool of buyers and the pressure is on. We're close, we're at the final push, but we have to fall in line. It pisses me off that I'm even playing their game."

He shoved a hand through his hair and I nodded. It was good to know that we were only doing this because he had no other options. And just for a short while. It was harder to let my thoughts run away from me this way.

"But these undeveloped teams are the best way to go," he said. "Otherwise, I'm bringing in a whole lot more investors and giving up most of the vision we've already established."

"And you're willing to get married," I said. "To get these teams."

He started to respond but stopped himself. His gaze flicked to me before he drained his water and snagged a few grapes from the plate. After a moment, he said, "Yeah, I am. But only to you." He shoved a few more grapes in his mouth. "It's our history that makes it believable. I wouldn't be able to do this with anyone else."

"I guess it's nice to know I'm not at the bottom of your list or something depressing like that."

He met my eyes. "You're the list, Em. You're it."

I scratched at a dried bit of something on the table with my fingernail. I hated that I liked being the only one he'd choose to be his fake fiancée. I couldn't believe I was operating at this level of pathetic.

"How does this even work, Ryan?"

"It works however you want it to work," he said, an edge in his words. "Decide how you want it to be and that's what we'll do."

"What are we going to tell people? What are we going to tell our *families*?"

He pressed his fingertips to his eyelids as a breath rattled out of him. "We'll get to that," he said, though it sounded quite a bit like *I have no fucking clue*. "We should go over the events I have coming up —and the ones that you have too. I want to make sure I have those blocked out for you. This isn't just about me. We're getting you all the revenge you want and then a little extra from me."

"I've always admired your vindictive side."

"The basis of all good marriages."

I eyed him. What the hell were we doing? "You think?"

His shoulders lifted. "Let's test the theory."

I left him in the kitchen to get my planner. It only took a second but I leaned against my bedroom door and pushed long, deep breaths out through my mouth.

What the hell was I doing?

I needed someone to come and explain my life to me. To tell me what to do because clearly I was not the person qualified to make my decisions.

What would they say? *Your oldest friend in the world needs you to marry him for a business deal and there's nothing you wouldn't do for him, even if you know that there's no way for you to fake your way through this and you will get hurt when it's over.*

On second thought, I didn't need anyone telling me what to do. I could muddle through just fine.

When I returned to the table, Ryan eyed me like he saw straight through my walls. The trouble was, I knew he could.

He waited while I flipped through the pages. "I have a charity event coming up in April," he said, pulling out his phone. "Here in Boston. You'll need a dress."

"Not a pajama party, then."

"My assistant will schedule a visit with a stylist who will do all your shopping," he said. "On my tab, of course."

"As your future wife, I'd expect nothing less."

He dragged his gaze up from his phone to meet my eyes, his lips parted. He coughed a bit, still staring at me. Eventually, he thumped a fist against his chest and murmured, "Sorry about that. Something—just something in my throat."

I grabbed his glass to refill it. "I have a student who tries to swallow his tongue every day. I've told him it's not going to work and it wouldn't be a great choice overall but he doesn't want to hear it. He chokes on his own spit a couple of times a week."

"I don't know how you handle that sort of thing."

"It's an art," I said, my hand under my chin. "Though this year has been mostly about crowd control and the art is often lost in the shuffle."

"You're good at it though. And I can tell you like it. Even when it's tough."

I was a little too deep in my dark, sulky corner to do anything with compliments so I said, "It keeps me busy."

Ryan took the glass and drank half of it in two chugs. "My publicist reminded me that I need to do some goodwill visits in the area. Mostly photo ops to shake hands and drop off a check."

I returned to my seat, grimacing. "You must hate that."

He rolled his eyes toward the ceiling. "So much. But what if I came to your school? I could talk some sense into your class."

"It's cute that you think you'd be able to do that." I folded my arms over my chest. The idea of Ryan in my classroom sent a rush of anticipation through me. I didn't know why I liked that so much, but suddenly I couldn't wait to show him the world of second grade. "I'm sure my principal would love to have you visit. Especially if there's a donation involved."

He tapped the April spread on my planner. "Talk to her and then shoot me some dates that would work for you. I'll get my publicist on it."

"I hope you know what you're in for," I said.

"I have no clue," he replied with a laugh. He handed over his phone, a draft email on the screen with a series of dates spanning the next few months. "These are my most important events through the end of the summer."

I went to work recording all of his galas and award banquets. They all slotted in between Grace's dress fittings and couples' showers and end-of-the-year picnics like my life was supposed to contain these multitudes.

"My assistant will handle your travel arrangements," he said as I flipped to August. "We should be able to work around your school schedule without any problem since we're taking my plane."

"Your plane," I echoed. "When did you get a *plane*?"

He shrugged this off as if we all had planes so why was I pestering him about his? "I have an endorsement deal with a private jet company."

I handed his phone back. "Quite the life you lead, my friend."

"It's not what it seems." He pointed to my planner. "Your turn. What do you need?"

A slightly hysterical laugh bubbled out of me. "Can you read a book for me about investigative experiments in early elementary science? Do you know anyone who can get Ines an internship? Or someone who can plan a field day for three hundred kids? Because that would be great." I shook my head, still laughing at the mortifying state of my life. "That shit show aside, it would be cool if my fake fiancé could give my ex murder eyes at Grace and Ben's housewarming party, a shower-slash-pub-crawl, and their wedding weekend. It's in Rhode Island, but don't worry. We won't need your private jet."

"Put me down for the murder eyes, but what's going on with Ines?"

I gave him the highlights of that situation. "She's so smart and I just wish these interviewers could see that instead of getting hung up on asking what kind of tree she would be because they're missing the good stuff. She's going to fall apart if she can't start her grad program in the fall and I really don't want that." I glanced away as I twined my fingers together. I hated admitting this part. Hated it for Ines but also for me because I wasn't so different. "And there's no one else to help her. I have to do it."

He tapped his phone a few times, his lips pulled into a thoughtful frown. He was going to be late for his dinner though I couldn't find it in me to be upset about that.

"Send me her CV," he said. "I'll see what I can do."

I laughed as I closed my planner. "Don't tell me you have an endorsement deal with an engineering firm."

He pushed to his feet and shot a parting glare at the sloped ceiling. "I don't, but I know people who know people."

I followed him to the door, saying, "If you can take care of Ines for the summer, I promise I'll marry you *and* make it look good."

He backed onto the landing, the rough hint of a smile brightening his face. "And if not? How will you make it look?"

"Oh, it'll still be good," I drawled, "but I'm skipping the painful-yet-effective push-up bra. The one that screams *barely contained barmaid*."

Then again, every day was *barely contained barmaid* day when you were a 36F.

His gaze flew to my chest before blinking away. He cleared his throat and rubbed the back of his neck. "Skip the bra either way." Another glance at my cleavage and he groaned to himself, adding, "I mean, you don't need to be uncomfortable. Not—not for my benefit."

I leaned against the doorframe, laughing. My opinion of myself wasn't so high that I couldn't enjoy some light objectification. At this point, it was all I had going for me. "Good to know."

"I'll text you tomorrow," he said. "We'll get that visit to your classroom set up."

Ryan made no move to go. I peered up at him for a moment, willing him to blow off his meeting and stay here with me. Talk with me like we used to. Tell me what he was really thinking, because just as he could see through my walls, I saw through his, and I knew this wasn't as simple as he wanted me to believe.

"Sorry to get stuck in the details," I said, "but what happens next? With the whole marriage thing."

He stowed his phone in his back pocket and nodded to himself, like he was making a decision he didn't feel the need to share with me. "What would you want to happen next?"

"I don't know." I tossed my hands out and started talking with all of my limbs. "Are you telling people we're engaged?"

"Do you want to?"

"I just want to know the plan," I said. "What are we saying? Who knows about this? Am I registering for a waffle iron? These are the important questions."

The corners of his eyes creased as he asked, "A waffle iron?"

"Yes, and I can only conspire with you if I know the whole conspiracy," I said.

He brought his fingers to his temples and kneaded his brow for a moment. Then, "Let's wait until next month to say anything. After the school visit and the charity ball." He leaned in and brushed some lint away from my hair. His phone buzzed, but he didn't seem to notice. "It won't seem so sudden."

A month seemed plenty sudden, but that was the difference between our worlds. "What about your family? How are you going to explain this to them?"

He stared into my eyes like he was trying to find something in there. Better judgment and common sense, perhaps. "There's nothing to explain. They'll get it."

I couldn't imagine Cecelia Ralston accepting that her only son wanted to fake a whole damn marriage just to buy some soccer teams, but I had my own parents to worry about. At least with them, I knew the value they both placed on marriage was low enough to not care one way or another.

"Are we eloping? Or are we planning a wedding?" I asked.

He went back to the hair spilling over my shoulder and dragged his fingers through it. I must've had a lot of fuzz from my scarf in there again. "What do you want?"

"I—I haven't thought about it," I admitted, and it was the truth.

"Well, I have," he said, his words low, like a secret. "And I know I want to marry you as soon as I can."

Right. That made sense. I should've known he couldn't wait months or even years to plan a traditional wedding. That didn't work for his world domination plans.

"But I also know I want to have a big party," he continued as his phone went on buzzing. "Something in the off-season. A huge blowout bash. Hundreds of people. A twenty-tier cake. A really good band. Fireworks."

"A tequila luge," I added.

"Fuck yes," he said with a growl. "That's what I want."

I realized I was smiling. "Okay," I said. "Then I guess I'll just get started on finding a luge vendor—"

"No," he said quickly. His phone buzzed again. "You have enough going on and—and we could do both." When I only blinked, fighting for my life to catch this train of thought, he continued. "Yeah. That makes more sense. Elope then have a big party."

"Right, right, right." I nodded like this was all one hop, skip, and jump of perfectly good logic. Maybe it was? Maybe I just didn't know anything about the right way to get fake-married? "And when are we eloping? Are we talking about some city hall setup or a proper Vegas event? Or some wild and crazy third option I can't even imagine?"

More buzzing. "We'll figure it out over the next month and then we'll hire a wedding planner to take care of the rest."

"Wedding planners, stylists, private jets," I teased. "You sure know how to spoil a girl."

"Yeah, I'm counting on it," he said under his breath.

I laughed, but when he looked up at me, his gaze was cool and steady. "Sorry for keeping you so late."

"Don't be." He gave a sharp shake of his head and took a step backward. He wasn't going to skip that dinner and stay with me, and I couldn't be upset about that. "Thank you," he said. "For doing this."

"Make sure your lawyer writes a good prenup," I said. "Otherwise, I'll take the plane when this is all over."

"I'd give it to you." He rocked forward and I let myself believe he was looking for a reason to stay. "About that field day," he said, rapping his knuckles on the doorframe. "Leave it to me."

Nothing should've surprised me at this point but... "Leave it to you?"

"Yeah. I'll take care of it for you." A small smile broke across his face. "Wife."

My lips parted and I reached for the pearls I still wasn't wearing as he jogged down the stairs.

chapter seven

Ryan

Today's Learning Objective:
Students will play dangerous games.

I WAS SO FUCKED IT WASN'T EVEN FUNNY.

The elevator doors opened onto the forty-ninth floor of the Prudential Center as I exhaled like I was white-knuckling my way out of vomiting. That wasn't so far from the truth.

Fucked fucked fucked.

I waved to the receptionist and headed straight for the small conference room in the back, the one with the views toward Fenway Park. I kept the lid of my baseball cap low and my gaze on the destination. While I'd mastered the *do not talk to me* vibes at an early age, some people were immune.

Most notably, Emmeline Ahlborg. The source of all fuckery in my life and the sole reason I was so fucking fucked right now.

I flung open the conference room's glass door and paced in front of the windows. I needed somewhere to put all this goddamn energy. Instead of resting my shoulder as advised by literally everyone who had something riding on my arm, I'd spent the past two weeks lifting like I still had the recovery time of a twenty-year-old. Supposed to be going easy on my hip too, but that didn't stop me from running six, seven, eight miles a day. Just to get out of my fucking head.

I never should've touched her hair. Not the first time, definitely not the second.

What the actual fuck was I going to do?

For once in my life, I didn't know the right move and it scared the shit out of me.

The door whooshed open at my back, but I didn't stop pacing. I heard the slide of Jakobi Jones's custom-made loafers against the carpet, followed by a rueful chuckle that scraped at my gray matter. My manager dropped into a seat while I stared out at the blindingly bright spring day, clear skies of endless blue.

I wanted to launch myself straight into the sun.

"I thought you said it went well." He paused and I had to assume it was to roll his eyes at me. "Even for you, this mood doesn't paint a positive picture."

As I saw it, there were two options available to me here.

On the one hand, I could put a stop to this right now. Blow up the tracks before the train could run away. Would it screw with our bid for those soccer franchises? Yeah, probably. And would it leave a weird dent in my relationship with Emme? Most likely. Even if she shrugged it off and made a joke out of it the same way she did with everything she pretended not to care about, the damage was already done.

On the other, stopping this meant we could never come back here again. We'd consider that pact from high school—one *she'd* proposed when we had no idea what the world had waiting for us and when thirty seemed like a distant future—void and fully forgotten if I walked away now.

But if we did this, I'd get everything I'd ever wanted. And I'd ruin my entire life in the process.

My gut churned as I laced my fingers together at the back of my neck. Two options, but the outcomes, they weren't so different.

I didn't recognize my voice as I said to Jakobi, "She's on board."

He cleared his throat. "Then you told her everything."

The city nearly glittered in this light. The Charles River snaked off into the distance like a deep blue artery. The lush green of new growth filled the trees and even the long strings of brownstones seemed sun-warmed and stately today.

I'd resented this city for so long. Resented Boston's position in the draft the year I turned pro. Resented that I was here, so close to home it was like I'd never fucking left, when I could've had the thousands of miles of distance that I required to take a deep breath without feeling every old ache and never-healed wound.

But in this moment right now, there was nowhere in the world I'd rather be.

I glanced over my shoulder but didn't meet Jakobi's eyes. "Not quite."

The tension headache that had haunted me since leaving Emme and her wide, hazel eyes at her door last night clanged around the base of my skull.

He huffed out a laugh. "What happened to the plan?"

The plan went up in flames the minute I saw her. It turned to ash when I touched her. And now, with our calendars organized like this was some kind of group project, there was a blacked-out burn hole in my memory where the plan should've been.

"Called an audible," I said, still chasing my gaze down Huntington Street.

"Care to fill me in, or do you intend to be a cryptic motherfucker all day?"

I shoved my hands in my pockets and ignored the question. "She has some requirements."

"Consider them met."

I turned away from the window and stalked to the table. Hands braced on the chair in front of me, I said, "Bold of you to assume you'll be able to get this done without finding out what she wants first."

He motioned to the belly of the office behind him and the nonstop hustle of associates, coordinators, and assistants as they managed the biggest names in sports. All under his command. "I always get it done."

"If that were true, the Wallace deal would've been closed months ago and I wouldn't be turning my life upside down to hold it together."

"If you had smiled for the cameras even once while you were dating Poppy Hemphill, the world wouldn't think you're as cold and arrogant as you look, and I wouldn't need the entirety of Stella Allesandro's public relations team to make nice after you."

The problem with partnering Jakobi on this franchise deal—hell, on anything—was that neither of us knew how to lose. We didn't know how to back down. We lived with the singular goal of plowing our opponents into the turf so hard they limped away with yard markings staining their faces. The number of times we'd holed up in this conference room and fought each other over every last stupid thing was greater than I cared to admit.

It was a damn good thing that, for the brief time our pro careers overlapped, we played for the same team. And that was why, despite the verbal beatdowns, he was among the best people in all of pro sports. Jakobi Jones was the only one I trusted enough to go after these soccer clubs with me. He was a stubborn son of a bitch and my closest friend.

With a grunt that had more to do with overworking my hip this morning than the tension between us, I took a seat at the table. Jakobi ran a mahogany hand down the length of his silk tie and arched a dark brow, silently screaming at me to get the fuck on with business.

"I need to attend a friend's wedding with her. With Emme," I amended. She had a name, and soon everyone would know it. "And a few other parties over the next few months. I don't care what we have to reschedule to make it happen. It's important that I'm there."

It was also important that I find an opportunity to push Emme's ex down a flight of stairs.

Jakobi pulled a silver pen from inside the breast of his suit jacket and made a note on his pad. "Do you have these dates or will I be assigning someone to dig this information up?"

"Yeah, I'll forward them to you. Marcie might've already sent them."

My assistant made her own schedule and I didn't ask questions because she was fantastic and, on the rare occasion that I did mention her middle-of-the-night emails, she'd say something like "The menopause wakes me up at three thirty, there's no helping it."

He ran a broad palm over his bald head. "Excellent. What else?"

"There's a sister. Stepsister. She needs a summer job."

He nodded toward the bullpen. "I can always use another intern."

"No, she's an engineer. MIT student. Smart kid, bad at interviews. She needs a job in engineering."

He glanced up from his pad with a slow blink. "That will take a minute but all right. What else?"

"I need to clear my schedule next week to do a visit at Emme's school," I said.

"Stella must be thrilled," he said under his breath. He was right about that. My publicist was over the moon. "Hopefully she's generating some talking points for you because you're going to do more harm than good if you walk into a classroom and glare at the children."

"I will not *glare* at the children," I replied. "Stella said I could read a story about sports and perseverance, or some other bullshit."

He set his pen down and exhaled loudly. "As you're aware, there's not a lot you could do to make the people of this town turn against you. They don't mind that you have the personality of a moss-covered rock because your passing stats are superhuman. They don't care nearly as much about Poppy's songs as they do about winning championships. However, if their kids come home from school crying about the mean man who growled a story at them, we're going to have a real problem on our hands."

"First of all, I will not be mean or growl at them," I growled. "And second, Emme would never let that fly. She'd take over before anyone started crying and then slap me upside the head."

He peered at me, his head cocked. He was silent for a long moment, a smile gradually splitting his face. He ran his fingers over his mustache. "I'm going to like her, aren't I?"

"So much." I'd wondered about her classroom last night. What it would look like, what it would feel like to be in Miss Ahlborg's class. Every time I thought about second grade, I was reminded of how simple life was back then. But second grade wasn't simple for Emme, not this year. I was going to fix that. I was going to fix a lot of things.

While I could.

Jakobi cleared his throat. "You're smiling."

"Unlikely." I snapped my fingers. "I need to make a donation too," I added. "What's the right number for that? Half a million? More? I don't want to lowball this."

Jakobi closed his eyes and rubbed his temples. "A donation for what purpose?"

"For—for whatever. I don't care. Schools always need money and there's nothing cold or arrogant about hanging around with some kids and leaving a pile of cash."

Jakobi made a note, muttering to himself and shaking his head. "Let's do some research. I'll send someone down there to put eyes on the playground and athletic fields. Get a sense of what they need so we can make something up about your charitable vision. That way, it at least looks like we have a reason to throw money at your girl's school."

My girl.

Liquid heat spread through my chest. It felt good for a minute, but then the truth of it seared straight through my skin and all the way down to my bones. It fucking hurt.

Just like it always had.

"There's one more thing." I tapped my phone and turned it toward Jakobi. "We might need to buy this building."

Another slow blink, a slight pinch of his brows. "She's requesting real estate?"

"No," I said carefully, "and she can't know that I'm looking into this."

"Oh, Jesus," he muttered.

"Her apartment should be condemned. The windows are literally falling apart. I'm pretty sure someone died on the kitchen floor. If we get so much as a sprinkle of rain, the ceiling is going to disintegrate like a paper towel."

He copied down the address. "Then why is it you want to buy the place?"

"Because then I can repair the roof and windows and whatever else the fuck is wrong with it. I offered up my condo, but she blew that off like a multimillion-dollar penthouse had nothing on her quirky corner of the North End. So what am I supposed to do? Sit on my fucking hands?"

With a thoughtful nod, Jakobi closed his folio and returned his pen to his suit coat. He draped an arm over the back of the chair beside him and studied me with an expression I couldn't decipher. It was like curiosity—yet smug about it. "I'll be damned."

"What?" I snarled.

He smiled at me then, wide and toothy and definitely smug. "Ryan Ralston has a heart," he said. "I haven't seen it until now because you left it with her."

I stared down at the table. My hip ached and my skull was full of iron spikes and I couldn't stop thinking about the way Emme's eyes went soft and dreamy when I told her how I imagined our wedding. Like there was a slim chance that she'd want that, and not for a business deal or to get back at a shitty ex.

Jakobi pushed to his feet. "Does she have any idea?"

I raked my teeth over my bottom lip. "No, and we're going to keep it that way."

chapter eight

Emme

Today's Learning Objective:
Students will examine historical documents.

"If we go out for recess early," I said, flipping through my plans for the day, "then we'll have plenty of time for small group reading and writing conferences before lunch."

Grace tapped a purple pen to my schedule. "I have three kids out for speech at that time."

"And I have two at occupational therapy," Jamie added.

"Fuuuuck," I groaned. Ryan was visiting the school today and while it was all very exciting, it was also screwing up our flexible group schedule. "Okay, then we do a super quick morning meeting and go right into writing conferences. Keep recess at the usual time and then we're rotating for reading. Whatever time we have left before lunch we can use for read-aloud or freewriting or something."

Grace hummed. "That might work."

"Let's go with this plan," Jamie said, scribbling down the changes on a sticky note. "Even if we discover five new problems along the way, we're just going to make the best of it."

I nodded. There would definitely be surprise problems. "Yeah, and—"

"Emme."

Ryan approached from the end of the hall near the front office. He looked thoroughly out of place among the colorful bulletin boards hung at elementary height. His long strides ate up the distance in no time at all. Beside me, I heard Jamie let out a breathy, "Wow."

"Hi," he said, holding out two paper cups. "Iced coffee and a smoothie. Since you're not making them at home."

"The only way to live is with a drink in both hands." I took a hearty sip of the coffee—I needed that more than the vitamins and nutrients right now—and motioned toward my friends. "Ryan, I'm sure you remember Grace."

The corner of his mouth tipped up as he took in my friend, dressed head to toe in black as usual. "As if I could forget."

"We call her Miss Kilmeade around here," I said. "And this is Jamie Rouselle. She teaches first grade. Jamie, this is Ryan Ralston."

Jamie gave him her biggest, brightest smile. She was good at smiling, as strange as that was to say. She had a way of putting people at ease. "Such a pleasure to meet you."

He nodded and slipped his hands into his pockets. "Thanks for making time for me today."

Jamie fanned herself with the sticky note. "You're welcome here any time."

She was also great at making an innuendo out of anything. I gave her a look that she specifically ignored.

"If it wouldn't be too much trouble," Grace started in that dangerously sweet tone of hers that promised to fuck up anyone who crossed her, "it would be great if you mentioned to these kids that playing professional sports is an extremely rare occurrence, and even if they do wind up in your shoes some day, they'll appreciate having a solid education behind them."

"I'd be the first one to tell them that," he said. "I didn't choose the college with the winningest team or the best coach. I chose the academic program I wanted above all else."

And the location. He'd wanted to go as far from home as the scholarships would allow. It still brought out a twinge of pain to think about him leaving. About the time between the start of college training camp and when I left for the University of Vermont, and how stunningly alone I'd been. There were friends who were around for a good time and lots of laughs and then there were friends who burrowed into your cells and altered your genetic code, and Ryan would always be the latter.

"I'm just saying, no big promises," Grace said.

Ryan nodded. "Understood."

Jamie kept staring like she wanted to take a bite out of him. I swallowed a laugh.

"I could show you around," I said. "Or—"

"There he is!"

At the end of the hall, a dark-haired woman waved at Ryan from where she stood with Lauren, the school principal.

"I think they're looking for you," I said.

"They are." He waved to her in response. "That's Stella. My publicist."

He didn't sound excited about that, but the scowl was nowhere to be seen. He wrapped an arm around my shoulders and pulled me in for a side hug. I felt his lips brush my temple as he shifted away.

"I'll see you later," he said softly. To Grace and Jamie, he added, "Good to see you both."

He turned and strolled down the hall. I slumped back against the wall when he joined the women waiting for him. Immediately, Grace and Jamie closed in around me.

Grace extended her arm, pointing toward the front office. "What the hell was that?"

I gazed down at my beverage options. Was caffeine really the answer? I wasn't sure. "What? Nothing! What do you mean?"

"I mean he kissed your forehead," Grace whisper-yelled.

"That's...that's not a big deal," I said.

"Wait a second," Jamie said. "Wait just a second." She waved the sticky note at me. "You never told me what happened at the dinner."

"What dinner?" Grace asked.

Shit. I never mentioned that to her. The last we'd spent any real time together, not a few minutes between classes or random texts, we'd gotten carried away with work on the seating chart for her wedding reception. For once, I'd succeeded at shoving Ryan into the mental box at the back of my closet.

"A few weeks ago," I said as casually as possible with two interrogators breathing down my neck. "Right after his birthday."

"Start at the beginning," Jamie said. "Leave nothing out."

"There's nothing to tell." I forced a laugh into my words. Even if I could, what would I say? "He's had some downtime in his schedule and he's been in town lately, so we've hung out."

And we're slightly engaged. I think.

"And now you're friends who give forehead kisses," Jamie said.

"And get drink deliveries," Grace added.

I pressed my shoulders into the wall. These two were human lie detectors. "We are making this into more than it is."

"Or we saw the way Daddy Football was looking at you and know we could've been hula-hooping topless and he wouldn't have noticed," Jamie said.

"He wanted to put you in his pocket and carry you around all day."

I didn't think that was anywhere near true, but it was cute that she thought so.

Grace stared at me straight on. It was the kind of stare that kept her third graders in line and had earned her the nickname Killer from her fiancé. "We're going to talk about this at lunch."

The sharp click of heels sounded against the linoleum floors and Audrey Saunders hurried toward us with a huff. The fourth-grade teacher threw an impatient glare toward the ceiling and tucked her white-blonde hair over her ear. "The third floor copier hates me."

"It hates us all," Jamie said.

"We'll be gathering in Emme's room for lunch today," Grace said, her stare gentle now. She wouldn't say it, but I knew she was hurt that I hadn't told her about seeing Ryan. Not a lot, nothing major, but it was another one of the many growing pains of not living together and sharing every ounce of our lives with each other. It was a weird shift after being joined at the hip since college. "She has some fun new developments she'd like to discuss with us."

Audrey glanced between us. She had no idea what was happening here. As if anyone could walk into this ten minutes late and understand a damn thing anyway. "I made cinnamon roll blondies last night."

"I already know that's going to solve all of my problems," Jamie said. "And even a few I didn't know I had."

Children started pouring down the hall, all lively chatter and squeaky sneakers. Grace took a step toward the door of her classroom. "Writing conferences, recess, small group reading," she said.

"Right." I bobbed my head more than necessary.

If I was going to be a convincing fake fiancée, I was going to have to get a lot better at standing up to questioning from my closest friends.

Lunch arrived as usual, at once too early for an adult to eat and too late for kids who desperately needed to get their wiggles out. I'd managed to catch a few glimpses of Ryan as he toured the school with Lauren and Stella, and again when the phys ed teacher invited him to join some activities with the kindergarten class.

Ryan's jumping jacks were outstanding.

When I got back to my room after dropping my class off in the cafeteria, Grace, Jamie, and Audrey were already waiting for me at the back table like a friendly little firing squad.

My ass hadn't even met the seat when Grace said, "Something happened with you and the dude."

I took my time unpacking my lunch and opening a can of seltzer. I didn't really know what to tell them because I didn't know the answer myself. And I didn't want to disclose too much and mess things up for Ryan's business deals. These women were not about to call up a sports podcast and drop the inside knowledge, but if this was serious enough to get married, it was probably serious enough to keep to myself.

But I had to tell them something. It would be weird to show up here in a few weeks and announce we were engaged after insisting we were just friends. So, I stayed as close to the truth as possible.

"When we were in high school," I started, tearing my kinda-stale pita into triangles, "we promised to marry each other if we weren't already married at thirty." I wrenched open the container of hummus without glancing up at them. "He hit thirty at the end of March. I'll be there in June. And neither of us are anywhere near married."

I stuffed a huge chunk of pita into my mouth and shrugged.

"I'm sorry," Grace said. "What?"

"You're in a marriage pact," Audrey said, pointing a celery stick at me. "With *Ryan Ralston*."

"I believe you," Jamie said. "Obviously, I love you and trust you and would never doubt you. But if anyone else told me that story, I'd say it was a darling work of fiction."

"Believe me, it's the truth." I scooped an obscene amount of hummus onto my pita. "I have it in writing."

"You—you what?" Grace stared at me like she'd never seen me before. "Like, a contract?"

I scrolled through my photos, going way back to high school again, and swiped until I found it. "Like I said, we made a promise at the end of high school. And we wrote it down."

I put my phone on the table and they leaned in to see the photo of my inscription in Ryan's yearbook. A minute passed while they read and I ate the mismatched snacks I'd grabbed on my way out of the apartment this morning.

"Why was the cutoff thirty?" Audrey asked.

"Because we were infants and we thought we knew everything," I said. "Thirty seemed a million years away."

"You signed it, 'Love forever, Your (probably) future wife,'" Jamie said, zooming in on the screen. "You also wrote that it was a binding contract and even if he tossed his yearbook off a pier, you'd always have proof."

I held out my hands. "Yes, to answer your question, I have always been excessively dramatic."

"You know that sort of thing isn't binding unless a witch blessed the bargain," Jamie said.

I laughed. "I didn't know that, but he agreed to the deal." I reached for my phone and swiped to the next photo, the one Ryan had texted to me all those years ago as *his* proof. It simply read, *I'll hold you to it. Your husband.*

"Goddammit that's romantic," Audrey sighed.

Grace brought a hand to her mouth. "Wow."

"He's here," Jamie said, awe in her voice, "because he's come to collect. You texted him on his birthday and he wanted to see you *that* weekend."

"He waited until it was time," Audrey said. "After all these years."

"He wants to go through with it," Grace said.

I managed a bumbly nod. "I mean, yeah, that's kind of what we've been talking about recently."

"How serious is this?" Grace asked. "Are you actually considering it?"

The thing about Grace that most people misunderstood was that she wasn't critical just to scratch a bitchy itch. She asked direct questions and framed things in ways that weren't always soft or comfortable because that was how she cared. She was fiercely protective. She didn't want anything bad to happen to the people she cared about.

And she also enjoyed busting balls when it was deserved. *Killer* really wasn't that far off base for her.

"I am," I said carefully. "But I want to be really clear that this isn't me rebounding from Teddy. I'm not jumping headfirst into the first lukewarm offer to come my way."

Or that was what I kept telling myself.

"I wasn't thinking that," Grace said carefully. "I was thinking that you've always had a very…close relationship with Ryan, and I know how much he means to you. There's a lot on the line."

"I know," I said, and I really did.

"If…anything happened," she continued, "I wouldn't want you to lose that relationship."

"I know," I repeated. "It's something I think about a lot."

Audrey peeled the lid off a Pyrex dish. "Cinnamon roll blondies," she said. "Eat them so I don't take them home."

I stared at her for a moment, studying her light tan trousers and cream-colored turtleneck sweater. I didn't know how she made it through a school day dressed like that. And do it in heels. My god, I'd die. I couldn't make it through the morning without jabbing myself with whiteboard markers.

"Would you actually go through with it?" Grace asked. "Would you actually marry him because of this pact?"

"Only because of the pact? No. I'm excessive, but I'm not completely irrational," I said. "There needs to be more."

Like some soccer franchises owned by a disgustingly wealthy family that makes everyone's personal lives a business matter and a blindingly vicious desire to make my ex regret his choices.

"So, what happens next?" Audrey asked as she cut a tiny cube of blondie for herself.

"I don't really know. We're hanging out right now. I'm going to some of his work events and he's coming to the wedding with me. We're just going to figure it out as we go. We'll see if it makes sense."

As I said it, I realized how it must sound to them. Like this was a fun little lark that probably wouldn't lead to anything. Like we might realize this was nothing more than a silly teenage vow made at the edge of our lives.

Everyone was quiet for a long minute.

"What happens if you realize it makes total sense?" Audrey asked.

"It looked like it made sense this morning," Grace said.

"The way he looked at you made all kinds of sense," Jamie said.

I shoved a blondie into my mouth.

chapter nine

Ryan

*Today's Learning Objective:
Students will take calculated risks.*

NERVOUS WASN'T A FEELING I EXPERIENCED.

Even before the playoffs and championship games, I'd be pumped, hyped, *focused*. Never nervous.

My coach in college liked to say I was fearless. That I didn't break a sweat when the biggest, baddest defensive ends had me in their sights. That I put everything into the game and left it all on the field.

And yet here I was, holed up in a school principal's office with sweaty palms and a swirl of adrenaline in my belly that made it impossible to stand still.

The last time I'd been this nervous—well, that'd involved Emme too. I should've known it would always be like this.

Stella collected me from the office before I could turn myself into a real wreck. She kept up conversation as we walked down the corridor with the principal, who had been nothing but nice, but she was not the person I wanted to see right now.

At the other end of the hall, I spotted Emme walking with her class. She said something to them and they chorused back in response. Her dark hair was swept over one shoulder, and with her navy dress, she wore a cardigan in a deep shade of orange that was probably called something like persimmon or marmalade.

"Miss Ahlborg will get the students settled and then introduce you," the principal said. Lauren was her name, though I'd lost track of her last name hours ago. It was Mrs. Something-Something, and if I hadn't been preoccupied with trying to catch a glimpse of Emme everywhere I went, I would've remembered. "This group is a bit more high energy than some others you've visited today, but Miss Ahlborg and I will be in the room the entire time to handle any issues."

I nodded while flashing a glimpse toward the media crew waiting outside Emme's classroom. It was a solid bunch. No surprise Stella had invited only the pros and none of those hacky assholes who thought they could get me to slip up and shit-talk the coach, the manager, the entire organization.

If the wear and tear on my body hadn't been enough for me to make retirement plans, the media games and league politics would've been enough all on their own.

I straightened as Emme approached with her class. Most of the kids goggled at the camera equipment. Others didn't give us the time of day and I respected that. If a media crew had shown up in my second-grade classroom, I probably would've glared at them too.

Emme leaned against the threshold, glancing at her students before grinning up at me. "Are we ready to do this?"

I kept telling myself this didn't matter. That I could fumble the whole thing and bore these kids out of their skulls, and no one would care because I gave them a bunch of money today. But I wanted to be good for Emme.

"If you are," I said, watching while one kid karate-kicked his way across the room.

"Then here we go." She patted my arm and breezed inside. "All right, my friends. Raise your hand if you remember me talking about a very special guest coming to visit us today." She raised her hand while pressing one finger to her lips as the kids started murmuring to each other. "Our visitor's name is Ryan Ralston and I think some of my friends might've heard of him before because he is a *very* famous New England football player."

Shit. She didn't even roll her eyes at that. Her teacher face could give my game face a run for its money.

"Give me two thumbs up if you've heard of Mr. Ralston before. Okay, I see so many thumbs! Now, wiggle your pinkies if you like football."

Stella chuckled beside me as hands and fingers all waved in the air. "Oh my god, Ryan, she's the cutest thing in the world. I want to gobble her up," she whispered.

"Love it, love it," Emme drawled. "Now, my friends, let's make sure we show Mr. Ralston the best, shiniest versions of ourselves today. That means we listen by keeping our lips zipped and our listening ears open. We raise our hands if we have questions and we wait silently for Mr. Ralston to call on us. Even though we have lots of visitors in the back of the room"—every head swiveled toward the media crew assembled against the wall like a defensive line—"we are going to keep our eyes up here. Got it?"

"Good," they chorused.

"Great," she replied. "Let's take twelve seconds to organize our spaces so we don't have anything distracting us while Mr. Ralston is speaking. Go!"

"How do you know her again?" Stella asked.

I watched Emme help the karate-kicker tuck a disaster of papers in his desk. When she was finished, she gave me a nod. I felt my lips turning up into a smile. The obvious answer was *from back home, from high school, from ninth-grade biology, from listening to music in her car during lunch all of senior year so I didn't have to talk to anyone.* But I heard myself say, "She's my favorite thing in the world."

I stepped away from Stella and made my way through the tight clusters of desks as Emme said, "Friends, let's give a big welcome to Mr. Ralston."

I met Emme on the rainbow rug at the front of the room and dropped a hand on her shoulder as I greeted the students. I knew the cameras had followed my hand. That was the plan.

"I'll leave you to it," she said.

My gaze followed Emme as she retreated to a wooden desk overflowing with green plants and several mugs filled with pens in the back corner of the room. She tucked herself behind the desk, her arms crossed in that sweet persimmon sweater, her hair cascading over her shoulder, and she turned an expectant grin in my direction.

I opened my mouth, but I couldn't remember what I was supposed to say. This time, she didn't hesitate to roll her eyes at the ceiling.

My smile widened and it wasn't the *I'm working very hard at being neutral and not a snarly beast* expression I usually forced in front of the cameras. Emme smiled right back at me and all the nerves died down. It was like we were connected in a way that science and logic hadn't figured out how to define, but I knew without a doubt was true.

I glanced at the obscenely small chair she'd set out for me and knew right away it wasn't an option. Even if I didn't break that little thing, I'd look like a jackass. Couldn't have that.

I started off with the same introduction I'd given all the other classes and presented a condensed, child-friendly version of my journey through college and pro football. I mentioned growing up on the New Hampshire seacoast, studying economics at the University of Arizona, and how I hadn't originally intended to enter the NFL draft because I liked numbers more than football. That detail was met with a frenzy of "What!" and "Why not?" from the class and a pointed side-eye from my future wife.

"It was my grandmother who changed my mind on that," I said. "She's a very smart woman. I always listen to her advice." I waited out the rumble of murmurs about grandmothers. General consensus: everyone listened to their grannies. "My grandmother reminded me that, as long as I had my education, I could always use it. No one could ever take that away from me. But football? Not the same. Most players have five, maybe ten good years in the game. So, she told me to play while I could and then go back to numbers, math, and business."

I watched as Emme dropped her gaze to her desk. She rolled her lips together and started organizing some of the papers there. She remembered those conversations—all the doubt and uncertainty I'd felt about skipping out on grad school, all the times I'd told her she was the only person I really trusted, all the times she'd gently asked, "Who are you really doing this for?"

Since that wasn't a mirror I'd been ready to face, I'd let Gramma CeCe's common sense guide the way. Play for a few years, earn big and take care of my mother and sisters, and then do whatever the hell I wanted.

It'd seemed like the right choice and it probably was, but almost eight years later, I still couldn't take the field without hearing Emme in my head, saying, "You're going to be one of the great ones. I just hope that's good enough for you."

She glanced up at me then, her teeth scraping over her full bottom lip, and I forgot to breathe. I had to clear my throat and reach for one of the bottled waters Stella's team had marked for me before getting back on track.

"The most important thing you can do is learn. Any guesses what the second most important thing is?" I fielded a mixed bag of responses before saying, "The second most important thing is keeping your body healthy." I glanced back to Emme, pausing until she met my eyes again. "Can we do some activities? Get up? Move around?"

"Yeah, of course," she said. "Friends, let's stand up and tuck in our chairs."

I motioned to Emme. "We always need to follow Miss Ahlborg's directions. She's the quarterback here. She calls the plays, she makes the decisions. To be a winning team, we have to listen to our QB all the time."

I rolled up my sleeves and led the kids in a few sets of jumping jacks, squats, and stretches. Then, with Emme's permission, I took them to run around the building a few times.

The media crew went crazy for it. They ate it up like there was something novel about jogging with little kids. Then they pulled me into an unplanned interview while the kids returned to the classroom and packed up for the day. I kept shooting Stella *what the fuck is this?* glares but she liked the questions and ignored my cries for help.

My publicist was a sadist. A straight-up, soul-eating sadist.

She came off as happy and bubbly, but she lived to torture her clients.

When it was all over and the crew was on the road and Stella knew I wouldn't be talking to anyone for a solid fucking week, I went looking for Emme. The halls were quiet, save for the ever-present whirl and chug of copy machines. Her room was empty but her phone was on her desk along with some purse-looking bags. She was still here, somewhere.

I turned in a slow circle to finally take in her classroom. It was bright and cheerful, and more aggressively organized than seemed natural for Emme. The University of Vermont catamount was clearly the class mascot, which meant I was legally required to send them a ton of Arizona Wildcats swag in response. It was only appropriate.

I had my phone out to call my assistant with a request for twenty-five stuffed wildcats and maybe an obnoxiously large one too when I noticed the bulletin board at the back of the room. The paper border hung limply from the frame and several star cutouts were scattered on the floor.

The crew had done this. Between the gear and all the people back here, they probably hadn't noticed, but they'd fucked it up just the same. I crouched down, gathering the stars and then trying to get the border back in place.

"Whaaaa—what are you doing?"

I glanced over my shoulder to find Emme stopped in the doorway, her hands on her hips. I couldn't look too long or I'd stare. I'd never been able to look at her for more than a few seconds without feeling like my chest was about to cave in or my head turn to sand.

I pointed to the bulletin board. "I'm fixing this," I said, reaching for the stapler on her desk.

"It's fine," she said, finally unsticking herself from the doorway. "I'll take care of it tomorrow."

I held up the stars. "Where do these go?"

She snatched them from my hand. "They—you don't have to do this."

"My crew fucked up your wall. I'm gonna fix it." I shook the stapler at her. "You can either tell me where these star things go or I'll figure it out by myself."

She huffed out a breath and passed me a star. "There," she said, pointing beside a planet cutout with *Laribel* written on it. Her knee brushed the back of my arm and I had to shut my eyes for a second.

My ability to be close to her and continue to function had been cut in half. I didn't know when it'd happened, but there was no denying it had happened. Whatever resistance I'd had in the past was gone now.

I really was ruining my whole life with this scheme and I could already feel it breaking me.

We continued like that until we returned the rest of the stars to their proper places. I mended the border, but that made little improvement.

When I gained my feet, she frowned up at me. "Sometimes I forget you're twenty-nine feet tall."

I ignored that and hooked an arm around her shoulders. "How much of your day did I ruin?"

"Only most of it," she said, resting her head against my biceps. "But the kids had a lot of fun and everyone was on their best behavior, so I have no complaints."

All I had to do was turn my head a few degrees and the scent of Emme's hair filled my lungs. It was subtle but warm. Something like vanilla. I'd been chasing that scent all day.

"Let me take you out to dinner," I said.

"It's three thirty," she said.

"We'll start with drinks and apps."

She laughed. "As much as I'd like to start drinking at three thirty on a weekday, I have to meet your stylist to pick up my dress for Saturday."

The charity ball. I'd almost deluded myself into forgetting about that. "Why isn't this stylist delivering everything to you?"

"I don't know. Maybe because I'm not home during the day to accept a delivery?"

"Trust me, Muggs. They can work around your schedule." I'd have my assistant straighten that out first thing tomorrow. "I'll take you to get your dress and then we'll grab something to eat."

Another laugh. "I have to help Ines prepare for an interview tonight."

I couldn't believe she hadn't pulled away yet. I couldn't believe I was standing here with her pressed up against no less than twenty percent of my body while I drowned myself in the scent of her hair. This was all I needed. All I'd ever ask. I could survive on this and I could be happy. Or something resembling that.

"We'll go back to your place, then. I'll order something," I said. "We should talk about the event this weekend."

That did it. That burst the bubble.

A breath rushed out of Emme and she stepped away from me, her eyes lowered as she moved to her desk and sorted through the papers there. "What...is there to talk about?" She shuffled the papers without looking at them. "You're picking me up at eight, right?"

"Yeah." I leaned against the side of her desk, my arms crossed. "How should we—hmm—how do you want us to interact?" When she cut a sidelong glance at me, I added, "Am I allowed to touch you?"

"Of course," she said.

"Like you're my wife?"

I held my gaze on her hands because I wasn't prepared to see the reaction on her face.

I was even less prepared to hear her say, "I think you mean fiancée. You're getting ahead of yourself."

I realized then that Emme was going to make me work. Even if this deal of ours was all about getting back at her ex and winning over the Wallaces, I still had to put in the work and fucking *earn* her. And I would. I *wanted* to.

I was no stranger to hard work. I'd graduated with top honors while also leading an underdog team to back-to-back Bowl Championship Series titles. I made a habit of studying my opponents so thoroughly I could recite their playbooks to them, flipping tractor tires to warm up every morning, and training harder and smarter than anyone else in the game.

So, when I found myself staring into the eyes of the only woman I'd ever loved, I knew it wouldn't feel like work at all.

chapter ten

Emme

*Today's Learning Objective:
Students will get carried away.*

"That looks uncomfortable."

Ines eyed me up and down, a grimace dug into her face. I glanced at her in the mirror as I tried to even out my cleavage. They'd sewn a heavy-duty bra into this dress for me which was amazing because I couldn't get away with free-boobing. But I must've done something wrong because one side looked deflated while the other was right where it should be.

"It's not bad," I said, scooping and shifting as best I could in a sequin-studded dress that was tailored to the point that I didn't dare take a deep breath. I figured it was good that it was this tight. At least I wouldn't worry about gravity taking over and flashing some nip.

"It looks like there was an explosion of citrus." She pushed her glasses up her nose and made a face that suggested we didn't care for explosive citrus. "Or—"

"I get what you're saying," I said.

"How much did it cost?"

"A lot," was all I was willing to say.

Ines nodded gravely. I wasn't sure she understood the mindfuck that was wearing a dress that could've covered three month's rent but I accepted it.

"You look better," she said.

I *humphed* down at my cleavage. "Well, it's not there yet, but it's more even."

"No, I mean, you look better than you did a few weeks ago. Like you're back from the dead." She shook her head, sending her pin-straight dark hair swishing. "Must be all the Vitamin C. From the citrus."

I sputtered a laugh. I loved Ines's jokes and her insistence on explaining them. "Must be."

"It's good that you're doing this. If you didn't get out there soon, I was going to drag you along to my kung fu classes and Magic: The Gathering tournaments. It's not good to stay in bed and be sad all the time." With a shrug, she added, "It wasn't worth moping around over that rat-faced man-pig, anyway."

I stopped fussing with my dress to peer at her. "Wait. When did you meet him?"

"I didn't, but I know he was a dick to you and that makes him a rat-faced man-pig to me."

I turned away from the mirror so she wouldn't see the tears that'd filled my eyes. "Thanks," I managed.

"You do look nice," she said, trailing the back of her finger over the bodice. "It's the kind of dress that regular people never get to wear."

I knew she was right and I also knew Teddy would've hated it. He would've made that sour milk face and told me to change into something that fit. Or he would've eyed my plumped-up breasts and said I looked like an overstuffed sausage. If he really wanted to shut me down, he would've poked a finger into my belly or hips and simply walked away with a disgusted shake of his head.

Once again, I exited Teddy from my mind with a mental scream of *Fuck you and the horse you rode in on*. He didn't belong there. His voice had no place in my inner monologue. He deserved none of my energy. "I love the yellow and orange. It felt...fun. And I didn't want to wear black."

"You deserve some fun," she said.

The truth was, I'd hated almost all the dresses Ryan's stylist Wren had selected for me. They were *so boring*. All the same silhouettes, all the same colors. What was the point of shopping for an actual ball if I didn't have a good time with it?

Black, gray, and navy blue were my day-to-day staples, but I'd always spiced it up with something bright and bold. Maybe I was living this dress-up fantasy a little too loudly, but I wanted to look like myself tonight. Just...fancy.

And that was how I'd landed on this sequined dress of deep, rich marigold with subtle swirls of sunset orange and pale yellow. It'd taken Wren a second to come around, but when I'd tried this one on, she'd agreed. I didn't know if it was my dark hair or the light olive of my skin or some other fashion thing I'd never understand, but exploding citrus worked for me.

When I had my chest even and organized, I gave my hair another fluff. I'd splurged on a blowout this afternoon because my hair was longer than I usually let it go, and the only thing I could reliably do with it at this length was twist it up with a claw clip and I didn't think that was the vibe tonight.

Jamie was right about it being time for a cut. I'd put it off because I hadn't cared enough about how I looked to want something new and I hadn't wanted to feed into the *new do, new you* storyline. That would've required me to make an effort at getting out there again, and I knew deep in my heart that if it wasn't for Ryan, I wouldn't be going anywhere.

"Aren't you going to be cold?" Ines asked. "You're basically half naked."

I glanced down at the dress pooled around my bare feet. "How is this half naked?"

She motioned to her shoulders. "You're...bare."

"I'm okay with this," I said. "But there's a cape that came with the dress if I really want to—"

"If you have a cape, you wear a cape," she cried. "Put on the cape!"

I froze with a bottle of setting spray held in front of my face. Aside from the ongoing train wreck of her internship situation, Ines did not have huge reactions to much of anything. She was reliably neutral. It was her operating system.

So, I found myself startled when she yelled at me about the cape.

"Where is this cape?" she asked. "I must see it."

I pointed to the short doorway that led to the strange annex off my room that functioned as a closet for me. My best guess was that it was used as a nursery back when this building was one grand home. It was too small even for an extremely narrow bed and—

"Oh my god you have to wear this." Ines returned holding the cape up by the hanger, her eyes wide and her mouth open. "If I had something like this, I'd wear it every day."

I studied the matching marigold satin with its delicate bursts of sparkling color, and tried to imagine Ines trudging through Kendall Square with this cape flung over her backpack.

It wouldn't be the most unusual thing to pass through Kendall Square on a given day. Not even in the top ten.

"I'll wear the cape," I said, taking the hanger from her. I'd meant to skip it because it seemed a little excessive, and as much as I loved some excess, I wasn't convinced I wanted to draw that much attention to myself. Though I probably should've gone with one of the simple black dresses if I was hung up on subtlety. "And we'll find you something equally rad. Okay?"

She helped me get the cape situated without messing up my hair and asked, "Can I take a picture? To send my mom? She'd love this."

I hesitated. Ines's mom was an extension of my mom. They had a little sisterhood, all of Gary's exes, and they were closer to each other than any of their subsequent husbands. Hell, half of them were filming a reality show together right now.

But my mother would find out about Ryan soon enough. Her phone blew up any time a high-earning player in any pro league went off the market. She'd make time in her schedule to attend the wedding. Whenever that was. And she'd definitely be there when all of this ended, all too eager to train me in the ways of the pro sports divorcée.

"Sure," I said weakly.

Her mom was sweet and she'd always been kind to me. Even if she'd sworn for years that Ines was just a quirky free spirit who didn't like living by society's rules, and not a kid who needed someone to accept and support her neurodivergent brain. But I could put that grudge aside for a minute.

I stepped into my shoes and struck the exact pose Wren had shown me. "Tell her I say hi."

"She's going to be so happy," Ines said. "She always likes hearing about you."

Among the many unhelpful comments from Ines's mother were often ones about how she wished she'd had a daughter like me. Yep, she'd say that shit right in front of her living, breathing, brilliant daughter. It always made me want to spill a cold drink down her shirt.

Since I didn't want to make a face I'd have to explain to her, I glanced at my phone while she sent off the photos. "Ryan's going to be here in a minute," I said, shooting off a response that he didn't have to come up to the apartment. "Could you help me down the stairs? I keep having visions of my skirt getting stuck on a loose floorboard or something and ripping the whole thing."

"You should be more concerned about falling down the stairs and snapping your neck than the state of your dress," she said, returning to her cool solemnity.

"Right, well, that too." I grabbed my clutch and shuffled toward the door. I couldn't move very fast in this dress. A knock sounded. I stared at it and sighed. "I told you not to come up," I shouted.

"And as you can tell, I didn't listen," Ryan shouted back.

Ines abandoned me to open the door, revealing Ryan in a devastating tuxedo. I'd seen him in skintight football gear and swim trunks, and there was no doubt in my mind that this was better. So much better. He looked crisp and precise in a way that was all Ryan, but something about him tonight exuded raw power. The man was a danger to society. I honestly didn't know what would happen when we went out in public. Swooning, fainting, underwear thrown at his feet. All possible. Likely, even.

Hell, I might get in on it too.

"Jesus Christ," he muttered, running a hand over his mouth. "You look—"

"Like citrus," Ines said. "The only thing missing is the lime."

I lifted my skirt just enough to show off my strappy heels encrusted with light green rhinestones. Peridot, Wren had called them. "Nope, I'm fully committed to the bit."

"No scurvy here," Ines said. "Because of the Vitamin C. From the fruit."

Ryan braced his hands on either side of the doorframe and nodded to himself for a second. His jaw was sharp enough that I was certain I'd cut my hand if I reached out and touched him.

He cleared his throat. "Bowen's downstairs," he said, extending a hand but keeping his gaze low. "We should go."

Okay, so not a fan of the yellow. Got it.

Maybe I should've shown it to him when we picked it up the other day. I didn't think he'd care much one way or another. It wasn't like he'd expect me to blend in with all the other silk ball gowns. He knew me better than that.

His gaze shifted to my neck. "I instructed Wren to select jewelry for you."

I fluttered my hand at the base of my throat. "Yeah. She did. But it seemed like too much. The earrings weren't my style and the necklace looked like something out of a heist movie. I didn't want you to spend all the money just to have some witty bandits cut the power and yank it off me in the dark."

"Next time," he said, "tell Wren you'd like to see something different."

"Please." I waved a hand at my skirt. "The last thing I need is more sparkle. It would've been a waste of money."

Ryan tucked my hair over one ear and frowned at the diamond studs there. They were the nicest things I had, and good-sized stones too, a birthday gift I was positive my stepmother had picked out. My father never would've gone for something so simple or elegant.

But more to the point, he never would've sent me a birthday gift.

"Next time, waste the money," he said, a few strands of my hair twisted around his finger. "I'll be disappointed if you don't."

"You want me to just...buy jewelry."

He nodded as he rubbed my hair between his index finger and thumb. "Yes."

"Does it have to be jewelry?"

"Is there something else you want?"

I stared at the crisp lines of his bow tie. I didn't know why, but I wanted to pull it loose. I wanted to make a mess of him. "What about books? I need a new class set of *The Miraculous Journey of Edward Tulane*. Most of them are more tape than book these days."

"Buy whatever you want. I'll add you to my Amex account."

A startled laugh burst out of me. "I was kidding about—about the books. I don't need—"

"If you don't order the books, I will."

He wasn't being serious. About any of it. I knew that. Even so, I said, "Okay, but don't be surprised if you see some major bookstore charges coming your way."

"Even if you ordered class sets of every second-grade book you could ever want, that would still cost less than the jewelry Wren selected for you."

Such an attitude with this one tonight. I rolled my eyes. "Aren't you supposed to be saving up to buy some soccer teams? Maybe it's not a great idea to be throwing around the cash like it's confetti."

He dragged his fingers down the length of my hair, pulling just enough to send a wave of tingles running over my scalp and down my neck. "I'm going to spend a little over sixty million on these teams when the ink is dry," he said, the words low and husky. "That's less than what I earn in a year before postseason bonuses, before endorsements." He released my hair and let his fingers trail down my bare arm to circle my wrist. "Buy all the books you want, wife."

I swallowed hard, but didn't say anything for a minute. Ines coughed from the other side of the kitchen but made herself look busy when we glanced in that direction. Eventually, I managed, "Don't get ahead of yourself, Wildcat. We're not married yet."

"I'm getting warmed up," he said. "You know how I am about practice."

"You guys are going to be late," Ines called.

Ignoring her, Ryan leaned in close, saying, "In the future, I'll take care of the jewelry."

I didn't know what to say, so I nodded as another round of tingles softened my skull.

Ines held the tail of the cape while I gripped Ryan's forearm and moved toward the stairs. "Wait, wait just a second," I said, carefully gathering my skirt. I tried descending the step again, but I felt the same tension in the dress that screamed *I'm gonna rip!*

"What's wrong?" he asked, staring down the curve of the stairwell.

I pulled the skirt up as high as the fabric would allow—which wasn't much. Still no progress. "I guess I should've gotten dressed on the sidewalk."

"Emme," he sighed. "I don't know what that means."

I drew in a shallow breath because it was all I could manage with this skirt bunched all the way up to my knees and the bodice slicing into my rib cage. "There's not enough room in this skirt to make it down the stairs. They're too steep and the dress is too tight."

"Fuck it," he growled. "We'll stay here. We don't need to go to this thing."

"That is *not* the answer," I said at the same moment Ines cried, "But the cape!"

"You said this was important," I continued. "That you needed to be at this event."

"It costs five thousand dollars to attend," Ines said.

"Oh, we're going," I said. "I am surgically attached to this dress, my hair's been blown out, and I have twenty-nine different products on my face. We are going to this party even if I have to parachute out a window." I motioned to my face and hair. "There's no way I'm letting you waste five *thousand* dollars per plate tickets and all of this."

"She spends most Saturday nights in bed, eating cheese and yelling at movies," Ines added. "She needs to get out of the house."

"Thank you for that," I snapped. "No one needed to know those details, but thank you so much for announcing them to everyone." Turning back to Ryan, I said, "I'll just change out of the dress now and duck into the hotel lobby bathroom when we get there for a quick switcheroo. Just drop me off at a side door or something."

"I'm firing this fucking stylist," he said under his breath. He shoved a hand through his hair and sighed in a way that made me long for lung capacity. Fists propped on his hips, he turned around and I could see in his face that he was in quarterback mode. He waved a hand at the cape. "Can you take that off? Until we get downstairs?"

"Yeah, but—"

"Good. Do that." To Ines, he said, "You'll carry that thing and the little bag." He snatched the clutch away from me and passed it to her before shrugging out of his jacket. "And if you don't mind, this." He pressed himself back against the wall, adding, "You're running ahead. I'm gonna need you to clear the way and open the doors."

When she was a few steps below, Ryan dragged a thoughtful gaze over my dress, lingering on the flare of my hips.

"Here's what we're doing." He gestured to the backs of my knees and under my arms. It looked like he was calling a play. "I'm going to carry you—"

"You're gonna fucking what?"

Fully unbothered by my screeching, he continued, "But there are some narrow turns. I need you to keep your head here"—he patted his chest—"and your legs tucked in tight."

"And what about the part where this is the fifth floor and I am not a small woman?"

"If I wasn't worried about nailing your head on the banister or messing up your hair, I'd throw you over my shoulder and run." He slipped an arm around my waist and the other behind my knees, and scooped me off the stair. "Be a good girl for me and keep your head down."

I curled in on myself as much as this dress would allow and tucked my head under his chin. He shifted his hold on me a bit and I waited for some kind of grunt or groan, a *this is quite a hefty package* or *you're a sturdy one*, but none came.

"Ines," he said, not even an ounce of distress in that commanding tone, "let's roll."

And true to his word, he damn near jogged down every flight of these steep, narrow stairs and out onto the sidewalk. He wasn't even breathing heavily when he set me down. No sheen of sweat on his brow, no flush of pink coloring his cheeks.

He stared at me while he slipped on his jacket and straightened his cuffs. When he was finished, he took a step closer, and then another. In the corner of my eye, I saw Ines hand him the cape. He swept a hand under my hair and I felt the soft fabric settle over my shoulders, against the backs of my arms.

"You look like the first day of spring after the coldest, most brutal winter," he said. "No one is going to be able to take their eyes off you."

"Oh," I sighed.

With his fingers at my throat, he snapped the clasp into place as he stared down at me. "There," he whispered. "*Very* good."

I didn't know this until Ryan asked Bowen to take the long way to the hotel, but we were arriving late to this party. On purpose.

"I see the oppositional defiance still runs strong in you," I said.

He glanced over at me with something like a smile. "I hate red carpets," he said.

"And yet you appear on so many of them."

"Contracts," he muttered.

"What? What does that mean?"

He cleared his throat and tugged at his collar. "Most of the time, those appearances are required by an endorsement contract."

"Like, the watch brand?" I pointed to the thick metal face poking out from his sleeve.

"No, I actually like this watch," he said, adjusting it on his wrist. "It's the less obvious ones. The car company, the mattress brand." He blinked like he had to flip through his mental account book. "The private jets."

"They like it when you show up at fancy things and look pretty for them," I said.

He nodded and left it at that. These appearances had to get exhausting for him. Idle chatter killed him slowly, and while I was certain all these years of being the face of Boston football had trained the worst of it out of him, that didn't make it any easier.

By the time we arrived, the red carpet and backdrop branded with the charity's logo were still in place, but the entrance was empty save for hotel staff.

"Ninety minutes," Ryan said to Bowen as we pulled up at the luxury Back Bay hotel.

"That's it?" I asked as Ryan opened my door. He curled an arm around my waist and scooped me out of the car, which was cool because my only other option was flinging myself off the seat and hoping for the best.

"That's more than enough," he said, dragging his lips over my cheek.

I swallowed hard. We'd joked around the other day about getting close in public, but I guess I wasn't prepared for the reality of it. Not that I was *un*prepared. We'd always been affectionate and I'd thought nothing of it. Hugging, sharing food, sitting close together.

Maybe it was the short supply of oxygen to my brain, but this felt different. *Completely* different.

Rather than watching me struggle to climb the handful of steps to the door, Ryan picked me up and deposited me at the entrance like I was a sequined piece of luggage.

"You gotta warn me," I said, wagging my clutch at the steps. "I can't have you tossing me around like a sack of potatoes."

Ryan tucked my arm into his and led me to the elevator. Two bellhops held the doors open for us and went to the trouble of pressing the button for the correct floor. "You're a lot prettier than a sack of potatoes. Softer too."

"That's nice and all," I said, "but the point is that you can't pick people up whenever you feel like it."

He tugged at his collar when we stepped off the elevator and found no fewer than ten hotel employees waiting nearby, all face-splitting smiles and helpful gestures toward the festivities.

"All right, here's the plan," he said, his voice low enough to stay between us. "One full turn around the room, stop long enough to take some photos with a few people, maybe some of the guys from the team, and then get the hell out before they serve dinner."

"No! I really want to know what a five-thousand-dollar dinner tastes like," I said.

"It's nothing special," he said.

"Says the guy with the private plane."

"I'll have them box up a plate for you," he said.

"It's not the same," I wailed.

He drew in a breath and it rattled like a warning. "I swear to god,

Emme, if you make me sit through a fucking five-course menu with a full roster of speeches in the middle, I-I—"

We stopped at the doors of the ballroom, the opulent storybook theme spilling out into the hall with exaggerated toadstools and thick branches wrapped in the dreamiest floral garlands. I beamed up at Ryan, waiting for him to land on the consequence he'd never cash in. "Yes?" I fluttered my lashes. "What will you do to me?"

I felt people watching us. I sensed the energy of their attention from every side, and from the corner of my eye, I saw someone aim a camera at us. Then another. A flash went off. It was strange, and if I gave myself a minute to think about it, I'd find a lot of reasons to be uncomfortable. But right now, here, with his hands flexing at his sides and his dark eyes eating me up, I couldn't bring myself to care.

A snarl sounded in his throat as he shook his head once, looping an arm around my waist. I flattened my hands on his chest to keep my balance while he dragged a hand up my back and over my shoulders to rest at the base of my neck.

"Fuck it," he growled.

He tipped my head back, and within the space between blinks, he went from staring at me to kissing me. At first it was a slow, firm press but then a quiet, strangled noise vibrated between us and I understood what he'd meant about coming out of a long, cold winter because I felt like the world was new again and I was too.

I linked my hands behind his neck and let him press me closer, *closer* while murmurs rose and camera shutters clicked around us. I couldn't let myself think about the audience. I told myself it was Ryan they were after and I was an irrelevant side note in the whole thing. None of it mattered much anyway because I wasn't sure my feet were still connected to the ground and my head was definitely floating off into space and my belly was—well, there was a lot of swooping and fluttering in there.

Another important note: I was kissing my oldest friend and it wasn't at all what I'd imagined.

This was not where I'd expected things to go tonight, but if the options were kissing Ryan or not kissing Ryan, I was good with this situation. I was a floating, flailing mess, but I was *good*.

No one had ever kissed me like this before. Like they were damn certain they wanted to kiss *me*.

I didn't even care that he was making the most of the media gathered nearby and checking off the girlfriend box. He was pretending in his way. I'd pretend in mine.

And then, just barely, he eased back. His forehead tipped against mine and his chest heaving, he whispered, "Fine. Dinner. But we're leaving before dessert."

I bounced on the balls of my feet. "Dessert is the best part!"

He closed his eyes like I was causing him real pain. "Emme."

Before I could defend dessert, his lips covered mine again, urgently now, as if this was the last moment to make the play.

Flashes went off around us.

It was my turn to stutter out the incoherent noises, and Ryan tore himself away from me with a gasp. He brought both hands to my neck, sweeping his thumbs over my cheeks. "I'll have every dessert in this city delivered to you tonight. I'll have a pastry chef on call to make you whatever the hell you want. But we're not staying a minute longer than necessary."

Ryan kept his arm around my waist and led me into the ballroom. He resumed that cool, steady mask that looked like disdain or even disinterest to the rest of the world but I knew to be the placid surface of a raging sea.

As for me, I didn't even have to force the smile in response to all the people who'd turned to look at us. I was as bright as this shiny, sequined dress.

chapter eleven
Emme

Today's Learning Objective:
Students will understand the assignment.

I HATED TO ADMIT IT BUT THE MEAL WAS NOT FIVE THOUSAND DOLLARS impressive. It was very good, definitely better than anything I would've thrown together, but it didn't come close to my expectations.

The expectations might've been the problem. I'd had it in my mind that every bite would be a gold-flecked orgasm or something. Maybe the gold-flecked orgasms were reserved for the twenty-five-thousand-dollar dinners.

Here was what I thought would happen: Lots of air-kiss schmoozing with snooty people who had snooty things to say while drinking snooty cocktails like rye on the rocks or pisco sours. Ryan would just glad-hand his way through it like the media-trained superstar he was while I'd smile and make innocuous chatter like *such an important cause* and *aren't the flowers a wonder?*

What actually happened: There was a small stampede to get a photo with Ryan, and *everyone*—even the actually snooty people with their foamy pisco sours—wanted all the insider football gossip. They wanted the drama going down between the coaches, managers, and owners, they wanted the scoop on trades and draft picks, they wanted to know if the fast receiver with good hands was on the road to recovery after another knee surgery or if the tight end who had a knack for being everywhere Ryan needed him on the field would be extending his contract.

And god love him, Ryan handled every question like he hadn't already answered it forty-seven times. He had a patient, natural way about him as he clapped people on the back and leaned in close to repeat the same evasive yet fully chummy response that he'd given everyone else, and these people *ate it up*.

Once again, I was in every photo, but at least I didn't have to say a single word about flowers. And it was a good thing, because with the lengths Ryan was taking all this performative affection, my body was stirring up some thoughts that I'd left alone for the past few months. I could feel the red staining my cheeks when he pulled me in close for a photo or he kissed my temple or he fitted one of those big hands around the curve of my hip and gave it a squeeze like he did that all the time—but with a whole lot less clothes. Every time his fingers traced the ball of my shoulder or followed the line of my dress across my back, more heat pooled low in my belly.

Of course I was having naked feelings from some absent-minded petting—and a few kisses for the cameras that'd hit harder than any real kisses I'd ever received. The past few months had been lonely. I hadn't bounced back from Teddy with any random hookups. Maybe I should've because I was damn near climbing out of my skin.

Surprising no one at all, I wasn't helping myself in shutting these naked feelings down. I responded to all this coziness by slipping my hand under Ryan's jacket and walking my fingers up and down the corded muscle in his back. Or dropping a loving hand to his chest and then letting it slowly slide down the solid length of his torso to the abs that felt like cobblestones. I kept my hand there through several tedious conversations until Ryan snatched it up and lifted it to his lips only to growl, "That's enough. We're leaving right fucking now."

"But—"

"No." He led us to the door in long, quick strides that had me struggling to keep up. "We're done here."

"But dessert," I whined.

We were almost to the elevator when we heard, "Ralston, get your ass back here."

"Motherfuck," he muttered. He cut a sidelong glance at me. "This will only take a minute."

Turning around, I found half the New England offensive line ambling toward us, bow ties loose and beer bottles in hand. I hadn't spotted any of these guys during cocktail hour and I would've, since they stuck out like sore thumbs. Very tall, very broad, very confident thumbs.

I pulled in a breath and let my eyes close for one final moment of peace before football crashed into my life all over again.

"Where the fuck did you fools come from?" Ryan asked, leaning in for one-armed embraces. He hadn't released my hand from his hold.

"I thought I was supposed to pick up Wilcox," said Crawson Bigelow, pointing to the running back, a thick-shouldered Black man with the kind of perma-smile that could thaw ice.

"I thought *I* was picking *him* up," Jaden Wilcox replied, pointing a baseball-mitt hand at the left tackle. Bigelows's chest was about as wide as a freeway and he had a dusting of freckles across the light brown of his cheeks. Adorable. "So I was waiting outside his place for an hour, but he was at my house."

"And both those motherfuckers forgot us," said Trenton Hersberler, slapping Damon McKerry on the back.

"But we were playing Mario Kart and didn't notice," said McKerry, tossing his long, braided locs over his shoulder.

Hersberler, the tight end everyone loved and wanted to see on the field with Ryan for another season, extended a lightly suntanned hand toward me. "Hello," he drawled, a stunning smile on his face. "Trenton Hersberler, though my friends call me Trent."

"Your friends call you Pumpkin Dick," Wilcox said.

He bared his teeth at Wilcox. "That's not—no. That's not true. It happened one time. No one calls me that."

McKerry snorted out a burly laugh. The boy was half bear, there was no doubt in my mind. Just like all the other left guards in the League. "We do," he said to me with a glazed grin that told me he was enjoying the hell out of his off-season. "Wanna know why?"

"My girl does *not* need to hear that story," Ryan said. He curled his thick arm over my shoulder, his palm flat on my chest while his thumb and forefinger bracketed the base of my throat like he could deflect the silly filth of locker room talk.

"No, actually, I'd love to hear that," I said, beckoning to McKerry to hit me with the dirt. I glanced up at Ryan. "I won't be able to leave here without getting that story. I'm in it now, and so are you."

"I hope you know what you're asking for," he said.

"I have no idea and that's the best part." To McKerry, I rolled my hand, saying, "Lemme have it."

"Here we go," Bigelow said under his breath, slapping a hand on Hersberler's chest.

"Fuckin' love this," Wilcox said, bouncing on the balls of his feet like he was ready to get in the game.

McKerry said through halting giggles, "My boy here accidentally jerked off with a bottle of self-tanner."

Bigelow and Wilcox dissolved into hysterical, wheezing laughter. Hersberler crossed his arms and glared up at the ceiling. "Fuck you all," he muttered.

"Let's clarify which part of this was the accident," I said. "Was it the jerking off or was it the self-tanner? Because I have some questions if it was an accidental jerk-off. Like, how? Just how? I mean, I'm going to have questions either way, but I want to get to the root"—Bigelow clutched his side and barked out a laugh as he crashed into Wilcox so hard they hit the floor—"of the issue here."

"I fucking hate you guys," Hersberler grumbled.

"It gets better," McKerry said, tears streaking down his round, teddy bear cheeks. Beside me, Ryan shook with laughter. Ah, not so stoic after all. "It was game day, and he went out and blew up his receiving yards. So, he had to keep it going. All fuckin' season with the self-tanner."

"Yeah, of course," I said. There was no reasoning with athletes and their superstitions. My second stepdad Jim was the worst with that. Always had to watch a very specific episode of *The Simpsons* while eating oatmeal with exactly seventeen blueberries the day of a game. And he hated *The Simpsons*.

"Now," McKerry went on, still cracking himself up, "his dick is..."

"Orange," I said when it didn't seem like the bear could continue.

"And sparkly," McKerry cried.

I pressed my lips together while they howled with laughter and Hersberler muttered to himself about having shitbag friends. Ryan huffed out a laugh that I felt on the back of my neck. "And why do you know that, McKerry? What are you doing close enough to this guy's dick to see it sparkle?"

That was the last straw for McKerry. He bent at the waist, his hands on his knees as he fought to suck in air. "He didn't know how to get the glitter off. He asked me if I thought he needed a doctor."

I glanced at Hersberler, who'd tipped his head back to drain his beer. "Same procedure," I said to him. "But instead of the tanning lotion"—I used the universal sign for jerking off—"soap and water."

Ryan stroked his thumb up the line of my neck. "Never change, Muggsy."

I wanted to laugh at that, but I was a bit preoccupied with the fact he hadn't taken his hands off me in the past two hours and my body just couldn't distinguish fact from fiction.

"Ma'am," Wilcox said from the floor, his hand extended toward me, "I don't know your name, but I know I love you."

McKerry slapped him away. "Get your fuckin' hands away from this angel. She's obviously mine."

"Not even close to yours, McKerry." Ryan motioned to me, saying, "Boys, meet Emme Ahlborg."

Wilcox frowned as he gained his feet. "As in—"

Bigelow shook his head like he hadn't heard right. "Any relation to the Chicago Ahlborgs?"

"Yeah, same," I said, feeling every muscle in me draw tight. "My dad."

I knew this moment was coming. There was no way for me to spend time in Ryan's world without dragging along the baggage that came with my last name. It was a wonder I'd made it this far.

Hersberler groaned as he rubbed his eyes. "You fucking tools told *Charles Ahlborg's daughter* that my dick is orange and sparkly."

That was what it always boiled down to. I was nothing more than my father's daughter, a branch in a great tree that had its roots in the earliest days of American football. Someone far back in my father's family had played on one of the first college squads at Penn. Then, a few years and probably some brain damage later, someone else in the gene pool decided to develop a regional pro league that would eventually turn into one of the four founding teams of the League as we knew it today. More than a hundred years later, the family still owned that team. My father and his sons—my half brothers—ran the organization today.

I wasn't involved.

"No sweat," I said to Hersberler. "The secret's safe with me. But seriously about the soap and water. It'll do you good."

"I will do anything you ask if you'll forget that whole story," he said, a hand over his heart as he stepped closer. "Emme—can I call you Emme?"

"As far as you're concerned, it's Mrs. Ralston and back the fuck up while you're at it," Ryan said, waving him off.

Oh. So...we really are practicing tonight.

It was going to take me a minute to get used to this.

"Excuse me but did you just say *Mrs. Ralston*?" Bigelow cried.

"When did that happen?" Wilcox asked.

"Soon enough," Ryan replied.

"Can I be the ring bearer?" McKerry asked. "I'm being so for real—you know I'd be good at it."

"Can we focus on me, please?" Hersberler clapped his hands together. "I'm the one in crisis here. If that story gets out and I'm traded to Chicago, I'll never play again."

My father had a bit of a reputation. He wasn't known for being the warmest, fuzziest guy. He was great to those who played well for him, but he could be mean, petty, and vindictive. He would waste a trade on benching an all-star player like Hersberler if he thought it proved a point or fucked someone else over.

"As much fun as we had here tonight with this little story," I said, "I can't think of a single reason why I'd ever tell another soul about you and your pumpkin spice sparkle. Least of all my father. I rarely talk to him about anyone's dick. It's kind of a rule I have."

"Thank you," Hersberler said, "but if—"

"Calm the fuck down, man," Ryan said to him. "If you'd stopped dicking around with your contract, you wouldn't need to worry about ending up in Chicago. Solve some of your own fucking problems and leave my girl out of it, all right?"

"That makes you a princess," McKerry said suddenly, glancing around to the other guys. "She's the princess—of football. Right?" He nodded vigorously, sending his loose bow tie flying like small, useless wings. "Am I wrong? She's our princess." He slapped a hand to his forehead. "I just told the princess about Pumpkin Dick. I said *jerking off* to the princess. Multiple times."

I smiled though I didn't mean it. I was hardly a princess in my father's world. I was barely the princess of my own apartment.

"You did," Wilcox said, slapping him on the back. "Well done, dude."

"If I was gonna talk about dick to the gridiron princess," Bigelow said, "I'd make sure it was my own and not fuckin' Hersberler's jack-o-lantern shit."

"I seriously hate you guys," Hersberler muttered.

"You love us so much," McKerry said, pulling him into a rowdy embrace.

A photographer stopped by then and corralled us into a group shot. Ryan and I stood on the end, his chest warm and solid at my back and his hands on my waist. "If we aren't inside an elevator in the next minute, I'm throwing you over my shoulder and running for the stairs. Just keep your head down. You'll be fine."

"You don't want to hang with the team for a bit?"

His hands flexed on my waist. "Why? I hang out with them enough. Do you need more dick stories? Because they have them."

"I've probably had enough dick for tonight, thanks."

Beside me, Wilcox busted into laughter and took McKerry and Bigelow down with him. Hersberler made a beeline for the bar. To the photographer, Ryan said, "Thanks for your time. Have a good night."

After another round of man-hugs punctuated by McKerry's incessant giggling, we stepped into the elevator. Ryan pulled me up against him, my back tucked tight to his chest. I startled when he slung an arm low across my waist. There was no one around to see this.

He pointed his phone at the mirrored doors and snapped a few photos. "Pick one," he said.

I swiped back and forth through the photos, zooming in on the tiny differences in each. His fingers were splayed wider across my belly in one, my lips were parted like I was gasping in another. My chin was tipped at a strange angle or there was the slightest hint of a smile on his face. But more than any of those barely noticeable details, we looked like we were together. Like I was meant to fit up against his body this way and his hand belonged on my hip and the hunger in his gaze was real.

"This one," I said, tapping that smile of his as the doors opened at the lobby.

We headed toward the sidewalk where Bowen and the SUV sat waiting for us. "I'm picking you up and putting you in the car," Ryan said. "Consider this fair warning."

"The rest of my dresses need to have full range of motion," I said as we reached the hotel doors. "If I can't kick and squat and lunge, I'm not wearing it." I rustled the sequined fabric. "Maybe I just need a slit up the thigh. That would've made a huge difference."

"Don't do that to me," Ryan murmured as he scooped me up and dropped me in the seat before jogging around the car and sliding in on the opposite side. "The North End," he said to Bowen.

"You promised me dessert," I said.

He rubbed his brows. "What do you want?"

"Something with chocolate," I said.

"Bowen," he called.

"On it," the driver replied.

Ryan went back to his phone. "Not that one?" He swiped to the image where I'd aimed a sharp, smirking glance over my shoulder. "I like that one."

"I like the other one."

With a shrug, he posted the photo to his social media accounts. No caption, but he did tag the charity. My stomach gave a hard flip at the idea of being perceived at such a massive level. Photos at the ball were one thing. Ryan's personal social accounts were several enormous things.

I told myself it didn't matter and gulped it all down. I'd tried to block this part out of the fake engagement plan. I knew I'd appear in public with him, I knew the connection to my father would become known, and I knew I'd give up my privacy—at least while we kept this going.

My hand shaking, I reached for Ryan's forearm and squeezed. His gaze followed my hand and stared at it for a long moment. Then he shuffled closer, his arm coming around my shoulder and my head resting on his chest.

"You can choose not to care," he said, pressing a kiss to my temple. "I know because you taught me how."

I murmured in agreement. That was true. But it also wasn't. Not caring wasn't the same as not feeling. "Yeah."

"Want to watch a movie or something?" he asked. "I'm told that's what you do on Saturday nights."

I bobbed my head. I didn't take the bait. "Yeah."

The car slowed on a side street and Bowen rolled down the driver's side window. "Thanks," he called to a person dressed in a chef's coat. He set two large paper bags in the front seat and sped off.

"What was that?" I asked.

"I texted Bowen an hour ago to order everything on the dessert menu and have it ready to pick up," Ryan said. "I never forget my promises to you."

Ryan helped me out of the car and I could say with absolute certainty that I didn't enjoy being a doll. It sounded really cute in theory—sweep me off my feet, hand-deliver me from one place to another, protect my delicate lady sensibilities from anything as crude as climbing out of a vehicle—but in practice, it was much less fun. My dress was cleaving my internal organs, my boobs were shoved up into my throat and suffocating me, and worst of all, I felt helpless. It wasn't a good time.

Now, standing outside my building while thick layers of spring fog pressed down around us, I realized we'd have to do it all over again. I watched Ryan unlock the door—I was busy holding the desserts—and gave a few test steps to see if the dress had stretched out at all. There was a bit more give than I'd had earlier. It could be enough.

"What the fuck is wrong with you?" he asked the lock, still jiggling the key. That thing was always a problem.

When he finally had the door open, I said, "I think I can manage the stairs."

Eyes wide, he stared at my dress for a beat. "What?"

I motioned to my thighs. "I think I'll be able to make it up the stairs by myself. It might be slow but I have a little extra wiggle room now. It would help if I opened the zipper too."

"It's not going to"—he shoved a hand through his hair—"fall off?"

"Hardly. I'm strapped into this thing five ways to the weekend."

Another hand through his hair. "I can carry you."

"Oh, I'm aware," I said.

He blew out an impatient breath and knelt down beside me, saying, "Pull up your skirt."

It was my turn to blink at him. "What?"

"You're not taking the stairs in these shoes." He slipped his hand under my skirt and circled my ankle. His fingers were warm and the touch jolted a small squeak out of me. "Up."

When I lifted the skirt, he went to work unfastening the tiny buckles. He held my elbow as I stepped out and then hooked them around his fingers. He motioned for me to turn around, and when I did, he tugged the zipper down to my waist. His knuckles bumped over the hooks of my bra and along the small of my back.

I shivered. There was no way he didn't notice. I'd tried so hard to keep my reactions in check tonight, but now, with all this oxygen rushing to my head and the complete lack of an audience gobbling up our every move, I found I couldn't hold back anymore.

That was the fear at the core of all this. I didn't trust myself to hold back. I didn't trust myself to keep my feelings out of the fake marriage. I didn't believe it could ever be anything but real for me, and thinking about that broke my heart in advance.

His knuckles disappeared and he reached for the carryout bags in my hand, saying, "I'll take those."

We made slow work of the stairs but Ryan stayed a few steps behind me, silent with a steady hand low on my back the entire time.

Rounding the landing on the third floor, I asked, "What do you want to watch?"

"What do you usually watch with your cheese?"

"Just so you know, it's not like I'm gnawing on a block of cheddar."

"But it's so much more amusing to me that way."

"Anything to force you to smile," I said.

He yawned. "I'll watch whatever you want. It's up to you."

"In other words, you don't want to choose but you will complain unless it's *Indiana Jones*, *The Hobbit*, or *Top Gun*."

"You forgot *The Mummy* and *Black Panther*."

"Ohhhh, *The Mummy*," I said. "Definitely that."

The apartment was dark when I let us in, no light seeping out from beneath Ines's room. Probably still out. I closed the door behind us and motioned for Ryan to follow me to the other end of the apartment.

"I need to change into something completely shapeless and soft before my ribs get stuck this way," I said, heading toward the closet. "My laptop is plugged in over there. Make yourself comfy."

It took me a few minutes to wrestle my way out of the sewn-in bra and the shapewear shorts Wren had recommended for *smooth lines*. I pulled on sweats and a hoodie and ducked into the bathroom to wash off my makeup.

When I returned, Ryan had ditched the shoes, jacket, and bow tie, and opened his collar at the throat. He stood by the bed, his hands in his pockets as he stared at the old water spots on the ceiling. "You're sure you don't want to hang out at my place? I have an eighty-inch TV and the rain never makes its way inside."

I settled on the bed and started unpacking the desserts. "I'm good." I patted the spot beside me. "You're not going to be able to see the movie from over there."

He hesitated a moment and then climbed up. He raised his arm as if he was about to wrap it around me but stopped himself, instead saying,

"You were incredible tonight. It was everything I needed and more. Thank you."

I felt my cheeks heat. I tapped the screen to start the movie. "Anytime, husband."

He made a noise as the opening credits rolled, something between coughing and clearing his throat. Then, "And thanks for putting up with the guys."

"Oh, come on. They were easy."

"Easy, perhaps," he said. "But that doesn't mean you'd choose it. I know you don't want anything to do with that world."

I nodded as I organized the desserts. "As long as I don't run into my dad at any of these events, I'll be fine."

"I'll make sure you don't."

"That's good enough for me to bust out the barmaid bra."

A long breath gusted out of him as he settled back against the pillows. "The less I know about your bras, Em, the better off I will be."

I was about to ask him about the kiss we shared tonight and whether he'd noticed how true and *right* it'd felt when those words hit me. I didn't hear them at first but like raindrops slowly soaking through your clothes, they chilled me down to the bone.

As the movie played, I watched as Ryan drifted off to sleep, his hands clasped over his stomach and his jaw relaxed for the first time all night. It wasn't long before he shifted toward me, his arm around my waist and his face pressed up against my side.

This—*this* was true. It was real but only when no one was looking. We didn't want the same things and I knew that. I *knew* it but my silly little imagination ran away with itself tonight just as I'd feared it would.

chapter twelve

Ryan

*Today's Learning Objective:
Students will keep the good times rolling.*

I KNEW IT WAS MORNING AND I HAD TO GET MY ASS TO THE GYM BUT I didn't want to open my eyes. Not yet. All I needed was five more minutes of feeling...not awful. My shoulder didn't ache, my hip wasn't shooting daggers down my leg, my joints weren't made of rust. For once, nothing hurt enough to get me moving.

I just wanted to exist in this bliss a couple minutes longer. Then, I'd take care of the hard—

Fuck.

It was then that I realized the pressure on my cock was real. It wasn't the remnants of a dream. It was happening right now and it was from Emme's ass in my lap—and the only things separating us were a blanket, her sweats, and my trousers. It might seem like a lot but I could be rid of all of it in less than thirty seconds.

I stared at her, still asleep beside me with her dark hair in braids and my hand tucked under her sweatshirt, resting loosely on her belly. My cock gave a painful throb and I had to swallow a loud groan.

It took everything in me to keep from jackknifing up and out of the bed. No one needed that kind of reaction. Uncalled for. And those antics would only draw attention to the fact we'd slept together—rather we'd slept apart while in the same bed—and I'd had an obvious physical reaction to that.

With all the regret in the world, I pulled away. Her torso was too short and my hands were too big for this to continue. One slight shift in either direction and I'd be in dangerous territory.

Slowly, I shifted to my back and shoved myself into a mental ice bath. Not that it helped much. Not now that I knew how perfect her backside felt against my cock. After touching her like she belonged to me for *hours*.

After kissing her.

Yeah, fuck, that one had changed things.

I'd told myself it wouldn't matter. That I could find the perfect moment with just enough cameras on us, and I'd get it done. Get it out of the way and move on.

I'd known *all* of that was bullshit but it was easier to believe the bullshit than the alternative. So, I'd kissed her. And then I couldn't stop. If I'd talked to anyone the whole night, I didn't remember because all I'd done was stare at her mouth and think about how I'd made a huge fucking mistake by telling myself I could play this game with her.

This was going to ruin me. I knew it. I knew it as well as I knew I wanted to roll over and drag her back to my lap.

The funny part was that my watch showed some of the best bio-data I'd had in months. Maybe years. I couldn't remember the last time I'd slept this well.

Emme shifted under the blankets and I knew she was awake. She took a few minutes to stretch and yawn before rolling over to face me.

"You were out so quick," she said around another yawn. "Do you remember seeing any of the movie?"

I shook my head. "Sorry. Didn't mean to crash here like that."

She brushed some loose hairs off her face. "It was better this way. I didn't have to share any of the desserts with you."

"You should've woken me up," I said. "Sent me home."

"I didn't mind," she said, stretching her arms over her head and sending that sweatshirt riding up the soft line of her belly.

I looked away. "Have you seen my phone?"

She kicked off the blankets and headed toward the door. "Over there. I plugged it in."

I knew better than to expect any kind of *what does it mean?* reaction from Emme this morning but I still wanted one. I wanted her to say something about last night, about sleeping together, about this whole fucking thing. To give me any small sign that she'd felt the earth move when we kissed. That she'd wanted to snuggle up to me in the night and she'd noticed how I reacted to her. Any opening she gave me, I'd take.

But I wasn't holding my breath for one.

I waited until I heard the bathroom door close before climbing out of the bed. I didn't trust my dick not to spring back to life at the sight of Emme and her three-sizes-too-large sweatpants. Though I was thankful for those sweatpants. As much as she liked sweeping things aside—like the fact *we slept together last night*—it would've been a lot tougher to pretend this was merely a friendly sleepover if she'd worn some little shorts or just an oversized t-shirt.

My notifications were more chaotic than usual and it took me a minute of blinking at the screen to figure out why everyone needed to talk to me right away.

"Fuck," I groaned.

The elevator pic.

I wanted to punch myself in the face for throwing Emme to the internet wolves but it seemed I was alone with that sentiment. Jakobi was pleased with the response and Stella was too, though her team had worked through the night getting rid of the more unhinged comments. My family, of course, had the most unhinged comments.

Claudia had been the first in the family group chat, sharing a screenshot of my social post sometime around five this morning. For reasons I didn't care to understand, they'd all been awake then and immediately chimed in with responses and hadn't let up in the hours since.

> Claudia: Explain yourself, brother.
>
> Mom: Is that Emme Ahlborg??
>
> Amber: Holy shit, it is Emme
>
> Mom: I hope this is real!
>
> Chloe: Well, I just screamed my husband awake
>
> Mom: Did you make this up, Claudia? Is this AI?
>
> Claudia: This is your son's page, Mom. Go look for yourself.
>
> Gramma CeCe: It's about damn time!
>
> Ruthie: Which event was this?
>
> Mom: Please tell me this isn't a joke!
>
> Amber: I knew it!
>
> Claudia: You must breathe, Mother. If you can't handle that, you'll never survive what I have for you next.

My youngest sister then posted *twenty-seven photos* of me and Emme scrounged from the charity ball's posts and the socials of anyone we took pics with. She grabbed the Boston newspaper's photos with all the guys from the team too.

> Chloe: Is it really happening? Is this it?
>
> Gramma CeCe: It's been 84 years…

> Amber: omg lol
>
> Claudia: The timing is impeccable as always, Gram
>
> Mom: I'm just so happy <18 sobbing emojis>
>
> Mom: FINALLY!! <10 praise hands emojis>
>
> Gramma CeCe: It was only a matter of time
>
> Ruthie: I have some questions
>
> Claudia: DAMMIT RUTH. Can't you let people be happy for a minute?
>
> Ruthie: I can and choose not to
>
> Mom: Put your questions away, Ruthie. This might be my only chance at grandchildren!
>
> Chloe: You have 2 grandchildren. My kids. Remember them?
>
> Mom: Obviously I meant grandchildren from Ryan
>
> Gramma CeCe: I wouldn't worry about babies. With the way he's looking at her in these photographs, that horse might already be trotting down the lane
>
> Ruthie: Let's not jump to those conclusions until we have all the facts
>
> Mom: Ryan, please tell your sister she doesn't need to litigate anything today
>
> Amber: Even if he does comment, she'll find fault with it
>
> Claudia: My evidence is stronger than your skepticism, Ruth.

Claudia dropped another dozen photos into the chat, including a blurry one where Emme's hand was flat on my abs and I was staring at her like I wanted to devour her.

Which was not wrong.

The group thread had continued on but I noticed a message outside the chat waiting for me from Ruthie.

> Ruthie: You and your new-old girlfriend are taking me to brunch this morning
>
> Ruthie: Buttermilk & Bourbon at noon
>
> Ruthie: Will you attract enough attention there or would you prefer someplace busier?

Emme returned, her hands curled up inside the arms of her sweatshirt. Her eyes were sleepy and the urge to take her back to bed shot through me. "What's up?" she asked, tipping her chin toward my phone.

"Well, two things," I said with a wince. "First, the entire world saw my post last night. You might want to turn off your phone for the day."

She jolted when she saw all the notifications waiting for her. "I guess it's a really good thing all of my social accounts were already private."

"It's the only way," I said, taking the phone from her. It wouldn't help to look too closely. "And, um, Ruthie wants to hang out. If you're up for brunch."

"Always up for brunch and I'd love to see Ruthie," she said, wandering into her closet. "Where are we going? I'll get ready and meet you there."

"I'll wait for you," I called.

She poked her head out but that didn't hide the fact she'd lost the sweatpants. The sweatshirt *just* covered the curve of her ass. The one I'd become all too acquainted with this morning. "You can get away with a lot but I don't think last night's tux is the look you want this morning."

"We'll stop at my place," I said, turning to look out the window so I didn't have to talk myself out of another erection this morning.

"Seems like it would be easier to meet you there," she said.

I glanced over my shoulder as she emerged in a bathrobe that was many terrible things. Short, thin, soft. And her hair in those braids. Terrible. I went back to staring at Charlestown off in the distance.

"Ruthie likes to play the cynic," I said.

"Oh, so this is a test." Emme nodded as she loosened her braids. "Gotcha." She stopped midway through one braid. "She's doubting *me*?"

I shrugged. "It seems that way."

"This kid isn't going to know what hit her," she said. "She's going to walk out stuffed with waffles and the knowledge that I'm actually your soul mate."

I gulped. "That's the spirit."

But then she frowned and jabbed at the air between us. "Wait. So, you actually want your family to believe this is real?"

I knew how to take hard hits. I knew how to fall. I knew how to play through blinding pain.

And yet none of that prepared me to hear those words without taking it like a direct blow to the chest.

This was how I'd ruin my life. This was what would do it to me. It wouldn't be the thunderclap fallout at the end. It would be all the paper-cut moments where I died a little while she had no idea.

"Yeah." I went back to my phone. "Is that okay?"

She hesitated long enough for me to glance up. "I don't want to hurt them," she said.

When it ends.

She didn't say that but it was obvious.

"We won't," I said.

We stared at each other. I knew she was thinking we *would* hurt my family when we split up. But I was thinking we could spare everyone and just keep this ruse going for the next fifty, sixty years.

"It's going to be all right," I said. "I don't know how but I know it will be."

With a nod, Emme headed toward the bathroom. I flopped onto her bed and groaned into her pillow. It smelled like her which only forced another groan.

> Ryan: Noon sounds great

> Ryan: Emme is very excited about brunch. She's also excited about seeing you but I can't understand why

> Ruthie: Love you too

RUTHIE WAS HALFWAY THROUGH A BLOODY MARY WHEN WE ARRIVED at the restaurant. Her gaze dropped to where I had Emme's hand closed in mine and she unfurled a cutthroat smile that said she saw straight through this little act and she intended to nail me to the wall for it.

But then she popped up from her seat and folded Emme into a tight embrace. They yelled at each other about how long it'd been and how good the other looked and a hundred other things I didn't catch because they'd gone ultrasonic at some point.

When we finally sat down, Emme plastered herself right up against me. I had no choice but to sling an arm around her shoulders. It wasn't strictly necessary to twist the ends of her hair around my fingers but when Emme made a show of dropping a hand to my thigh, *everything* became necessary.

"This is new," Ruthie drawled, Bloody Mary in hand. "When did it all start?"

"Around Ryan's birthday," Emme said easily. She skimmed the menu, tapping her finger beside the description for a frozen Irish coffee that had enough whiskey to make her silly with a few sips.

"Mmm. You'd like that," I said to her.

"Then not long," Ruthie said. "Just about a month, really."

"We met up one night to celebrate and...yeah, it happened fast,"

Emme said, a metric ton of suggestion in her tone. My sister's steely gaze dulled a bit at the implication Emme and I had been tearing up the sheets. "But how else would it be with us? We've known each other forever and—you know, it was just the right moment. Everything fell into place and"—she looked up at me, her eyes heavy with hunger—"here we are. At last."

She raised her fingertips to my jaw and drew me closer. I arched a brow in question and she gave a quick dip of her chin. This woman, fuck. She could read my moves from a mile away. I closed the narrow gap between us and kissed her while my sister loudly slurped up the rest of her drink.

The backs of Emme's fingers traveled over the line of my jaw and I'd swear to god the whole restaurant went silent. Her touch, light and lazy as though it was an afterthought, had heat pooling in my chest, my arms. I didn't think I'd ever be cold again.

Ruthie plunked her glass down on the table hard enough to rattle the silverware. I pulled back to say to Emme, "I think my sister feels neglected."

"Probably." She nodded in a way that had her lips brushing mine and it took everything in the world to keep from hauling her into my lap and just fucking keeping her there. "We should've stayed in bed."

I had to close my eyes because if I looked at her, if I looked at those pert, pouty lips for another minute, I'd find myself hard and miserable *in public* with *my sister watching*. Since none of that could occur, I cleared my throat and blinked down at the menu. "What are you in the mood for, Muggsy?"

She gave my thigh a light slap. "Behave yourself."

"Well, shit. Okay. I was wrong. I get it. This is real as fuck and you love each other in sick, serious ways." My sister rolled her eyes. "I'm sold and I'm expecting a plus-one to the wedding. But I am drowning in the pheromones here. We are in a busy restaurant on a Sunday morning and you two are a hiccup away from making a baby in front of me. I am *begging* you to turn it down before I suffocate and die."

Ruthie lifted her glass, calling to the nearest waiter, "Another round over here? And keep 'em coming. Thanks."

Because I was both an idiot and a masochist, I trapped Emme's hand on my leg. Just brilliant. "*I'm* behaving. You're the one causing problems."

"The jalapeño grits sound good," Ruthie said, sounding bored. "The crab cake benedict too."

"No. Get something else," I said, shifting to stare across the table at my sister. "Em's allergic to shellfish."

"Oh—I'm sorry," Ruthie said, dropping the hardened cynic stare for once. "I totally forgot about that."

"No, it's okay. I'll be fine as long as we keep the crab on one side of the table," Emme said.

"At a minimum, you'll start coughing." I leaned around Emme to grab her purse off the bench. "Actually, where's your EpiPen? I want to know where to find it if I need it."

When I unzipped the little bag, she pointed to the injector nestled between her phone and wallet. "See? Easy peasy. Nothing to worry about."

I pointed at Ruthie. "No crab cakes."

She held up her hands in surrender. "Understood."

I glanced over at Emme but found her frowning, her gaze distant. I rubbed my palm up and down her arm but that didn't shake her out of it. After a minute, I asked, "What looks good to you?"

She shifted on the bench just enough to angle her shoulder between us as she studied the menu. "Not sure yet," she murmured. Before I could press any further, she beamed a smile at Ruthie. "Tell me everything about the new job. Ryan says it's really intense. But you love it, right?"

My sister launched into a long summary of her life as a junior associate at a corporate law firm and all I could do was watch while Emme seemed to pull into herself and away from me.

chapter thirteen
Emme

*Today's Learning Objective:
Students will fly in fancy jets and catch confusing feels.*

AFTER THE CHARITY BALL, RYAN WAS TIED UP WITH MEETINGS IN LOS Angeles, Vancouver, Tampa, and back again to LA. He still found time to get me a key to his condo and a shiny black Amex that I'd been instructed to use for anything I wanted.

When I'd asked for clarification on what *anything I wanted* might include, Ryan suggested I hire some movers, put the key to good use, and relocate to his condo where I'd be less likely to wake up buried under the ceiling.

I suggested a miniature Shetland pony and an endless supply of antibacterial wipes for my classroom instead.

The next day at school, I received a lovely bird's nest fern, a hardcover class set of *Edward Tulane* so pristine I wouldn't let my kids within five feet of the books, and a stuffed Shetland wearing an Arizona Wildcats jersey.

And two *thousand* rolls of antibacterial wipes.

He was busy that day and didn't get around to returning any of my *OMG WHAT DID YOU DO?!?!?* texts until I was half asleep. He'd insisted it was nothing, and while that was partially true—he had enough money and enough people working for him to make these things happen with barely a thought—it was that he had thought. He'd remembered *Edward Tulane* and he'd remembered the plants on my desk.

I felt...special.

I had a hard time trusting that emotion because it had a terrible way of proving itself to be an illusion but he'd remembered the books, the plants, all of it.

He'd remembered *me*.

It was risky, letting myself spend time with that thought. As risky as everything else we were doing though probably worse since it lulled me into believing these gestures had nothing to do with our fake relationship.

It made me wonder if this was fake at all.

THE INTERNET CLAMOR QUIETED BY THE END OF THE WEEK, WHICH WAS great, though my students were suddenly very interested in my love life. Lots of questions about everyone's friend Mr. Ralston. A few questions about my ability to get everyone tickets to home games. And one kid asked if I knew where Hersberler was with his contract negotiations.

I didn't mind that part. It was harmless, and soon enough, the fascination had worn off. Kids were great like that.

It was the messages from brands wanting to send me everything from clothes and shoes to detox teas and collagen powders that felt like I'd tumbled into someone else's life. It was the requests from magazines and newspapers asking for interviews that taught me to swallow my coffee first and read emails second to avoid choking. It was the texts from folks I hadn't heard from in ages who made it seem like we were the best of friends and didn't even pretend they weren't looking for gossip.

It was overwhelming. Jamie tasked herself with shutting off the direct messages on all of my apps, closing comments on any old posts, and making my profiles as invisible as possible. When she was done with that, she dug into my email to weed through the invitations and offers and assorted outreach. She informed me I'd need an assistant just to handle my emails if I ended up marrying Ryan.

She still referred to him as Daddy Football and I still died a little every time I heard it.

I'd managed to avoid getting a close look at the dark side of it all—the unbelievable vitriol that came with being the topic of conversation on the internet and everything that went along for the ride—and I hoped I could keep it that way as long as possible.

When my mom had married her fourth husband, part of her plan was to become a regular on some reality series featuring pro sports wives and girlfriends. After three disappointing marriages where she had to pretend to give a shit about football, baseball, and then hockey, I didn't blame her for leveraging her next husband's status for a bit of her own.

Dell Hanshauer was a retired basketball Hall of Famer who was kind of a jackass and always called me Emma but he was a household name. Even people who knew nothing about basketball knew about Dell. He had a plum prime-time gig on the leading sports network and a podcast deal that was worth more than the cozy town on the New Hampshire seacoast he called home.

All of this was great—the ongoing Emma incidents aside—except for the part where my mother became a reality TV star when I was a teenager, and this drama-obsessed world of ours formed *and announced* their opinions on every last thing about her.

I'd never wanted to be in the spotlight like that.

This flood of attention washing over me right now, it was different than her reality series. It wasn't television, it wasn't manufactured conflict. I told myself it wouldn't be like that. My situation, my choices—they weren't the same as my mother's.

Although.

The one thing I'd always hoped my mother would do was build a life that wasn't about a man. All those years we'd spent between the marriages, the times when we had to pick up and start over somewhere new—I'd wanted her to stop looking for the next one. I'd wanted her to exist as a fully formed person first and not as someone's wife or ex-wife.

My life wasn't about a man. But now I saw how it could be.

Ryan's winning streak didn't stop with books and antibacterial wipes.

Ines was invited to visit an engineering firm that specialized in robots and thermal things—I didn't catch most of the details—and they offered her an internship on the spot. Ines, being Ines, asked for a few days to consider the terms.

Once we'd agreed it was a fantastic opportunity with the side benefit of relieving a ton of stress, I blew up Ryan's phone with long, gushing texts thanking him for his help. He claimed he knew nothing about it but offers like this one didn't fall out of the sky.

Grace and Ben were visiting some family of his, so Jamie came with me over the weekend to finally chop off a few inches of hair. On an impulse, I added a few deep burgundy overtones to my dark brown base too. I panicked a little when the hairstylist turned me around for the big reveal. I smiled and made noises about how much I loved it while silently promising myself I could always change the color back and the length would grow out.

Within a few days, my hair only crossed my mind when I realized I had less to twist up with a clip or the feathery fringe pieces fell into my eyes. Though I was too busy at school to pay much attention to how I looked. There was a miraculous string of days—*consecutive* days!—when my class didn't attempt any sort of mutiny. I didn't want to jinx anything but it seemed like we were turning a corner.

Still, there were times when I wondered what it'd be like if I'd picked a job that didn't require me to be "on" every day. Something where I could sneak in a little late and half listen during meetings that could've been emails. Maybe it would be boring and maybe I'd end up with a list of reasons why teaching was actually the better gig but at least no one would ball up their assignment, throw it at another kid's head, and yell that they weren't going to do any of this stupid math junk.

It was enough to make me want to settle into a rocking chair and mutter "Kids these days."

Jamie had always known she wanted to teach but I didn't come to that conclusion until college, and mostly because it made my dad furious. According to him, the only worthwhile majors involved business. Pre-law if I wanted to push my luck. He'd spent all four of my years at the University of Vermont trying to talk me out of my education degree. It was a waste of my time and his money, he'd said.

That pretty much summed up my relationship with my father.

The only thing better than the sudden shift for the positive in my classroom was the promise of spending the weekend with Ryan. We were going to the Kentucky Derby, and though that wouldn't have been otherwise high on my interest list, I felt like I was in a different universe when I was with him. In many ways, it *was* an entirely different universe, but it wasn't the posh parties that did it for me. It was that my old friend was the safest place in the whole world. I could be a wreck, I could be at my all-time lowest, and that didn't change anything for him.

I could even kiss him at a busy brunch spot with his sister and all of Boston looking on, and that still wouldn't change anything.

"What...is this?" Grace asked, tipping the headpiece from side to side. "It's giving Medusa."

"It's a fascinator," I said, running through my packing list for the weekend. "People wear them to the Derby."

"Is it a choice that many make or a requirement?"

"Honestly, I don't know. But Wren insisted I bring three so it sounds like a requirement." I motioned to the hatbox sitting open on my bed. "That one's the most over-the-top."

She gave me a meaningful glance. "Set it aside for me when you're done with it. I love a good Medusa moment."

"You really do." I pointed to a pink peony fascinator. It was smaller but still whimsical. "I'll probably wear that one. I like the way it plays off my dress."

I'd ended up with another yellow dress but this one had a full, flowy skirt with pale pink flowers embroidered throughout. This dress not only allowed me to breathe *and* navigate stairs but also high kick to my heart's content.

Unless I got up close and personal with a whole lot of Kentucky bourbon, I didn't see any reason I'd be high kicking but I liked having the option. A girl's gotta live.

"You're right. That is cute." She held the pink headpiece up to the dress hanging over the back of my door. "And you won't accidentally turn anyone to stone."

"You say that like it would've been a problem," I said, checking off items on my list. "I'd enjoy wielding that kind of power."

"I mean, yeah, same." She opened a shoe box and frowned at the nude strappy heels that looked like a sprained ankle in the making. "I'm sorry you've had to do all of this by yourself."

I set the list down. "All of what?"

She waved at the packages piled up beside my bed but shook her head and said, "Everything with Teddy and now this thing with Ryan. I've been distant and scattered and self-centered, and you've been getting semi-engaged all on your own. I'm sorry."

"It's okay," I said, and I meant that. In truth, she had been distant and scattered. But she'd also threatened, with no amount of hyperbole, to call off her wedding if it saved me from some discomfort. It would've made me responsible for the future of her marriage and that was a pretty huge burden to put all on my shoulders, but I knew she cared. "You can keep talking about how much you love me and all the reasons you hate living with a boy but I'm going to try this on for you because I'm worried it makes me look like a muffin."

"He starts projects and then—I don't know, he just forgets about them," she called as I undressed in the closet. "I am *not* going to micromanage his tasks but I've thought about putting him on a sticker chart."

"Not to infantilize your fiancé or anything but he'd probably like that," I said, fighting my way through this dress to find daylight. "Also, let's introduce him to Ines. Maybe they'll finish each other's projects."

"I like my oven too much to risk that," she said.

I emerged from the closet, a hand at the back of my neck to keep the dress's halter ties in place. "What's the verdict? Am I a muffin?"

"Not a muffin," she said, frowning at the short pink dress with a very full, ruffly skirt. "But some kind of pastry. I want to say cream puff but I'm not sure that's accurate."

I fluffed the skirt. "That's all I needed to know. It's okay. This was just a backup option."

As I returned this dress to the garment bag, Grace called, "You're kind of famous now. I'm not sure I like that."

"Because you're worried I'm going to forget my humble roots? Hate to break it to you but hiking up five flights of stairs to my pastrami-scented apartment every day pretty much guarantees it'll never slip my mind."

"Because people know who you are now," she said. "People can be weird and creepy."

That was true. Nothing weird or creepy had happened but I didn't feel quite so anonymous in the world anymore. I told myself it was mostly in my head but then someone would stare at me a beat too long at the grocery store and I'd question everything.

Before leaving town, Ryan had insisted on having Bowen drive me to and from school. Something about public transportation having "too many variables." I didn't argue with him. Who wouldn't prefer door-to-door service over crowded subway lines with constant delays and breakdowns? Even better, Bowen always had coffee *and* a smoothie waiting for me. A prince among men, that Bowen.

Or perhaps his boss was the real prince.

Grace continued, "I don't want your life to become social media fodder."

I returned to the room, presenting another dress for inspection. As I turned in a circle, I said, "I don't think it will go that far."

"Which part? The internet's interest in you"—she adjusted the dress's straps and then nodded her approval—"or the marriage?"

I went back to the closet instead of answering the question.

I LEFT FOR THE PRIVATE AIRSTRIP OUTSIDE THE CITY IMMEDIATELY after school on Friday. Ryan was flying in from somewhere—I'd lost track of all the cities and time zones—and we were traveling to Louisville on his plane together.

I wasn't sure what his meetings were about but I knew from the minute I saw him jogging down the plane's stairs that he was pissed. His jaw looked like it was going to snap at any minute.

But then he closed the distance between us, wrapped one arm around my waist and brushed his free hand through my hair, saying, "I like it."

It took me a minute of blinking at him while he studied the black cherry strands tucked over my ear to figure out what he meant. "Oh! Yeah? Really? I wasn't sure—"

"Yes," he growled.

I stared up at him as my belly flipped over. Heat spilled over my shoulders and down my spine. I could feel the warmth flooding my face. "I thought about changing it back."

"Don't," he said, skimming his fingers through my hair, over my cheeks. "Don't change it. Unless you're not happy. But I think it's gorgeous."

My face was definitely red now.

I knew I had to stop reacting to Ryan this way. It wouldn't do me any good and I ended up looking like I'd put my blush on in the dark. He was a secretly sweet guy who'd always said breathtakingly sweet things to me, and I couldn't let myself choke on all that sugar.

We boarded the plane, a sleek eight-seater with plush carpet and glossy wood paneling. The captain's chair seats were arranged in quartets and appointed in smooth, sumptuous leather. The bathroom was nicer than the one in my apartment—by a lot—and there was a cozy kitchenette where a pant-suited flight attendant offered me freshly baked chocolate chip cookies, a chicken Caesar salad, or salmon en croûte.

"Mrs. Ralston would prefer the tangerines I ordered," Ryan called from behind me. "Give her the whole bowl."

I hooked a glance at him but he was busy with something on his phone and didn't notice. Still, I stared at him for a long moment, waiting for one of his half smiles or some light teasing about this curious little situation of ours.

"Could I get you anything to drink, Mrs. Ralston?"

I blinked back at the flight attendant. It took me a second but I asked, "What do you have back there?"

She tapped a manicured finger to her lips as she eyed me. "Hmm. How do you feel about lavender-scented neck wraps?"

As I reclined with a glass of sparkling water, a crystal bowl filled with tangerines, and a heated wrap draped over my shoulders, I knew I'd never travel this comfortably again.

I wasn't even sure I wanted to travel if it wouldn't be like this.

Ryan settled on the other side of the narrow aisle as we took off for Louisville. He plowed his way through a family-sized chicken Caesar salad while asking about my day, my kids, my friends' classes. He asked about Jamie, Grace, and Audrey by name, and that made some small part of me bloom.

He listened to complicated stories about the things I liked about my curriculum but also wanted to completely change while I devoured the tangerines. He let me complain about standardized testing and how there wasn't enough time for play and social development and other things neither of us could fix. He told me to stop taking the bad days so seriously—and so personally—when I said I doubted my longevity for the classroom if I kept having tough years like this one, and then he thumbed orange stains off my face like I was a precious child.

After the pilot announced we'd be landing in twenty minutes, Ryan slid off his seat to kneel in front of me. I started to join him because what the hell did I know? Maybe this was what you did on private planes.

But Ryan settled his hands above my knees and held me in place. A slight smile pulled at the corner of his lips as he said, "Stay there. Let me do this."

"Do what?"

He laughed and blew out a breath. Then, "This probably isn't what you had in mind for yourself and I am sorry for that but believe me when I say there is no one else in the world I'd rather marry. I just hope there's some part of you that wants to marry me."

He pulled a velvet box from his pocket and thumbed it open to reveal a diamond large enough to seat a family of four. "*Ohmygod*," I gasped.

Ryan took my hand and slipped the ring onto my orange-sticky finger. The band was thin, almost dainty, with smaller stones glittering down the sides. "If you don't like it—"

"It's the most incredible thing I've ever seen," I breathed.

"Okay." He adjusted it on my finger. The weight of the stone had it lolling to the side. "But if you decide you want something different, it's no problem."

"It's *enormous*," I said.

He lifted a shoulder. "Were you expecting something less?"

I stared at the stone as I turned his words over in my head. I guess it had to be the size of a jawbreaker to be believable. No one with his contract, his endorsement deals could get away with anything less than four carats. Not without raising eyebrows.

"As long as it's convincing, that's all that matters. Right?"

"What matters to me is that you like it," he said. "I chose this. For you. I saw this one, kind of round but also square, and it made me think of you."

"Because I am both round and square?" I teased as I motioned between my hips and breasts.

"Because you're many things at once," he said with a laugh.

I pointed at him. "Smooth."

He shrugged as he leaned back on his heels. Straightening the ring once again, he said, "Is that a yes?"

"You have to ask?"

He dragged his lower lip between his teeth as he met my gaze. "I wanted to give you another chance to back out."

I dropped down to the floor and pulled him into a hug. "Nah. I'm a sure thing."

He shook his head against my shoulder. "Not even close."

chapter fourteen

Emme

Today's Learning Objective:
Students will take the one-bed loss like a win.

WHEN WE ARRIVED AT OUR HOTEL, THE FAMOUS GALT HOUSE ON THE Ohio River, we didn't do anything as mainstream as checking in. We were met at the door by someone whose entire job was to wait for us to show up, hand us our room keys, and escort us to the elevator.

We didn't even bring our own bags which was probably for the best because I couldn't be responsible for anything other than staring at the ring perched on my hand.

The sparkle was unbelievable. It was so bright, I was convinced everyone in the hotel lobby could see the light radiating off it. But it wasn't just the ring. I felt like a crystal sun catcher hanging in the perfect window, light and color streaming out of me and leaving tiny dancing rainbows everywhere I went.

I was *engaged*.

Yes, there were many technicalities and complications, but I didn't need to think about that right now. Not when I was still reeling from the proposal.

I hadn't expected a proposal of any kind. Certainly not one on bended knee. If I'd thought about it, I would've anticipated the big, shiny ring but it was all the other pieces that made me feel like a disco ball.

I'd replayed Ryan's words on the drive from the airport and still found myself stuck on the earnestness of them. It was as though he'd meant what he said.

Part of me—a very, very dangerous part—wanted him to mean it. That same part of me could hear my heart thundering in my chest like a stampede with no end.

"Ready?" my fiancé asked, nodding toward the elevator. Two hotel staffers held the doors open. Another offered us water, mint juleps, or champagne.

This, I could get used to.

I reached for a champagne flute, watching the way my ring gleamed under the warm light of the chandeliers. I glanced to Ryan and discovered him staring too. When he slowly shifted his gaze to my face, a smile warmed the corners of his lips and he reached for my free hand.

The stampede in my chest gained speed. I felt it shake all the way down to my bones and blaring through my veins. It was so much, so intense—and somehow I wanted more. I wanted to feel all of these things until I forgot what it was like to be sad and alone.

With our fingers laced together, I said, "Lead the way."

THIS PLACE REMINDED ME OF ALL THE CHRISTMASES SPENT WITH MY dad and his family. They were all about private islands in the Caribbean or ultra-premium luxury resorts in Aspen or Whistler. The more exclusive, the better.

I always felt like I was betraying my mom when I was with them. That family he'd created with his new wife Danielle and my half brothers was the one my mother had envisioned for herself, the one I knew she still mourned. It was the one she would've had if my father hadn't been an unapologetic cheater with lawyers who wrote bear-trap prenups.

A staffer met us at our floor and escorted us to our suite. Ryan pressed a crisp bill into his hand and sent him on his way once we were inside, and I appreciated that he knew those maneuvers. Even if this wasn't exactly new to me, it would've taken me five full minutes to realize I should tip the guy and another five to dig cash out of the bottom of my bag. If I even had cash, which I usually didn't.

"Take whichever room you want," Ryan said, gesturing down the hallway. "I have to return some messages before we leave for the party."

There were a million parties this weekend and we were scheduled to make appearances at all of them. I didn't know what constituted an appearance. Was it literally just a pop-in or were we doing time at each venue? Or was it more a matter of flashing the engagement ring at the right people?

Regardless of how it worked out, I was going to look good at these parties. The muffin/cream puff dress aside, Wren and I understood each other now. I hadn't expected to enjoy working with a stylist so much—or letting Ryan buy all my clothes—but it was great having someone do all the legwork and then present the best options. We didn't shy away from color, I had enough room in every skirt to break into a dead sprint if needed, and I felt confident again.

I'd missed that.

My thumb twisted the band on my ring finger as I wandered down the hall and glanced into the first bedroom. The bed was the size of a city block. I expected the next to be the same, but when I opened the door I found only a closet stocked with extra blankets and pillows.

Convinced that I'd missed something, I opened every door in the suite and made two passes through the living and dining rooms. Ryan arched a brow in question but said nothing, his phone pressed to his ear.

I hurried back to the first bedroom—the *only* bedroom—with Ryan trailing behind me, still on the phone. I heard him say to someone, "Just make a decision and get it done."

He ended the call and watched as I rounded the bed. This wasn't a problem. It really was a big bed. His entire offensive line could snuggle up in here. Hersberler would end up on the floor but that had more to do with his personality than the fit.

"What's up?" Ryan asked, his arms crossed over his chest.

My gaze snagged on his thick forearms and the lines inked there. It took some effort to drag my attention away because my fiancé—regardless of whether I was supposed to notice this or not—was devastatingly hot. "This is the only room."

"It's a two-bedroom suite," he said.

"I've checked every cupboard, cabinet, and closet. I assure you it's not."

His eyes snapped to the bed between us. He swallowed hard. "I'll call Marcie. She'll handle it."

I worried the back of my ring again. "Who's Marcie?"

"My assistant."

He tapped his phone and paced away, leaving me staring down at the bed. I heard him speaking though I could only make out the tense tone, not the words. I bet his jaw was back to being a concrete block. His dentist probably had a nice summer home just from looking after those molars.

I'd never known Ryan to be anything but tense. I met him in ninth grade and I remembered immediately wondering why he was so damn serious. He had tons of friends and was involved in everything and he had a sly sense of humor but there was also a dark energy tethered to him like rings to Saturn.

As it turned out, his father had been dying. Slowly but also quickly, in sudden, devastating bursts that upended his family. By that time, the first floor of their home had a hospital bed, oxygen tanks and compressors, and a constant stream of nurses and health aides. The ALS took him the summer before our last year of high school.

I still thought about whether the Ryan of today, the Ryan I'd always known, would be the same or different if his father was alive and well. Different, of course, in all the ways that sickness and loss and grief jackknifed their way through an otherwise ordinary life. But what if Ryan was a serious, solemn soul because it was his fundamental nature and not simply because it'd been demanded of him at such a young age?

I didn't know if there was any point to carrying on that debate with myself. All I knew was there were times when I had to remind him that he didn't have to hold the weight of the world on his back. That it was okay to be happy and to do things simply because he wanted to, and not because his mom needed the help or his sisters needed to pay for college or any other reason he had to ignore his inner compass.

"This is the only room," he said from the doorway, his phone still pressed to his ear.

I glanced up from the pristine bed linens. "A-plus on the comprehension and recall."

"No," he said, running a hand down his face. "This is the only room *here*. It's the only room anywhere. In the whole fucking town."

"Well, isn't this event a pretty big deal around here? It stands to reason there wouldn't be much availability."

He held up a finger as someone spoke to him. "You're telling me every vacation rental is booked too, Marcie? Every last one?" He blew out a breath as she replied. "Are there any houses for sale? Some kind of quick, all cash deal?"

"Don't be ridiculous," I said.

Marcie must've echoed that sentiment because Ryan held up a hand. "All right, all right, I won't buy a house tonight. Forget it." Then, in a low, lethal voice I didn't think I'd ever heard from him before, he said, "Let them know I'm not pleased."

It appeared he *really* didn't want to share this bed with me.

Such an efficient way to chase off my sunbeams and heart stampedes.

He exhaled every molecule of oxygen from his body and folded his arms. I could actually hear his jaw popping from the other side of the room.

I stared at him, still fiddling with the band of my ring. "I think you're overreacting."

"But—" He slashed a hand toward the bed.

"What about it?" I asked. "You didn't have a problem staying at my place a few weeks ago and this bed is twice the size. We could get a third person in here if you wanted an adventure. Is McKerry in town this weekend? Or Wilcox? I bet one of them would be down."

The phone fell from his hand, clattered to the floor. The veins in his neck appeared to bulge and that seemed like something to be concerned about. Medically, perhaps. "You want to run that by me again?"

"I'm just saying we have plenty of room and you don't need to be weird about it."

"By suggesting we invite McKerry to—to *what*, exactly?"

"It was a joke. I know you're familiar with the concept." I tossed up my hands and stomped to the living space to grab my luggage. Ryan was exactly where I'd left him when I returned to the room.

"I don't want you to be uncomfortable," he said. I wasn't sure how he was able to speak through that clenched jaw but he was known for doing impossible things.

"If you'd listen to me, you'd hear me saying that I'm not uncomfortable."

"I'll sleep on the couch."

I rolled my eyes. "Don't be ridiculous. You don't *fit* on the couch."

"Then the floor."

"Oh my god, would you stop it? I'll take the couch before you take the floor."

"I'm not letting you do that."

"You don't decide what I do." I flattened my palms to his chest and gave him a shove. Of course, he barely moved. "Get out of here so I can get dressed."

I slammed the door behind him because my inner child was a moody teenager. Grabbing my makeup bag, I headed for the bathroom. In the bright lights, my ring glittered up at me.

I guess that made this our first fight as an engaged couple.

Tonight was like a bar crawl of the most lavish estates in and around Louisville. We pulled up at a few parties and made quick work of seeing people on some mental checklist Ryan was working through.

For the most part, all I had to do was smile and talk about how nice everyone looked and how gorgeous the decorations were. As a lawn ornament, no one expected much of me and they didn't go looking for more. I couldn't decide whether I liked that but I did like the earrings Ryan gave me before we left.

He grumbled something about making good on his promise to pick out the jewelry and tossed the glossy red box on the solitary bed in our suite. The multicolored gemstones were like a bouquet of wildflowers that climbed up my lobe and dangled low enough to nearly brush my bare shoulders.

I *adored* them. They were unusual enough to feel like something I would've selected for myself and they went perfectly with my long, full-skirted dress covered in bright embroidered florals.

On the way to the last stop of the night, Ryan warned me we'd be staying a bit longer and seeing more people. I warned him I'd be ordering the entire room service menu when we returned to the hotel and not sharing any of it.

We hadn't revisited the topic of sleeping arrangements.

This party was held at a suburban mansion that was pretty much the size of the entire North End. I didn't know what set this party apart from all the others, but right away I understood that it was very different. If I thought Ryan had kept me close before, he basically shoved me in his pocket now.

If I was being naked-in-a-nightmare honest with myself, I didn't hate it.

I actually kind of liked it.

These past few months, I'd been so lonely. I missed being close to another person. I missed being wanted—even if it was just the performance of desire and a distant relative of the real thing.

But there was another part, one that had nothing to do with the dark days since everything went to hell with Teddy. A part that liked the way it felt when Ryan touched me—and much more than friends were supposed to like each other.

So, I went along, even if I was still annoyed about that little fight and hungry enough to scarf down anything on a passing server's tray, regardless of whether they could confirm the shellfish status.

I beamed up at Ryan every time he introduced me as his fiancée, every time he said, "My fiancée is the best second-grade teacher in the world," every time he stopped a server to say, "My fiancée would like another mint julep."

I curled into him, a hand always on his back, his shoulders, his chest. I'd let my palm slide down to his abs, but he was quick to grab my wrist and show off that new ring.

"When's the big day?" asked a woman wearing a necklace that looked like my ring multiplied by forty.

Her husband, a hedge fund manager whose name I'd immediately forgotten, asked Ryan something about whether he'd looked at the new numbers. Instead of responding to him, Ryan said, "Soon, we hope." He glanced at me with a slight smile. "Probably before training camp."

"That soon?" I asked with a laugh. Camp started in late July.

His gaze dropped to my lips. "If you'll have me."

Another laugh. I didn't know why he kept acting like I was going to back out at any minute. "I think you know I will."

The hedge fund couple excused themselves and, for the first time since arriving, no one swooped in to fill the space. In fact, we were strangely alone in this moment, which was what made his next question even more confusing.

He trailed a finger down the length of one earring. "Do you like them?"

I arched a brow but I didn't think he noticed because he was still staring at the gems. "I think you know I do."

Humming in agreement, he gave a slight nod. "They look good on you." He brought his hand to my jaw, swept his thumb over my cheek. "Can I kiss you?"

I tipped my chin up. If only he knew how long I'd waited for him to ask. "Always."

And when he touched his lips to mine, I pretended—just for now—that all of this was real.

WE DIDN'T TALK ABOUT THE KISS OR HOW IT WENT ON LONGER THAN polite for the setting. Or how we were breathless when it ended. Or how we kept swaying toward each other like our bodies knew something we didn't.

We didn't say anything and we didn't share another kiss the rest of the night.

It was better that way. Nothing good would come of this growing into something more…complicated. With our history and all. And our lives were different. So totally different.

We returned to the hotel after midnight, bleary-eyed and hungry. I had Ryan's jacket draped over my shoulders to ward off the chill in the air and his tie hung loose around his neck. He held my hand as we shuffled to the elevator and swept me close once we were inside.

"Still ordering the whole room service menu?" he mumbled into my hair.

"No," I said, letting my head rest on his chest. "I'm not bothering with anything sensible. Just give me a bucket of fries."

I heard him rustling in his pocket and then the snap of a camera's shutter. Another pic for the socials. He held it up for my approval. I gave a tired nod.

"Will you share the fries?"

The elevator came to a stop. Neither of us moved. "If you give me all the burnt and ugly fries."

"I always save those for you," he said.

I bobbed my head. "Okay, then."

The room had been tidied since we'd left. Lamps were lit, the bed linens turned down, and the complete explosion of my makeup on the bathroom counter now looked like something out of an organization video.

"There's champagne," Ryan called from the living area.

"Really don't think I need more alcohol," I said as I kicked off my shoes. These fucking things. Wren and I were going to have a long talk about my tolerance for shoe-induced pain the next time I saw her. "If the rest of the weekend is anything like tonight, I'm gonna be sweating mint julep until the summer solstice."

"There's also chocolate-covered strawberries," he said.

"You shall bring them to me now."

I stepped out of my dress and groaned in relief once I had the strapless bra unhooked. I wanted to fling it straight into the sun but I only had myself to blame. I'd chosen the X-strap dress knowing full well that my bust required a level of support that could only come from a perilous combination of steel and spandex. If I wanted to fight gravity, I'd have to accept some reorganization of my ribs.

I turned to get a look at my back in the bathroom mirror before pulling on a sweatshirt. Deep, red grooves in my skin glared back at me. One spot on my side looked particularly miserable. It would be gone in the morning, and if it wasn't, I always had diaper cream on me. That stuff fixed everything.

"There's also chocolate-dipped orange segments, which I wasn't sure about but I tried one and I'm—oh, Jesus, fuck, Em, I'm sorry."

I glanced away from the mirror to find Ryan in the bedroom, his back to me with a silver platter in one hand while he shoved the other through his hair. And I was wearing only undies and a hoodie clutched to my chest.

"It's all good," I drawled as if we walked in on each other mostly naked all the time.

He let out a tight laugh but he didn't leave. "For fuck's sake, Em." He fisted his hand in his hair while I pulled the sweatshirt over my head. "What happened?" he asked. "To your back."

"Oh," I said, reaching for the sleep shorts I should've put on five minutes ago. "It's from my bra." I stared at the hand still tugging at his hair. His knuckles were white. "I'm dressed now. Sorry about that. I should've closed the doors."

"You should've had your own room," he grumbled.

"We'll just have to blame the Derby for that."

He hung his head and blew out a ragged breath. "I'll take the sofa."

"You will not," I said. "Don't invent bad solutions to things that aren't problems. We'll find something to watch, eat fries and chocolate-covered fruit, and build a great wall of pillows down the middle of the bed to protect your virtue."

He shot a glance over his shoulder but didn't meet my eyes.

"I don't have any virtue so there's nothing to protect." I babbled when I was overtired, overstimulated, and underfed, so I went on. "I'm the opposite of virtue. Whatever virtue is these days, I'm not it. I mean, I packed two different vibrators just for this two-night stay and—"

"You gotta stop saying these things to me."

"—it's not like I can't get by on my own but sometimes you just don't want to get in there and do the work."

He gripped the back of his neck. "We don't have to talk about this."

"But you have to keep the happy hormones flowing. Grow that serotonin at home with an orgasm a day. That's what they say." The words kept coming but my brain had no involvement. No brakes for this runaway truck. "Not that I have any plan on doing that. On using them. Like, here. Because—well, you know. Just the one bed. And I already checked the box this morning so I'm good. I'm great."

Ryan set the platter down on the bed and bent at the waist, his hands on his knees and his chest heaving. It took me a minute but I realized he was laughing. It sounded more like drowning on dry land.

I could've been embarrassed. Could've curled into a small, mortified ball and found a corner to hide in for the night. And maybe I would've done all of that if I'd spewed all those inside thoughts on anyone else but this was Ryan.

"Get a hold of yourself," I said, smacking him on the back. "You're the one who wanted to marry me. You're legally required to put up with my weirdness now."

He wrapped an arm around my thighs, still bent at the waist, still shaking with laughter. He rested his head above my knee. "There was just so much of it at once."

"I suggest you get used to it." I smoothed a hand down his back. "It will only get weirder."

"I'm sorry I walked in on you like that," he said.

I shrugged. "I'm sorry I left the doors open."

I felt him blow out a breath. "Your bucket of fries will be here any minute now."

"Consider yourself absolved of all crimes," I said.

With another ragged breath, he glanced up at me. "Why is a bra making it look like you've been whipped?"

I made a cupping gesture in front of my breasts. "It takes a lot of heave-ho to make this work. It leaves marks."

He patted my thigh and straightened, his brows pulled together tight. "Is there something we can do to fix that?"

"I'm used to it," I said. "And it fades pretty quickly."

He extended a hand toward me but snatched it back and shoved it in his pocket. "Does it hurt?"

I shook my head. "It's not that bad. It just looks gnarly for a bit." Gesturing to him, I said, "I'll let you change. I hear it's helpful to close the doors while doing that."

Ryan flipped open his cuffs, then the buttons on his shirt. "From the same people who recommend an orgasm a day?"

I blinked as he shrugged out of his shirt. And there he was, muscle and ink and tanned skin. I cleared my throat. "Surprisingly, no. Different schools of thought."

He tossed the shirt to a chair near the window. "Understandable."

His hand dropped to his belt and something clicked in my head. I had to get out of here right now unless I wanted... Unless. "Think about which movie you want to watch tonight," I said, crossing to the door.

"We never finished *The Mummy*," he said.

I didn't stop, didn't spare a backward glance when I heard his belt hit the floor. "Gonna stay awake this time, husband?"

"Bet on it, wife."

And once again, Ryan was asleep within the first ten minutes of the movie.

I hadn't bothered to build the wall of pillows just as he hadn't bothered to put on a shirt. All of this became a pressing matter of concern when the slumbering bear beside me decided to roll across the great expanse of this bed and throw his arm around my waist.

It was the first time I'd been able to study his tattoos at this range. Swirling lines, almost like stylized ocean waves, ran from his shoulder down to his wrist. There were trees and flowers, clouds and constellations. It was beautiful. A layered work of art.

When I knew he was deep asleep and holding me like he'd never, ever let go, I traced the lines with the tip of my finger. Just like last time, he didn't stir.

chapter fifteen

Ryan.

Today's Learning Objective:
Students will take old relationships to new heights.

DERBY DAY WAS AT ONCE THE BEST AND WORST DAY OF MY LIFE.

Best: I woke up wrapped around Emme again.

Worst: I was so hard that when I pried myself away from her and out of the bed, I had to grab onto a chair because I was dizzy.

Best: I knew she preferred to start each day with an orgasm.

Worst: I wasn't involved in any part of that and thinking about it had me on edge, every muscle in my body drawn painfully tight.

Best: I talked to just about everyone on the long, long list of people Jakobi and I prioritized for this trip, and Emme was charming them into pleasant submission. I'd sign up for all this glad-handing and backslapping and boozing bullshit every day of the year if I could do it with her.

Worst: There were multiple occasions when I should've been following a conversation but was instead staring at Emme like I couldn't decide if I was dreaming or awake. She had this ability to ask people questions about themselves and make it sound like she truly cared—an ability I did not share—and it made everyone eat out of her palm while she did it.

Including me.

My mind wasn't built for an event that started and ended within two minutes. I understood the development of a defense in response to the other team and the mechanisms of offensive plays within a game. The race was impressive as hell, though as someone who played a sixty-minute game over the course of three hours, I had a hard time with *blink and you'll miss it* sporting events.

We made the rounds at a handful of parties after the race, and while I could've quit the whole thing hours ago, there was one last elusive name on my list. One person who *had* to meet Emme this weekend if this plan was going to work for me.

We hadn't technically been invited to the final party we stopped at though I didn't see that as a roadblock. It was late enough that no one would be guarding the doors too aggressively and—while this was arrogant as fuck to admit—I didn't *need* an invitation.

As expected, we strolled right in. Less than five minutes later, Wally Wallace—that was his real, legal name—sauntered across the covered patio toward us, a hungry little smile on his face. The guy never failed to come across as a complete creep.

I gripped Emme's waist a little tighter than necessary when his gaze shifted toward her. "I'm going to apologize in advance for what's about to happen," I said under my breath.

She glanced up at me, eyes wide. "For—what?"

"My dear Mr. Ralston," Wally drawled, wagging his jeweled walking stick at me. "I had no idea I'd bump into you at this soiree." He leaned on the stick, leering at me with his small, watery eyes and a smile that was all teeth, no warmth. Jakobi had once referred to him as a groundhog and I couldn't unsee that. "How fortuitous."

I nodded. As a rule, I hated pretending to like people for the bullshit reason of it being good for business. If I had to gargle someone's balls just to close a deal, I didn't want the deal that much. And it wasn't just pretending to *like* people that killed me but also associating with known creeps and passively approving of that creepy behavior.

Case in point: Here I was, throwing Emme to that fucking groundhog.

"Good to see you, Wally," I said. "How about that race?"

He made a puttering noise, like an old VW Bug trying to get up a hill, but then patted the breast pocket of his linen jacket. Probably full of cash from his winnings. "Oh, it was all right, Mr. Ralston. It was all right indeed." His attention turned to Emme then and he rapped his stick on the slate floor like a judge bringing court into session. "And who is this lovely lily?"

Again, I squeezed her waist. "Wally Wallace, this is my fiancée, Emmeline."

"Well, my dear, allow me to extend my warmest felicitations on your impending nuptials." Wally held out a hand to Emme while baldly eye-fucking her tits. Instead of shaking her hand like a non-deranged human being, he kissed his way across her knuckles. I gave him until the count of three in my head and it was a damn good thing he put his tongue back in his mouth before I reached three.

"Thank you," she said while he licked his lips. Such a fucking creep.

"Aren't you just a dove?" he purred, ghosting a hand over her cheek. He was lucky I let him keep that hand. "I'm sure I've seen this face before. You're on that television program, the one with the lady doctors, isn't it?"

Emme laughed. "Oh, no, I'm a teacher."

"A schoolteacher," he gasped. "What do you teach, Miss Emmeline?"

"Second grade." She paused, waiting for his next question, but he was busy staring at her cleavage again. "It's a really fun age," she added.

"And you're making an honest man out of Mr. Ralston here," Wally said. "I suppose it would take someone who knows how to dole out the discipline."

Emme cocked her head to the side but her smile never slipped. "I'm sure I don't know what you mean."

Wally belted out a laugh and didn't trouble himself with noticing that Emme and I hadn't joined in. When he was finished, he pulled a handkerchief from his pocket and blotted the corners of his eyes. "What a delight you are," he said to Emme. To me, he tapped the handle of his stick against my chest and added, "It's a fine thing to see you're settling down. It'll do you good."

Wally made a show of bowing his head and kissing Emme's knuckles again, and then found someone else to harass. Not a minute too soon.

When he was on the other side of the patio, Emme whispered, "What the fuck just happened here?"

"You just got me one very big step closer to sealing my franchise deal," I said. "Which means we're leaving right the fuck now."

"OPEN YOUR MOUTH."

I stared up at Emme and the hands she held poised over my face. "Where did you learn this again?"

"Just do it," she said, her fingers wiggling. "You'll feel so much better."

Little did she know, lying on a massive bed with my head in her lap while we shared a bottle of wine already had me feeling pretty great. "Remind me what it is you think you're fixing."

"Your jaw," she cried. "All the clenching and grinding. You're giving yourself headaches."

"Not that I've noticed."

She gave me a flat stare. "Probably because it's turned into one long, constant headache and you've just accepted the pain as part of your everyday life."

When I didn't respond—because she wouldn't believe the amount of pain that I'd accepted as part of my life—she brought fingers to either side of my face, right near my ears. She pressed her fingertips down the line of my cheeks, moving in small circles as she went.

"Open," she said, digging a bent finger into my cheek.

I gave up the fight. I didn't care if she'd learned this from some snake oil science video she found on social media. I didn't want her to stop.

"And close," she said, slowly dragging that finger down the ridge of my jaw.

A sound grunted out of me as the motion unspooled some ancient store of pressure. "What the hell was that?"

She brought two fingers to either side of my jaw, slipping through my scruff and working up to my ear and then back down. "Just me being right once again."

"Hmm. Should've known."

I continued opening and closing my mouth on command, and Emme continued kneading and molding me. It reminded me of all those times when we were younger that she'd plop down beside me and announce I needed a hand massage after a long written exam or I should try a pumpkin face mask with her or something like that. Those were my favorite moments with Emme. I'd faked so many hand cramps the last year of high school that she looked up wrist exercises.

"What was the deal with the guy?" she asked after a few minutes. "The one who just needed a monocle to complete the rich villain look."

"His grandparents started a bunch of gas stations across the southeast like a hundred years ago," I said. "His dad turned it into a chain of highway off-ramp convenience store destinations but also bought big stakes in other businesses. Trucking companies, logistics, cardboard manufacturing. And now Wally is chairman of the board but has no hand in day-to-day operations. He sits on a pile of cash that he uses to buy whatever amuses him, among which currently includes soccer club franchise licenses."

"And somehow he finds time to shove his tongue between random women's fingers," she mused. "Easy, easy there. Don't go clenching that jaw up on me after I worked out some of those rocks."

"I'm sorry you had to deal with that." I glanced up at her as she went to work on my temples. "If there was any other way—"

"I knew what I was getting into when we started playing fake fiancé," she said. "You forget I'm very familiar with that old money crowd and all their weirdness."

"I'm still sorry about it. Especially the slobber he left on your hand."

"Why soccer?" she asked. "Did someone say fútbol so you went along with it and you didn't realize the mistake until it was too late?"

"Funny." I watched as she grinned, amused with herself. She was so damn cute. "You know why."

She gave a shake of her head that said she wasn't playing ball tonight. "If I knew, I wouldn't ask."

A few strands of hair slipped over her ear and brushed her cheek. I loved the shorter length. She'd always worn it long but there was something that punched me in the gut about it now. I reached up, caught those strands between two fingers. "Because I actually like soccer."

"Mmm. That would help."

"What? No, *I told you so*?"

Another obstinate head shake. "Nope." But then, because she'd never been able to walk away from this topic without getting the last word in, she added, "But it's good you're excited about life after football."

"I am," I said, willing her to meet my eyes. She didn't.

"It's good you're finally doing something because it's what you want," she said.

"I finally can."

She rolled her eyes toward the ceiling. I felt her soft sigh on my forehead. "You can tell me you *had* to go to Arizona and you *had* to enter the draft all you want but I know what's true and what you've let everyone else believe is true."

I closed my eyes as her knuckles pressed the hinge of my jaw. "That's not fair, Em. I had to take care of my family."

"What's not fair is how every game you've ever played has been about your dad first and you a distant second," she said. "The only reason you played in college is because everyone told you how proud he would've been, how all he'd ever wanted was to see you make it to that level, how much it would mean to him. Not a single person stopped to ask if you wanted that. They just told you how much your dad would've loved cheering for a Big 12 team."

My father spent nearly half of my life dying. It was a slow avalanche that consumed everything in its path for years until it gained speed and wiped out everything.

He'd always been larger than life. He did everything, knew everyone, helped everywhere. He was the guy who'd come over to help you patch your roof after a storm, the one who hosted the best tailgate parties for any game, and the one who coached both girls' field hockey and peewee football until he couldn't stand on the sidelines any longer. There were photos of him carrying all four of my sisters through the snow one year, and another, from an earlier era, of him lifting a full keg one-handed.

When he was sick, everything we did was for him. Rearranging our bedrooms so he didn't have to climb the stairs, rearranging schedules so someone would always be with him, rearranging the ways we thought about what it meant to be alive.

The least I could do was take the field every Friday night and play the game of my life. My father needed that joy, that hope. We *all* needed it. And I'd needed the purpose.

But then we rearranged our lives again, and that time it was to make room for grief and loss.

Those Friday nights turned into a tribute. Every game was played in his honor, a memorial service in many parts. My family—the whole town, really—had grieved and celebrated his life through those games but it'd never worked that way for me.

When the scholarships rolled in, I went as far from home as I could get. As far from the soft-eyed expressions and "Your dad's up there cheering you on!" as I could get.

But it wasn't far enough because college sports news reporters were obsessed with my backstory. There were four or five different human interest packages they played every game day. The worst was the one about me finally winning the state high school football championship less than five months after my father's death and I'd dedicated the game to him. Never once had I dedicated a game to anyone, and my *team* won that game. But as far as that reel was concerned, my arm and I were the only things that mattered.

Pro ball had never appealed to me but my mom was going to have to sell the house in order to swing all the payment plans for Dad's medical expenses and my sisters' college tuition. She hadn't let me worry about those things at U of A but when I realized the scope of the debt bearing down on her, I couldn't come up with a better option.

So, I kept playing with the ghost at my back. The human interest stories never stopped. Draft day was—well, fuck, I'd dissociated through most of it but my origin story video nearly drowned itself in its own tears.

Now I was on the board for the leading ALS foundation in the US. I was their celebrity spokesperson and helped raise millions of dollars for them each year and matched every penny. I appeared in their commercials along with a photo montage of my dad coaching my peewee teams and I voiced a line about me carrying on his legacy of sportsmanship that made my stomach drop every time I heard it. I would've done it regardless of whether anyone knew my story, but goddamn, Emme was right.

She'd always been right.

I didn't want to live in a life written by loss—and I knew now that my dad wouldn't have wanted that either.

"And allow me to add," Emme went on, "that there were years between the time he passed and when you got your draft day signing bonus. If taking care of your family was your biggest concern, you would've skipped college ball and gone to work on a lobster boat."

"I wouldn't have lasted a week on a lobster boat."

"You know what I mean."

"Think of it this way," I said. "If I hadn't entered the draft against your very specific advice, I wouldn't be buying these teams which means I wouldn't have asked you to marry me." I turned my head and rubbed my face against her belly. She pushed her fingers through my hair. I wanted to pry my ribs open and show her my heart because I'd swear to god it only beat like this for her. "I'm not complaining. You don't have to either."

"I'll stop bringing it up," she said, "if you stop doing things you hate."

"I don't hate football." When she didn't volley that comment back to me, I added, "I started seeing a sports therapist three—four?—years ago. Whenever we lost to Minnesota in the Super Bowl."

"That was five years ago, my friend."

"Shit, really?" I tried to get ahold of time but her fingers on my skin were making it hard to think. "I started seeing this guy a couple of months after because I couldn't reconcile the loss. It wasn't—it didn't make sense to me. It didn't add up."

"You did choke pretty hard in the third quarter."

"I thought you didn't watch my games."

"It was like you forgot how to read your coverage and couldn't find your receivers on the field."

"Love you too," I said. She gave me a smirked smile that made me think of lemony sunshine and sinking my teeth into her thigh. "He helped me think about things differently. To separate out all the things

I'd packed into football and figure out which ones I need, which ones I don't."

"Has it helped?"

"I signed a contract extension, didn't I?" I asked. "I could've walked away. I thought about it. I had enough money for my whole family to live comfortably the rest of their lives. I didn't need anything else from the game."

"Then why did you?"

"Because I realized I don't hate football," I said simply. "It was possible I never did but it'd all grown so cluttered and complicated."

"So, you chose it. For once."

"Yeah." I shifted to wrap an arm around her waist. "You're the only person who ever noticed that it wasn't my choice. I never forgot that, even when I did the exact opposite of what you wanted."

"I just wanted you to—gah. Never mind. I'm happy it's better for you and I'm happy there are good things waiting for you in the future."

You're the only good thing that matters.

"Did therapy help with everything at home?"

A stitch pulled too tight in my chest. That was always the spot. My therapist liked to say big emotions took up space inside us, and while I'd rejected that theory for longer than necessary, I knew now that my grief lived under my breastbone. I felt it swell every August as the memories of his final days crowded around me and again every time Mom and Gramma CeCe lobbied for me to come home for the holidays. Things were better when I kept my distance.

And I could afford to take them and my sisters on tropical holiday vacations so it all worked out.

"Yeah," I said, though it sounded halfhearted even to me. "Still working on it."

"That's okay." She gave me the same reassuring smile she'd given me all through high school but especially that last year when most days I couldn't remember how to breathe. "I haven't figured out things at home either."

"We'll figure it out together." I burrowed into her belly again. I loved how soft and luscious she felt. "We always do."

She ran the backs of her fingers from my forehead to my chin and up again, and I thought I was going to float away. I hadn't been this chill in a decade. Longer, probably. "It's fun being your fake fiancée," she continued. "I've missed hanging out with you and now I get to do it while glaring at anyone who shakes their boobs in your face."

"I don't think that…happened," was all I could say.

"I know you're not blind, Ryan. You're fully aware it happens *all* the time."

I shrugged. I wasn't debating this while her nails scraped at my scalp. Certainly not touching the fake fiancé comments.

"We make a good team," she said, reaching for her glass on the nightstand. "And drinking absurdly expensive wine in fancy hotels with you isn't bad either."

"We are a good team," I said, watching as her tongue peeked out to catch a drop of wine. "I always knew we would be."

EMME WAS *NOT* IN A GOOD MOOD WHEN SHE WOKE UP THE NEXT morning.

She emerged from the shower wearing a hotel robe that didn't look like it fit too well and her hair twisted up in a towel. A cloud of steam billowed out behind her like a personal army of fog.

She barely spoke to me as we packed for the airport, and tossed a few pillows to the floor that'd angered her in some way. I figured she was hungover. After nonstop liquor and not nearly enough food or water to soak it up this weekend, anyone would be in rough shape. And we'd made the genius decision to top it all off with red wine last night.

"I'm cold," Emme said, snatching a hooded sweater out of my hands. "Need to borrow this."

She returned a few minutes later wearing the sweater with a pair of leggings. She looked...amazing. So good I couldn't speak. I had to turn around while she dried her hair so she wouldn't see the smile on my face.

The ride to the airport was quiet, which I attributed to the hangover. I didn't think much of it because we were both on the struggle bus. I couldn't even think about a mint julep without my stomach sloshing.

But when we boarded the plane, Emme more or less collapsed into her seat and curled herself into a ball. I didn't know what to make of that. I kept an eye on her as we took off, glancing over the frame of my iPad every few minutes.

Once we were airborne, she pulled the hood up, tucked her knees into the sweater, and dropped her head to her folded arms. She was pale, none of her usual rosiness riding high on her cheeks. Even her lips were pale.

I leaned forward, my arms braced on my thighs. "What's goin' on over there, Muggsy?"

She shook her head but kept her eyes closed. "Cramps."

Ah.

Well.

Okay.

I could work with that.

She'd always had a bad time with cramps. Gone in for surgery during college because of it too. Endometriosis. They'd said she'd probably need more surgeries. I didn't know if she was at that point again. I just wanted to make it better.

I went to the back of the cabin to grab a few things from my bag and put the attendant to work making some hot chocolate. Kneeling in front of Emme, I pried her hand open and dropped a few tablets in her palm. "Take these," I said, holding a glass of water for her. She accepted it with shaky fingers. "Good girl. How about some blankets?"

I slipped my hand under the sweater and pressed my palm to the small of her back. She'd always liked that when she had cramps in high school. She'd called me her hot water bottle. I'd been dumped twice—no, three times—by girls who'd found that troubling.

Maybe they'd been right but I'd never cared much. It wasn't like I'd gone looking for girlfriends. They'd always appointed themselves to that role.

"You're so warm," she groaned.

"Then come sit with me while the meds kick in," I said.

She considered this for several long seconds before giving me a resigned shrug. "Only if you tell me if it's uncomfortable for you."

I was more likely to chew my arm off, but I said, "Yeah."

I reclined the seat all the way back and Emme settled on her side, her head on my chest and a leg thrown over one of mine. I tucked the blanket around her and rubbed her back while she dozed.

The hot chocolate was ready but I decided against waking Emme. We could always reheat it. Or make more. To my mind, the only reason to have this much money was to give the people in my life every single thing they needed, exactly when they needed it.

If my girl wanted a fresh cup of hot chocolate, she got a fresh cup of hot chocolate.

I stared at the ring on her finger as she slept. I'd spent an entire week looking for the right one. Jakobi almost strangled me. Apparently, other people didn't need to visit eighteen jewelers in four cities to find the right ring. I doubted other people were hoping their fake fiancée actually fell in love with them before the jig was up.

Emme shifted a few times, which was only fair because I was about as soft as a concrete basement. Eventually, after some blanket fluffing and several frustrated huffs about the armrest being in her way, she ended up straddling my thigh.

We could've gotten away with this the same way we got away with a lot of the handsy shit we did—by systematically ignoring it—but something about this was different from kissing for cameras and jaw massages.

And that something was the way I started rocking her against my thigh as I rubbed her back.

At first I was just trying to shift the position of my irritable hip, but her breath caught and she pressed her face deep into my shoulder when we connected at a certain angle.

So I did it again.

It was gentle, barely more than a nudge when I stroked my palm up her spine. I kept that up for a few minutes, saying not a fucking word and keeping my gaze on the ceiling. The last thing we needed was some eye contact to make this too real.

Then Emme decided to participate.

When my hand moved up her back, she rolled her hips to meet the pressure. There was no way she didn't notice my sharp inhale or the hard flex of my fingers against her skin.

The hood concealed most of her face and I was sure she preferred it that way. As much as I wanted to see her eyes glaze over with need, it was enough to watch her hips moving under the blanket and hear her tiny, half-swallowed sighs of pleasure.

Those little sighs lit up every corner and fold of my brain. I loved them. Wanted to hear them every day for the rest of my life.

But I couldn't think about anything but the warm, glorious place where she rubbed herself against my leg. My joggers were thin enough that I could feel the heat radiating out of her and I was hit with a staggering need to slip my hand under those leggings and find out how wet she was.

I didn't, but god, I wanted to.

I wanted *so* much. Wanted to get a handful of her ass and show her exactly how to ride this out. Wanted her tits in my face. Wanted to take her hand and show her how hard she'd made me.

But she learned all about hard when she started sliding her leg up and down my shaft.

I shifted a hand to her hip to give it to her just the way she needed and the responding groan that vibrated through her body almost had me popping off. I had to wait, had to hold out, but she wasn't making it easy.

The hungry roll of her hips against my leg was almost too much to watch. I knew how those hips would bounce on my dick, how they'd jiggle when I pounded into her from behind.

In my head, I had her stripped of everything but my sweater. I nipped at her breasts through the wool while she sank down on me. Kissed her neck, her jaw, her shoulders while she bucked and screamed. Held her tight while she came, even tighter while I came.

I forced my eyes open and saw her tongue dart out to wet her lips. Fuck, I hadn't even thought about her tongue yet.

My hold on her hip was unforgiving, my fingers digging into the plush skin there and driving her harder, faster. But she met every rock with a roll of her own, with shuddering breaths and deep, perfect moans.

I wanted to say something. Anything. I wanted her to know how gorgeous she was, how incredible she felt, how much I wanted this— how I'd *always* wanted this.

Though it didn't matter what I wanted because Emme's thighs tightened around me as she whispered, "Oh god, oh god, oh god. Yes, fuck, *yes.*"

"That's right," I said, low and easy like we weren't rewriting everything we were to each other. "Let me make you feel better."

I rolled my lips together as she went on rocking against me, slower and a little shaky now but still blindingly hot. She dragged the flat of her thigh over my cock with enough pressure and friction to make me forget my name.

Something like "Right there" and "Don't you fucking stop" babbled out of me as I came so hard and so long I was concerned I'd damaged something. Never before had I felt my body hollow itself out —and then keep going.

Neither of us moved. We didn't say anything. I just stroked her back and kissed the top of her head and let myself enjoy the aftershocks. Her skin was damp under my palm and I loved how hard she'd worked for it. Even though she'd kept her face from me, she wasn't shy.

There was nothing shy about dry humping.

My shirt was soaked like I'd been hit with several water balloons and I could survive the discomfort but Emme was having a hell of a time staying out of the mess. After one last kiss to her hair, I climbed out of the seat and tucked the blanket around her. "I'm gonna change. Stay right here."

When I finished cleaning up, I found Emme curled up in her seat and working very hard at feigning sleep.

I sat down and braced my elbows on my thighs. I was still woozy from the orgasm, from all of it, and I wanted to pick her up and bring her back to my seat but she'd chosen this. She knew what I wanted and she made a different choice for herself.

I had to respect that. I couldn't bully my way in—no more than I already had—just because rubbing up against her while fully clothed was the best sex of my life.

chapter sixteen

Emme

Today's Learning Objective:
Students will have a quick little breakdown in the bath.

IT WASN'T ENOUGH TO FAKE SLEEPING THROUGH THE LAST HOUR OF THE flight.

No, I had to take this game of avoidance to the most unhinged level possible.

I sat up with a theatrical stretch and yawn and "Oh wow, we're already landing?" when the plane hit the runway. As if I hadn't been counting down the seconds during the descent. When Ryan caught me staring at his change of clothes, I decided to ramble for a solid twenty minutes about needing to work on my lesson plans tonight and how I liked our curriculum well enough but still felt the need to unpack and adapt everything to my preferences.

There were a few moments when he glanced at me, his brows pitched high and his flat expression asking, *Are you listening to yourself?*

The answer was yes, I was listening to every mortifying bit, but it was also no, and neither should you.

In the car, I talked at excruciating speed *and* length about Ben and

Grace's upcoming housewarming party. The work they'd done on the house, the wedding plans, the people who would be there along with extended personal histories. I went so far as to rattle off every item I was planning for the charcuterie board I'd bring, where I'd buy it all, and how I'd arrange the cheese into a cute B and G.

I kind of wanted to throw myself down a well and stay there for six to eight years until I'd shifted into some kind of watery goblin and forgotten all about my human shame.

"Audrey always brings a dessert or two," I went on, staring out the car window at the gray skies and pouring rain. "She got started with gluten-free baking because her doctors thought she was intolerant but it turned out she was just in a really toxic marriage and once she got rid of that guy and all the stress that came with him, her body slowly healed. Crazy how that can happen."

"Crazy," he murmured.

"She actually had a whole gluten-free baking site for a while and she'd test out her recipes on us and—"

Ryan dropped a hand on my thigh and leaned over, pointing out my window. "Is that Ines?"

"What? No. Where? I mean—what? I don't think—where? No. Probably not." I stopped flailing for a second and realized he was right. And she was wearing my yellow satin cape. "Oh. Yeah. That's her. That's Ines."

"What the hell is she carrying?" he asked. "Bowen, can you slow down up here?"

Ryan's hand was still on my thigh, his index finger busy tracing the seam of my leggings as if I was capable of enduring such things in these circumstances. I was not.

Bowen cut across North End traffic and pulled to the side as he approached a waterlogged Ines, her glasses bleary from the rain and the cape soaked through.

"Ines," I called, though she didn't seem to hear me. "I'll get out and talk to her."

"Please don't," Ryan said before switching on his deep, commanding QB voice. *"Ines."*

That did the trick. He was good like that. She whirled around, half blind from the rain and struggling to carry—I didn't even know what.

"Ines, it's me, Emme. And Ryan." I added, "And Bowen too. Hurry, get in here. Get out of the rain."

"The rain is part of the problem," she said, stepping up to the SUV. "That's why I needed all the rice."

"What do you mean, you needed rice?" I pushed the door open and shuffled closer to Ryan. He only gripped my thigh tighter, as if that would help anything.

"To save your laptop." She heaved a twenty-pound bag of basmati rice onto the seat. "Because it's raining inside too."

RYAN SURVEYED MY ROOM WITH HIS FISTS PROPPED ON HIS HIPS. Chunks of ceiling plaster covered my desk, my bed, the floor, and a steady stream of water poured in through two or three spots. My bookshelf and everything on it was destroyed. There was nothing to be saved on my desk. School papers, books, bills—all of it wet to the point of disintegration. My closet took the worst of it with a whole waterfall coursing down one wall and soaking just about every piece of clothing I owned. My shoes floated and bobbed in the flood.

With a nod, Ryan said, "Time to go." Pulled out his phone and swiped through a few screens. "Grab anything you can salvage. I'll have Bowen pull around in a few minutes."

I picked up a shirt I'd left on the bed, now caked with plaster and other debris I couldn't identify. I didn't even know how to clean something that'd drowned in gross ceiling water. It smelled like an old basement. Was there a special detergent for that or was it more like fifty washes with the regular stuff?

Another chunk of ceiling hit the floor with a squelch and I glanced at Ryan. "I'm sorry, what did you say?"

Phone pressed to his ear, Ryan said, "Get whatever you need so you can leave in the next five minutes. I'm taking you home with me."

I motioned to the ruptures in the ceiling. "But—"

"You can't stay here, Muggsy. You know that." He gave me a look that begged me to stop fucking around and get moving. "Ines has already talked to the landlord and warned your downstairs neighbors too. There's nothing else we can do here, and standing around and waiting for the rest of the ceiling to give out isn't a great idea."

"I can't leave Ines."

Her room was as dry as a bone. She only discovered the flood in mine when the water started spreading out into the kitchen.

"She's coming with us," he said, holding up a hand when a voice boomed through his phone. "Jakobi, hey. No, we'll deal with that later. I need you to hop in your truck and get over to the North End. No. No, Em's apartment is underwater and I need a hand getting her roommate moved out."

Ryan gave me a *hurry up* hand gesture and paced into the kitchen, still talking to his manager, Jakobi.

I stared at my room for a long moment, still too stunned to process any of it. This weird little place I'd called home for the past few years couldn't be mine anymore. Not now, maybe not ever again.

I toyed with the band of my ring, still slightly foreign against my skin. If I was being honest with myself, it hadn't been home since Grace moved out. It was still *my* place but it wasn't *our* place anymore, and that part mattered more than I ever thought it would.

From the other side of the apartment, I heard Ryan say, "Okay, Ines. We need to make some decisions. What are we packing right now?"

I pressed a fist to my mouth to smother a manic laugh. Not twenty minutes ago I was busy wringing the oxygen out of every molecule in reach in the daft hope of suffocating that interaction on the plane from memory. All I'd wanted was to climb into bed and hide under the covers for a minimum of sixteen hours. *Alone.*

And here we were, waiting on Jakobi's truck and figuring out if there was anything, even one tiny thing from this place, that I could take with me to Ryan's condo.

Where I wouldn't be able to hide at all.

"Did you buy or lease?"

Ryan set eight reusable grocery bags on the marble island, all of which he'd insisted on carrying into the high-rise condo himself, and cut a glance toward Ines. "Buy."

"How much did you pay?"

"Ines," I whisper-yelled.

She held up her hands. "What?"

"It's rude to ask those things," I said.

Ryan shook his head. "It's fine. Reporters write about it all the time. My grandmother gives me a ton of shit about it too." To Ines, he said, "About fifteen million."

"Dollars?"

He shrugged as he unpacked a bag. We'd cleared out the fridge and cupboards before leaving. "The seller wasn't willing to take jelly beans."

She pushed her glasses up. "What's the square footage?"

"A little over four thousand inside, another thousand on the deck."

I glanced past the comfortable living room and dining room with a table to seat eight, toward the deck. The clouds pressed in close, heavy and dense. The city all but disappeared.

If it wasn't still raining like the end of days and my uterus wasn't clawing its wallpaper off, I'd disappear too. I just needed to figure a few things out and I couldn't do that during Ines's interrogation of

Ryan or his wildly precise approach to shelving peanut butter and black beans.

I had a tote bag loaded with vitamins, hair stuff, and any random thing that wasn't wet. My heating pad, which came as a huge relief seeing as my period decided to visit five whole days early. A few bras, some t-shirts, jeans that fit only sometimes. But that was it. I needed to wash my clothes from the weekend so I had something to wear to work tomorrow and—god help me—my lesson plans were still a mystery. And the laptop I needed to access my instructional materials was chilling in twenty pounds of rice.

"When are you and Emme getting married?"

"Ines, my sunshine," I whispered, pressing fingertips to my eyelids. "It's a good question, one I've asked several times myself, but can we put a pin in this chat until after I have a cute little panic attack because I have no computer, no underwear, and no idea how I'm supposed to function tomorrow?"

"That's cool," she said as she turned a curious eye to the barista-quality espresso machine on the countertop.

"You're not having a panic attack," Ryan said, moving on to the cheeses. I noted a bit of judgment in his eyes when he had them all laid out on the counter. "We're going to get everything fixed, and replace anything you lost."

"Yeah, but how? *How* does that happen? My landlord is a guy in a bodega. We're not talking about responsive property management here."

"You're not saying anything I don't already know," he said, eyeing the wedges of gouda and brie. "That kind of damage takes time to fix. It's not going to be resolved this week. Probably not this month." He shrugged like this was fine. "So, stay here."

I glanced down the long line of the kitchen island to Ines. She was entertaining herself with the espresso machine. "But this is *your* place."

"Legally, it'll be yours soon enough."

I searched and searched but found no adequate response to that. I just...I hadn't even thought of it that way.

"Listen. You have two options," Ryan said to me, taking real care to organize the cheddars. "One, we leave now to pick up a new laptop for you and then swing by some shops for your—for whatever you need."

"And the second option?" I asked.

He closed the fridge and turned, meeting my gaze. "Or I call Marcie and Wren right now and tell them to have everything you need delivered tonight. It might take Wren a few days to replace your entire wardrobe but she can get you taken care of for tomorrow."

"I can't let you do that," I said. It was enough that he and Jakobi had made quick work of packing Ines's room and then hauling her into her new—though much more temporary—accommodations. Even if Ryan said she was welcome here indefinitely, I couldn't imagine he wanted her taking apart his oven. Or that espresso machine.

"Yes, you can." He folded his arms over his chest as he stared at me. "You can argue with me about it all you want but that's not going to solve any of these problems and it won't make you feel better so don't." He turned, opened a drawer. He pulled out a small bottle and shook two tablets into his hand. "Come here. It's time for another dose. You need to stay ahead of the pain."

I shuffled over and accepted the pills while he filled a glass of water. "Thanks," I mumbled.

He watched me swallow before asking, "What'll it be? Are we going out or am I making a call?"

I knew the money was nothing to him. Some clothes, a laptop—it was pocket change. And I knew that if our roles were reversed—if I was famous and outrageously wealthy and he was a refugee of his flooded apartment—I'd haunt the shit out of him until he let me help. I'd be so fucking mad if he tried to put on a brave, self-sufficient face about it.

And that was why I stopped fighting him. Why I didn't pull out my pride and let it be the only thing keeping me warm while I suffered.

"I guess you can call them."

"That's my girl," he said, a slight smile pulling at his lips.

"When you do get married," Ines started, "can I play the harp at the ceremony?"

We shared a glance before turning to her. Ryan asked, "You play the harp?"

"No, but it's not realistic to assume you'll be able to coordinate a large wedding with less than twelve months of lead time and I've always wanted to take lessons."

We shared another glance. He shrugged. I gave a quiet laugh as I rubbed at the band of my ring.

"Will you learn 'You've Lost That Lovin' Feelin''?"

Ines squinted at him. "What's that?"

I snorted out a laugh. "It's the song from *Top Gun*." Shaking my head at him, I said, "You can't be serious."

"I never joke about *Top Gun*." He had the audacity to look offended. "It's a great song. The *best* song."

"It's about falling out of love," I argued.

"It's about putting it all on the line before it's lost," he replied. "It's about fighting right to the end, even when you can't get a single point on the board."

"A football song, then. Gotcha." I gave him a cheeky thumbs-up that had him muttering about my willful misunderstanding. "You can have your sad song if I can walk down the aisle to 'Maneater.'"

He slapped a hand over his heart. "Muggs, I'd require it."

"Okay so that's 'You've Lost That Lovin' Feelin'' and"—Ines eyed me, a brow quirked over the rim of her glasses—"'Maneater.' Do I have that right?"

"What? Would you prefer something from *Les Mis*?"

"Yeah, I don't know much about weddings," she started, "but is the French Revolution's death opera really the vibe you're going for?"

"It is not a *death opera*," I cried. "And it's set several decades *after* the French Revolution, thank you kindly."

Ryan leaned against the island and crossed his arms. "'On My Own' is not the soundtrack to a happy marriage. And I know because I've listened to it with you no fewer than six thousand times."

"That seems like an exaggeration," I said. "If we take lonely little Eponine from 'On My Own' and the guy who knows his gal won't be getting the lovin' feelin' back anytime soon, and toss them together, there's a chance they'll be very happy. Or much worse off. Who are we to tell?"

Ryan stared at me like he had something to say but he shook his head and turned to Ines. "Take those lessons."

"Awesome. Thanks." Ines pumped a fist and grabbed her backpack from the floor. "Am I allowed to use the gym? Don't worry, I won't touch anything and I won't get in your way. It would just be cool to practice without taking two buses to do it."

He nodded. "Yeah, anytime."

Another fist pump. "This place is great." Giving me a baleful look, she added, "Our place was great too. Just great in a primitive, cave-dwelling kind of way."

I tried to laugh but I ended up sounding like a bullfrog.

"I'm going to take apart your laptop now and see if any of it can be saved," Ines continued. "In case it wasn't clear enough, I'm gonna close my door and mind my own business for the rest of the night. You two can do whatever lovey cringey woo-woo stuff you want."

She wandered down the hall in the direction of the home gym, den, and spare bedroom where Ryan and Jakobi had unloaded her things.

All I had was my luggage from the weekend and the tote bag of despair, and both of those things still sat at the edge of the kitchen. There was one very obvious answer as to where I'd be sleeping though I still expected to hear something about a pull-out couch in the den or a daybed in the gym. If the topic didn't come up soon enough, I was going to have to do the awkward thing and ask.

"Is she really going to learn the harp?" he asked, back to organizing the cheese.

I banded an arm across my torso. My body was trying to kill me today. "Probably."

Ryan glanced over his shoulder at me, clocked my hunched stance with a scowl. "Just so you know, there's a soaking tub the size of a swimming pool in my bathroom and it has eighty-four jets. It's brought me back from the dead more than a few times."

That was an opening if I'd ever seen one.

"If that's your way of asking me to get naked in your room, you should've said something a lot sooner."

Several wedges of cheese tumbled out of his hands and hit the floor. He dropped his head as a raspy breath rattled out of him. "Emmeline."

"It was always going to be weird," I said. "I just kicked it in the ass to get it moving. Now we can get it over with."

He scooped up the cheese and dumped it into a drawer, abandoning all organizational schemes. Closing the fridge, he said, "I can leave. If you'd be more comfortable."

"Don't be ridiculous," I said. "Where would you even go?"

"I have a place near the stadium. I usually stay there unless I have a reason to be in the city."

I shook my head. "I don't want you to leave."

"Why?"

A moment passed and then another while I searched for the words. He turned his attention to another bag and I got the distinct sense he didn't want to look at me right now. I laced my fingers together, aware all over again of my ring—and the lines we'd crossed today.

In all these years, we'd never done anything like that.

Although.

Although...

We'd kissed—a lot. And not only when there were eyes on us.

We'd shared a bed—a few times. And we always ended up climbing each other in the night like vines.

Then there was everything else. Massaging his jaw. Flashing him the other night. Asking him to unzip my dress after the charity event. Letting him carry me down the stairs. Jumping into his arms when we met for dinner. Hugging every time we parted like we were about to be separated for years.

And there was no forgetting that I'd let him pick up the soggy tatters of my life, move me into his penthouse, and replace everything I owned with a few quick calls.

Maybe...maybe we'd never crossed *this* line before but there were a lot of other lines leading up to it.

Maybe this wasn't weird or awkward or a reason to become a well-water goblin. Maybe this—and by *this*, I did mean dry humping my oldest friend on a private jet—was the next logical step.

If that was the case, that meant I had to take another step, cross another line.

"How many—" Ryan scowled as he pulled another two jars of jam from the bag and added them to the others gathered on his countertop. "Why do you have so much jam?"

"Because Shay's husband's a jam farmer and he always sends us home with a bunch when we visit. I swear, he grows the best jam in the entire world."

"I'm aware that you're fucking with me," he said, folding the reusable bags into crisp squares, "because I know that you know that jam isn't something one farms. I know what you're doing and I know why you're doing it and I love you but can you stop and have a real conversation with me for one fucking minute?"

I crossed to the island, grabbed a bag from his hands and tossed it aside. I reached for him, a hand on the back of his neck, the other cupping his granite jaw. Pushing up on my toes, I touched my lips to his. It wasn't really a kiss, it was a gentle brush and *Hi. I'm here.*

He sucked in a sudden breath and he lifted the arms that'd been frozen at his sides to my waist, holding me tight against him. His teeth grazed my bottom lip and it felt like *Good. I've been waiting.*

We stared at each other for a moment, the silence tight around us until I said, "Stay. I want you here."

His jaw softened under my palm. I pressed one kiss to his lips before he picked me up and deposited me on the countertop. He stepped between my legs, saying, "Did you really think I'd leave?"

I shrugged. He slipped a hand under my sweater and stroked small circles low on my back. "You would though. If I said it was what I wanted."

"But you don't want that."

I shook my head. He left a line of kisses from my jaw to the tender spot where my neck met my shoulder. "Who would yell at me about jam farming if you left?"

He dropped his head to my shoulder with a sigh. "Jam doesn't grow on trees, Muggsy."

"But peaches do and they make really nice preserves."

We stayed there for a minute, his palm warm on my back and my fingers raking up his nape, and I didn't trouble myself with questions about what this was or what it meant or where it would go. I didn't have to spend my time worrying about how this would end or what we'd be like when we were friends who'd been married.

Trouble would come and find me when it was time. It always did.

Eventually, Ryan said, "I wasn't expecting you to stay in my room. There's another suite upstairs."

I glanced around. I didn't see a staircase anywhere. "There's an upstairs?"

"Yeah, on the other side of the gym. It's bigger and more private. It has a sauna and a cold plunge. Oh, and another deck, some storage, and a family room."

"I'm going to need a map to get around this place."

"I'll draw you one after I make some calls," he said. "I mean it though. Stay wherever you want. Take my room. Kick me out for all I care."

"I'm not kicking you out of your bedroom, you incorrigible man."

"I'm on the road most of this week anyway and I do have the better bathtub."

With a breath, I put some space between us. "Where are you going?"

"Minnesota." He rubbed a hand over the back of his neck. "I'm meeting with a group of strength and conditioning coaches. Trying to get my arm in shape."

"Oh, that's a relief," I murmured. "I thought I was the only one who'd noticed your pass completion rate had dipped."

He dropped his hands on either side of me and stared straight into my eyes. "I love how hard you ride me." His tongue peeked out, just a bit, and ran along the line of his teeth. "About my stats."

My loud gulp seemed to bounce off the walls in this wide, spacious room. My cheeks were rosy red and it would've been safer to take this in a different direction but I said, "Someone has to."

We went on watching each other, leaning in by inches as the moments passed. We could've stayed there until we closed the distance and crashed into each other again but a brutal stab of pain shot through my back, between my hips, and down my legs. The only way to withstand this was to curl in on myself and breathe like I could exhale the hellcat currently possessing my uterus.

I couldn't, but it was better than screaming or accidentally tearing a towel bar off the wall. The towel bar thing only happened once and it was when I was sixteen. It was the one time my stepdad had been notably impressed with me.

Ryan pulled me into him and stroked a hand down my back. "I'm going to get the bath started," he said, his lips on my temple. "I'll bring your things in there so you can change. You can keep everything there —if you want."

A breath shuddered out of me and I nodded. "Give me some time to think about it."

"Can I watch while you think?"

"In the bath? No." I brought my hand to his solid chest, experimented with touching him this way simply because I liked it. "Good try but no. I don't have a spare minute for anything like that. I'm positively overbooked at bath time. I need to cry, panic about what I'm going to teach this week, and then zone out while obsessing about pointless things. I couldn't squeeze you in even if I wanted to."

"And you don't want to?"

He asked this in a plain, unassuming way. There was no heat, no innuendo. No expectation. And I loved that so much because I knew my response wouldn't change anything between us. There wouldn't be pressure or disappointment. There wouldn't be any loaded comments about the weekend ahead or the next time we traveled for one of his events.

We'd be okay if we never crossed another line together—and that was everything I needed. We could only cross these lines if we could turn around and walk back to the start at any point.

"Not right now." I motioned to my abdomen. "There's a teardown project taking place in my uterus. Authorized personnel only."

He reached between us, pressed a hand to my belly. He was so deliciously warm, I couldn't help but lean deeper into his touch. "Is there something you need? Supplies or anything else?"

I shook my head. "No, but...thanks. For everything. You really didn't have to do all of this for me and Ines."

"It wasn't like I was going to leave you two there." He kissed my temple, my forehead. "At least not without a canoe."

"That would've solved many problems though invented a few others."

"Couldn't have that." He scooped me off the counter, set me on my feet. "Come on. Let me introduce you to all the different pain-relief bath soaks I keep on hand."

"No hotter words have ever been spoken," I said, lacing my fingers with his.

chapter seventeen

Ryan

*Today's Learning Objective:
Students will be able to read the room.*

EMME CHOSE THE ROOM UPSTAIRS.

It was probably the better direction to go, all things considered. We all needed to retreat to our separate corners and recalibrate for a night. Plus, she didn't feel well and I doubted I'd succeed in staying on my side of the bed. I hadn't managed it yet, and after this morning I couldn't see the odds getting any better.

We shared a meal upstairs in the family room and then she worked on her plans for school while I watched a few hockey games. I needed to pack for my trip to Minnesota tomorrow and I owed Jakobi a call—my grandmother too—but nothing in the world could get me off this couch. No fewer than six hundred times did I stop myself from asking *Can we do this forever?*

Goddamn, that was all I wanted. Just like this and for as long as possible.

Though I didn't know where we went from here. If we went anywhere. She'd kissed me in the kitchen and neither of us were pretending it had anything to do with wifeing up my reputation.

But it'd ended and she'd drawn some boundaries. That part didn't surprise me. I knew Emme so I knew it was coming.

I remembered two things from my four years of high school. The first was the dark, suffocating blanket of my father's illness and the way I still felt trapped beneath it every time I went home.

The second, and the one that stuck with me like an old splinter, was sitting by while Emme bounced from relationship to relationship. She dated a lot though never seriously. Nothing lasted more than a month or two and it always ended when there was a threshold she wasn't interested in crossing. Some thresholds were big, others nothing at all. But she only crossed the lines she chose to cross.

In ninth grade it was Christmas. The guy she was with—Ethan Mace, a year ahead of us and not a complete prick but I resented his presence on this planet very much—wanted her to join his entire extended family on Christmas Eve. There were like sixty people coming to this thing and they took their traditions very seriously. She wanted nothing to do with it and he didn't recognize that insisting it would be fun and chill—with sixty people and a baby Jesus in the manger skit—only made her run faster for the exit.

In tenth grade it was Marcus Denflower and the homecoming dance. She wanted to go with a group of friends. He wanted to go with *her*. They split up one day before the dance. I lucked out in that situation because she used me as a human shield against Denflower's attempts at smoothing things over. Fortunately for all of us, he knew better than to fuck with me.

In eleventh grade it was Jaxon Perrent, and that silly motherfucker wanted Emme to watch him play chess at lunch every day. She didn't even bother with a backward glance in Jaxon's direction when he swore he hadn't meant it as an ultimatum. She was done and that was the end of it. She ate lunch with *me*. That single point on the board—and those lunches—had kept me going through some hard times.

In twelfth grade it was Kivan Waleswood and he wanted her to go to his parents' lake cabin with him after the prom. It was obvious what

Kivan was looking for with that. I knew Emme had...done things but there was a big difference between some time behind closed doors at a house party and a whole fucking weekend alone in the woods with someone. Emme—*thank god*—wasn't interested in the cabin or even going to the prom with Kivan anymore.

Then she blew my entire mind and announced we'd go together. It was supposed to be a joke, and I didn't understand how or why or what that was supposed to mean but I didn't care. It was the closest I could come in that grueling time to getting what I wanted.

And I knew now that if I wanted Emme, I had to let her make the decisions. If I wanted her to wrap herself around me the way she had this morning, if I ever wanted to feel her shake and pant with pleasure again, I had to wait until she was ready.

I had to give her time to cross the line.

If there was one thing I had when it came to Emmeline Ahlborg, it was patience. After fifteen years of watching her date the weakest link in every chain, a week or two was nothing. I could do that in my fantasy-soaked sleep.

Hang on. There was a third thing I remembered from high school. It was working out with the football team before school started and hearing Brett Kincaid, the senior quarterback who lost his starting position to me three weeks later, yell *Dibs on the new girl* when Emme walked past the field. We all knew he had a hard time hearing the word *no*. He was a fucking asshole who thought everyone owed him something.

Everyone knew this except Emme.

I would've noticed her regardless of Brett's announcement. She was gorgeous and new, two things we didn't get much of in my town. I might've talked to her though I didn't do much of that in those days. I would've liked her and I probably would've let her sweep me into her orbit too.

But I knew there was something undeniably right, something *specific* about her that fit me like a key in a rusty old lock when I told her to watch out for Kincaid and she replied, "You mean the punk with the slippery hands and slow feet? Yeah, he outed himself as a dick waffle this morning. I asked him if this was his first season on the field. Surprises all around because it's not. Then I asked whether he knew he wasn't supposed to be throwing interceptions." She leaned in, close enough for me to smell the citrus on her. Close enough for that scent to imprint itself on my nervous system. "He made some noise about me not understanding the game and I told him to worry less about my understanding and more about the yards lost to all his sacks."

She'd dropped her hand to my arm like we'd known each other forever and I remembered walking around all day with the heat of her touch burning me like a brand. I remembered looking at my skin and expecting to see a mark there. But it was the last thing she'd said that stayed with me even longer.

"And then, since he was getting all fired up, I explained that I just don't go out with players. It's a homegrown rule. My dad owns a whole-ass football team"—that was back before he destroyed his relationship with her—"so believe me, I have rock-solid reasons."

I nodded along like *yes, I understand this* but I was busy snapping off the early buds of hope that'd sprouted at the arrival of this unbelievable girl who knew football and smelled like oranges and laughed at people who tried to give her shit. I foreclosed every possibility that'd surged to the surface when she smiled at me, leaned close to me, touched me.

I could still feel that key breaking in my lock.

Because I had to play. There was no other choice on the table for me. I had to suit up and take the field on Friday nights because it was the one thing my father looked forward to. He'd already lost so much, already struggled with the hopelessness of an ALS diagnosis. The least I could do was play the game he loved. Give him an hour or two where life wasn't completely fucking awful.

And I was counting on the game to get me out of that town. There wouldn't be money for me to go to college, not when everything was going into round-the-clock care for my dad, and not when there were four other kids in my family.

I had to play.

It didn't matter whether this irreverent, fast-talking, half-pint of a girl had crashed into my life and all I wanted was to stay close enough to her that she might touch me again and make me feel a million confusing things at once. She made it seem like we were the only ones in the world, and that world wasn't nearly as terrible as the one I went home to every night.

I had to play and she didn't go out with players.

That was how it went with us. Inseparable from that point forward but never *together*. The difference was slight, the sort of thing that didn't translate cleanly. I learned every nook and facet of jealousy. I taught myself how to swallow down desire and walk away from possessive envy. I stewed in resentment of the guys she dated—always the most deplorable candidates the species had to offer—but I never let myself resent her.

The thing about that key was that when it broke, it stayed inside me. Waiting for her to come back, to find the remnants and finally turn it.

I'd already asked for so much and probably taken more than I deserved. I wasn't going to rush her tonight.

Not when I was going to ask for much more very soon.

Claudia: "Boston's star QB Ryan Ralston announces engagement to girlfriend Emily Ahlborg at Kentucky Derby"

Claudia: <link to Bleacher Report>

Amber: ok wow so this is really happening

Ruthie: they never get her name right

Chloe: at the Derby?

Mom: RYAN

Chloe: I can think of better places to get engaged

Mom: !!!!!!

Amber: The article just says she was wearing the ring at Derby parties so maybe he popped the question before?

Mom: Is this real?

Gramma CeCe: It's about damn time

Mom: Ryan, answer your phone!

Ruthie: I'd offer to draft a prenup for you but I don't want my head ripped off

Mom: RYAN PICK UP YOUR PHONE

Gramma CeCe: Leave the betrothed alone, dear, or you'll never get that grandbaby you want

Chloe: For the record, she does have grandbabies

Claudia: Here's a pic from some fancy party

Claudia: If you zoom in, you can see the ring

Gramma CeCe: Didn't need to zoom in much! That thing's the size of an egg!

Ruthie: Yeah, an ostrich egg

Ruthie: Give that prenup a thought, okay?

Claudia: He's not getting a prenup, Ruth. You know he'll give her everything.

Mom: They aren't even married yet and you're talking about their divorce????

Amber: Do we actually know they're not married yet?

> Mom: What does that mean????
>
> Gramma CeCe: You know how your son works, Cecelia. He won't say a word until he's ready.

THE FIRST THING JAKOBI SAID WHEN HE ANSWERED MY CALL THAT night was, "You're in so much trouble."

"That's the least useful thing you've said all day."

"That little lady has you wrapped around every one of her fingers and all her toes," he drawled. "And you love it."

I flipped on the lights in my home gym and headed for the weight rack. Earbuds in place, I asked, "Is there a point to any of this?"

He hooted with laughter. "Is the sister part of the package?"

I closed my fingers around a pair of fifties. "You saw the place. Couldn't leave her there."

"Maybe not, but I wouldn't have taken her home with me. This city is full of apartments. You could've found one for the sister before the day was out and been done with it."

"Emme never would've gone for that."

A noise trilled low in his throat. "You and that heart of yours. You fooled everyone into believing you don't have one, but after the weekend you've had, they'll think you're a man reborn. Nicely done."

Leaning my chest against the bench, I started in on a series of trap raises. "If you're done with the pearls of wisdom for the night, do you think you could update me on the pending issues we have? Or are you just going to shovel shit at me until you find something else to amuse you?"

"Stella will be pleased," Jakobi continued. "She knew we'd be able to turn your image around but I think she'll be surprised at how fast those tides turned." He chuckled to himself. "She's a good choice, this friend of yours. Excellent, actually. Couldn't have done better myself."

Grunting as I reached the end of the set, I managed, "Any news from the Wallaces?"

"Wally's personal assistant informed me that he's leaving for a month-long family holiday tomorrow and he'll be making his final decision on the franchise bids when he returns."

"A timeline," I panted. "It's about fucking time."

"We'd suspected this all along but the confirmation is appreciated." After a pause, Jakobi added, "The assistant suggested our bid was the strongest. Barring any unforeseen events, we could have this wrapped up before preseason games start."

That news came with a wave of relief but then there was something else—an odd prickle of disappointment. If we succeeded in buying the rights to these teams, I wouldn't need to drag Emme to every party and charity event on my calendar. Wouldn't need to perform for the cameras and anyone else watching. Wouldn't need to do any of this.

The truth was I didn't have an exit strategy with Emme. My best guess was that it would blow up in my face and destroy every shred of connection we shared. But if that didn't happen and we managed to survive the next few months, maybe we'd keep the fun going a little longer. Maybe we'd just stay together. Forever.

I forced my arms back harder than necessary and sucked in a breath when a ripple of pain went through my shoulder. "Dammit," I murmured, dropping the weights.

"If you're messing with that arm again, I'll call your fiancée and inform her you require supervision. Something tells me she's quite the disciplinarian."

"Don't bother her unless I'm dead," I snapped. "The arm's fine. Just pushed it a bit too far."

"You're going to push yourself right out of another Super Bowl ring if you're not careful."

I dropped into a plank rather than argue with him.

"We'll talk later this week," Jakobi said. "Before I let you go—

what's the story with the sister? Ines. She's lovely—and fascinating. Brilliant. She's the engineer who needed the summer gig, yes?"

I dropped my head between my arms and groaned. "She's twenty-two."

"I figured as much." He murmured to himself. Probably justifying a twelve-year age gap with something about women maturing more quickly. They certainly matured more quickly than former NFL running backs. "Would it be a problem if I—"

"She's Gary Rockwell's daughter."

"Well, fuck." He huffed out a laugh. Gary was a nice guy but he was a fucking train wreck. It was one of the worst kept secrets in pro sports. "You always know when he's in big trouble with a bookie because he starts showing up on all the networks for color commentary."

I sat back on my knees for a moment before starting the next plank. "He's not around much but I've heard he's protective of Ines."

"Not nearly enough if he let his daughter live in that moldy attic your fiancée called an apartment."

"Now do you understand why I wanted to buy the building?"

After a moment, he asked, "Are you seriously warning me off from her?"

I stared at the mat as I counted to sixty. Jakobi could wait for his answer. "I'm warning you to be on your best behavior. Ines is —special."

"You don't think I noticed that?"

"Listen, man, a lot of things happened today. I'm not making assumptions about a fuckin' thing. I'm just trying to keep my head above water." I blew out a rough breath as I settled in for another sixty seconds. "She's also trained in the art of kung fu so I might not have to kick your ass if you fuck it up. She'll do it for me."

A deep laugh rumbled across the line. "I'd savor the opportunity."

Before I could think better of it, I added, "She wants to learn to play the harp."

"Interesting. I can work with that." I heard the shuffle of papers and then, "Just look at us. Teammates yesterday, business partners today, brothers-in-law tomorrow."

"Are you drunk or high?" I sat back on my knees. "You met her today. You talked to her for a maximum of fifteen minutes. It's early to lose your head. Find out if she's remotely interested first."

"Ah, but that's where you and I differ."

I pinched the bridge of my nose. "I don't think I care but what the fuck are you talking about?"

"I see what I want and I go for it. I see the win before the game even starts and I put everything into clinching it," he said. "You see what you want and spend fifteen years running down the clock. You wait until the win is in sight."

"A win is a win," I said, annoyed to find any shred of accuracy in his words.

"Come on, now. We both know that's not true."

I didn't say anything. I just knew I'd do anything for that win.

chapter eighteen
Emme

Today's Learning Objective:
Students will keep the wheels turning.

"That boy wasted no time." Jamie reached across the table to grab my hand. "He's quick but he has excellent taste."

"Oh my god," Audrey breathed, leaning in to get a look. "Love a cushion cut."

Grace watched me as she unpacked her lunch. She'd been excited last night when I'd messaged her with all the news—the engagement, the flooded apartment, the move to Ryan's place—but also asked more than once if I was sure about this, if this was what I wanted.

It was easy to say yes, for two reasons. First, I was sure—in a very wobbly, deer-in-the-headlights sort of way. Especially when Ryan let loose comments about me being legally entitled to condos and god only knew what else. As if there was any corner of my mind where that information belonged. I was closer to reconciling with the fact that there were feelings between us that weren't purely platonic.

Second—and definitely not the most well-adjusted reason—I'd learned since breaking up with Teddy how to give Grace exactly enough information for her to believe I was doing all right and not ask too many questions. I had to be okay, because if I wasn't, she'd start making noises about calling off her wedding again.

Carrying that responsibility on my shoulders was the hardest thing I'd ever done for her, and that was saying something because back in college I tweezed eight ticks from her thighs and butt cheeks.

If college taught me anything, it was to liberally apply bug spray *all over* when camping (and having sex while camping) in the Vermont woods during the summer.

Setting aside my work as Tick Tweezer Extraordinaire, it was a damn good thing that I wasn't still rotting in bed and ranting at romcoms because I would've run myself into the ground hiding it from her.

That first month or two without her in the apartment had been so tough. I'd missed her like a limb—and I knew it was the same for her because we'd spent hours on the phone every night. We'd video call to eat dinner together or watch our usual TV shows. Or we'd talk about nothing while folding laundry or scrolling apps.

We didn't do that anymore.

Part of me wondered whether this was the natural evolution of things. Even under perfect circumstances, things were bound to change as we grew up, moved, settled into serious relationships.

But the other part of me wondered whether Grace heard herself all those times she threatened to cancel the wedding. If she knew what it meant to put that weight on me. If she understood that it wasn't fair to ask that of me.

We'd always said we'd never let a man come between us.

Strange to think how Teddy was the asshat to prove us wrong.

We'd chatted as I settled into the second-floor suite, which I'd chosen mostly because my body was not in friendly form. I required some space and some privacy, and the flexibility to visit the bathroom as many times throughout the night as necessary and without explanation. And I'd needed time to sort through the endless stream of packages from boutiques and high-end department stores to find something suitable for second-grade life.

"I don't want to get engaged but I wouldn't complain about someone giving me a ring like this," Jamie said. "How do I arrange that? How did *you* pull it off?"

"He adores her," Grace said simply.

I smiled at her though I shook my head. "Don't exaggerate. We've been friends since—"

"He always has," Grace repeated. "Come on, you know it's true."

"She's right," Jamie said. "I knew it was serious when he rolled up with her coffee *and* juice. Don't even get me started on the forehead kiss."

"Why do I always miss these things?" Audrey grumbled. "I love forehead kisses."

I poked at my lunch while they mythologized Ryan's visit to the school. For once, I had an actual lunch of fruits and crackers, cheeses and meats that appeared in his fridge sometime during my hour-long soak in the bath of wonder and amazement. If he'd introduced me to that tub two months ago, I would've agreed to marry him on the spot.

"Not to be that bitch but has this moved a little quick?" Jamie asked. "I'm not saying it's wrong. You know I'm all in and I have been since the start but have y'all come up for air?"

"We've known each other for a little more than half our lives," I said. "It's not like we're starting at the ground floor. I think that makes a big difference."

"They know everything about each other," Grace said. "They know each other's families with encyclopedic detail. Their inside jokes have inside jokes."

"I can't decide if that's really fucking rad or something to be studied by scientists," Jamie said.

"It's rad," Grace said. "The first time I met Ryan, I found myself getting annoyed at how often he interrupted her but then I realized she was doing it just as much. They constantly jump into each other's thoughts."

"Putting on my older sister cap for a second," Audrey said. "Relationship timelines tend to shorten in your thirties. You know if there's a connection on the first date, you know if there's a future by the third. It's not unusual to hear from my friends that they were talking about marriage, kids, all of it early on."

"I had no idea instalove was a byproduct of aging," Jamie said. "Fascinating species, the monogamous."

"I mean, is it instalove or is it being real?" Grace asked. "Remember how Ben was in a situation with someone else when I met him and—"

"Oh, that's right," Jamie said. "I always forget you were the other woman."

"No, I wasn't," Grace said, laughing. She wasn't the other woman. She was a villain but not like that. "I told him to fix his shit and come talk to me when he was done. But the point is, we knew there was something from the start and we didn't play games."

"Second date," I said, holding up two fingers. "She came home and told me it was very serious."

Nodding, Grace said, "Within a month, we were talking about the future. We dated for a while before getting engaged but we knew we were headed there."

Audrey grinned at me. "I don't think you're moving too fast." She nudged a chocolate butterscotch cookie toward me. "Have you guys set a date or were you too busy riding the high of your engagement to go there yet?"

I cringed so hard at the mention of *riding* anything that I shuddered. "We didn't get that far," I said, shoving aside Ryan's comments about tying the knot before training camp. If we did end up eloping, I wanted that one to be just for us.

"I'm sure Shay would reserve a date for you at the farm," Jamie said.

"We should all get married at the farm," Grace said with a clap of her hands.

"Ohhhhh no," Jamie said, laughing. "You know I'm not getting married."

"You say that," Grace started, wagging a carrot stick at Jamie, "but I don't buy it."

"It doesn't matter if you buy it," Jamie replied sweetly. "I'm giving it away for free. Take it. Shove it in your back pocket or anywhere else that suits your fancy."

"I think it's possible you'll find yourself exploring more at some point," Grace said. "You've broadened your interests before. Who's to say you won't do it again? Who's to say you won't find yourself in a triad or some other pairing, and you'll want to test out a bit of permanence?"

"Me," Jamie replied. "I'm to say. And, in fact, I'm saying it right now, there's not a single reason in the world that I'd choose to legally tie myself to a relationship."

Grace shrugged. "Okay. I can be wrong."

"Since when?" I teased. Smiling, she rolled her eyes and made a show of going back to her sandwich.

Jamie shot a glance to Audrey. "Don't trust that act. She's coming for you next."

"I'm not coming for anyone," Grace drawled. "I just want my favorite people to have all the love they deserve. You both have such big, kind hearts"—she glanced between Jamie and Audrey—"and I want you to have someone to love you as much in return."

"With the love from my big, kind heart," Audrey said, her delicate brows arched high, "count me out. I've been through it once. Barely survived. Not going back for seconds."

I shared a meaningful glance with Grace. For such a hard-ass, she was unbelievably sentimental. "But we could recycle the bridesmaid dresses."

"Okay, now you have my interest," Audrey said.

"You'd get married just so we could put these dresses to use one more time?" Jamie asked, laughing.

"Not an actual marriage," she said. "Someone who needs health insurance or citizenship or something." She thought about it for a second. "I'd make a great fake wife for someone who needed a hetero-looking relationship."

I was suddenly very interested in peeling my tangerine. No fake wives to see here.

"Lavender marriages are a necessity for some," Jamie said.

"The two of you," Grace muttered.

I shoved some fruit in my mouth to keep from laughing out loud.

"Would Ryan want a wedding at the farm?" Jamie asked. "Is that something he'd be into?"

"We know we want a big party and good food," I said. "And a tequila luge. Everything else is to be determined."

"I can't keep my drawers on when there's tequila involved," Jamie said.

"Honey, you don't keep your drawers on when there's water involved," Audrey said.

"That's true," Jamie mused.

Grace asked, "Will Ryan want to invite a lot of the guys from his team?"

Some water went up my nose as I thought about taking McKerry up on his offer to be our ring bearer. And Hersberler hitting on everything with two legs. "Yeah, probably."

Jamie reached for her Diet Coke, nodding slowly. "It's a good thing Grace will be your maid of honor because I'm warning you right now —I don't think I'll be on my best behavior at your wedding with all those boys and all that tequila."

I met Grace's eyes across the table. She beamed at me, saying, "I'm ready for it. Or, I will be once I get through with *my* wedding."

I nodded and told myself to smile back. There was no doubt in my mind that things would be different on the other side of her wedding. We'd be okay again.

Or something like it.

On the way down to the cafeteria to pick up our students, Jamie hooked her arm in mine, saying quietly, "Your face says you've been naughty."

I couldn't stop the big, full-cheeked smile that swallowed me whole. "A little," I admitted.

We stopped at the top of the staircase, letting the others go ahead without us. "It was a good weekend, I take it?"

Jamie and I didn't usually talk about sex. Well, Jamie talked about sex and I asked intro-level questions about polyamory and the etiquette of orgies and cuddle puddles. But I needed to talk to someone about the events that took place on the plane.

After I'd stopped thinking about throwing myself down a well, it hit me that while I liked sex and I'd had plenty of it with a handful of satisfying partners over the years, I'd never done *that* before.

The specifics of it aside, I wasn't one to initiate. I could drop a hint—or a hand high on his thigh—but I didn't take the lead or provide a ton of direction between the sheets. It wasn't the most mature thing to admit but I was more comfortable letting my partner tell me what he wanted than making my desire the focus.

I didn't have any big reason for it other than the fact I didn't trust most people enough to be completely vulnerable in that way.

Apparently I trusted Ryan enough to mount his leg.

"Well. On the flight home yesterday," I started, feeling the heat rise to my cheeks again. "I wasn't feeling good—cramps, hangover—and we were just chilling under a blanket. And then that turned into rubbing up against each other." Every cell in my body pulsed at the memory of how hard I'd fought for that orgasm, of my heaving breath, my sweat-damp skin. How I'd thought of nothing but getting myself there. How I'd *used* him to do it and he'd liked it. He'd wanted it. "I basically rode him like a birthday party pony."

"It sounds like this marriage is getting off on a phenomenal foot," she said with a wink. "Many happy returns."

Quietly, I said, "But I made it all about me."

"Well done," she replied. "I admire that kind of energy."

"But it wasn't—you know—reciprocal."

She arched a brow. "He didn't finish?"

"Oh, he did," I said, bobbing my head at the memory of the very soggy shirt to go with the equally soggy joggers. Thank god for carry-on luggage. "But I didn't do anything for him to—"

"Let Auntie Jamie stop you right there." She dropped her hands to my shoulders. "Emme, my love, my glorious, silly tempest, I promise you did everything right. If he was able to reach completion"—she spread her hands out in front of her—"without you lifting a finger, you did so many things right that you've won sex."

"I've *won* sex?"

"Yes, you've won. You're the best. And you might've won sex but that boy of yours is realizing he won at life. He gets engaged and comes in his pants all in one weekend? He's searching up mating bonds and wondering if you have any other hidden powers."

Another wave of heat climbed up my neck. I'd spent the whole night tossing and turning with the sound of Ryan's low growls in my head. Couldn't forget the way he'd gripped my waist and moved me like he knew how my body worked better than I did. The way he'd said, *Don't you fucking stop* like he was desperate for me.

I'd wanted to creep down the stairs, slide into his bed, and hear it all over again.

I felt Jamie peering at me, her dark brows low. "You liked it, right? It was good for you?"

I stared down at my ring. "I had no idea it could be that good."

"It's amazing what you can accomplish without even getting your pants off." She gave my forearm a squeeze. "What did he think about your hair?"

I absently ran a hand through the strands. "He liked it." I hesitated to add, "He said it was gorgeous."

She drew a checkmark in the air. "Oh, yeah. We're keeping Daddy Football."

BOWEN WAS WAITING FOR ME WHEN I LEFT SCHOOL FOR THE DAY. He passed me a cup of hot chocolate and a box of brownies from a bakery on the opposite side of the city. The drink was piping hot and tasted like rich, milky heaven.

I offered Bowen half a brownie, and thankfully he accepted. It seemed like the least I could do for him after he helped Ryan evacuate me and Ines from the flood yesterday.

We drove to Ryan's building near the Common without much chatter, which I appreciated after an interminably long day of cramps and begging seven- and eight-year-olds to follow directions.

When we pulled into the underground garage, he mentioned something about picking up some packages from the mail room and bringing them upstairs for me. I didn't know what I was expecting but as I stood in the kitchen surrounded by gifts from just about everyone in pro sports, I knew it wasn't this. Flowers, chocolates, blankets and bath towels, even matching Cartier watches.

And *five* sets of iPads with our names engraved on them. That was ten iPads altogether.

Those were coming to school with me tomorrow. I didn't care whose names were carved into the case.

On his last trip to the penthouse, Bowen handed me a small leather case. "From Mr. Ralston," he said.

I unzipped the case to find another black credit card, a spare set of access cards for the building and garage, and a shiny new phone. Before I could figure out how to respond to any of this, my phone—the real one, not the platinum-dipped status symbol—flashed with my stepmother's face.

I didn't usually ignore Danielle's calls. She was the neutral bridge between me and my dad, somehow, and she always respected my limits. Illogical as they seemed to be.

I didn't have a lot of emotional energy to speak with her right now but I knew I had to. Danielle was too polite to call repeatedly or blow up my phone with texts but she would worry, which turned my dad into the bloodthirsty defensive tackle of his earlier days. Old habits and all.

The last thing I needed was a voicemail from my father reminding me that I was an ungrateful bitch.

"I have to take this," I said to Bowen, pointing to my phone. "Any chance you want this hot honey collection? I will never need this quantity of honey."

He studied the elaborately packed gift. "I'll give it a shot and report back. I'll see ya tomorrow."

"Thanks, Bowen." When he closed the front door behind him, I tapped Danielle's call and plopped down on the cozy blue sectional sofa. "Hey, Dani."

"Congratulations!" she cried, dragging the word out so long it was more like a subway train with bad brakes. "We're so happy for you!"

"Oh, thank you." I sounded like someone had poured mud into my palm and told me it was a great honor.

"When did this all happen? Tell me everything. I want the whole story!"

The problem with Danielle—and it really was a problem for me because it complicated the shit out of my life—was that I liked her. She was outrageously nice. More than anyone who'd been on the receiving end of my viciously cold shoulders had any right to be.

She liked to send me clothes that "just didn't work" for her but we weren't the same sizes and didn't have the same style. She always included me in holiday plans even though I hadn't visited in years. She'd send calendar invites for birthday parties and barbeques, and respond with *Maybe next time!* when I declined. She'd call to check in and casually mention that my dad was going in for another knee surgery or that my half brothers would be in Boston for a business trip soon if I was available for dinner or drinks. She constantly shipped little packages from specialty shops with cups and pillows and cashmere blankets bearing puns and sayings on them because she thought they fit my humor. They didn't, but I appreciated the thoughtfulness. I always kept them.

I also knew, in a very fundamental way, that I could call Danielle in the middle of the night and the *first* thing out of her mouth would be, "I'll be right there."

I didn't like to admit how much it hurt that she was the closest thing I had to a truly parental figure in my life.

"I mean, it happened kind of fast," I said, reaching back for the talking points I'd honed this weekend. "Ryan and I, you know—"

"I think you two were meant for each other right from the start," she cut in.

"We do go way back." I tried to punch some life into my words but ended up sounding like I was annoyed. All-around failing at this functional human thing again.

"I really think it's important to be friends first," she said.

I kicked off my shoes and settled deeper into the sofa. I should've brought the brownies with me but I was down now and not getting back up. "Yeah," I said. "Really important."

"Okay, girlie." I heard her clap her hands and click a pen. "Fill me in on the plans. What are we thinking? Are we staying local? Are we going places? Is this a destination wedding? Do you have a coordinator—because I can take care of that for you tonight. If you want, no pressure. You know I'm not here to stress you out about *anything*. Okay?" Before I could respond, she went on. "Do you have a season in mind? Or anything you just love and know you have to incorporate? Or maybe you want to say fuck it all and just elope, which is not wrong." She snorted out a laugh. "I should probably ask what Ralston wants but let's be honest here, all the boys need to be happy are pigs-in-a-blanket during cocktail hour. Ask me how I know."

She hooted out a laugh. I tried to join in—good sport and such—but all I managed was a burpy throat noise.

My dad and Danielle got married when I was six, just one week after finalizing his divorce from my mother. Danielle was twenty-one, a former cheerleader for the very team my father owned, and, as my mother had drilled into every conversation about her successor, Danielle was five months pregnant on their wedding day. These pieces came together to form a less-than-flattering picture of Danielle—and Mom certainly preferred the harshest angles—but that wasn't the only story here.

"Honestly, I don't know what we want yet," I said, and I hoped she believed that. "We haven't talked about it much. It just happened this weekend."

"I will be thrilled for you either way but please tell me he didn't propose at the Derby."

"No," I said, choking on an actual laugh. "Before. On the flight down there."

"Much better. Love that. I'm so excited for you two." She squealed and breathed a happy sigh, and I knew she was smiling. I realized I was smiling too. "Your dad's so excited, even if you're marrying the enemy."

It was a joke. I wanted to take it that way. Just like I wanted to take some of my father's phone calls too. I wasn't there yet. Wasn't ready.

All I could manage was a sarcastic quip about Chicago's D-line crumbling like a sleeve of crackers against Ryan's team last season. I pulled an artfully arranged blanket off the back of the sofa and did my best to wrap myself like a burrito as I said, "I think they are their own enemies first and foremost. We don't even need to bring my fiancé into the equation."

She gave a hearty laugh. "If that man of yours is interested in a few seasons in Chicago, I think we can—"

"No," I said, much harder than necessary. "That's not—we're not getting into that."

"Of course not, sweetie," she said, fully unbothered. "And everyone knows he's a Boston boy. They're not giving him up for anything."

She was always the gentle parent—for me, for her own kids, for my dad. On certain occasions, my mother. We could be atrocious versions of ourselves and she'd take our hands and say it was okay to have huge, uncomfortable feelings.

"No, and you need to save the money to buy yourselves a decent rushing game," I said. "And a QB who doesn't spend all his time flattened under a pile of defensive ends."

"You know you're telling this to the wrong person," she sang. "He'd love to give you a peek at what they have in store for next season."

"I have a lot of work to do. I should probably get to that," I said. "After the Derby, I wasn't prepared to teach today and it showed."

She laughed easily and said, "Before you go, I just want you to know I would love to host a shower for you. Or a luncheon or cocktail party or whatever you'd like if you don't want an old-fashioned shower." When I didn't respond immediately, she filled the silence. "We could do it in Boston or you could come to Chicago or we could pick a cute location. I'll fly all of your bridesmaids in with you, of course. I'd *never* expect you to come all on your lonesome."

Every conversation with Danielle was studded with small acts of penance. Today we were repenting for all the holidays and summers when my parents' custody agreement required me to visit my father's new family halfway across the country and I'd spent all that time being an outsider. As I grew up, I'd asked to bring a friend along only for my father to tell me that I was on *his* goddamn time and if I had such a problem with it, I could be the one to tell my mother she wouldn't receive another penny in child support from him.

Every conversation with Danielle also featured casual updates on my father's newest mood-stabilizing meds or his newfound commitment to mental health counseling. Any minute now, she'd mention that he'd be late to dinner tonight because he was meeting with his therapist or that he'd said something a few weeks ago that'd really stuck with her as proof of his progress.

It wasn't that I didn't believe her. I did—and that actually made it so much worse.

He'd left me enough choked-up voicemails in the past few years for me to know that someone was asking him hard questions. But that didn't mean I wanted to have a hard conversation with him.

I'd had enough of those already.

"I don't want to interfere with any plans your friends or Ralston's family or your mom already have for a shower," Danielle added. "If you want to give me your maid of honor's number, I'll take it from there. I'll follow her lead and foot the bill."

"That's really sweet of you and really generous, Dani." I drew in a breath to steady myself. I'd faffed my way through this conversation long enough. "I need to talk to Ryan first. I'm not sure about his schedule and—"

"Will you be traveling with him next season?" She practically screamed this down the line.

"Oh, I—I'm not sure. I don't know how that would work with my school schedule."

"You're going to continue teaching, then?"

"That-that's the plan," I stammered, though I had no idea what state my life would be in at the end of the summer. I'd be married and…then what? How long was that supposed to last? *Was* he expecting me to attend his games?

Ryan and I were long overdue for a little chat about the details of this arrangement.

"Good for you." I heard her slap something. Probably a marble countertop. "Okay, beautiful girl. I'm sure you're inundated with well-wishes and congratulations right now so I won't keep you any longer. If I can help you with anything…"

I thought about the kitchen and the piles of gifts waiting for me. Dani would know how to handle it all.

Then again, so would my mom.

But she didn't make a point of calling me the way Dani did. She hardly called me at all. Not when her show was taping. And when she was finished taping, there were promo requirements.

I didn't mind it, really. It was good that she had something to keep her busy. Something that finally mattered to her more than making my dad miserable for the way their marriage ended.

And I already knew what she'd say about all of this. She'd tell me they cheat and they lie, and even if he promised me the world, I'd be safer if I kept my expectations small and my attorney on retainer.

"People are sending things," I blurted out. "Flowers and iPads and stuff. Diamond watches? Ryan's not here this week. I'm not sure what I'm supposed to do. I can barely walk through the foyer."

"We'll go through it together," she said. "I can be there first thing in the morning."

"You don't need to do that," I said, and in the back of my head I could hear my mother raging at me about choosing *that common whore* over her. The panicked shakiness I'd always thought of as carbonated bubbles in my blood came fizzing back like I'd never chased it away. "I have to work and—and it's not a big deal. I'll figure it out."

She was quiet for a moment and I worried I'd offended her until she said, "I never doubted you for a second, hon. Don't forget that Ralston has an entire staff just waiting to make your life easier. I promise you his assistant can get handwritten thank-you notes in the mail by the end of the week if you ask. She'll have all the addresses you need too."

Oh—right. Marcie. Why hadn't I thought of that route?

"Here's a little tip," Danielle said. "Have the gifts forwarded to

Ralston's office. His people will know what to do. Don't give up your foyer."

I rubbed my forehead. I hated the headaches that followed that surge of panic. It was like being a shaken-up bottle of soda, all those bubbles pressing together at the top. I just wanted to close my eyes and let it all fade away. "Thanks, Dani."

"Are you kidding me? Thank *you* for letting me talk your ear off." I heard her moving around, the soft clack of heels against hardwood. "Before I forget," she added, "your dad wants you to know he won't put in a competing offer."

"Okay," I said at length.

I didn't know what we were talking about and Ines chose that moment to arrive home and yell at the very top of her lungs, "Emme! Where the hell did the floor go?"

"We'll talk later," Danielle said. "I just want you to know I'm so happy for you."

"Thanks," I said. "I'm happy too."

The strange thing was, I meant that. I sank deeper into the sofa, wrapped in the blanket and my stress tremors, and I let myself fall asleep while Ines rooted through the gifts.

chapter nineteen
Emme

Today's Learning Objective:
Students will swim in shallow waters.

Wildcat: Call me when you have some time tonight. I want to run something by you.

Emme: That falls under the umbrella of "we need to talk" so thank you in advance for the anxiety

Wildcat: No anxiety, everything's fine

Emme: "everything is fine" is just extra-strength anxiety

Wildcat: I swear there's nothing for you to worry about

Emme: Then run it by me now

Wildcat: Are you free to talk?

Emme: That depends whether it's something Grace can hear because we're at her hair and makeup trial

> Wildcat: A trial like...a qualifying round?

> Emme: Yeah, she has makeup artists competing to see which one can create the best smoky eye in less than 90 seconds

> Wildcat: Are you fucking with me?

> Emme: A little

> Wildcat: Call me when you're home

"Wow." Grace turned in a slow circle as she took in Ryan's condo. "You weren't kidding about—" She waved a hand at the long wall of full-length windows and the city stretched out before us. "I thought it was going to be cold the way all these ultramodern places are but"—she smiled at the blue sofa, the casual dining table, the white kitchen—"it's like actual people live here."

"Do you want to see the den? The bookcases go all the way up to the ceiling. There's one of those roll-y ladder things."

She pinned me with a stare made more fierce than usual by the heavy-handed makeup and elegant updo. "I can't believe you have to ask."

We wandered through the rooms—she had her Belle in the Beast's library moment on the rolling ladder—and I pointed out all the luxurious features. The towel warmer in the bathroom, the ice machine that produced twenty different shapes, the windows with adjustable transparency levels to block out light.

When we settled on the roof deck with a bottle of wine to catch the last of the sunset, she said, "This suits you."

"What? The penthouse condo? Or weeknight drinking?"

"You know what I mean." She ghosted a hand over the short sleeve of my dress, a cute little thing included in the items selected by Wren. "You look really nice."

"Thanks." I was pleasantly surprised by Wren's work on replacing my clothes. The pieces looked like something I'd choose—but better. More polished, more refined. And the wild thing was that I felt better too. I felt put together and confident, and those things made a difference.

Grace shot a glance toward my ring and smiled. "I'm happy he finally made a move."

"That he—oh. Yeah." I bobbed my head too many times and stared into my glass as something twisted inside me. It'd been months of shaving down the truth to keep her wedding on track and it still ached like a muscle stretched in the wrong direction for too long. "Me too."

"I know you live in a completely different world now." She gestured to the fireplace that unfolded itself from the wall at the press of a button and the skyline outlined in the last light of day. "But you're still my best friend. You can't get rid of me so don't try."

"Why would I try?"

Her shoulders lifted to her ears and she cut her gaze to the stone-tiled floor. "I don't know. You wouldn't, I guess."

I wasn't used to seeing insecurity from Grace. Nothing shook her confidence. Even when she was uncertain, she stood strong.

"It's been different, you know, since I moved out." She set her glass on a side table and clasped her hands between her long legs. "And then since Teddy and even more since Ryan. I didn't notice it at first because I've become exactly who I said I wouldn't and now the only thing I can think about is my wedding but I haven't been a good friend to you in a long time and I miss you so much. I don't want to lose you."

I perched on the arm of her chair and gathered her in an awkward hug. "You won't."

She held me for a long moment before saying, "I don't know how to tell you this."

My stomach dropped. "Whatever it is, we'll be okay. We always are."

She shook her head and scraped her teeth over her bottom lip. "I interviewed for a third-grade position at the school in our neighborhood last month." She glanced away. "They offered me the position this morning."

My stomach tossed itself off the deck and down fifty-nine floors to the street below. "Oh."

"The commute is killing me," she hurried to say. "It's at least ninety minutes each way. And I thought it would be okay, I thought I'd have so much time for audiobooks and pods, but it's sucking the life out of me and I can *walk* to this school. We talked about moving but we just finished work on the house. And it was Ben's grandmother's house and it matters too much to him."

Despite my stomach flopping around on the street and my head filling with static, I nodded. I hadn't realized the commute was taking such a toll. "Of course the house matters to him. It matters to you too. And it's going to hurt like hell to see you go but it's a good kind of hurt. It's a happy change." I squeezed her shoulders. "I'm happy for you."

"I haven't told anyone else yet." She took a sip of her wine and blew out a breath. "I wanted to talk to you first."

Again, she needed me to be all right. So, I would. "Audrey will develop a brunch, happy hour, and girls' dinner party calendar, and she'll politely enforce it." I settled back on my seat because the armrest had left my butt partially numb. "Jamie will have a small tantrum and then beg you to take her with you."

"Shay will cry," Grace said with a laugh. "Even though she was the first one to leave."

"She will cry," I agreed.

"And what about you? What will you do?"

I ran a hand over the soft hem of my dress as I thought about teaching without Grace across the hall from me next year. We'd been together so long I could hardly imagine it. But that wasn't what she needed to hear. No, she needed me to give her permission to grow and change, even if that took us down different roads. Even if I felt like I was being torn in half. "I'm going to hope and pray that your fiancé can round up some of his big, strong firefighter buddies to pack your classroom because I'm not qualified for that kind of hard labor. And then"—I held up my hands, let them fall to my lap—"I'll help decorate your new room. I'll listen to you complain about your new principal and how the other teachers aren't nearly as fun as we were, and I won't even say *I told you so*. Not once."

We laughed for a moment but then Grace sobered. "Thank you for understanding."

I smiled and gave her hand a squeeze. "Don't thank me too hard. I *have* to understand. Otherwise, I'd just be a cold-hearted bitch and that's your role in this relationship."

A laugh tore out of her and she flopped back in her chair, kicking her feet up in front of her. "Oh my god, what am I going to do without you?" She wiped tears from her eyes as she went on laughing.

"You'll probably be tried as a witch," I said. "At the minimum, a heretic."

Still laugh-sobbing, she asked, "And what about you?"

"Oh, well, I'll probably need a few months to recover from the Stockholm Syndrome you've had me under all these years but I'll be okay. I will have to watch the poor soul who takes over your class and inherits Satan's finest soldiers next year but I'll make sure Jamie keeps her little fridge stocked with emotional support snacks for them."

"It's the least you can do."

We watched the city lights for a few minutes before Grace asked, "Will you take pics of me on the ladder before I leave?"

"Yeah, of course. We need to make the most of your camera-ready face."

"I knew you'd understand."

After Grace headed home, I changed into a hoodie and sleep shorts and went downstairs to grab a fresh load of laundry from the dryer. I tossed my phone on top of my warm clothes and called Ryan. He answered on the second ring.

"How's the arm?" I asked immediately. I refilled my water bottle in the kitchen and headed down the hall toward the stairs.

"Tired," he said, and that was exactly how he sounded. "But solid. They've had great advice. Made some good tweaks."

"That's good because I won't marry a QB averaging fewer than two hundred passing yards a game."

"One, you know my average is two-seventy and two, let's get married this weekend."

I dropped the laundry basket halfway up the staircase, sending everything tumbling down. My stainless steel water bottle bounded down each step with a noisy clank and my phone went with it.

"Hold on," I yelled, scrambling to the landing to grab the basket and then scooping up my sweatshirts and undies. The only saving grace was that my water bottle had stayed closed. "I just need to find the phone. Everything's fine. It's here somewhere. One moment please." I heard the muffled sound of my name and realized my phone was somewhere *in* my clothes. It took a few frantic moments before I found it hiding in the arm of my favorite dark orange cardigan. "Okay. We're back. We're good."

"Muggsy," he said with a sigh. "What the fuck just happened?"

"Nothing," I said, a little breathless. "Just a small laundry situation. On the stairs. Where my phone was eaten. By a sweater."

He was quiet for a second. "Are you fucking with me again?"

"This time, no, I'm not."

Another pause. "Are you all right?"

"Yeah, of course." I sounded like I'd just run a mile. "You were saying something about this weekend?"

"Do me a favor and sit down first," he said.

I made my way up to my room and set the basket down. Leaning back against the pillows, I said, "Go ahead. I'm safe in my bed."

"You're—oh. Yeah." I heard him swallow a gulp of something and then clear his throat. "Let's get married this weekend."

The word "Okay" fell out of my mouth automatically and then, after a hazy blink, "Wait. Grace's housewarming party is on Saturday and—and we can't miss that."

"We won't miss it." He shifted and I heard a rough exhale. He was probably sore after all that practice. "Friday, then."

I pressed my fingers to my lips. Friday was the day after tomorrow. Two sleeps from now. Two sleeps until my *wedding day*?

We had to talk about so many things. Everything, really. The rules and the timeline and the expectations. Rather than doing a single thing to help myself and cut down on my confusion, I said, "Let's do it."

"Yeah?" I could hear the smile in his voice. I liked that I'd put it there.

"Yeah. Yes. Friday," I replied. "What do you need me to do?"

He hesitated. "Do you trust me?"

"Unless you're talking about us jumping out of an airplane or engaging in ritualistic sacrifice, I think you know I do."

"Neither of those apply here," he said. "Let me take care of everything. All you have to do is come home after school and we'll go from there."

I dragged the laundry basket toward me and started folding clothes. "It's not that I don't trust you but what the hell does that mean?"

He made an impatient noise. I *adored* those sounds. Loved pushing him. "It means I'll hire an officiant, get the license, and ask Wren to send over dress options for you. We can do this out on the deck. Sunset, how about that?"

"Do I have to wear white?"

"Wear whatever you want, Muggsy."

The questions kept pouring out of me then. "What about cake? Don't we have to cut a cake? It doesn't count if we don't have a cake."

"My wife wants a cake, we get a cake."

I shook out a sweater and then immediately abandoned it to ask, "Who's going to be there? Is it just you and me? Or other people?"

He cleared his throat again. "That's your call."

I thought about Grace and my friends, and how they'd filled in the holes where family should've been. I thought about Danielle and how she'd be on my doorstep tonight if I asked. And I thought about Ryan's family and how their grief was like a hand that held him underwater, even all these years later.

This one would be for us. We'd have the traditional ceremony and the big party, and that one would be for everyone else.

"Just you and me," I said. "Oh—what about Ines?"

"She'll be our witness," he said. "And harpist for the big event."

"What about rings? I need to find a ring for you, don't I?"

"Don't worry about that now. I want to get a band made for you anyway. Something to fit with your ring."

For the millionth time today, I stared at my engagement ring. It really was lovely. "I don't think my finger can manage much more than this."

He laughed. "I knew you'd say that, which is why we need to design something for your child-like fingers."

"Can we actually pull this off in two days?"

"If I wasn't in Minnesota, I could pull it off tomorrow."

"You've grown arrogant in your old age," I said.

"I prefer realistically confident."

I glanced down at the clothes I hadn't folded. Most of it would have to be fluffed again. "I know you need this for your business deals and everything but I really don't want to take anything away from Grace right now. They're having their party this weekend and the wedding is right around the corner. This is *her* moment."

"Her moment is five weeks long?"

"It doesn't matter to me if it doesn't make sense to you. It's important to me." I started flinging clothes back into the basket. I'd tell him about Grace's announcement after we got through this. I couldn't mix the chaos in my life and expect to keep any of it straight. "All I'm saying is I don't want to make this weekend all about us. Maybe we should wait."

"Or we do it Friday and don't say anything for a couple of weeks," he said.

"Hmm. That—that's not a bad solution," I admitted. "That gives us time to get rings too."

"We could drop the news the week school finishes for the summer. When we head to Vegas for that awards banquet. We'll have a media circus on our hands and Stella might strangle me but she'll have time to prep."

I set the basket on a chair and crawled under the covers. After a moment, I asked, "You really want to do this with me?"

"I wouldn't do it with anyone else."

Warm pressure filled my chest and spread down to my belly. "Just so you know, I wouldn't fake-marry anyone else either." I heard him shift like he was stretching and then a pained grunt. "Did they push you too hard or is your conditioning that bad that you're suffering from a few days of workouts?"

"I'm all right." His tone suggested otherwise. "Long day, that's all. I just need to soak in some boiling water."

I nestled deeper into my blankets. "I'll let you go."

"Fuck no, you won't." I heard him moving around and then the rush of water. "Talk to me while I turn into stew. I need to hear about the makeup trial. Was there a winner?"

"We have some strong contenders though it'll be a game-day decision."

"Risky but I respect it."

He hissed and I heard water lapping around him. It occurred to me that he was quite naked on the other end of this call and...I did not dislike that. "You never did stick with the planned plays."

"Because I knew the play they wanted me to run wasn't going to work against the defense read on the field," he said.

"So sure of yourself," I mused.

"Well...yeah," he replied, a touch of hard-earned prerogative in his voice. "I know what I'm doing out there."

I wanted to say something quick and quippy, but instead, I let out a sad sigh. "Grace is leaving. She got a new job for next year."

"Shit," he murmured. "Are you okay?"

"It doesn't feel real yet. It probably won't until the new school year starts up and I have to be nice to the stranger who takes over her classroom." I brushed some hair away from my face. "But I don't want to talk about it right now. My feelings are too messy."

"I don't care. Be messy."

I was quiet for a moment, busy twisting the bedsheet around my finger and letting it go. "It just hurts, you know?"

"I do." I heard the water shut off. "It sucks when people leave, even if they leave for valid reasons."

"Yeah." We didn't say anything for a minute but the silence was comfortable. It was easy. I decided to shatter it with, "How's the tub there? Designed for your oversized species?"

A surprised huff burst from him and then, "What?"

"I mean, I'm only asking because it's not like you fit in the average bathtub. I'm just picturing those gangly limbs of yours packed in there while you sit in an inch of water."

I heard water moving around him as if he'd scooped it up and let it splash over his body. His chest, probably. Even if it was a huge tub, he probably wouldn't have room to sink all the way to his neck. Which meant—at this very moment—beads of water were rolling down the broad expanse of his chest, curving around the rise of his pecs and snaking between his abs toward—

Oh.

Oh—no.

"It's more than an inch," he said. "But I think you already knew that."

I ceased to exist.

The pulsing between my legs seemed to suggest I was very much alive but the rest of me was deceased. And my first realization in the afterlife was that flirting was new for us. We didn't do this. There'd always been affection between us but this was something different.

And I liked it.

"The tub is deep. Comfortable." He made a raspy, growly sound. "Bet it could fit two."

"But you like being alone." I almost slapped myself for that. I didn't know what was wrong with me. Probably something to do with being dead.

"Not always."

"Oh. Hmm. Yeah."

"It's a nice place," he went on, immune to my sputtering. "Great pillows. I might ask them to send some home with me. I like a good pillow." I could still hear the water as if he was pouring one handful after another down his chest. Like he intended for me to hear that. "Big bed. I like that too."

I thought about last weekend at the hotel in Kentucky—and the night he'd stayed at my apartment. I didn't remember the size making much of a difference when we'd chased each other even as we'd slept. "You are something of a beast so that's understandable."

"Is that what you think?"

"Am I wrong?" I asked, all indignant teasing.

Another splash. A sound like skin running over skin. And then, "You have no idea."

I swallowed hard. I didn't know what this was or where it would go if we kept on this path. And I didn't know why it made heat rush through my veins and energy buzz over every last inch of me. I didn't know how one bath time phone call could zap the life back into me.

But it wasn't just one phone call. It was my new hair and his visit to my school. It was moving Ines to his condo and my tangerines on the plane. It was being able to take a deep enough breath to hold my head up and feeling like I mattered enough to someone to order a fuck-ton of antibacterial wipes for their classroom.

And it was getting myself off on his leg last weekend too. I hadn't been the only one playing then, just as I wasn't now.

I didn't know what it meant for us but I knew I'd finally roused enough of my old self to feel like this life was worth living. Like I was worth it.

And the man I was going to marry was worth it too.

I smiled as I said, "I think I have some idea."

He sucked in a breath and I knew—I *knew* there was no turning back from here. The Ryan and Emme of the past were gone and this new version of us, this couple, were much more than childhood friends.

I didn't know what lived in the dark unknown of that *much more* but I knew we'd figure it out—together. Like we always did.

"Have you softened up yet?" I asked.

A choked sound echoed around him. "Not even close." He cleared his throat and then turned the water on again. "You told me a few months ago you wanted to be married. You wanted to be settled."

"Yeah," I said, snuggling into the pillows. "I do."

"What does that look like for you? Is it a house and kids? A backyard for some dogs to run around? Or a brownstone in the city and traveling every chance you get? What is it?"

It took me a minute to find the right words. "I don't care about the house, the backyard. The place, the things—they don't matter. They've never mattered. I just want something that belongs to me. Something that's permanent."

"And the kids?"

I scowled at the bottles of vitamins, supplements, pain relievers, and hormones lined up on the bedside table. "That's complicated."

"Why? Because of your condition?" he asked. "Or because you haven't decided about kids?"

"The world is a riotous, melting disaster and I'm truly concerned about handing over that shit show to anyone," I said. "But I've always been told getting pregnant could be difficult. For me. So. I'm not sure."

"I can make some calls and get you in to see better doctors if that's what you need. If you decide that it's what you want, I'll find the specialists. We can—we can do anything, Em."

I hummed as I thought about this. There wasn't a lot anyone could do. There wasn't a cure for endometriosis. The treatments were limited. The options were split between semi-constant pain and surgery—and I'd already gone under the laparoscopic knife once. I was probably due for another nip and tuck of my errant endometrial tissue. It had an annoying tendency to attach itself to places it didn't belong, filling me with something akin to painful, diseased cobwebs. Or they could chuck my uterus right in the bin.

That was an option but…I always saw myself with children. They were in the far-off future when my apartment wasn't the site of a great flood and I wasn't fake-marrying my best friend to exact some revenge, but they were there. Two, maybe three. I didn't have a master plan for any of these things but I knew I wanted to give my kid some siblings. I didn't want them to be alone the way I'd been alone.

I knew there would be medical challenges though, and I had to block out those worries before they convinced me it'd never happen and it wasn't worth trying. I tried to manage my expectations because I wasn't great at handling disappointment. And it wasn't like I was in any state to start that process. In my mind, I was still a kid myself. It didn't matter that thirty was coming up. This was a problem I'd solve another day. When I grew up.

"Are we talking about your big-headed babies again?" I asked. "Because I have some questions about how that'd work."

"No one's had the talk with you yet?" I could hear the sharp grin in his voice. "Don't worry. I'll explain everything."

I laughed though something stirred inside me at his words. Something that wanted—no, *needed*—to hear him explain how we'd fit together. The images in my head appeared all at once and I tried to blink them away but I couldn't escape the sight of him braced over me, one hand in my hair while the other moved between my legs.

Suddenly I was hot, much too hot for this sweatshirt. I had to set the phone aside to fling it off and find something lighter.

"What are you doing?" he asked.

"Changing into pajamas," I said, because I wasn't going to explain the real issue.

"You're—Jesus, Emme." A groan, a ragged exhale, and then the water turned off. "I'm warning you right now I'm not in the mood for another one of your fuck-arounds."

"You're not in the mood? Please. Don't you think I have better things to do?" I asked as I pulled a tank top over my head. "I mean, I'm getting married in two days and I might have to birth some giant babies bred for the backfield. Fucking with you about whether I'm wandering around my room topless—"

"Emmeline."

"—is the least of my priorities." I smiled to myself as I climbed back on the bed. I loved it when he called me that. I'd never tell him as much because pushing his very large and easy to locate buttons was my absolute favorite thing in the world and I only heard my proper name when he was fully exasperated with me.

I heard a long, muffled growl and then, "If you're not fucking with me, switch over to video."

Without thinking any of this through, I tapped the icon and found myself staring at Ryan. Naked. Glistening. Submerged halfway up his chest. All of which was to be expected in a bathtub.

Brighter minds might've caught on to this before initiating a video call.

"Hello there." I blinked a few times too many as I drank in his wet chest, wet shoulders, wet hair. And all that ink on display. I really wanted to know about those flowers tucked in between the trees and waves and everything else. With an exaggerated gesture to my shirt, I said, "Pajamas."

His scowl was a line of craggy granite, his brows rough peaks. He tipped his head to the side as he eyed me. "I can see that."

I folded my legs in front of me and leaned back against the pillows. I knew this shirt was thin and, in the right light, a touch see-through. His gaze dropped to the V-neck, then lower. His eyes flared and I had to ask, "Are you happy now?"

"Like you wouldn't believe," he growled.

I watched his gaze devour me and he didn't even try to hide it. The attention turned my nipples to tight, rosy points right around the time I noticed his free hand had disappeared under the water. His shoulder shifted and there was a slight bunch and pull in his biceps.

I had a good idea where that hand had gone and what it was doing —even if I didn't know what we were doing.

I didn't know if it would be like this when he came home on Friday, if we'd flirt and tease and press into each other, but I hoped so. I wanted to feel this again. And I wanted to feel it with him.

And I didn't really care what we called it or how long we had before the time ran out. Nothing in my life ever lasted very long and this arrangement could be over before the end of summer. I had to wrap my arms around it and hold it close while I could. That was the only way to make it through.

His lips parted on a sigh and a stray thought hit me. "Oh! What about flowers?"

His gaze narrowed but his arm didn't stop. "Flowers for what?"

"For Friday," I said. "For our little wedding."

"I told you I had it under control." At this, I shrugged, sending the V of my shirt a little deeper. His eyes snapped shut and he said with a huge exhale, "Either you trust me to do this or you don't."

"Okay, okay, calm down." I snuggled deep into the blankets, grinning like crazy. There were times when I wondered if I was something of an unhinged bitch or just a lovable brat who liked to pester her deeply pester-able friend. It was probably a mashup of both. "You know I trust you."

"Yeah." He ran a wet hand down his face. "It's a good thing I trust you too, Muggs."

chapter twenty
Emme

Today's Learning Objective:
Students will say "I do."

BY THE TIME I WAS FIFTEEN, I'D BEEN IN SIX WEDDINGS. ONE FOR MY father, three for my mother—Gary, then Jim, then Dell—and two for Ines's mom, who was my mother's best friend. I'd been a flower girl a few times, a junior bridesmaid a few others. I still had the silk flower crown I'd worn when Mom married Jim, even though he was awful and that marriage barely lasted two NHL seasons. I loved a flower crown.

Even with all these weddings behind me, I'd never thought much about my wedding. Never in any specific terms. There were the basics of beach versus ballroom, but little beyond that. No vision in white. No wedding daydream.

Which didn't help me at all as I sifted through the two racks of dresses Wren had sent to Ryan's place. There was everything from exquisite Cinderella gowns that wouldn't fit through the door to beaded minidresses to simple summery shifts.

"This is incredible," Ines breathed, holding up a short satin dress in ochre with a series of crisp, pleated ruffles running over the shoulders and crisscrossing down the bodice.

It reminded me of a velociraptor but if she liked it— "Try it on."

She shook her head. "These are for you."

"I can only wear one at a time and I know I won't wear that one." I motioned to the hall, toward her room. "The ruffles aren't for me but they'd look cute on you. You might as well try it."

That was enough convincing for Ines. She hurried off to her room, leaving me alone to choose my wedding dress.

Maybe it was silly—or straight-up delusional—but I couldn't convince myself this was a *wedding*. It was something Ryan and I were doing just like that charity event and party-hopping at the Derby. We were playing dress-up and make-believe and—and even if I wished for some piece of it to be real, it wasn't.

That fool-hearted wish had me pulling a buttery yellow dress from the rack. It had a full, flouncy skirt that would skim my knees and long tulle ribbons for straps that would drape over my shoulders, almost like a veil. Wonky embroidered flowers and raw hem lace made the dress fun and that was the vibe I wanted for this night.

We'd have fun getting married. That seemed like the way it should be.

WHEN I VENTURED DOWNSTAIRS WITH INES—WHO ROCKED THE velociraptor dress—the condo looked nothing like it had a few hours ago when I'd returned from school.

I glanced to Ines. "Did you know about this?"

"All I knew was that I had to keep you upstairs until seven." She ran a hand through her bobbed hair and fussed with her glasses. "No one said anything about all that."

She flung her arms at the trees and flowers, the candles and twinkle lights covering nearly every inch of the living space. Though it wasn't a living space tonight. It was a secret garden floating in the clouds, high atop the city.

Ryan emerged from the den, his hard, stoic expression warming into a smile as he approached. He wore a dark blue suit and an immaculately tailored white shirt with a faint pattern I couldn't make out. His collar was open at his throat and his jacket already discarded.

"You look—" He stared at me, shaking his head. He took my hand and I did what anyone wearing a flouncy skirt would—I twirled. Brushing a finger along the ribbon ties at my shoulder, he added quietly, "I like this. It's you."

"I thought so too."

I went for another twirl, laughing as the warm evening air whooshed around me. Tonight *would* be fun. All of it would be fun.

Ryan swept his thumb over the back of my hand and nodded toward the enchanted forest around us. "Is this okay?"

I took in the trees dripping with lanterns and lights, the rose-wreathed candelabras crowding every surface, the garlands draped from one end of the deck to the other. I couldn't believe it was real or that all of it had been assembled in just a few hours.

"I'm going to be one hundred percent honest with you, Wildcat. When I asked about flowers, I was thinking something like a little bouquet. Never in a million years would it've occurred to me to get a bunch of trees."

"We can get rid of the trees." He pulled his phone from the back pocket of his dark trousers. "Give me five minutes and we'll—"

I snatched the phone away. "The trees are amazing. They're insane —all of this is insane—but I love it. I-I can't believe you did this. In two days."

He cocked an arrogant brow. "Told you I would."

I glanced around, finding new arrangements in every corner. It was magical. Even with years to plan and all the most brilliant designers in the world, I never would've come up with this. I didn't understand how it was possible for this to be exactly what I wanted when I'd had no idea what I wanted until I saw it.

"Still want to do this?" He crossed his arms and that shirt pulled deliciously tight across his chest and arms.

Nodding, I ran a finger over his rippling forearm. "What's this pattern? The stitching is so delicate, I can't tell."

"It's a flower," he said. "Jasmine, I think. I don't know. Something like that."

I followed the pattern up to his bicep, his shoulder. "It's so pretty. You should get more of these shirts."

He closed his hand around my fingers before I tracked the pattern down his chest. "I will."

A deep, booming laugh rang out from the other side of the condo and we both shifted to stare at Jakobi and Ines in the entryway. He leaned against the door, his long legs crossed at the ankles, and beamed down at her like his entire reason for being was to shower her in light. He listened—*truly listened*—as she told a story. Her eyes sparkled as she spoke and I couldn't remember ever seeing her so animated before.

"What's happening over there?" I asked, still captivated. As far as I knew, Ines was interested only in Bruce Lee, and she split that interest evenly between the kung fu and the frequency with which he was shirtless in his films. There'd been a boyfriend one summer at space camp and then someone in her first year or two of college but the details were hazy. She responded to most of my questions about dating with "It just seems like a waste of time."

You're not wrong, honey.

"That's gonna need to simmer for a little while before anyone knows what it is." Ryan trailed his knuckles over the line of my jaw, turning my attention back to him. "You didn't answer me before. When I asked if you still wanted to do this."

I twisted on the balls of my feet, sending the dress swirling around me. "I want to do this," I said, still shimmying. I knew I didn't feel like a bride but I did feel happy, and maybe it was better that way. "Do you?"

He dragged his bottom lip between his teeth as he stared at me. A storm cloud passed over his features but it was gone within a blink. After a steady moment of watching me sway, he said, "As long as we're still on for the big party too."

"I mean, yeah, we kind of promised Ines the coveted spot of headlining harpist. Backing out now would be poor form."

"You're right." He shrugged into his suit coat and then plucked something off a nearby table. My eyes almost popped out of my head when he pushed the bouquet into my hands. "I hope you like this."

"Oh my god. You put an artichoke in a bouquet." I blinked between Ryan and the weird, wonderful bouquet. There were plum peonies, purply-gray sea holly, long, trailing veronica, and one huge flowering artichoke. I never would've come up with this and somehow it was the only thing I'd ever wanted. I clutched it to my chest. "I love it."

"Yeah? I have a backup if you don't."

"This is the most perfect bouquet ever created. This is the start of us as an artichoke family." I grabbed his hand, tugged him toward the open doors of the deck. "Come on. Let's do this thing. We've waited long enough."

Ryan squeezed my hand as we stepped outside. Jakobi and Ines were right behind us, still talking softly about robots and *Star Trek* and an ice cream shop that'd opened in the Seaport.

The sunset blazed through the evening sky and warm spring air mixed with the heady florals all around us. I smiled down at my dress and how the prickly sea holly fit right in with the raw lace, and the shades in the artichoke complemented the pale yellow. All these pieces, they fit together just so.

I gripped the flowers as the officiant got right down to business welcoming us to this ceremony of marriage. "Ryan, do you take Emmeline to be your—"

"I do." He brought his free hand to the bouquet, lacing his fingers with mine as I laughed. A grin started at the corner of his mouth and it unfurled into a wide smile that had my heart pounding in my chest and a few overwhelmed tears fogging my eyes. After all these years, I was *marrying* this sweet, broody boy. "Yes to all of it. Everything. I do."

"Not wasting any time. I like it." The officiant chuckled. "Emmeline, do you take Ryan to be your—"

"I do too," I said, still laughing.

"Then I won't make you wait another minute. By the power vested in me by the Commonwealth of Massachusetts—"

There was more to that sentence but it was lost to me when Ryan brought his hand to the back of my neck and sealed his lips to mine. I wrapped my arms around his shoulders and sank into the kiss, holding this moment as tight as possible.

Ines and Jakobi cheered when we came up for air but we couldn't stop staring at each other. It was as if the words no longer mattered because we had something better, something deeper.

"Cake," Ryan whispered, his lips barely a breath from mine. "I promised you cake."

I ran a hand down the back of his neck. His eyes fluttered shut and the growly noise in his chest made me think about the way my fingers felt as they tripped over velvet. "It's a requirement. We're not legally married without sharing some cake."

"Yes, a wise woman told me all about that." He laughed as he straightened the ribbons at my shoulders. "Let me show you what we came up with."

Ryan led me to the other end of the deck and I gasped when I saw the small cake, sculpted and decorated to look like a tower of tangerines. "I can't believe you did this," I cried, leaning in close to see the dimpled skin, the woody stems, the green leaves. "This is art. I can't eat this!"

Ryan ran a hand down my back and settled on my hip, his fingers stretching across my belly. Heat radiated out from each fingertip and spiraled through me. "I'd like to make this official so you're going to have to."

"And I really want a piece too," Ines called.

I relented and Ryan and I sliced the cake together, sharing a chunk of tangerine that was actually chocolate cake with coffee buttercream frosting. It bent my brain. I loved everything about it.

Ryan ducked his head to mine, saying, "You have a little something here."

He kissed the corner of my mouth, and not for the first time today I wondered what happened next. I knew what I wanted but I didn't know how to get from here to there. Even with all the sexual tension we'd built up over the past week, I couldn't figure out how we'd take the next step. Maybe we needed to fool around under a blanket again.

That was assuming Ryan even wanted to fool around under a blanket. Or anywhere else. He'd flirted like he wanted that but we were new at this and I didn't know how to interpret it yet.

"I could spend all night here," he whispered, kissing down my neck and across the crook of my shoulder. He squeezed my hip, jerking me closer to him. "All night."

So, maybe I didn't have to overthink it.

Once we'd all sampled the cake and shared some champagne, Jakobi leaned in to kiss my cheek and then held his hand out for Ryan to shake. "Congratulations to the newlyweds. Since I've kept him away from you all week, I believe you two deserve some alone time." To Ines, he asked, "How do you like observatories?"

She pushed up her glasses. "I like them when they're not busy. I can't focus when there's too much noise."

A wide smile filled his face. "Then you're in luck because I have a private tour scheduled at the observatory at Boston University tonight. You'll have to come along."

"That's one of my favorite observatories."

"Mine too." He glanced at his watch. "I have a dinner reservation in the Back Bay before the tour. Would you join me?"

She pointed to the velociraptor dress. "Do I have to change or can I wear this?"

"Don't you change a damn thing, beautiful," he crooned.

If Jakobi's words had the impact on Ines that I thought he'd intended, it didn't show. She simply grabbed her favorite windbreaker and belt bag from near the door, stepped out of her heels and into a pair of beat-up Vans, and turned the full wattage of her excitement back on him.

I shot a warning glance at Jakobi before saying to her, "Call me if you need anything. Promise?"

"Promise." She'd barely formed the word before diving into a speech about her favorite telescopes, and Jakobi led her from the condo with a hand low on her back.

"Is this what it feels like to watch your teenage daughter go out on her first date?" I asked.

"I don't know," he replied. "But I don't think we need to wait up for her."

I laced my fingers with his and held up our joined hands though I remembered at the last second we hadn't exchanged rings. We didn't have anything to prove what we'd promised tonight. "Then what should we do?"

He stared at me, a slow, devastating smile pulling at his lips. "Do you trust me?"

I grinned at him. "You know I do."

chapter twenty-one

Ryan

Today's Learning Objective:
Students will be able to make moves.

WE CAUGHT THE LAST HALF OF A RED SOX GAME AT FENWAY PARK and scream-sang "Sweet Caroline" and "Dirty Water" from the cheap seats. Emme yelled at the pitchers and drank my beer even though she swore she didn't want one. She ran a fingertip over the ink on my forearm and promised she'd figure out what it all meant eventually. I kissed my way across her shoulder in response. When she snapped a selfie, the bright lights of the ballpark shining down on us while the crowd cheered, I stole it to post on my social platforms.

We flooded the streets along with the rest of Boston after the game, and every time I looked at her I knew I'd never before felt this alive. I couldn't keep my hands away from those silky ribbons at her shoulders. All I could think of was untying them and watching the dress hit the floor.

I'd changed out of my suit but Emme stuck with the flowery dress that looked like it was made entirely of summer daisies. I liked that she wore it out. I liked that she was mine to show off tonight. I wanted the whole city to see her—and to know that she belonged to me.

We posed for hundreds of photos with people who yelled things like "It's Ryan fuckin' Ralston!" and "We named our dog after you!" and "Jesus Christ, my father's never gonna believe this." We didn't turn anyone down when they approached. It was like we knew we needed to crowdsource our wedding album.

We wandered through the bars near Lansdowne and Boston University like it didn't matter who knew us, drinking and dancing and singing along with every song until they turned off the lights.

We ended up in the back of a car around two in the morning. We stared at each other with drowsy eyes and warm smiles lit by the golden glow of streetlights, and I knew I'd be all right if this was how our wedding night ended. Even if I wanted more—so much more—I had everything I needed.

Then the driver turned under an overpass and for a singular moment, everything went dark.

I didn't know who made the first move. I didn't care. We found each other in the darkness and we moved together like we'd been doing this forever. Like we were made for this. She was beside me, then in my lap, then straddling me, her knees pressing into my hips and her skirt floating around us like a fog. My hands were under Emme's dress and her lips were everywhere and there was nothing else in my head—not a single fucking thing—other than getting her home.

The ride back to my building was short, and when we arrived, we dashed through the lobby like a clock was ticking down the seconds until the spell lifted and everything went back to the way it'd always been between us.

We didn't say a word—or come up for air—once we were in the elevator. I kissed her as I untied the ribbons at her shoulders, and though the dress didn't fall off, it gave me entirely new regions of skin to taste. I boosted her up against the wall, rocked hard into the heat between her thighs, and scraped my teeth over her bottom lip. She purred into my mouth and my brain shorted out. It was enough to make me worried about this ending all too soon.

I didn't put her down when we reached my floor and she made no attempt to unwind her legs from around my waist which was everything I needed to know.

The condo was dark though it still smelled of green and flowers. As if I needed the reminder that I'd married this girl tonight. As if there was any chance I'd ever forget.

Emme pulled my shirt up and off one arm as I carried her to the bedroom, our lips still locked and her tiny sounds still driving me wild. I had one hand down the back of her underwear and the other frantically searching for a zipper, and though I wanted her naked for this, I could still get the job done with her skirt shoved up around her waist.

At least for the first time.

I set her on the bed and pulled my shirt the rest of the way off before whipping my belt from the loops. It landed with a clank on the other side of the room as I reached for my button-fly but Emme was already there, her tongue snared between her teeth as she pulled my jeans open.

Before I could say a word, before I could even breathe, she shoved my clothes down, wrapped a hand around my shaft, and took me into the unbelievable heaven of her mouth. My heart stopped for a whole minute, but when it started up again, every muscle in my body pulled painfully tight. Without thinking, I surged all the way to the back of her throat and earned myself a sudden slap on the ass as she gagged.

Pulling back, I dug my fingers through her silky hair and cupped a hand under her jaw. I felt the tense and pull of her muscles as she worked me all the way down to the root and back up to the head like she'd crawled inside my mind and opened up the file on the fastest way to tear me apart.

I let my hand run down her neck and chest, and slipped my fingers under the top of her dress. I traced the luscious round of her breast until I found a perfectly pebbled nipple waiting for me and I knew I wouldn't know peace until I'd felt it against my tongue.

"Off," I barked, tugging at the front of her dress.

She looked up at me then, her eyes bright and her mouth stretched wide to take my cock, and I realized I was about thirty seconds from coming all over her face. Call me old-fashioned but that was not how I wanted to start off my wedding night.

I tried to take a step away, tried to regain some control, but she returned a hand to my backside and dug her nails in hard enough to leave her mark there. I dropped my head and bellowed at the ceiling as her tongue wrapped around my head with the kind of pressure that nearly knocked me over.

"Not like this," I said, gathering her hair in my hand. I tugged her back but that only made her suck harder. After a moment of complete torture, she pulled off with a pop that reverberated between us. "Get that dress off."

She leaned back, her palms flat on the bed and her lips shiny and swollen. She watched while I kicked off my jeans and boxers and stepped between her legs, her gaze raking over me with the kind of intensity that made goose bumps ripple over the back of my neck. She stared at my cock, her gaze of open, unfiltered appraisal enough to make me ache from the inside out.

"Are you going to make me beg for you?" I asked as I tipped her head back and traced my thumb over those plump lips. "I will. I'll get on my knees. I'll worship you."

She gave the floor a meaningful glance and I didn't waste a second dropping down in front of her. I reached under her dress and skimmed those little, skintight shorts down her legs.

"My turn," I said, shouldering my way between her thighs.

Emme pulled her skirt up to her waist in slow, agonizing inches, her eyes locked on mine the entire time. When I finally dropped my gaze between her legs, I knew I'd found the center of my universe. I didn't even need to touch her, taste her. I just knew—as if it was inevitable. My whole life was a series of moments leading up to this one.

Leading up to Emme.

I ran my thumbs down the center of her, parting her just enough to swipe my tongue over her clit. She shuddered out a breathy moan that made me feel like a fucking god and I went back for more.

Her fingers soon twisted in my hair and her hips arched toward my mouth and her arousal ran down to my wrist. Her arms gave out and she flopped back against the bed, and I realized I wanted *that*—I want to exhaust her entire body—for the rest of my fucking life.

She didn't say anything besides the occasional murmurs of *yes* and *there* and *oh my god*, and I knew I could come just from listening to her. Within minutes, her body tightened and she bucked against my mouth, and I went on licking and petting her until the gasps subsided and her grip on my hair loosened.

"I'll come back here again tonight," I said. "But now, let's get you out of these clothes."

She pushed up on one hand and pointed to her side with the other. "Help me with the zipper."

Thrilled with the wobble I'd put into her voice, I drew the zipper down to her waist. The dress fell away and I pulled it over her head, leaving her breasts spilling out of a strapless bra. "This too?" I asked, climbing on the bed to kneel behind her.

She nodded, bowing her head as I swept her hair over one shoulder before going to work on the hooks. My shaft bobbed between us, hard like never before, and it was a wonder I could even think through the pounding, desperate need inside me. I wanted to devour this woman. Lick and bite and fuck and mark. I wanted it all, and after all this time, all these years of wanting, she was finally mine.

I slipped an arm across her breasts when I tossed the bra aside, holding her tight against me and stealing a moment to kiss my way down the line of her shoulder. I palmed her breast, my thumb circling her nipple as my other hand slipped between her legs.

"Let me have you now, wife," I said, my lips on her neck. "Let me give you what you need."

Emme nodded and some automatic, hyper-focused part of my brain took charge. I didn't think about shifting her to the center of the bed or grabbing a condom from the bedside table. It just happened. One move after the other until everything fell into place. It was like this during games too, the ones where everything clicked. All I had to do was react.

When I climbed over her, my cock hot on her soft belly and my fingers working between her legs, all that focus slowed way down. I saw every exhale, every curve of her lips, every dart of her eyes—and though I knew the answer, I needed to hear it one more time. "Yes?"

Her lips tipped up at the corners as her gaze dropped between our bodies, to where my cock was troublingly close to embarrassing me, and back up. "Fuck yes."

I shifted, letting my shaft slide through her wet seam. The head nudged her clit and she rocked against me, just like she had on the plane, and I made a noise that wasn't entirely human. She ran her hand up my spine and settled it on the back of my neck, and she urged me closer until our lips met.

Quietly, barely a gasp, she said, "I want my husband to fuck me."

It didn't really matter what I had inked on my skin. Not when I could hear those words on repeat in my head for the rest of my life.

I ran a hand down her thigh to the back of her knee and held her open as I watched her pussy take my cock. I would've stared at that perfect pink flesh and the way it stretched around me all night if she hadn't brought me back to her mouth.

I kissed her as she whispered, "It's too much," and I asked, "Am I hurting you?"

A single shake of her head. "No. You're just…a lot."

"Breathe for me, baby. Just a little more."

She did breathe though that meant I had to slap a hand to the headboard to hold myself steady while she shifted her hips to take me deeper. The wood creaked and I growled into her neck as the heat and pressure tested all of my strength.

I kissed her again and grabbed the hand she'd bunched in the sheets and brought it back to my neck. "Don't let me go," I said.

"I won't," she said, "if you don't."

It was the easiest thing in the world to say, "Never."

Again, I kissed her as we moved together, as I pinched her nipples and she dug her nails into my back. As she cried and shuddered and begged me to get her there. As she locked her legs around my waist and held me close while she shattered for me and all I could do was slam into her like I wanted to leave a mark. As I came so hard that part of the headboard cracked under my hand. As we laughed and shook and held each other.

I'd had years to imagine what this would be like. How it would feel to peel her clothes off and drink in her naked skin. To run my hands over her soft, luscious curves, to taste those places. I'd dreamed of what it would be like to have the right to touch her this way, to spread her legs and discover all her secret places. To make her writhe and gasp and claw at me. *For* me.

In none of those dreams did it start with her grabbing me by the cock and sucking me within an inch of my life. Never once did I think I'd spend every second kissing her like I couldn't let go. And I never thought it would feel so absolutely right. I'd known it would be good, that I'd make it good for her. But the sex wasn't simply good. It was *right*. And in those minutes that I'd been lost between her thighs, I was right too.

And if I could just hold on to this, hold on to Emme—well, I knew Emme and I knew tomorrow would be…strained. She'd retreat until she found her bearings, and if I played that game, she'd make her way back to me. Then I could figure out how to keep her.

Because I *had* to keep her. It was the only option. Not ending our marriage, not picking up where we'd left off as friends. I'd go on existing if I lost her but I'd never feel this way—I'd never be *right* —again.

When it was over and we determined the bed was broken but not so much that we needed to do anything about it now, I rolled Emme on top of me, my cock half hard and still pulsing inside her.

"This," I said, cupping her breasts in both hands, "is perfect."

"How are you—" She rocked her hips against me and my whole body twitched. "Still going strong?"

I wasn't about to correct her so I held her waist as I bucked up into her. "Because it's you, wifey."

"Be serious," she shot back.

I skimmed my hands up her sides and back to her breasts. I was going to spend hours getting to know these beauties. But first— "I am. I'm dead serious."

"You can just"—she glanced down at my torso—"keep going?"

So I'd have to explain a few things to her. All right. "I'm hard because I want to fuck you. Because you're gorgeous and sexy, and because I want to spend so much time in your cunt that you'll expect me to pay rent."

She circled her hips and her cheeks suddenly flushed pink. There was something about those rosy cheeks that did it to me every time. A new wave of arousal rushed through me and I thrust into her again. She dropped forward, her hands flat on my chest, and I seized that opportunity to get my tongue around her nipple.

"I can keep going," I said into the glory of her breasts, "because I have endurance like you've never seen, wife. Get used to it."

chapter twenty-two

Emme

Today's Learning Objective:
Students will get their game-faces on.

I woke up naked—and with Ryan's hand between my legs.

His touch was light, as if he was simply holding me...by the vagina. Which was to be expected because we'd had sex last night. Lots of sex. And we'd also gotten married.

All kinds of adventures for us.

He was asleep, if the slow, steady breathing on the back of my neck was any indication, though he was stunningly hard against my ass. Individually, I had no problem with any of this. The hand between my legs was strangely pleasant. Much better than the usual middle of the night boob grab. And there wasn't much that dick couldn't do.

But I needed to get the hell out of this bed because my brain required seven to ten business days to process all of yesterday and figure out who we were to each other now that we had naked sleep-overs. Now that I knew the feel of him hitting the back of my throat and bottoming out inside me. Now that we'd jumped from old friends to a fake engagement to a thoroughly consummated marriage. Now that we could never again say we were just friends.

Most of the time, I could roll with whatever happened. I didn't need a roadmap of everything up ahead. But right now, with my body straining to rock against that hand or lean into that hard shaft, and my head a jumble of hope and dread and affection, I needed to find my way through. This mattered—probably more than anything had ever mattered to me—and I had to get it right. Even if that meant I was weird as hell about it for days.

I had no doubt it would be fun to stay here and let him fuck me right through the mattress a few more times but I really needed to get up and turn into the kind of gangly, embarrassing creature who overthought so hard she set her own hair on fire. Also, I desperately needed to blow my nose.

"I'M GOING TO NEED YOUR MEDIA FACE TODAY," I SAID, FUSSING WITH my own face in the car's visor mirror. My eyes were bloodshot from everything that'd happened last night plus the blanket of pollen that'd fallen over the city. My nose too. Not cute. Not the look I wanted for this wonky new relationship of ours. Or seeing Teddy again.

"Which one?" Ryan grumbled from the driver's seat.

I'd teased him about driving us to Ben and Grace's house outside the city this evening and I'd succeeded in fully exasperating him within the first five minutes of this journey. It gave me something to do other than worrying about last night or having to see Teddy or—god help me—speak to my ex.

"If you're giving me a choice, let's skip the post-game press conference face. No one needs you sitting there with your arms crossed, a mean scowl, and a beanie pulled down halfway over your eyes."

"That's only when we lose."

I stared at him. I could tell from the smile that pulled at the corner of his lips that he knew I was looking at him but he kept his gaze on the road. I also knew he wasn't upset with me. A little disgruntled this morning, sure, but we'd settled into a workable rhythm of pretending everything was fine and never once referencing yesterday's events. Avoidance was so fun. "Are you sure about that?"

He jerked a shoulder. "Mostly."

"Right. Let's have the media face where you dig deep inside to find the strength to tolerate spending time with loads of people desperate to tell you how great you are. Just like all those Derby parties."

"Just like the Derby?" He glanced over at me with a meaningful arch of his brow.

I could almost hear him growl *Don't you fucking stop* with that eyebrow. I had to press my thighs together.

"Close enough," I managed.

He reached for my hand and his thumb traced the band of my ring, his attention back on the road. "I'll be good. Anything you want, I'll do it."

"I just need you to chat up the guys for a bit. You can go back to being dark and broody—"

"I am not *dark*."

"—once they agree you really are the god of football and my ex realizes he's as useful as a severed head."

"If anyone's dark here, it's you," he muttered.

"I am a ball of goddamn sunshine and don't you forget it," I yelled. Then I followed it up with an ugly sniffle.

He shook with laughter as he exited the highway. "I fuckin' love you, Muggsy."

"Don't forget that either." I dug in my bag for another allergy tablet and some tissues before going back to touching up my face. It was a warm day, and even without the allergies I had a tendency to look like a sun-dried tomato when left outside too long. That never stopped me from buying new products on the off chance one of them would keep my rosy cheeks in check. "Love you too...Wildcat."

I stopped myself from calling him *husband*. I didn't want to overthink this but I didn't want it to come out the wrong way. Especially after last night. And the way I'd crept out of his bed. And how I still felt the echoes of him between my legs.

"Why the hell do they live all the way out here?" he grumbled as he turned deeper into the residential neighborhood.

"It's Ben's grandmother's fault. She felt like leaving him a house was a good idea."

When we pulled up at the freshly painted ranch, I gave my lip color one last look before climbing out of the SUV. I was in a new dress today because the one I'd picked out for this occasion was hosting quite a lot of black mold at the moment. But I loved this long, yellow sundress with tiny dots and soft, ruffled straps just as much.

My apartment was still a disaster and the landlord had no information for us other than "Not today, sweetheart."

But I knew I looked good and I felt good. And it didn't matter what Teddy thought about any of it because he was the human equivalent of a sinkhole and I had a four-carat diamond on my hand from my Super Bowl MVP husband.

I was doing just fine.

When I had a gift bag looped around one arm and a large tray balanced in the other, I nudged my backside against the door to close it. It didn't shut all the way but just enough that I needed to free up a hand to do it. "Dammit," I muttered.

"I saw that." Ryan circled the front of the SUV and took care of the door. He glanced between me and the string of cars lining the block. "Ready?"

"Yeah, we'll go through the—oh, not again." I kicked my leg out from my skirt to find my lace-up sandals had unlaced themselves once more. I held out the tray toward Ryan. "Can you take this?"

He gave me a single shake of his head and crouched down in front of me. His t-shirt stretched tight across his back as he studied my shoes. It took a second but he figured out the procedure, testing each crisscross and the bow at the top twice.

Then, for no reason at all, he brought his palm to the back of my leg, right behind my knee, and skimmed it all the way up my thigh. He glanced up at me as his broad hand settled just under the curve of my ass while his fingertips drew tiny circles on my inner thigh, and he asked, "Is that what you needed?"

I managed a nod and some noise of agreement and he slowly—*so slowly*—trailed those fingers back down my leg and around my ankle. After another moment of nearly obscene caresses, he pushed to his feet and gave me a long, lazy kiss.

I wobbled where I stood and it had nothing to do with my shoes. Should've stayed in bed with him this morning. It would've only delayed the onset of my overthinking but at least I'd be too orgasm-drunk to get obsessive.

He took the tray from my hand, looped an arm around my shoulder, and said, "Let's get you that revenge, wifey."

THE PARTY SPILLED FROM THE OPEN-PLAN KITCHEN AND FAMILY ROOM out into the backyard. Groups congregated around the grill, the kitchen island, the patio table under the newly constructed pergola. I spotted Ben outside, pointing up at the roof with some grill tongs while talking to a guy wearing a Ladder 66 shirt. Audrey was busy slicing lime wedges near the sink while Jamie stirred a pitcher of something I prayed was her famous margarita recipe.

No one noticed us at first but then I saw the subtle chin jerks in our direction, the nudged elbows and pointed beer bottles, the gazes that landed on Ryan with a furrow followed by *Is that...?*

Grace rushed over when she saw us making our way through the family room. She waved us into the kitchen, tsking at the heavy bag I pressed into her hands and grumbling about how gifts weren't necessary.

"It was Ryan's idea so you'll need to blame him." I gave her a flippant shrug and took the tray from him. "Now, about the charcuterie. It didn't come out exactly as I'd planned because someone kept sneaking up and eating my salami roses."

"Mmm. I love having my salami rose eaten," Jamie called.

"I'm clearly spending too much time with you because I'm not even shocked by that comment," Audrey said, mostly to herself.

Grace surveyed the spread of cheeses, meats, crackers, and other goodies I'd put together. "It looks amazing."

Ryan came up behind me, wrapping an arm around my waist and banding the other across my torso, leaving his hand splayed over the bare expanse of my chest. His fingertips slipped under the shoulder of my dress and he traced the line of my bra strap. His lips on my neck, he said, "I'll make it up to you."

I felt a ripple of awareness move through the house and I knew all those eyes were on us. And I knew my ex was one of them. I'd spotted his big stupid truck the second we turned down this street and I'd heard his whiny laugh float in from the backyard.

He was watching now, I was sure of it, and I hoped he felt the same sad, sinking sensation that I'd experienced outside his door that night. Not because he was being hit with the fact that I'd moved on from him or even that he'd been wrong to treat me as he had. No, he was realizing he'd never be able to watch his favorite team play again, never be able to wear his Ralston jersey—without thinking of me and my husband.

But that wasn't why I brought my hand to the back of Ryan's neck and pulled him down for a kiss. That wasn't why I kept it going longer than necessary or why I let my fingers scrape along his scalp until he squeezed my hip *hard*.

He went back to my neck, holding me tight to his solid body as he growled, as he pressed his teeth to my skin. "What are you doing to me?" he whispered.

"I don't know," I whispered back. "What does it feel like?"

"You really want to know?"

When I tipped my chin up in challenge, he pressed his hips against my backside and—*oh*. I felt the hard heat of him through my dress and I blinked. Stiff and insistent and *huge*. All that from one kiss?

He gripped my hip again, but this time he put a breath of space between us. "Give me a minute," he rasped, his hand still under my bra strap. "Then I'll make your boy regret his entire existence."

I glanced up at him but found him staring at my breasts. This dress did have a certain milkmaid quality so I couldn't blame him. Though I didn't mind the attention just as I didn't mind the strong, sudden reaction to that kiss. Not when it made me feel like I'd been plugged in and turned back on after months—years?—of waiting for someone to finally *see* me. To want me, exactly as I was.

"He's not my boy," I said, running my knuckles along the scruffy line of his jaw. "He's not mine at all."

"Good." Ryan pulled me back to him again, a growl low in his throat. "Because I don't share."

THERE WERE TWO THINGS I KNEW TO BE TRUE RIGHT NOW.

First off, my husband was a really good guy. Probably the best guy. If there was a ranking system for this sort of thing, my guy would be at the top of the chart all day every day.

Two hours into this party, he was still taking photos, answering every random question thrown at him, and recounting his most recent championship win down to the minute. There was one point when he couldn't remember something about a play and called up Hersberler, put him on speaker, and had the tight end tell the story from his side of the field.

Ryan had so thoroughly captivated everyone that Grace, Audrey, Jamie, and I parked ourselves at the island with our bottomless margaritas and decimated the charcuterie. It was mostly margarita for me since I'd sampled enough of the cheese board while preparing it and that was just fine by me.

I kept seeing big, rugged firefighters share bright, soulful expressions and a shake of their head like *Can you believe we're talking to Ryan Ralston?* They slapped each other on the back or landed light blows on biceps when he revealed some insider info or said something like, "I had no idea whether that move would work but I was fucking thrilled when it did" or "That one was all luck. I couldn't have called that play if I'd tried."

Everyone except Teddy.

No, like the toenail fungus he was, he lingered on the fringe of the group and made himself look busy with his phone or the grill or literally anything else. He slid between scowling at Ryan and leaning one ear in to hear more of his stories.

It was almost funny. I couldn't drop all of my resentment to embrace that humor but it was enough. It was what I'd needed from today.

Until I raided Grace's medicine cabinet for anything to turn off these allergies and found myself staring at the woman last seen half naked in Teddy's apartment. I hadn't noticed her in the crowd though I'd never thought to look.

She was wearing more clothes now which was a nice change of pace but it forced me to notice that we had quite a lot in common. She was a couple of years younger than me but we were both short and dark-haired, full in the bust and fond of sundresses that showed it off.

And we both wore engagement rings.

Mine lazed toward my pinkie like usual and hers…well, I'd seen hers before.

Heat burned in my cheeks. I glanced away, motioning down the hall as I tried to squeeze into the slip of space between us. "Sorry. It's all yours."

But she blocked the way, saying, "Hi. I don't think we've met. Not the right way. I'm Clara."

"Clara," I repeated, my lips a tight line that couldn't pretend it was a smile. "Emme."

"I know," she said. "And I'm so sorry about—about everything."

I drew in a breath and stared down the hall, mentally willing anyone to come and rescue me. A long moment passed and I resigned myself to the fact I was stuck in this quicksand conversation. With a steadying breath, I forced myself to face her. My lips parted but nothing came out. Except a gross, wet sniffle.

Clara twined her fingers together as she hurried to say, "You should know it was my fault. I never asked Teddy whether he was seeing anyone else and I should've."

I'd never blinked so hard at anyone in my life. "Excuse me, what?"

"If I expect monogamy in a relationship, I have to ask for it," she went on. "I didn't and"—she shot me a small, pitying glance that made me want to rip the shingles off this house—"I guess you didn't either. I'm so sorry that we found ourselves on either side of that situation. I didn't want that and I hate that you were hurt in the process. I would've ended things with him if I'd known."

"You don't think he shares any of the responsibility?"

Her tanned shoulders rolled in an easy, unbothered gesture. "He could've said something sooner. He knows that was a mistake."

My heartbeat thundered in my chest. I couldn't comprehend how it was merely a mistake to her when that betrayal had overturned my entire life. "Then you're aware that he doesn't prioritize monogamy in a relationship. You know who he is," I snapped, "and you're still marrying him."

She glanced down at her ring. "Yeah, I do. And I am."

Clara finally stepped back, giving me enough room to get past her. But I studied her, desperate to understand how we could experience the same event in such wildly different ways.

Maybe I was wrong about it all. Maybe I was the presumptuous fool who'd never thought to ask whether we were seeing other people. We'd only been together for a year. What if I thought I deserved more than I did? The relationship had obviously meant much more to me than him so it would stand to reason that I'd just inflated the importance all around.

"Anyway, I just wanted to say hi and clear the air," Clara said. "We'll probably run into each other a lot and I hope we can be friends or something like that. Someday."

A loud cheer went up from the direction of the backyard and then a roar quickly followed. I had no idea what they were doing out there but I knew that like all great quarterbacks, Ryan—the best guy—was behind it. I also knew my ex, the one who'd convinced this woman it was pretty much okay for him to cheat because she hadn't asked a precise sequence of questions, was probably off kicking rocks in the corner.

At least there were those silver linings.

After a soft laugh toward the backyard, Clara glanced toward me. "I am sorry about how it happened and I wanted you to know it was unfair and wrong."

Those words weren't meant to wound me. The opposite, I was sure. They weren't meant to poke at the scabbed-over places where I'd folded in on myself just to get through the worst of it.

Yet all I could think was that revenge hardly mattered.

I'd hardly mattered, not if Teddy had planned to marry this woman all along and I'd been nothing more than the girl he hung out with when he wanted good food, fresh laundry, and a target for his shitty comments. Wasn't that the truth of it?

Another cheer spilled in through the open windows. I rubbed the band of my ring as I listened for more. Ryan probably had them doing combine drills. I'd bet anything he was sitting back with a beer and watching while these guys ran through ladder holes or sprinted the length of the backyard while dragging a loaded ice chest. And I loved him for it.

When I didn't respond, she asked, "Don't you think it all worked out for the best?"

If I looked at it a certain way, I could see what she meant. I'd stopped waiting on a douchebro who had zero fucks to give me and upgraded to a man who thought nothing of carrying my plump ass down five flights of stairs when my dress was too tight and begged me to let him fuck me last night.

But just like everything else in my life, it wouldn't last.

I PLOPPED MYSELF BETWEEN GRACE AND JAMIE AT THE ISLAND AND played at being distracted with my phone until I saw Clara return to the patio a few minutes later.

With a not so gentle elbow, I nudged Grace. "You forgot to mention the part where Teddy's engaged these days."

"He's what?" she yelped. "Since when?"

"I didn't get the whole proposal story from Clara on account of her ambushing me in the hall just now. She wanted to apologize to me. Since she was the one I found in bed with him and all."

Jamie pushed to her feet and craned her neck to survey the group outside. "Where is she? Never mind, I'll know. But don't forget y'all have to bail me out if this goes bad. I don't like spending the night in jail."

"Nothing is going bad because you're sitting down and not starting anything." I grabbed her skirt and pulled her onto the stool. With a wad of cocktail napkins in hand to deal with my runny nose, I said, "She was actually very nice and sweet, which I hate violently. She didn't have to approach me or apologize but she did, even if she's not the one who should be handing out the apologies."

"I didn't know," Grace said. "I would've warned you if I did." She stared off toward the patio. "Ben would've heard about it if I'd known."

I glanced outside to where strings of lights on the pergola glowed in the evening darkness. Ryan talked with a few people near the grill while watching while guys took turns box-jumping onto an ice chest. I reached for the margarita pitcher and topped off my glass. He wasn't dying of grouchy man misery and he was grown enough to tell me when he was done being the center of attention. "I know."

They studied me as I sipped my drink, and after a few moments of tense silence punctuated only by my nose-blowing, Jamie launched into a story about a sex party she attended where everyone wore varying amounts of bunny costumes.

"I went with a tail for obvious reasons," she said, "but then—"

"No, wait." Audrey held up both hands. "What are the obvious reasons?"

Jamie stared at Audrey like the answer was about to slap her in the face and she just needed to think about it for a second. When Audrey only shook her head, Grace added, "You're gonna have to walk us through it, honey."

With a goofy eye roll, Jamie zigzagged a finger over her torso. "There are only two ways to wear a tail. One of them is a G-string. The other"—she glanced between us, still hopeful we'd figure it out—"is a butt plug. Which is my preference."

Audrey lifted her glass to her mouth and drained the contents while Grace laughed.

"I will definitely regret this," I started, going back for another refill, "but why?"

"It's a lot of fun," Jamie said. "And I don't feel like I have a wedgie the whole time."

"No, not a wedgie but a whole...*thing* up there," Grace cried.

"That's the fun part," Jamie replied. "Trust me on this! You might not think you're into it but then you get a little toy and you realize it's a spicy good time."

"No—hold on. Stop. Where are your clothes?" Audrey asked.

"I'm not wearing any," Jamie said, laughing.

Audrey's mouth fell open. "Why not?"

"Because I'm there for a double stuffing of dick," she replied.

"Triple, if I like anyone enough to let them take the plug out of my ass."

A throat cleared behind us and we all turned at once to see Ryan staring at us, his arms crossed and his eyes narrowed. I started to laugh but a sloppy, tequila-flavored hiccup burst out of me instead as the liquor plowed into me all at once.

"All right there, Muggsy?"

I lifted my fist of napkins and almost empty glass in a wobbly salute and hiccuped again. "As good as I'm gonna get."

"Why does he call you that?" Audrey asked. "What does Muggsy mean?"

Ryan's brow lifted as he crossed the room toward me. Once he had a hand settled low on my back, he frowned down at me and brushed a thumb over my cheek. "You want to tell them? Or should I?"

"It's a dumb, tragic story." I shook my head but that sent everything swimming. I felt a hand on my shoulder, then sliding up and down my arm. "When I registered for school in New Hampshire, my name got messed up on the paperwork. Every year, on every teacher's class roster, it was Emmugglas. Like, Emme and Douglas smashed together for no good reason. They tried to correct it in the student database a million times but it never stuck. At graduation, they literally called Emmugglas Ahlborg."

"And everyone called you Muggsy because of that?" Jamie asked.

"No, they called me Bitsy, short for Big Tits, because everyone felt it was best to identify people by cup size. It sounds bad but let me tell ya, I had it better than the gal they called Beesting." I pointed at Ryan though I didn't do it well because he caught my wrist and brought it to my lap. "He's the only one who never called me Bitsy."

They stared at me for a moment. At least it seemed that way. I was having a very hard time focusing on anything right now.

Then, Audrey said, "I don't like any of that."

"Such misogynistic bullshit," Grace muttered.

"At least Daddy Football didn't sexually harass her," Jamie said.

"He didn't. Not even once." I shifted to stare up at him but his features all swam together. "I always hoped he'd slip up so I could make him admit he'd noticed me like that. Never did. Never ever ever."

I tried to loop an arm around his waist but lost my bearings and started to slip off the stool. Everyone cried out and rushed forward as Ryan caught me but the room never did stop spinning.

"What's going on with you?" He took a sip from my glass and grimaced. "Is this all you've had tonight? Any water? Food?"

"I've had all the broken crackers and a couple different allergy pills. And some Manchego."

"Allergy meds and margaritas are a special combo," Jamie murmured. "Especially if you enjoy sleeping like the dead."

Ryan braced himself behind me, an arm low around my waist and the other gripping the island as if I needed a guardrail. "Right. Okay. I'm taking you home now. Where's your bag?"

Grace hopped up. "I'll get it and follow you outside."

"But I need to hear about Jamie's bunny sex party," I argued.

"I got railed like six times and couldn't remember where I put the butt plug so I left without it," Jamie said with a limp fist pump. "It filled someone's goody bag."

"And you enjoyed all of that?" Audrey asked.

"It was okay. Most of the fun was getting ready and then walking around, seeing what was going on and what everyone was doing."

"Walking around naked," Audrey said.

Jamie grinned. "Yes, my darling, confirming once again I was bare as a babe."

Audrey circled both hands. "And that was the fun part?"

"Yeah. I mean, the sex was…fine. Nothing to check off the vision board but good enough. Then I woke up the next day with another UTI," she said. "Just a standard Saturday night for me."

"I bake bread on Saturday nights," Audrey said.

"You could come to a meet-up with me and see what it's like to have dozens of people fantasizing about you at the same time. It does wonders for the ego."

"I think I'm okay with the bread," Audrey replied.

"Whatever makes you happy, love," Jamie said. "I just want you to know there's someone out there who wants to butter that bread of yours."

"You really are a good friend," Audrey breathed.

"It's one of my many gifts," Jamie said.

Ryan cleared his throat. "Anything else you need?" he asked me.

"I'm sure there's more," I said, though I could hear the slur in my words now. Did I really drink that much? I didn't think so. Those glasses weren't especially big. There'd been some refills but—and what time was it? "We have really important things to talk about, you know."

"I know it, baby, but it's late and I want you to get some rest."

I bobbed my head. "If you say so."

"You're following directions now?" I felt his lips on my forehead. "That's new."

"Just like my shoes," I drawled. "And everything else because my house is a watery grave."

He pulled me to my feet and steered me toward the door as I called out my good-byes. When we reached the front steps, he said, "I love these shoes, Em, but you're gonna roll an ankle if I let you take another step. I'm going to carry you to the car. Hold on."

I tried to summon an argument for this but my eyelids refused to stay open and my mouth was like limey cotton. I felt him scoop me up, and then a blink later I heard the seat belt click around me. Another blink and the highway was flying past my window.

I turned my heavy head and stared at him. My *husband*. His jaw was like granite again. "Are we exclusive?"

He looked over, his brows pinched together and his forehead creased. His scowl was a harsh, irritable line dug into his face. "We're fucking *married*, Emmeline. Yeah, we're exclusive."

"Okay. Were we exclusive before that? Before last night?"

"We've been exclusive since the night I asked you to marry me." He shook his head. "Why would you even ask me something like that?"

I sank deeper into the seat and tucked my arms close to my chest. My eyes drifted shut again and I couldn't fight it off. "Because I learned two things today and one of them is that people will cheat unless you tell them not to."

chapter twenty-three

Ryan

Today's Learning Objective:
Students will reevaluate information once considered fact.

EMME DOZED MOST OF THE DRIVE HOME WHICH GAVE ME PLENTY OF time to tear apart everything I knew about the woman I'd spent fifteen years telling myself never wanted me as more than a friend.

I always hoped he'd slip up so I could make him admit he'd noticed me like that.

I glanced over as a snore trilled out of her. "I noticed. I always noticed."

All this time. All those years I'd told myself to push it down and shove it aside so I could be a true, decent friend to her and not some entitled dude waiting for any sign of an opening. All those years and she'd been waiting too?

I almost couldn't believe it.

If she'd said this two weeks ago, I *wouldn't* have believed it. Would've shrugged it off as the silly ramblings of a woman who liked to forget she couldn't hold her liquor.

But after what happened on the plane last weekend, after everything last night—I saw those moments in a bright new light.

Maybe this plan—this *marriage*—wasn't going to end in the ruin I'd imagined after all. There was a chance we could figure this out. Together.

I wanted to dive into the deep end right now. Wanted to tell her everything, even if it broke me, and I wanted her to promise we'd figure it out together.

But then she started snoring again.

I laughed to myself and skimmed a finger down her cheek, and told myself there was time. There'd always be time for us.

Now that there was an *us*.

A strange level of vindication came with hearing it hadn't been entirely one-sided. All the time I'd spent hating the guys she went out with, the agony I'd experienced from seeing her with them—maybe she'd shared a bit of that.

I wanted to go back in time and rewrite our history but I knew that if this part—this huge fucking fundamental part—had been different for us, it wouldn't change the rest of it.

Even if she hadn't laid down her no-players law from the start, I wouldn't have lasted more than a few weeks with her. A month or two if I'd respected the rules she never thought to share with her boyfriends. And that was assuming I'd had the time and mental bandwidth to do anything more than go to school, play football, and help keep my family from going off the rails before and after my dad died.

Most days I'd only had the bandwidth to watch Emme peel her tangerines and carefully pick bits of pith off the segments. I would've been another one of her worthless boyfriends who couldn't get it together to be the guy she deserved.

Goddamn. If I'd known…

But I knew now.

And if that was what she wanted—what she'd wanted since the start—then we could finally stop telling each other this arrangement was temporary. That it had anything to do with her ex or my business deals or even our pact. And we wouldn't have to act like last night had been a mistake or whatever the fuck was happening there.

Traffic was heavy for no apparent reason so when I took a break from dismantling the belief system underpinning our entire fucking relationship, I switched gears and freaked the fuck out about her asking if we were exclusive. What the fuck was that about?

When I was done with that, I spent ten minutes in standstill traffic shooting off emails to see whether I could cancel my West Coast meetings or any of the endorsement appearances scheduled for me this week because I wanted to stay in bed with my wife.

Very productive night for me.

It only improved when we returned home and, instead of insisting my half-conscious wife explain herself and the past decade and a half of our history, I steered her toward my room. It was closer to the front door and she was enough of a fall risk tonight without adding a whole staircase to the equation. We'd figure out which one would be *our* room later.

I steadied her in front of a dresser and dropped to my knees to handle the lace-up shoes that I was convinced had manifested themselves from a dark, filthy corner of my mind. She held her dress to her knees while I took my time trailing my fingers up the back of each calf and slowly unwrapping the ribbons from her legs.

Save for the city lights flowing in through the windows, it was dark in here though I could still see faint lines where the ribbons had pressed into her skin. I rubbed small circles into her calves and told myself it was probably the wrong time to duck my head under her skirt and lick my way up her thighs.

If there was one thing I could do for this woman, it was wait.

"I need to take this off," she grumbled, her fingers reaching for the zipper at the back of her dress.

I gained my feet and nudged her hand away when she missed a second, then third, time. "Let me." She dropped her head to the side like it was too heavy to hold up while I drew the zipper down. "Did you get everything you wanted from tonight?"

"Not really. I think I grabbed the nighttime allergy meds instead of the non-drowsy stuff," she said around a yawn. "I blame the bleary eye situation. Grace also takes everything out of its packaging and organizes it into little containers with dainty labels which actually makes things much more complicated so she gets some blame too."

I ran my knuckles down her bare back. She shivered, clutching the dress to her chest. "That's not what I meant."

A beat passed before she pulled in a wobbly breath. "You were great. Nice job on the media face. It never looked like you wanted to eat anyone's soul simply for existing which is leaps and bounds ahead of most of your press conferences. Very nice job on whatever the hell you had those guys doing in the backyard later on. I'm sure my ex nearly broke his own neck ignoring you but also hanging on your every word, and that's all I can ask for."

I dropped my hand to her hip. "Was it the revenge you wanted?"

Another breath, another yawn, and, "Can I borrow a hoodie? Or a t-shirt?"

Keeping that hand on her hip, I pulled open a drawer and grabbed some options for her. "Since when do you ask? Your thieving little fingers always steal my shirts."

"Not always." I could hear her pouting.

She held the sweatshirt to her chest and glanced back at me, an expectation of privacy in her eyes. I didn't think she'd need that after last night but I wasn't going to press the issue. I knew how she operated. Just another game of inches.

I paced to the windows facing Boston Common. I heard the dress swish to the floor and the shuffle of bra straps sliding down her arms. I shoved my hands into my pockets and stared at the city lights until all I could see was bright white halos.

I realized then I should've walked out when I had the chance. I couldn't just stand here with my dick hard and my head making the best and worst of everything I'd heard tonight when I knew damn well she'd be asleep within the next five minutes. And I knew this wasn't the night for another one of our sleepovers.

Not unless she asked for it.

After all these years, I finally knew what it sounded like when she came around my cock and I knew how it tasted to call her my wife. And I wasn't about to forget it—or cross another line until she was ready.

I needed to find some tissues and get her a big cup of water and then hit the treadmill until I couldn't feel my legs. Instead of doing any of that, I asked, "Where are we with the revenge plot?"

"I found out he's engaged now."

That fucking guy. It would've been amusing to watch him avoid me all night if not for the fact that I wanted to sack him so hard he lived the rest of his life with the taste of soil in the back of his throat. That opportunity didn't present itself to me though I glared so many holes through that boy he was a screen door by the time I was done with him.

"Which I discovered when I met his fiancée." I heard the rustle of sheets and a sad, salty laugh. "Well, I met her *again*."

I turned around. Discussing her ex smothered any arousal I felt real fast and I couldn't have this conversation without seeing her face. "What does that mean?"

"He's marrying the girl he cheated on me with." Her words dripped with the deceptive kind of sweet that women used when they wanted you to know they were furious and teetering on the edge of psychotic. "She didn't think it was too much of a problem. The cheating, that is. Because she never asked if he was seeing other people. Guess who else didn't ask? If you guessed me, then you're right! If only I'd asked, then —then what? I would've found out he was seeing girls on the side? No, actually, *I* was the girl on the side. I was the girl who put up with his shit and still cooked him dinner. That must make me the fool in this story. But don't worry about that because his fiancée wants us to be friends now."

That *fucking* guy.

There was no other option for me than to climb onto the bed and pull Emme into my arms. "You want me to send some linebackers to fuck him up?"

She made a ranty sound and pulled the hood up, tightening the strings under her chin. It was the cutest thing. I loved when she did that. She looked like a strange, beautiful doll. "That's not going to solve anything but I wouldn't lose sleep over it."

"You proved your point tonight and believe me, he heard it loud and clear." I rubbed a hand down her back. "You can't let him get to you."

"It's not that I'm letting him get to me," she said. "I'm just angry. About everything." She curled her hands into tiny, angry claws and shredded some invisible demon. "I see him and all I can think about is the mess he left behind, and I'm *furious*. I'm furious that he took so much from me and I'm furious that I let him. That a year of my life is gone but he gave up nothing. He walked away without a scratch on him and went on to convince this girl it was actually her fault he'd cheated."

"Then this isn't about him getting engaged?"

If her eyes could've killed me, I'd already be out there haunting old houses. "I don't give a single fuck about that. It's that he ruined so many things—he ruined *me*—"

"No, Em, he didn't. Not even close. This dickhead guy doesn't have what it takes to break you. He tried and look what he got. You crushed him like a bug tonight and you probably blew off his fiancée too."

"For your information, I was actually very nice to her."

"Mmm. Bet you were."

"Stop it with the judgy *mmm*. You weren't there," she snapped.

"I didn't have to watch it go down to know you intimidated the fuck out of her."

"I don't intimidate anyone. Not even my second graders. I'm five feet tall and sometimes I buy shoes from the kid's section."

"You have no idea"—I ran a finger along the line of her jaw and gently tipped her face up to catch her eyes—"how much power you wield just in the way you look at people."

She shook her head. "I don't—I don't think—"

"You can cut someone in half with a glance. I know because I've watched you do it for years. Just like I know you're the only one who doesn't recognize how strong you are."

She trailed a finger over the inked waves on my forearm and the red cupping circles around my elbow where the therapists in Minnesota had manipulated the joint this week. She was quiet for a long minute and I didn't mind because that fingertip was busy blowing up every nerve ending in my entire arm. When she made her way up to my bicep and under the sleeve of my shirt, I accepted the hard truth that I was completely powerless against her. She could turn me on with nothing more than the touch of one finger and I'd gladly beg for more.

Then, seemingly unaware of her impact on me, she yawned until her jaw clicked. "It's hard to keep being strong when nothing lasts. I feel like I never stop putting myself back together. Always starting over. Every time I think I'm okay, something new falls apart. It's everything, everyone. Even Grace is slipping away from me." She tapped that finger to the center of my chest. "And someday I'll lose you too."

"Not in this lifetime," I said, my voice suddenly strained. "Or the next one."

"You say that but..." She lifted her shoulders in a small, resigned shrug. "Nothing lasts. Not for me."

Notice me. Notice this. The way I always noticed you. The way I'll never stop noticing.

"We're going to last, Em." I laced my fingers with hers, held them to my chest. "I'm not going anywhere. There's no world where I exist without you and I don't want there to be one."

"It's hard," she said softly. "Always having to be strong. It's exhausting."

"Yeah. I know all about that." I dropped a line of light kisses across her cheek. "But I'll block the hits for you now. It's your turn to take it easy. You can rest."

A nod, another yawn. "I'm not an unhinged ex-girlfriend who can't let go."

"I know you're not." It was a risk but I added, "Though I need you to stop letting him have this hold over you. You don't deserve that and he's not worth the energy."

"I know but—"

"No," I said, brushing my lips along her jaw. "The best revenge is forgetting all about him. Can you do that for me?"

She dragged her fingers up my arm, back under my shirt. I almost ripped the thing off to let her explore but then she stopped, gathering the fabric in her fist.

"I'll forget him but that doesn't mean I'll ever forgive or that I'll stop being angry." She must've read something in my expression—probably the realization that she *would* murder people with her eyes if she had the capacity—because she went on. "Isn't there anyone in your life, any of your *many* exes—"

"There's not that many."

"—who never fails to make you want to scream and smash things with a baseball bat?"

I held her tight because she kept shifting and no one had invited a hard-on to this conversation. "Not really, no."

"It doesn't matter how long it's been but whenever you see them or hear about them, it's like chewing on tree bark. It's awful and you hate it and everything tastes terrible for the rest of the day. And you also want to smash things."

She turned her big eyes up at me. All I could think about was staring into those eyes when I'd laid her down and pushed inside her last night. Which wasn't useful or remotely appropriate at this moment but she was *right here* and she was touching me and I couldn't help it.

She drummed her fingers on my bicep. "It's not like that with Poppy?"

I blinked. "Who?"

"Poppy," she said, as if enunciating would jog my memory. "Singer. Purple hair. Posh little British accent."

"Oh, no." I scowled. "Why would you think that?"

"The song!" she cried, shifting her knees to either side of my lap to face me. The sweatshirt rode high on her thighs, concealing very, very little. Not a great development as far as my restraint went. "The one she wrote about you! Aren't you chewing on tree bark every time you see her?"

"No, and I'm going to explain why." I held up a finger and tapped it to her nose. "One. I can't remember the last time I saw her."

"Her music is everywhere. Including that song about you."

"Two," I went on, tapping two fingers to her top lip. I fucking loved that lip. "That song isn't about me." Her eyes flared and she wanted to argue but I held those fingers to her mouth. "And three, I'm not legally permitted to disclose this but we're married so I'll tell you that relationship consisted of carefully arranged public appearances and nothing more."

"Oh, so, you have experience with this setup," she said, gesturing between us. "Makes so much sense."

"Quiet, wife." I reached for her hand and straightened the ring perched on her finger. "You know that's not what we're doing."

She tried to roll her eyes but didn't pull off more than a lazy wink. "Why did you need a fake relationship with Poppy Hemphill, then?"

"I didn't. She did." I shrugged as I kissed her knuckles, her fingertips. Dragged the pad of her ring finger between my teeth and watched while her eyes widened when I bit down. "Her label needed to build her reputation up in the States. The label's parent company also owns the luxury car company that'd just offered me a massive endorsement deal. Do the math, Muggsy."

She shook her head like she needed to carefully sift that information into the rest of her consciousness. But she was still a little drunk and the headshake involved her entire body. "Then who's the song about?"

"I don't know and I don't care."

"But everyone thinks it's you!"

"And?" She waved her arms at me like I was intentionally missing the point, and what little patience I had for this topic snapped. "Is there a demographic that believes I'm a dick because some part of that song lines up with something they saw on the internet? Yeah. Aside from the issues with closing the franchise deal, I'm not losing sleep over it and neither should you."

"But what about other exes?" she asked. "There has to be someone you're still bitter about."

"We've never once talked about a woman I was seeing. I've never mentioned that I'd met someone or introduced you to a girlfriend. Why do you think that is?"

"I-I just thought you didn't want to talk to me about those things."

"Those things?" I echoed.

She leveled a stare at me that warned me to play nice. I had no intention of doing that and when I dropped my attention to her mouth, a frustrated noise rasped in her throat.

"There's never been a shortage of women in your life," she said. "There's models and actresses and singers and—"

"Em, I love you, but you're really fucking wrong about all of it. Those were public relations setups. Either it was a publicity event for a brand or a favor to someone. None of it was real."

"Then…you aren't plowing your way through all the young starlets."

I wanted to drag her bottom lip between my teeth and just move the fuck on from this mess but I talked myself out of that. For now. "No."

"But everyone thinks you are."

I lifted my shoulders. "If you say so."

"And that's why you needed"—she wiggled her ring finger at me—"this."

"I've always needed that." I took that hand and settled it on the back of my neck. "You've always known it too."

Her drowsy eyes narrowed and her lips turned down. "But what about—everything else? I know you've always been…active."

My brows lifted as a smile tugged at my lips. "But I never liked any of them."

"Why not?"

Finally, I brought my hands to her hips and pulled her in close, as close as we could get with these last few layers of clothes between us. Her gaze dropped, her nails pressed into my nape, and I knew she felt me stiff between her thighs. Even if she was only hearing half of what I was saying, I needed her to understand this. "I don't think it matters anymore."

She swallowed hard. "What do you mean?"

I waited, wanting her to see it for herself. "I'm married now."

She blinked several times. "Oh."

"And it seems"—I ran my thumb over the plump line of her lips—"you're married too. Time to leave those exes in the past where they belong. Can you do that for me?"

She nodded, her eyes growing heavier with each blink. "I think so."

"That's my girl."

She tucked her head against my shoulder and murmured something I didn't catch. The hood slipped off her head and I rubbed my face against her hair. Then, "I'm really tired."

I kissed her temple. "Yes, you are."

I rolled her down to the mattress and tried to pull the blankets up around her but she immediately kicked them away like the feral creature she was. The sweatshirt bunched up around her waist in the process, leaving me staring at hot pink panties with tiny white bows on either hip.

I managed to choke out, "I'll let you rest."

The plan was to get up, sit in the cold plunge until I calmed the fuck down, and then run flat out for an hour. Very simple, very effective. Or lock myself in the nearest bathroom and jerk off. Another straightforward solution. Either one would work.

But Emme grabbed my arm and asked, "Will you stay with me?"

She pulled my arm across her torso, tucked her backside into my lap, and nestled up into me until she found the perfect spot.

And all I could say was, "Always."

chapter twenty-four

Emme

*Today's Learning Objective:
Students will adapt to evolving situations.*

If this first week was any indication, I wasn't especially good at being married.

It started with the small coma I fell into after mixing my allergy meds with Jamie's death brew moonshine margaritas. I woke up the next *afternoon* with hair drool-plastered to my face and sinuses swollen enough to see from space. Ryan, my husband dearest, had already jogged a half marathon and picked up lunch from a cute little café nearby. They'd stopped serving breakfast hours ago, I was told.

He was polite enough to not mention my extra-strength meltdown in his bed the night before or the other night we'd spent in that bed, that one with less clothing and more wild sex. I returned the favor by asking zero questions about the very thick, very hard dick I'd felt rubbing up against me as I fell asleep. That was none of my business.

And then there was the issue of me waiting around for him to come back to the condo on Monday night, my calls and texts going unanswered for hours, only to discover he was filming a commercial outside of Vancouver. Somehow, I'd misplaced the knowledge that my husband left the country.

I'd wanted to talk to him about everything that night. I assigned my class a long, involved independent project that gave me enough time to sit at my desk and blankly stare at my computer while I decided what I was going to do about Ryan—and all the lines we'd crossed.

The responsible answer was to define some boundaries and ground rules. It was the only smart thing to do now that our relationship had taken one helluva left turn. We should've done it from the start, way back when we first floated the idea of this arrangement, but we didn't and we were paying for it now.

It was possible that I was paying for it much more than Ryan was. Or it seemed that way. I was the one who'd escaped his bed and flown into *everything is fine* mode the next day when we could've sat down and talked about what this meant for us.

I didn't think I possessed the skills to have a conversation like that but it was really fun to pretend I could. It was like saying I could water ski because I'd heard of both water and skis.

Still, I'd needed to say something on Monday. Needed an idea of how we continued existing together in this marriage with our new history crowding around us. Most of all, I needed to hear from Ryan. Aside from the massive erection he'd nestled between my butt cheeks like it belonged there, I didn't know what he was thinking. He was being ridiculously polite and giving me all the space in the world since he'd flown off to Vancouver but none of it did me any good because it wasn't all about me anymore.

But if it was, if *I* had to write the rules for us, I'd have a really hard time convincing myself that our friendship would survive another night like that one. It was the absolute best of my entire life but if that became an everyday occurrence for us, I didn't see how we'd ever find our way out of this marriage when the time came to end it. And it would end. That was the whole plan.

I just didn't want to make it hurt any worse than I already knew it would. It wasn't an easy conclusion to reach but I knew I needed my friend more than I needed life-altering sex.

I mean, it couldn't always be life-altering. Right? That was a one-time situation. Highly unusual circumstances. A perfect storm of drunk and lusty and kinda married. No one was having that kind of sex on a regular basis. It wasn't possible. Not even golden-armed football gods like Ryan.

At least that was what I was telling myself.

The next morning, when I'd decided I needed to stay home from school but didn't think to notify anyone other than my principal before going back to sleep, I ended up with forty-two missed calls from my husband and Bowen banging on my bedroom door. Apparently the combo of not answering my phone and not showing up for the drive to school meant everyone agreed I was dead. Or something equally dire.

Poor Bowen though, he'd never be the same after getting the full effect of me screaming my lungs out at him when I opened the door plus, all the side boob my oversized tank top had to offer. He deserved a lot of credit for putting up with me. He waited at the condo while Ryan sent some doctor he casually had on speed dial over for a house call and then went out to pick up lemon-lime soda and bagel crackers for me.

I was a little less spacy once I had some antibiotics for the allergies that'd turned into a sinus infection but not before missing a dress fitting appointment with Wren. The bigger problem was that, in my snotty-throbby-bleary state, I'd also forgotten about this weekend's event. The team's Super Bowl ring party was Saturday on Nantucket and my dress still needed to be tailored.

Of all the events to forget, this one was *not* it.

When Friday afternoon rolled around, I was doing better. I was packed and prepped and could breathe through my nose again. Breathing was so underrated. I'd girded myself for two solid days of football talk and shored my defenses against the inevitable comments about my father.

Though as I headed to the airport where I was due to meet Ryan, it took three rounds of Bowen trying to get my attention for me to realize *I* was Mrs. Ralston.

"Mrs. Ralston," he said once again, impatience touching on each carefully articulated syllable, "Mr. Ralston is on the line for you."

Terrible at marriage. Just terrible.

"Oh. What?" I glanced down at the phone in my hand. I hadn't missed any calls this time. I leaned forward, toward the front seat. "What's going on?"

"Em, we had to land outside Philly." Ryan's voice boomed through the car speakers. "Some kind of mechanical issue."

"Are you okay?" I asked.

"Is that the princess?" McKerry's deep voice came over the line. Ryan had him and a few other offensive linemen with him today for a magazine photoshoot in Dallas. "Lemme talk to her. Princess! How you doin', girl?"

"Go the hell away. My wife doesn't need you bothering her," Ryan said.

"He's fine," I said, laughing.

"See? I'm *fine*," McKerry hollered. "If you ever get tired of this cranky old man, you come talk to me, sweetheart."

"Don't make me fucking kill you, McKerry," Ryan said. He didn't sound murderous. He just sounded tired. I could almost see him rubbing his temples. "Listen, this is going to take a few hours. I'm waiting to hear back about any available planes in the area, but if that doesn't work, we're going to grab a commercial flight."

Bowen and I shared an amused glance at that. I could only imagine the sight of Ryan and his starting O-line wedging themselves into the last available middle row seats of a commercial flight.

In the background, I heard McKerry say, "Can you ask her if she likes jerky? Because I brought a super big bag with three different kinds from this dude that I know who makes it and it's primo quality and I'd share if she wants to hang out."

To me, Ryan said, "Hold on a second." Then, to someone else, "Can you take him, please? No, I don't care. Have him do some wind sprints on the runway. It *is* your problem because I'll leave you here with him if you don't let me talk to my wife for five fucking minutes."

Bowen swallowed a laugh.

"Fuck me," Ryan muttered, though it didn't seem like he intended that for me or Bowen. Then, "Okay Muggs, here's the deal. No matter how this shakes out, we probably won't be able to stop in Boston to pick you up and I don't want you waiting around in a terminal at the off chance that we can. Marcie's working on getting you booked on a commercial flight to Nantucket and I'll find a way to meet you there later tonight. Assuming I haven't been arrested for strangling McKerry and Hersberler."

"Let's do what we can to avoid that," I said.

"Believe me, I'm working on it."

"I'm afraid to ask about Wilcox and Bigelow. Are they fighting over a parachute or tied up in the cargo hold?"

"They're deep into a video game battle. I don't think they've even noticed we landed." I heard a door close and then, "I'm sorry this is such a mess."

"It's really not a big deal," I said. "Isn't there a ferry? I could take the ferry."

"Yeah, it leaves out of New Bedford," Bowen added.

"You're not taking a ferry," Ryan said. "Listen, I just got a text from Marcie that we're getting you on the seven o'clock to Nantucket. You'll have an email any minute now. There will be a driver waiting to pick you up and take you to the house we have for the weekend. The house should be stocked but if there's anything you need, just call Marcie and—"

"You do realize that I've lived on my own—in a major city—for a number of years, right? And that I did keep myself alive through all of those years?" Ryan didn't respond though I was positive the muscles in his jaw were doing a lot of work. "You have nothing to worry about. Everything will be just fine."

Everything was not fine.

In fact, everything went wrong in big ways. What should've been a quick trip over Cape Cod to the islands turned into a national security incident.

When I arrived at the house three hours later than expected, I found Ryan jogging down a carpeted staircase, scowling whole thunderclouds at his phone. I slammed the door behind me.

"I've been looking for you for the past ten minutes," he said, jabbing a hand at me. "Where've you been?"

"I just got here."

"But...how did I beat you here?" he asked as he crossed the room toward me.

When he skimmed a hand down my back, I stared up at him for a second. "You might want to sit down for this."

His eyes went wide. "For what?"

"You probably won't believe any of this and you should know this story comes at a great personal cost," I said, pacing away from the foyer. "But I'm going to tell you anyway."

"Emmeline. What the fuck happened?"

I gestured to a crisp white sofa. After a moment of intense staring —which I won—he went to the sofa and sat down.

I spread my hands out in front of me. "There was a delay."

He pointed to his phone. "But you took off and landed on time. I tracked your flight."

"I can see how this might be confusing. I'm also confused." I wandered in a short circuit between a pair of wingback chairs. "The delay was after the landing. And just for me. Because my vibrator turned on during the flight. And it didn't look like a regular vibrator to anyone involved so I had to explain what it was, and then it wouldn't turn off even when five different people tried to disable it. And everyone on the flight went crazy—crying, praying, screaming. And they called in some really important people with badges and guns because the vibration pattern sounded like a countdown and they thought someone was remotely controlling a detonator. In my vibrator."

Ryan leaned forward, his arms braced on his knees. "Holy shit."

"Yes, that's the correct sentiment." I bobbed my head many times. "I got to talk to a bunch of dudes who took everything very seriously and they had a lot of questions for me about where my vibrator has been—"

"Oh, fuck, no." He pressed his steepled hands to his lips.

"—and the last time I used it—"

"Oh my god. Em." Closed his eyes.

"—and who has access to it."

"Fuuuuck." Shook his head slowly.

"Pretty much, yeah." I went on pacing. "While that little conversation took place, they searched all my stuff. Like, all of it. Thoroughly. Then they decided I'm not a terrorist bomber or anything terrible like that. I tried to tell them from the start I'm just a girl who buys knock-off sex toys that malfunction at the worst possible times but I guess they had to reach that conclusion on their own."

Ryan blew out a long breath and clasped his hands together between his knees. "Are you all right?"

"Yeah." Tears filled my eyes and spilled right over before I could do anything to pull them back. I hadn't let myself experience any of the panic I'd felt until now and it hit me all at once. "But they confiscated the vibrator."

"I'll buy you a new one," he said.

"That's not the point," I sobbed. "I woke up late this morning and didn't have time for—well, that doesn't matter but everything's just a mess now. And I was supposed to work on my plans for field day on the flight but this happened and my life flashed before my eyes. Now I have field day to organize and lesson plans to write for next week, and I might be on the no-fly list. I know the lesson plans don't matter as much because it's the end of the year and that's a shit show anyway but I need to make it look like I'm trying to be good at my job. Especially if my principal finds out I was involved in a sex toy bomb scare."

When I wiped the tears from my face and took a long, shuddering breath, Ryan just watched me, shaking his head. His shoulders started bouncing before the sharp crack of his laughter filled the living room. He fell sideways on the cushions, his face buried in a collection of decorative pillows embroidered with sayings like *Seas the Day* and *Sea, Sand, Surf*.

"It's not funny," I cried. "I was *interrogated*."

He barely made a sound but his entire body shook with the force of his laughter. He clutched the pillows to him as he went on wheezing. Stomping to the sofa, I grabbed a pillow reading *The Beach is My Happy Place* and whacked his denim-clad ass with it.

"I wouldn't react this way if it'd happened to you," I said, snatching away one of his pillows to wail him with it.

"Not only would you laugh your whole ass off," he said, chest heaving, tears running down his cheeks, "you'd never let me forget about it."

I walloped him in the gut. "For your information, I'd be very sympathetic."

"You'd throw me a birthday party with a sex toy bomb scare theme. The invitation would be a fake mug shot and you'd hand out Fleshlights as favors."

"You're a very mean boy." I pulled the last few pillows out from his grip, pounding him with each one. "I'm standing here *crying* because I was detained by like five different government agencies and you're *laughing* about—"

He caught me around the waist and had me pinned beneath him on the sofa before I could even thump him with either of the pillows in my grip. He reached for my wrists, gathering them over my head and holding them flat against the cushions. When he dropped his hips to mine, I shifted against him and his gaze snapped up. I'd only meant to test how much wiggle room I had but it seemed like I'd tested something else altogether.

"I'm not making fun of you," he said softly. "I just—this might be the greatest Emme fuck-around of all time."

I jerked against his hold on my wrists but he didn't let go. "I'm not making this up!"

"I know you aren't," he said, "but it would only happen to you. This one definitely tops the time you got arrested in Montreal."

"I don't think a voicemail from Gary would've gotten me out of it."

"No, but my lawyers would've." When I only blinked at him, he asked, "Why didn't you call me?"

"I don't know. Everything was happening so fast."

He nodded like he understood exactly how it went with bomb scares and cheap vibrators. "Next time, call your husband."

Leaning down, he brushed his lips over mine and I didn't stop him. Not at first. Not when he deepened the kiss and rocked against my hips. But then I remembered myself, remembered that friends were more important than fake-marriage fuck buddies, and I wrenched a wrist free and whomped him with a pillow.

He stared at me, no amusement to be found in his expression. "Something you'd like to say, wifey?"

"I just need— I think we should— Maybe this isn't a good idea?"

It took a minute but a shadow of understanding slowly moved across his features. "What, precisely, isn't a good idea?"

I set a hand on his broad chest, selfishly letting my fingers spread out over the solid plane. "Maybe the physical stuff?" I pushed against his chest, and after a moment he shifted to his knees, taking all his delicious heat and pressure with him. "Boundaries might be good. And maybe some rules too?"

The muscle in his cheek pulsed and his brow lifted. "You don't sound too sure about that."

"I—I am." I wasn't. I desperately wanted to drag him back to me and let someone else worry about what would happen when this marriage ended. I wanted to hook a leg around his waist and see how he performed on a squishy sofa. "It's just that I don't want us to get hurt. Later on."

He glanced away and I knew those words had hit the intended target. He didn't want a messy ending any more than I did. Climbing off the sofa, he cleared his throat and pushed a hand through his hair. "Yeah. No problem."

For better or worse, I stayed stretched out on the sofa, one leg dangling to the floor, the other bent at a sharp angle to give Ryan the room he'd needed between my thighs. Though he marched into the kitchen and didn't look back at me. Guess he didn't want to look our new boundaries in the eye.

I heard the refrigerator open and then, "Muggsy?"

I tucked my hair over my ears. "Yeah?"

"You're never flying without me again."

Since that seemed like the only thing we'd agree on tonight, I called, "Okay. Maybe we give that ferry Bowen mentioned a try. That sounded pretty nonconfrontational."

I heard the refrigerator shut and then the pop of a beer bottle. "I'll think about it."

chapter twenty-five
Emme

Today's Learning Objective:
Students will draw lines and define limits.

IT TOOK ME A MINUTE TO REALIZE IT BUT EVERYTHING IN THIS HOUSE was white. There was a little blue, a little gray, but overwhelmingly white. And now there was also some pink in that palette from the blush that'd rubbed off my face and onto the crisp white duvet cover from flopping onto the huge, fluffy bed in my room.

Once I scrubbed makeup from my skin and made a half-assed attempt at organizing my looks for tomorrow, I opened my laptop to work on my lesson plans but quickly gave up on being productive to watch a cooking competition.

I figured I deserved a minute to recover from the day. From the whole damn week.

The competition was almost over when Ryan knocked on my door. I didn't know which of the remaining five bedrooms he'd selected for himself or why he'd rented such a large house for the two of us, but I knew I had to get up and go to the door. I couldn't stay in bed and invite him inside. Unless I wanted to *invite him inside*.

I shuffled across the extra-plush white rug, regretting my threadbare sleep shorts, equally thin henley shirt, and no bra as I went. None of it said *Let's keep it in the friend zone.*

I opened the door to find Ryan leaning there, his arms braced on either side of the doorframe and his head ducked between his shoulders, like he was doing some sort of standing push-ups. He shifted his jaw, his cheek hollowing with the movement. He didn't look at me when I asked, "What's up?"

"Everything good in here?"

I crossed my arms over my chest. No need to involve the nipples in this. "Yep."

He glimpsed up before returning to his study of the floor. "And you like this room?"

"Yeah. It's great." He nodded but didn't say anything else. After a tense minute, I said, "Listen, if it's going to be weird between us because I—"

"Let me help you," he said, his voice low. "I know how serious you are about getting that orgasm a day. You missed it this morning and the government took your toy so, fuck it. Use me."

"Ex...cuse me?"

"Use me," he repeated, finally dragging his eyes up to my face. No, to my mouth. "It's worked well for you before. Do it again."

"Wh-what does that mean?"

His hand dropped to my waist, pulled me close. "I don't think you need an explanation but I'll talk you through every inch if that's what you want."

"But what about—you know—we should talk about—"

"You know what you need and it's not some fucking boundaries," he said. "Let me give it to you, wife."

Everything inside me softened—and then clenched hard. I gulped down a whole boulder and felt heat spread across my chest, up my neck. Between my legs. And all those smart, responsible reasons for drawing this line between us breezed right out of my head. But I couldn't stop myself from saying, "Just this one time. Just tonight."

"If that's what you need to tell yourself." He pulled a strip of condoms from one pocket and a bottle of lube from the other. Tossed them both to the bed. My eyes all but popped out of my skull. "Anything else you need to talk about?"

I couldn't tear my gaze away from the condoms. And the lube. "I meant, like, logistically, how are we—"

"Let me show you how."

He brought a hand to the back of my neck and the other to the base of my spine, and pulled me tight to his chest as his lips met mine. My body, my stupid, needy, traitorous body melted into him like I'd been waiting for this all week.

"I'm taking these off," Ryan said against the corner of my mouth. My sleep shorts hit the floor as he walked me backward toward the bed. A laugh huffed out of him when he realized I wasn't wearing any undies. "You can tell me how you want to put me to work or I can figure it out for myself. Your choice."

I lifted a hand to the back of his neck to steady myself. As if anything could steady the pulsing, rolling need that'd surged to life inside me. As if there was anything to be done about my body's sudden awareness of Ryan and his heat, his touch. His unbelievably thick erection burning its way through my shirt.

"I'm not sure—" My words trailed off. I didn't even know what I was trying to say. I couldn't think. I was too busy hearing *Use me* on a dark, low loop in my mind. And I realized I didn't care about being responsible anymore.

"What would you do if you were alone?" He dragged his lips down my neck and nipped the crook of my shoulder. One hand traveled over my hip to squeeze my bare backside while the other gathered up my hair in a rough grip that made my scalp prickle. "How would you take care of yourself?"

I pressed my forehead to his chest. A red, burning flush stole across my cheeks. "I just use a toy," I said, the words crammed tight together.

"Is that all you want tonight?" He grabbed my hand, slipped it between my legs. Our twined fingers traced the damp line of my slit. "You want to lie back and enjoy the ride?"

He led our fingers to my clit and it only took a few circles before I moaned into his chest. I couldn't be expected to answer questions. Not in this condition.

"I don't know," I admitted.

A growly noise rasped in his throat as he bared his teeth on my shoulder. "Then let's find out."

My henley flew off and then I was on the bed, floating on a cloud of pillows while I watched Ryan unbutton his shirt. He draped it over a bench at the foot of the bed and his trousers soon followed though he made no move to drop his slim-fitting black boxer briefs.

He collected the condoms and lube and set them on the bedside table, and then shifted to face me, his hands on his hips. Something about the stark efficiency of those moves reminded me that I was naked, completely uncovered and not all that graceful about it. I tucked my knees up and crossed an arm over my torso, concealing a bit of my belly pudge and corralling my breasts in the process. I knew my angles.

And I also knew Ryan had seen me naked last weekend, but in my mind that was more like a dark, moody montage of nudity. Some might even call it tasteful. But this—with two lamps lit, light spilling in from the adjoining bathroom, and the incandescent glow of these white sheets, nothing was left to the imagination.

"Don't do that." He arched a brow at my arm, fully exasperated. "You don't hide when you're all by yourself, a toy between your legs and—what else? What do you use to get you there?" He tapped an index finger on the waistband of his boxers, a mere inch from where the head of his cock strained against the fabric. "Do you watch something? Read something?"

My tongue darted out to wet my suddenly parched lips and I shifted to cover even more of my belly because I was comfortable like this and it gave me something to do other than tell my fake husband about the carefully curated bookmarks I kept in a folder titled Recipe Ideas on my phone.

Another one of those growly, raspy noises from him filled the room and I watched his finger connect with that black waistband, the same finger he'd used to tease my clit a minute ago.

"If that's what you want." He jerked a shoulder up. "We'll see how long it lasts."

He climbed over me, his knees sinking deep into the bed. His hard shaft tented his boxers and everything inside me demanded I reach out, I take hold of him, but he caught my wrist before I could.

"Not yet, little wife." It sounded like a scolding. I would've needled him on that but I forgot everything when he pushed my bent legs apart and settled on his belly between my thighs. Wasting not a second, he spread me open with his thumbs. "Tell me about this toy. What did it do for you?"

He dragged his tongue over my clit like he had all night to tease me. The unhurried pressure of it startled a moan from me and I knew I wouldn't be able to hold back. At this moment, I couldn't remember *why* I'd wanted to hold back to begin with.

"Tell me," he said again, stroking his knuckles down my inner thigh. "How'd it work?"

"Suction," I gasped out as he licked me.

He hummed and the vibration spiraled deep inside me. As if he knew what he was doing to me—he probably did, that arrogant bastard—he ran a hand over my belly, up to my breasts. He pulled a nipple between his fingers and tugged as he licked. "Where do you like to be sucked?"

A wave of pleasure engulfed me quickly and I could barely keep my eyes open, barely breathe. "Clit," I managed.

"Hmm. Let's see about that."

Ryan shifted, pushing my legs wider. He rested his head on my thigh and—and I stopped being able to form words when he sucked at my clit, hard and steady. He kept one hand on my breast, still busy torturing a nipple, and the other between my legs, stroking everything but my aching core.

He pulled off and stared at me with a slight smile. "Yeah, you do like that." He ran a knuckle down the length of my seam, down between my cheeks and then back up again. "Is that all this toy did for you?"

His mouth was wet but he made no move to wipe it off. For a minute, it was the only thing I could focus on. Then I blurted out, "I can't come unless I have something inside me."

Ryan's brows went up and he nodded like we were discussing the type of potting soil I used for my succulents. He went on tracing me with that knuckle, his touch so light that I had to rock toward him to get more. "Like this?"

Two fingers pushed inside me at the same moment his mouth returned to my clit. My back arched off the bed when he drew me between his lips with firm, relentless pulls. Everything inside me tightened, twisted. It throbbed and ached. And I couldn't just lie there anymore. I had to—had to *do* something.

I shifted up, my hands lost in the millions of pillows as I tried to find a better angle, to open myself wider. Because I needed more and I was mindless for it.

"That's right," he said, glancing up at me. "Watch. See what I do to you."

From this angle, I could see his jaw ticking as he treated me to the kind of long, steady suction I love and the way his shoulder rolled with every thrust of his fingers inside me. I saw his hips bucking against the mattress too.

My belly swooped and a fresh new rush of heat moved through me at the sight. I didn't know this would have that kind of effect on him. And this wasn't any slow, lazy thrusting to take the edge off. It was rough, disorderly rutting.

I dragged my fingers through his hair, pulling a little to get his attention. He only sucked harder, leaving me hot, desperate, and clenching while I watched his rowdy hips grind into the mattress.

"I want to know how to get you there," he said, his words hoarse and his eyes hazy. "I need you to come on my tongue."

I gripped my knees, holding my legs open as wide as I could manage. The wet sound of his fingers, the feel of them filling me as he seemed to unravel every one of the nerves attached to my clit made me dizzy with need. I was almost there. Just another minute and all the pressure gathered low in my belly would overflow and he'd—he'd—

"Are you gonna come with me?" I barely recognized my voice, husky and heavy with meaning. He murmured against my damp flesh and nodded, his silky hair sliding against my thigh, and it was like he'd cut the tether holding me back. As the orgasm rippled through me, all I could say was "Oh, fuck, Ryan. *Please.*"

Unable to hold myself up any longer, I dissolved into the pillows, chest heaving and my core pulsing hard around his fingers. I felt like no part of me truly existed beyond that slick spot between my legs. Everything else was secondary. Arms, legs, head—none of it mattered. Just tools for making my body do this bright, stunning thing that I could barely call an orgasm because it eclipsed everything I thought I understood about the kinds of pleasure I could experience.

Then, as I twitched and shuddered through the last waves, Ryan dropped his head to my inner thigh and groaned with such force, I was certain it shook the foundation of the house. He rocked into the mattress at a frenzied pace and I felt his teeth on my skin. He thrust his fingers into me, his palm flat on my clit, and his entire body jerked so hard, his shoulders drove my legs wide open again.

His hips sank into the mattress as he released a long, ragged breath. We were a jumble of limbs with my legs splayed and half his hand buried inside me but neither of us made any move to change that. We didn't say a word, didn't even glance at each other for a minute.

But then I couldn't go another moment without asking, "How did you—I mean, just…from this?"

He tipped his face up to me, head still pillowed on my thigh. "Do you have any idea how hot you are?"

I rolled my eyes. "Let's not get carried away."

"I'm not." A wet noise filled the room as he withdrew his fingers, but instead of wiping them on the sheets, he went back to circling my clit. A shiver darted through me and I tried to twist away from those almost-painful tingles but he held me down with a forearm over my hips. "Don't lie to me and say you stop at one."

"Sometimes I do," I snapped.

He dropped his gaze to my cleft, watching as he tormented my aching clit. "You're not stopping at one tonight."

I wanted to argue with him. Tell him it wasn't his decision to make. But we both knew this wasn't about who called the shots. It was about letting go of the boundaries and rules I thought we needed and it was about letting go of the relationship we had before all of this started. Before we got married and consummated the hell out of it.

"You've made me come in my pants *twice*," he said, still staring at my most private place. "What's it going to take for you to understand that you're the hottest, sexiest, most alluring woman I've ever seen?"

I clutched a pillow to my face. "Don't say things like that."

"Why the fuck not?"

"Because I don't like playing make-believe. You're obviously exaggerating and—"

"I'm fucking *what*?" His brows pinched together and he scowled up at me but he kept stroking my clit. My head wanted to argue. My pussy wanted to be stuffed. It was very confusing. "I've never done this before"

"Done what?" I asked from behind the pillow.

"Gotten off just from going down on someone. And there were five different times when I almost blew it but I kept thinking you'd ask me to fuck you and I wanted you to use me any way you needed. I didn't let go until you'd come on my face."

I edged the pillow aside to catch his eye. "Are you being serious?"

He nodded, the rough scrape of his scruffy jaw on my thigh only making the pressure gathered behind my clit more intense. "There's nothing hotter in the whole fucking world than turning you on and getting you off. Tasting you too. God, you taste so fucking good. And watching you drop that sweet shy girl act? Fuuuuck. That's when I know it's time to go to work."

"It's not an act," I said. "I am shy. Sometimes."

He leaned down, teased my clit with his tongue until my hips started rolling in response. "You're not shy. You just need a minute to remember how it's going to be with us."

I didn't trust the orgasm building deep in my pelvis. My second and third orgasms were always small, more like epilogues of the first than whole new stories. But this didn't feel like an epilogue. It was heavy and low and unfamiliar. It was new—and strange enough that I almost wanted Ryan to stop.

Instead, I asked, "And how's it going to be?"

He shifted to his knees, one hand still moving between my thighs and summoning something from my darkest depths while he stretched over me and planted the other hand near my shoulder. Dipping down, he brushed his lips over mine. "You're my wife," he said. "You let me give you everything you need."

I chased his lips for another kiss. He gave me that—and his fingers inside me with the kind of quick, shallow thrusts I required right now. "Everything?"

"Everything. Always." He caught my bottom lip between his teeth, bit down just enough to send a zing of electricity to my core. "That's *my* rule."

I curled an arm around his neck when the first tremors of the orgasm started. The little waves moved outward from my clit but then I clenched hard around his fingers, hard enough for him to whisper, "Oh, *fuck*" and gaze down at my body like he could see those spasms as they happened. Maybe he could. Maybe I was too far gone to notice.

"You forgot." Ryan picked up my hand from where it rested on his carved abs and pressed his thumb to my palm. Same as I used to do for him after big written exams. "I told you I'd handle field day."

My eyelids felt heavy as I blinked at him. I knew I'd sleep like a stone if I could just stop trailing my fingertips over him, stop curling closer. But there was a ripple of electricity just beneath the surface of my skin and it sparked to life in every place where we touched. I feared it would stop if I fell asleep.

"Hmm. Yeah. I thought that meant you'd swing by and run around for a few minutes."

He shook his head, working the tight muscles between my thumb and index finger. I pulled the blankets up around us higher. "I have it all under control. Nothing for you to do."

I nestled deeper into the pillows to watch him. "But...what does that mean? Because this is kind of a big deal and it needs to be handled a certain way unless I want to tick off everyone. It might sound like a lot of fun for second graders to play dodgeball with McKerry but we have a lot of kids to entertain and a lot of teachers will run me out of town if I leave them with an hour or two to kill before the end of the day."

He huffed out a laugh. "I promise you that won't happen."

"For the sake of my relationships with these people, why don't you just tell me what *will* happen?"

He didn't respond right away. I watched him tenderizing my palm and let my gaze follow the lines of his tattoos up and around his arm, over his shoulder. I'd always wanted to study them like this. Now I wanted to know what they meant.

Eventually, Ryan said, "I played in college with a guy who runs training camps for student athletes. Mostly D1-bound football, basketball, and soccer players, but also swimmers, gymnasts, runners. I gave him a call, asked him to come up with something for a range of ages, and just blow the whole thing out."

I yanked my hand from his grasp so I could sit up to face him. Since we'd scooted to the other side of the bed—away from any damp spots—that basically required me to straddle his lap. His naked lap. We'd each taken a minute to tidy but it did leave us completely undressed. "You hired a pre-college athletic trainer to run field day?"

"If you hate it, we can change it. I had backup plans if that didn't—"

"It's amazing." I brought both hands to his face, cupping his jaw. "I can't believe you did that."

He pulled an irritable scowl. "Why not? You should expect me to follow through. Expect me to have decent plans when I commit to something. It's the barest fucking minimum."

"Your minimum might be a little higher than everyone else's."

"Get used to it either way." He closed his hands around my wrists. "The idea of your entire class going against McKerry in a dodgeball game does have its merits though."

I dropped my head to his shoulder as I laughed. "We'll make that happen." I settled deeper into the crook of his neck with a yawn. "Thank you."

He kissed my shoulder. "Of course."

When he banded his arms low on my hips, I felt the hard ridge of his shaft against my belly. It was as good an opportunity as any so I reached between us and curled my fingers around his length. "I told you a few secrets," I whispered, dragging the backs of my fingers down his arm. "Now it's your turn. Tell me what these mean."

"Mmm." The sound rumbled out of him and shook right through my chest. "I wish I could give you something as impressive as your story but there's not much to explain. The waves are from the seacoast, the trees from the rest of New Hampshire." He motioned to the numbers running down the length of his side. "Dates of my national championships. Not much else."

"But—" I tapped a finger to the scribbled words tucked in between the trees, around the spiral of the waves. And the small flowers raining down his chest between other designs. "What does this say?"

"Nothing, really. Bullshit that sounded cool in college. That sort of thing." When I just went on staring at him, he added, "My artist is really talented and comes up with a lot of great ideas to extend the existing pieces. It doesn't have to mean anything."

But that wasn't Ryan. Not at all. *Everything* meant something to him. Every decision was built upon a thousand others like a monument. And he'd done nothing, absolutely nothing at all, not even once, because it had sounded cool.

"Not that interesting." He cupped my backside and rocked against my core. I was sensitive but not sore, and that mattered. "You know what *is* interesting? How you still haven't told me what you're using with those toys to help you along."

"I can't see why that's something you need to know."

"But it is," he argued, completely serious. "If you're going to use me, you might as well make it an authentic experience."

"I think I'm good for the night." I rolled against his erection just to see if I could get some exasperation from him. Not even a flash. "I'm caught up now. Thanks."

The hand on my ass slipped between my legs to where I was wet all over again. "Are you though?" When I didn't respond, he went on. "You prefer mornings, right? You've said as much a few times. How does that go? Open your eyes, reach for your phone to turn off the alarm, and then—" He followed the quick glimpse I shot my phone on the bedside table. Fatal mistake. A slight smile brightened his eyes as he reached for the device. He held it to me while the other hand stroked my seam. "Show me."

"Why?"

He leaned in, brushed his lips over the shell of my ear. A shudder moved through me. "Because I want to know everything."

"Nothing in it for you?"

"It's all for you," he said, "but that only makes it better for me."

I didn't know if it was the orgasms or the ridiculous adrenaline of the day but those words did something to me. They told me to get moving because there was nothing to be embarrassed about, not after everything else that'd happened tonight. At this point, it would only be crazy to *not* share my porn preferences with my husband.

"I'm lazy," I said, climbing off his lap to a grunt of protest. I settled on my side and tugged him behind me. His arm went over my hip, his hand between my thighs like cupping me was his default position. "I roll over, grab a toy, and visit one of my favorites."

Ryan nudged his knee between my legs, opening me to him as I tapped through my bookmarks. His touch was light, almost absent-minded, as I swiped through the options. I heard him suck in a breath as the videos' titles and cover images flew by. His hips surged against my backside but he didn't say anything, only pressing his lips to the ball of my shoulder and keeping them there.

"Just so you know," I started, fully defensive, "I like a whole bunch of different things. That doesn't mean I want to do any of them. Don't get any ideas or make any wild assumptions. These are just things—"

"I understand how porn works, Emmeline. Pick something."

I tapped the first bookmark and propped my phone on a small pillow. The video opened on a yoga studio with a handful of participants rolling out their mats. The rough exhale on my shoulder told me he knew where this would end up.

"Would you have that toy where you want it by now?"

I nodded as the yoga students started stripping out of their clothes. This video didn't waste any time and I appreciated that. I also liked the amateurish vibe and the slightly above-average bodies that weren't stuffed with implants and waxed within an inch of their lives. It was like a real yoga class that just happened to devolve into an orgy within five minutes.

Ryan reached for something from the other table and returned with the condoms and lube just as the instructor paced the rows of mats.

"Then let's do that." I shifted toward him, onto my back, but he stilled me with a hand between my shoulder blades. "Stay there. So we can watch."

I rolled back to my side in time to catch the instructor stroke a pair of dicks while the students stood in tree pose. Remarkable balance on those two.

I heard Ryan tear open the condom and then the top click open on the lube bottle. He pushed two slippery fingers inside me as the instructor demonstrated the downward dog pose with the assistance of three students. I knew he felt me clench.

Then he was there, the broad head of his shaft pressing against my tender flesh. He rocked back for a second before sliding all the way in, filling me past the point of full, and I screamed at the perfect, overwhelming pressure.

"Shhh. I'm trying to listen," he said.

I wanted to respond with some sharp comment but this position made me feel like he was rearranging my organs and breathing was the most I could manage. I'd never been so thankful for lube as I was right now.

He skimmed a hand up my torso as the yoga class melted into a crush of bodies bucking, licking, stroking. Every possible pairing, every position. Taking my hand, he led me back to my clit. "Show me what you like."

I didn't think twice about obeying. It was *necessary*. When his fingers moved to my nipples and he pulled in time with each thrust, I knew I was a minute, maybe two away from coming. Even if I wanted to, I wouldn't be able to hold back.

"That is—" His words cut off as he groaned into my shoulder. He liked the three women taking turns helping each other with their bridge poses. Not that I could blame him. Incredible teamwork in action. His hips moved faster and I hoped he was close. I wanted this time to be good for him. "Fuck, I like your style, wife."

There was an extreme close-up of the instructor guiding several students at once—she was a really great multitasker—and I jolted as the combination of his fingers pinching my nipple and his cock shuttling into me at the best angle and his teeth on my shoulder knocked me right over the edge. Before I even knew what was happening, the orgasm twisted through me, pulsing and clenching everywhere.

Ryan lashed both arms around my torso and held me steady as he hammered into me. "That was what you needed, wasn't it?"

I managed a nod. I didn't think I could speak.

"Yeah, that's my girl."

He surged up into me once more and I'd swear the groan he shouted into my shoulder left a mark. I felt it just as I felt him swell and throb inside me.

"I have another rule," he rasped against my neck.

"Mmm?"

"This is our new morning routine."

"But what about when you're on the road? Which is very often. What do I do then?"

"You can do it without me," he said with a great deal of reluctance. "I won't like it but I'll accept it. My one condition is that you must tell me everything about it."

"While you're in a bathtub?"

"If I can manage it, yes."

At that, I giggled uncontrollably. I wanted to blame it on the sex but it was more than being fuck drunk. It was everything inside me feeling new and fresh and right, like I'd finally found a version of myself that fit on the first try.

Not for the last time, I said "Okay" to Ryan Ralston without really thinking about what I was agreeing to.

chapter twenty-six

Ryan

Today's Learning Objective:
Students will dismantle watery arguments.

I DIDN'T KNOW HOW EMME DID IT BUT SHE SLIPPED OUT OF BED without me noticing again. My girl wasn't especially quiet or stealthy which meant the only explanation I could piece together was that I slept like the fucking dead when I was beside her. As much as I wanted to notice when she left me, it seemed my brain had other plans.

This left me to wander the halls of this oceanfront estate in search of my wife. I heard the shower running in her room and headed in that direction. We'd abandoned her room last night after she spilled a glass of wine in bed though she blamed that on me because I bit her nipple. I had it on good authority that she liked it when I bit her nipples so the spill was on her.

I leaned against the doorframe, and while I'd decided to not be grouchy that she'd left the bed, returned to her room, and decided to shower without me, that didn't stop me from glaring at the soft, round shape of her in the steam. I didn't make a habit of dropping the tension in my shoulders and chest too often and letting myself see all of her. I did it last night—and last weekend—but I didn't know how to exist without reaching for that restraint.

I had to. I couldn't let myself believe that after all this time she was finally mine. There was always a chance this would blow up on us, on me, and nothing that'd happened in the past twelve hours could change that.

She could be mine for now. For today. For these moments in between the rest of our lives. And I would find a way to survive that the same as I'd survived everything else. There wasn't much else for me to do.

Although I intended to address a few important issues this morning.

The bathroom was thick with steam and the showerheads—there appeared to be five or six—roared like small waterfalls. Emme was busy scrubbing her hair and she still hadn't noticed me.

I kicked out of my athletic shorts and opened the glass door to step in behind her. "I don't like you sneaking out of bed, wifey. Makes me think I'm not doing enough to keep you there."

Emme screamed and a bottle fell from her hands. When I retrieved it, I found her with an arm over her breasts and her legs pressed together like she needed to hide herself from me. "You could've announced yourself," she shrieked.

"You could've noticed that I've been watching you since you started washing your hair."

"When did you turn into such a creep?" She flicked her free hand at me and her eyes widened when her gaze fell on the hard shaft jutting out toward her. As if I could help it. She was *wet*, for fuck's sake. "What do you think you're doing in here?"

"I think it's time for us to have a little conversation instead of you running off to your room or being very busy with cheese or pretending you're asleep for the rest of the flight."

Her lips parted and her eyes went even wider. I laughed. She really thought I hadn't noticed.

"And what would you like to talk about?" she asked. "In the shower, of all places."

"I'd like to start with this." I pried her arm away from her breasts. "No more hiding from me, Em."

"I'm chilly," she said primly. "You let in the cold air."

"It's a tropical fucking rainforest in here. You're all pink." I cupped her jaw, swept my thumb over her rosy cheek. "Let me walk you through what's going to happen next."

"This seems like a kitchen table conversation."

She shifted away from me and reached for a round plastic thing with little nubs on it. I didn't know what it was until she squirted some body wash on it and went to work scrubbing an arm.

It took me a second to snap out of the trance that was a soaped-up Emme but when I did, I grabbed the round thing and took over the job. "That's tough shit because we're having the conversation here. Now, I'm going to say a few things that you're not going to like but do me a favor and try to listen."

"Really setting yourself up for the win," she said.

"I meant everything I said last night."

"About field day? Great, because your version sounded a lot better than anything I've come up with and my ass is going to be toast if I have to pull everything together in two weeks by myself."

"About field day," I said, "and everything else too."

Emme dropped her gaze to the tiled floor. She was quiet for a minute while I washed her arms very, very thoroughly. "You said a lot of things."

"I meant all of them." I turned her to face the wall as I started on her back. "That's what I want. Now you have to tell me what you want."

I went into most games expecting to win but that wasn't going to work here. Instead, I devoted all of my attention to washing her back. I wasn't going to let myself think about what would happen if she turned around and said it felt like she'd waited years for this and life finally made sense. Just as I wasn't going to let myself think about what would happen if she decided she wanted to enforce those boundaries and rules again.

"I don't know," she said quietly. "I don't know what it means for us to…to complicate things like this. For our friendship and this fake-marriage thing."

I had to choke back an irritable growl at *this fake-marriage thing*. I'd sooner survive her reaching in and ripping my beating heart from my chest than I would hearing those words ever again.

"I'm worried it will make all of this a lot harder," she continued.

I stepped closer, letting my shaft slide into the plump curve of her backside. "It's going to be hard either way."

She slapped a hand to the wall, laughing. "I just—I don't want to lose you. I feel like it's already so much more complicated than we thought it would be and sex is jumping up to a whole new level of difficulty."

"I mean, if you do it right."

She laughed but it was an indulgent laugh, like she wanted me to know it was a good joke but I was pushing my luck right to the edge. "I don't want to lose you," she repeated. "That's my bottom line. When I think about the end of the summer, when your deals are closed and Grace is married, I get scared because I know this will end and I can't lose you in the process."

I stroked the scrubber down her sides as I weighed the risks in front of me. I could all but guarantee she shut me down or go on holding myself back until the end of my days. I was fucked either way so I asked, "What if it doesn't end after the summer?"

She whirled around, her expression panicked. "Sooner? Not before the wedding, right?"

"No, silly girl. I'm not missing that wedding for the world. I need to meet this jam farmer." I turned her back to the wall. "We talked about the end of the summer because we had to get through so much during that time."

She wagged a finger at me over her shoulder. "No, you wanted to get back to your life by the end of the summer and be done with this."

I swatted the finger away. "I never said any part of that."

"But—yes, you did! You said it that day in my apartment. When we were looking at our schedules and you screwed up my window."

I ran the scrubber down the line of her back and around the flare of her hips while I tried to figure out how the hell I gave her the impression I wanted to hustle my way through this marriage. "The window was already broken," I said, though it didn't matter and it wasn't going to fix this new issue of ours. "It continued to disintegrate when I looked at it a little too long."

After a pause, Emme said, "I thought you wanted to get this over with as quickly as possible. That you were just counting down the days and...and when your deal is done, we'll be done. And it hurts whenever I think about it because I *love* you, Ryan, and I miss you when you're not with me but I know I'll break if we spend the next month in bed together and then it's just over. I don't want to break and I don't want to lose you. I *can't*."

Blood whomped in my ears. I rested my head on her shoulder for a second before realizing the better place for me was on my knees. When I hit the tile, I skimmed my hands up the insides of her legs. She took a step out when I nudged her. "You won't lose me," I said, my mouth following the crease where her thigh met her cheek. "You will never, ever lose me."

"You can't promise that."

"I can." I swept the scrubber up her legs, over her ass. Across her toes, which made her giggle and jolt. Between her legs, my fingertips slid along the pulsing heat of her seam. Everything squeaky clean. Perfect for making a mess all over again. "We already have the summer planned. Let's just see where that goes."

"I think I know where that goes and it's to your bedroom."

I sank my teeth into the ripe round of her cheek and pressed two fingers inside her. She slapped the wall and dropped her head down. I licked my way up her crease. "That room's been nothing but good to you, wifey."

"You play dirty," she said on a moan.

"That's what you think? You have no idea how I play. I haven't even stepped on the field yet." She didn't say anything for a few minutes while I licked and bit and teased until her legs shook. Then, "No deadlines. Give me that and I'll give you what you want right now."

Her shoulders hitched and I had the distinct sense she was going to tell me to fuck right off. This was how it would end—my wife would leave me kneeling in a shower on Nantucket, and the one relationship that'd gotten me through the worst days would wither.

But then she held out a hand to me, saying, "Come here," and all the tightness in my chest dissolved.

I closed my arms around her torso, holding her tight as the water washed over us. "I love you too, Em." That bliss lasted for about ten seconds before I groaned up at the ceiling. "*Fuck.* I didn't bring a condom. I'll be right back. Don't move. No, actually, keep that clit warmed up for me and—"

"I can't get pregnant. I'm on a bunch of meds that shuts it all down." She glanced down at my cock, her lips pressed together in a disapproving frown. "But I don't know where that's been."

"It was in the back of your throat last weekend." The frown deepened. "All clear. Nothing for you to worry about."

She squeezed my hand. "Then don't leave me."

I parked myself on the tiled bench—*fuck*, that was cold—and led Emme to face forward in my lap. "Right here for me," I said, holding her waist as she scooted back. "There you go, gorgeous. That's my girl."

She gripped my forearms, bracing herself. My legs were slippery and her feet didn't touch the floor. She wobbled but I wasn't letting her go anywhere. "I've never done it like this. This position. It's kind of weird, not being able to see you."

"Do you want to stop?"

She shook her head and a spray of water droplets from her hair hit my chest. This bench sat right at a convergence point of all the showerheads. "No, but I don't want you to tease me if I do it wrong."

"Do you not understand how good sex is with you?" I held myself steady at her entrance, the head of my cock throbbing at her unrelenting heat. "It's not good. It's fucking insane. I'm thirty and it wasn't until our wedding night that I realized I could rebound that fast. I'll never be the same again and I can't even be mad at you for it. If you're doing it wrong, it's still going to rewire my nervous system. Are you ready yet?"

"Okay, okay, calm—*oh fuck*."

I banded my arms over her torso and rocked up into her as the shower spray hit right between her legs. Within a minute, she was already clenching hard around me.

"I can't help but notice," I said, her nipples clothespinned between my fingers, "but this shower could fit an entire yoga class."

Emme belted out a deep laugh and I knew I loved my wife—and there was a good chance she loved me the same way too.

Claudia: "Boston's bling party sparkles on Nantucket; Ralston's offensive line shines"

Claudia: <link to Barstool Sports>

Amber: how cute are they? oh my god it's too much

Claudia: isn't that dress gorgeous? That color would make me look seasick but it's incredible on Emme

Mom: She's an angel!!!!

Chloe: I love that she wears such fun dresses to these events

Mom: So much fun!!! Such a sweetheart!

Amber: someone needs to convince Ryan to bring her home so we can tell her these things

Ruthie: good luck convincing Ryan to do anything but precisely what he wants

Mom: You know he's very busy, Ruth

Gramma CeCe: let the boy live. He deserves some room to breathe. It's bad enough the whole world is watching this courtship.

Chloe: I'm just waiting for him to decide to take us on another family vacation. We'll get plenty of time with her then.

Amber: You mean another one of his holiday avoidance tactics? And yes, I'm waiting for that too

Claudia: fingers crossed for a nice, quiet cushion between games this Christmas

Ruthie: I'm praying for a bye week. I hate when he takes us all on vacation for the holidays but has to leave after a day or two

Claudia: <41 images attached>

Amber: how do you find all these photos?

Claudia: I'm a dark web huntress

Mom: Claudia! Don't joke about things like that!

Claudia: who said I'm joking?

Chloe: Ryan can't bring Emme home because he's too busy looking at her like he wants to unhinge his jaw and swallow her whole

Gramma CeCe: they'll make beautiful babies

Claudia: Gram, can we not instigate this early in the morning? Please I'm begging

Mom: I've been waiting so long for a grandbaby!

Chloe: I have no more words

Claudia: ...and look what we've started

Mom: I'm aware you have children, Chloe. I was there for all 39 hours of you laboring through the first delivery and 44 minutes for the second.

Chloe: then why do you keep talking about wanting a grandbaby? YOU HAVE 2

Mom: Good heavens. Don't you know when your children are sad and unhappy, Chloe?

Chloe: Of course but I'm also aware that they exist, which is all I'm asking you to do

Mom: Then you understand how helpless you feel as a mother when those babies are unhappy.

Mom: Your brother has been unhappy for a terribly long time. He's been so lonely. He has all of us but everything about family has been hard for him since we lost your father.

Chloe: Oh come on! That's not true! He's insanely rich and famous and before that, he was insanely popular. He has everything he could possibly need.

Mom: It might look that way but the money and fame can only fix so much.

Chloe: He doesn't even participate in the family group chat!

Ruthie: Remind me again who set up hefty college funds for those kids of yours?

Gramma CeCe: Mind yourself, Ruth.

Mom: The only time he wasn't lonely was when he was with Emme. A light would come on when he was with her and it would burn out when she left. I see these photos and the first thing I notice is that the shadows have finally cleared from his eyes. He looks like himself again and it's been too long since he did.

Mom: Now that they've found each other, all I want is for him to be happy. Maybe he can have a family to call his own. He needs more to love than football.

Claudia: excuse me why am I crying

Claudia: extremely rude for you to make me feel my own feelings

Amber: it's so funny how we only have these conversations over text. Like we'd never say a word of this face to face

Chloe: probably because we spent 5 years watching our father die on a hospital bed in the dining room and that shit never really goes away

Chloe: I'm sorry. Sometimes I'm a self-centered bitch.

Amber: yeah we know

Ruthie: It's probably good that we're getting all of this family mess out now. Less to horrify Emme with later.

Mom: He's been awfully generous to all of us. I think we can give him the time he needs to come around.

Claudia: or we could break into his condo and just wait for them to show up

Gramma CeCe: give him a few more weeks.

Claudia: then we'll break in!

Gramma CeCe: I'll bring the crow bar and hooch

Ruthie: It's not a great idea to put that in writing

Claudia: did it leave a scar, Ruth?

Ruth: what?

Claudia: when corporate law surgically removed the humor and joy from your body?

chapter twenty-seven

Emme

Today's Learning Objective:
Students will engage in structured play.

I couldn't explain it but I'd needed to wander around a grocery store this afternoon. Ryan had a prepared meal service and a grocery shopping service, and all of it was fine but I left school knowing I wanted something more.

Bowen pushed the cart after picking me up from school and we talked about his granny's pork butt recipe. It did sound pretty great but Ryan was training and traveling this week and Ines was never at the condo so I had no one to feed.

The strange part was that I wanted to feed someone. I hadn't felt that in a long time.

I returned home with a whole bunch of random—a ton of seasonal veggies, a wild rice blend, some fun herbs and spices, and a perfectly crusty loaf of grainy bread. I didn't know what I was going to do with it. There was no recipe or meal that came to mind but it was all too good to pass up.

I unpacked the items and smoothed my hands over the surface of the countertop. I'd lived here for more than a month but I hadn't cooked anything other than reheating leftovers or toasting a bagel. The meal service helped with that but also, I hadn't wanted to cook anything. The desire wasn't there anymore.

But now, seeing the veggies and herbs on the counter, I felt something.

Then my phone rang and my mother's face flashed on the screen, and all those feelings dried up. I grabbed a sparkling water before answering. "Hi, Mom."

"You would not believe that shoot I've had," she said, the breathless words coming quickly. Either on the treadmill or spin bike. Mom never did just one thing. "We can usually count on Aruba but it rained for twenty-one days straight. They had to fly us to St. Lucia just to find some sun. It was an enormous improvement as far as the weather went but they clearly weren't prepared for a production of this size."

I strolled out to the deck. The shoots for her reality show always had these issues. Not enough drama on-screen, gotta add some acts of god to the mix. "That must've been tough."

"I went weeks without reliable cell service," she said. "I would've called sooner if I'd known you were engaged. Congratulations!"

"Oh, yeah, thank you." I glanced at my ring. It was weird being married but keeping it a secret. I kept forgetting that no one else knew. "I didn't want to bother you while you were taping."

"Bother me? You're my *daughter* and you're getting *married*. It's no bother, Emme." There was a voice in the background announcing an increase in incline coming up. "I was just so surprised that I had to hear about it from that person your father married. She called to ask about my availability. Were you aware she's throwing you a little party?"

All at once, I felt like a shaken bottle of soda with pressure gaining force as it gathered at the top. My mother knew exactly what she was doing with phrases like *that person* and *little party* and *my availability*. She drew the lines and I was allowed to color inside them. Anything outside those lines was a betrayal of the worst kind. There was not an inch in between.

"Yeah, Danielle mentioned that," I said.

"I politely informed her that the *mother* of the bride would be the only one to host a gathering," Mom went on, still breathing hard but her sharp tone was enough to send a shiver of dread through me. This could very easily turn into her ranting about Danielle for two hours. And I was complicit. I'd *spoken* to her, of all the inexcusable things. "You just know anything she did would be so tacky. Not a drop of class in that girl. I really hope you didn't give her the impression you'd attend."

Whatever Danielle was planning, my mother would plan to double it. Triple it. Make it so huge and excessive that I disappeared from it entirely but she emerged with the satisfaction of winning a game where she was the only one keeping score.

Hell, she was the only one playing the game. Danielle did a good job of staying out of Mom's dance space but I also knew she didn't worry about anyone else's opinion of her. She said it was none of her business and that she'd never get out of bed if she tried to care about making everyone happy.

"I didn't really commit to anything," I said, aiming for a disinterested tone.

"That's a relief." After blowing out a labored breath, she went on. "I'm so happy for you, darling. It's such an exciting time. We'll have to put together a list of designers you like for your dress. Custom, of course. Everyone will want to know who you're wearing. Show your father and his child bride how well you've done for yourself."

"Those things cost more than my entire salary."

She scoffed. "That's what you have a fiancé for, my dear."

I took a long sip of water instead of responding.

My mother did well for herself these days. The reality shows, brand deals, and appearances gave her a fine income of her own, and her current husband Dell had money like Scrooge McDuck—he could swim in it. But it hadn't always been that way.

The child support situation from my dad wasn't great. He always gave me lavish gifts—clothes, electronics, a car when I turned sixteen—but he'd fought to pay my mother as little as possible. Things were worse after her second marriage to Gary, who couldn't keep a penny to his name. She learned some hard lessons and went into her third marriage with an excellent prenup. When that whole thing went to hell, she left with a golden parachute.

If I ever asked her for money, she'd help me. But my mother wasn't one to offer. There was no trust fund, no allowance. Not from her.

There was a trust fund from my father though, one he'd restructured to prevent me from accessing until I was *forty-five* because he wanted to keep my mother away from it as long as possible.

My mother had never forgiven him and I had some complicated feelings too, though it was the size and force of her reaction to that move rather than the events leading to it that hurt me most of all.

The trust fund wasn't amended until my last year of college, a few months before I was scheduled to gain access to it when I turned twenty-two. It came after a Christmas spent on a private island with my father, Danielle, and my half brothers. Though I didn't share the holiday with them since I was shipped home early.

I still couldn't remember what I'd said to set my father off. Probably some snarky comment or a petty complaint. Nothing that should've resulted in him throwing a heavy-bottomed rocks glass at my face and splitting my cheek.

By the time Danielle came back from the beach with the boys, glittering shards of crystal covered the tile floors. He hadn't stopped after the first glass. He went on screaming that I was spoiled and ungrateful. That I was turning into the same sort of manipulative whore my mother was.

My father was quick to anger and I'd heard all of it before but something broke in me that day. Any ability I'd had to tolerate that relationship dried up while blood and tears dripped down my face. Any connection we'd shared was severed when he told Danielle to get me out of his sight.

He'd barked orders at her about letting me find my own way home but she didn't listen. Somehow, his rage always bounced right off her. She fixed my face and promised to fix my father too, even if he was a mule who wouldn't change easy. She booked me a first-class seat, swore she'd do everything in her power to make it right, and hugged me harder than anyone had before.

A few weeks later, the letter arrived with a chunk of legal documents. He apologized for losing his temper though quickly transitioned to telling me I'd made inexcusably poor choices by pursuing education as a degree and sticking with it. Since I'd declined his invitation to work for him, he believed it was time for me to live with the consequences—and do it without the aid of a trust fund.

I hadn't spoken to him since that holiday. He'd left voicemails though I didn't listen to all of them. The first year or two, I deleted everything. I was too scarred, too exhausted from carving him out of my heart and cauterizing those wounds to try. But then Danielle insisted he was making changes. He was seeing a therapist, trying meds, cutting back on the alcohol. Some of the messages sounded like he was reading a script or he'd called to fulfill a requirement. Danielle's or the therapist's, I didn't know. He promised to do better, to clean up his act, to fix his mistakes. I wasn't sure he knew what all of those things entailed. Others were emotional. In the last year, he'd cried in all of them. It sounded like he'd discovered that one parent taking out their vendetta against the other parent on the kid wasn't healthy for anyone.

Sometimes, he suggested he'd be willing to turn over the trust fund if I visited him in Chicago. Maybe it was pointless to leave that money on the table but I couldn't bring myself to go crawling back to him. If he wanted to fix things, it wouldn't start with me making the first move.

Though the money would've been nice. It would've helped a lot, especially living in an unconscionably expensive town like Boston—and on a teacher's salary. But I managed. And through it all, my mother's primary contribution was outrage. There were endless tirades about his desire to use money to punish anyone who crossed him, and convoluted legal strategies she'd invented from talking to someone married to a lawyer. She couldn't let it go. Couldn't stop with her vendetta against him.

And now she wanted me to use Ryan's money to land another hit. As if any of it mattered.

I knew she was thinking Ryan would see to it that I had a custom gown. She knew what he earned, what his endorsements were worth. She was more plugged into the game than most of the analysts on sports networks. Nothing off the rack for the highest-paid player's bride.

"I'll think about it," I said.

"It's so sweet that you ended up with Ryan after all these years," she drawled. "But don't let that fool you. They all cheat. It's never a matter of if, it's when. They just can't help it. You wouldn't believe the amount of women throwing themselves at these boys."

I dropped my head back. The fizzy pressure inside me slowly turned acidic as it sloshed in my belly. "Good to know."

"I don't say any of this to take away from your happiness or discourage you one bit," she went on without a hint of irony. "You know firsthand how it is. This one won't be any different."

I didn't want to argue with her. I couldn't. There was no sense in telling her that Ryan simply wasn't like my father or any of my stepdads. She'd never believe it. She'd have too many examples to back up her claims. And the sad part was that I had seen it all.

"I'll put you in touch with my lawyer. We can't have you ending up in the middle of nowhere without two pennies to your name, the same way your father left us."

"I think I'm okay on the lawyer front," I said. "I'll take care of it."

"I started finding little things," she said, ignoring me. "First it was earrings. Then it was a silk scarf. A diamond watch. I thought he was saving them for my birthday or just a surprise for some rainy day." She drew in a breath and I could almost see the sad, faraway look she'd get in her eyes whenever she talked about the end of her first marriage. "But then my birthday would pass and the trinkets would be gone, and I knew he'd never meant them for me."

My stomach pitched and I had to press a hand to my mouth to talk myself down from the sudden wave of nausea. I knew all about trinkets that hadn't been meant for me.

"You can tell yourself he's different," she said. "He might be. Until he's not."

"Mom—"

"I know you're happy now, honey, and I'm happy for you. But you have to be smart too. Don't make my mistakes."

I let her talk through the rest of her workout, murmuring along as she debated the best months for a wedding and which wedding planners lived up to their reputations. Through it all, I told myself Ryan was different. I was different.

And this marriage was different too because it wasn't meant to last.

Or so I'd thought.

"I LIKE THIS FOR YOU, BUT IT'S NOT GOING TO FIT IN THE CHEST." I pulled a dress from the rack and handed it to Jamie. "I have another one in here somewhere that's sort of a wrap dress, but still fancy. That style might work better for you."

"I could always stuff my bra," Jamie said, holding the dresses up to herself and studying her reflection in the walk-in closet mirror. She volunteered with a community arts program and one of their major donors was hosting a special event. "Get some of those rubbery cutlets and shove 'em in there. I might do that just to see some poor dude's reaction to it at the end of the night."

"Or you could get the dress altered."

"It's *your* dress," she cried.

"I don't mind." I handed her the wrap dress. "I have more than I could possibly use and I'd rather see you wearing it than leave it to catch dust."

She gave the mirror a side-eye glance. "Still don't think I want to get your dress tailored."

"Try them on," I said as I heard the house phone ring, "and decide if you like them first. Then we'll make them fit."

I grabbed the wall phone in my bedroom and told the building's concierge to come up with the package they'd received for me. I still kept my things in the upstairs room. I was comfortable up here and Ryan's schedule was packed with endorsement work, business meetings, and conditioning for the upcoming season. From now until the start of training camp in July, he was on the road four or five nights a week. It made little sense to move myself downstairs, even if the bathtub was exceptional.

I ducked back into the closet—a room almost twice the size of my bedroom in the old North End apartment—and found Jamie frowning at her reflection. The dress was way too big in the chest, but everything else fit perfectly. "I have to run to the door to get a delivery," I said, "but that's adorable on you and I'm going to kick and scream if you don't take it."

"If only I had your knockers," she called after me.

"Trust me, you don't want this kind of trouble," I shouted back.

A buzz sounded at the door as I descended the stairs. The concierge insisted on bringing it inside for me—it really freaked them out whenever I tried to carry my own packages up from the front desk or the door—and I sent him off with a cranberry macadamia nut cookie.

Audrey had sent me home with a dozen, as if I needed to be alone with that many cookies. I still didn't know how she found the time to bake something new from scratch every day. I considered it an accomplishment if I made it through without an afternoon nap.

"Anything good?" Jamie asked as she came into the kitchen, one dress slung over her arm.

When I didn't respond, she pointed to the box on the island. "Oh, I don't know." I glanced at the mailing label and realized it was addressed to me. I didn't remember ordering anything, but that hardly mattered. Not a day went by without us receiving engagement gifts or promotional items from Ryan's endorsements or yet another soldering iron for Ines. "Not sure," I murmured, tearing into the package.

Another box sat inside the cardboard box, this one an elegant matte black with a soft satin ribbon and an envelope tucked under the bow. The card wasn't signed though I had a good idea who it was from.

WIFEY,
I'LL ALWAYS KEEP MY PROMISES TO YOU.

"Well, isn't that precious," Jamie said, reading over my shoulder. "What's the promise? What did he send?"

Once I had the ribbon untied and the black lid removed, I found a bunch of small boxes in different shapes and sizes. All tied with the same creamy ribbon. I tore into the first one and yelped when I found a thick, curved vibrator staring up at me.

I slammed the lid back in place. "Oh my god," I whispered to myself. "I can't believe he did this."

"Okay, so y'all make some spicy promises," Jamie drawled, peeking into the black box.

"No, no, it's from the other weekend when I almost ended up in prison because we confused a vibrator for a weapon of mass destruction."

"Well, that's been known to happen."

"And Ryan promised he'd replace the vibe." I motioned to the package. The one I realized was full of sex toys. "But he can't just send one, can he? He has to clear out a whole store."

"Sounds like fun. What else do we have in here?"

I rubbed my temples as Jamie set each individual box on the countertop. About twenty in all, bringing an increasingly deep blush to my face and neck as I loosened the ribbons and discovered the adult treasures waiting for me.

"He's in Toronto this week," I said, as if that explained anything. "Shooting an ad campaign for a car company. Or maybe it's the hair care products? Or is it both? Probably both. He likes to cram in as much as he can."

"Really," she said, holding up a butt plug with a sparkly gem on the end and a set of nipple clamps that were probably solid gold. "Never would've guessed."

"That's not what I meant," I said

She held up two more vibrators. "This is high-end shit. I hope you appreciate what you have here."

"I'll do my best." I closed the lids and gathered the discarded ribbons. I eyed one item before putting it away. "What's this about?"

Jamie glanced over at the series of round, black bands of varying sizes. "Cock rings," she said with a slow nod. "Keeps things...*robust*. Makes it last a little longer."

"What made him think we needed that?" I asked myself. "I'm going to have a talk with this boy when he's done for the day."

With a cackle, Jamie grabbed the dress she'd left on a kitchen stool. "You have plenty to amuse yourself with here, so I'll be on my way. Thank you again for helping me find something to wear. You're my savior."

"No cutlets! Get it tailored," I said. "Don't you dare bring it back to me."

She came in for a side hug. "Have fun with all this. Or with pestering him. Maybe that's part of it. Whatever works for you, sweet pea."

When the door closed behind Jamie, I reached for a cookie and surveyed these gifts. Some were surprising—the plugs and clamps weren't on my bingo card—while others were very interesting. There were several toys similar to the one I'd lost to the Air Marshals, and they all looked like a good time. A few clit toys in wacky shapes.

Strawberries, flowers, butterflies. They looked like something I'd enjoy. And there were a bunch of traditional vibes too. No stone unturned, not with these sex toys.

I bit into the cookie. "This husband of mine."

I WAS IN BED WHEN RYAN FINISHED FOR THE DAY. HE SENT A TEXT saying he was heading back to his hotel and then another asking if it was too late to talk. I laughed at that and glanced at the black box I'd left on the end of the bed.

"Not tonight," I murmured as I shot back a response.

He called a few minutes later, the screen mostly dark as he walked into his hotel room. "How's my wife tonight?"

I heard him flop into a high-backed chair and heave out a weary breath. He sounded tired. A light on the other side of the room cast his features in a soft, golden glow, though his eyes were still shadowed by the inky night.

"I'm all right," I said. "Long shoot?"

"Really fucking long." His hand went to the back of his neck. I watched the pull of his biceps as he kneaded the tension there. "But I want to hear about you. How was your day, Muggsy?"

I gave him a rundown on my class and their mid-week squirreliness, Jamie shopping my closet, and Audrey's cookies. He'd like them. He was a fan of throwing cranberries into every last thing. Such a New England boy. Then I went into detail about the amount of time Ines was spending with Jakobi (a lot) and Grace's ongoing debates with herself about ten different wedding issues (to distract herself from real issues).

"Anything else?" he asked, clearly pecking around for mention of his delivery.

"That covers it," I said, propping the phone up against a pillow beside me. "I want to hear about your stuff now. What did you do today?"

He ran a hand through his hair as he let out a dry laugh. "I sent you something."

"Oh, yeah, that." I bobbed my head. "It was delivered this afternoon."

"I'm aware of that."

"Hmm." I grinned, prodding him to continue.

He stared at me for a long moment. "I was notified the minute you received it. I've spent the past"—he turned his wrist to catch the time—"six hours thinking about you opening that package." His voice was suddenly low, rougher. I realized I'd pressed my thighs together and balled my fingers in the sheets at some point. "Tell me what you think of your new toys, wife."

"I think you're a little unhinged with all this," I said.

"*Unhinged* is having a vibrator confiscated by the air marshals." He stared at me, my shadowy room to the midnight quiet of his suite. "Do you have a favorite?"

"You can't possibly think I dropped everything to try them all out. Just one after the other, all day long. Nothing but me and my new toys." I stared at him for a moment, basking in this opportunity to torture him. "Or is that exactly what you're thinking?"

He tipped his head back against the chair, the long line of his throat exposed and his lips parted. "*Em*."

I wanted to climb into his lap and lick my way up that neck. "Yes?"

"Tell me." His groan echoed so loud, I almost believed he was in the room with me. "*Please. I'm dying here.*"

I climbed out from under the covers and dragged the box closer. I turned the screen to give him a look. "I was too busy organizing these items to try them out. And learning what half of them are," I added.

"Then you should explore," he growled.

I laughed. "What?"

"Pick one and give it a try," he said, his words clipped, "while I listen."

Another laugh. This one felt like a crumpled ball of tinfoil. "I...I'm not sure I can."

"I know you can."

I waved a hand at the box. "These things haven't been charged."

He shook his head, giving me a sharp smile that felt like his fingertips running down my spine. "Baby, did you think I'd send you toys only to have you wait to use them until they're charged? Fuck no. I wanted you to be able to play."

"Then how—" I didn't finish that sentence. I wasn't sure I wanted to know how that worked.

"White glove service," he said as if that explained everything.

"What if Ines comes home?" I asked, suddenly breathless. She divided her time between work, kung-fu, and Jakobi, but I didn't want to bet on that. "She could walk in."

"Explain to me then how you managed to get yourself off once a day without Ines interrupting any of those times," he said. "And in that postage stamp of an apartment."

"I don't know how it worked, Ryan," I snapped, all out of patience. "I just know that it did."

He arched a brow, gazing at me in challenge for a moment before saying, "The purple one? With the curved end? I think you might like that."

It was *exactly* like the toy I'd lost. As I turned the package over, I realized it was much better than my old toy. All of these were. No random vibes from Amazon that didn't hold a charge and would consistently die at the most crucial moments. These were ultra-premium sex toys, just like Jamie said. I was pretty sure one of those plugs was solid platinum.

"What are you thinking, Em?"

I made a vague noise while I sifted through the toys. "Did you pick all of these out? By yourself? Or did you put an assistant on the job?"

"I spent *hours* choosing those for you. I read all the specifications, the reviews. I thought about you reaching for them while I was away—

and then showing me how they worked when I came home. But I don't think I can wait that long." With a growl, he scraped a hand down his chest and I *felt* that touch. "Close the door. Lock it."

I didn't think before crossing the room, flattening a palm to the panel, and then flipping the lock. Didn't consider what I was doing when I opened the package and cleaned off the purple toy with the enclosed wipes. They smelled like cucumber and aloe, which was maddeningly pleasant, and yep, this bad boy was fully charged.

"Take off your clothes," he said. Another order. Another *growl*.

I set my phone on the side table while I yanked off my pajamas, giving Ryan a fantastic view of the ceiling and pulling another impatient rumble from his chest.

"Calm down," I said.

"Get in bed, Emmeline."

I slipped under the covers and propped up my phone beside me, bringing my husband back into view. "It's funny," I started, shifting against the pillows to get comfortable, "how I haven't heard you unzip anything yet."

His smile in the dim light seemed dangerous. "Is that what you want, wifey?"

A startled, breathy noise panted out of me. I felt tight everywhere, desperately so—and silly too. Like I could do any outrageous thing and I'd get another one of those rare, precious smiles from him. I could say *anything* and he'd beg me for more. That I'd always be safe with him.

And I knew I *adored* this man. That he was *mine*. That it didn't matter how any of this had started or where it was going because it was real and true, and he belonged to me. He'd *always* belonged to me.

"I love you," I said, the cracking out of me like an accusation. "I've always loved you but *I love you* and I had to-to—"

"I know, Emme. I love you too."

"Like I'm your wife?" I asked. "Is that how you love me?"

"You *are* my wife," he said, his voice like sandpaper. "And that's the only way I ever want to love you."

Tears welled in my eyes, but I couldn't stop smiling. "Then it only seems fair for you to play with me." I balled my fists under the sheets. I didn't want him to see the tremor in my hands. Didn't want him to know I felt like my chest was splitting open, like my heart wanted to break free from the cage of my ribs. "I don't want to be alone."

"Then you won't be." When he stood, he angled his phone down. It was too dark for me to make anything out more than shadowed outlines but he added, "Joggers. No zipper."

I couldn't help but sigh. His backside was downright biteable in those pants. "You're so cute in joggers. You should wear them more often."

"Baby, I'll wear whatever the fuck you want, but right now, I need you to get to work."

A shiver moved through me, a cool, spiraling snap of energy. "This one?" I held up the purple toy. I loved the look of the suction element. That thing was going to destroy me. And the vibe element had a nice, thick head. Combined, these features would scramble my brain in about a minute. "What do you want me to do with it?"

His head dropped back against the chair. "Just let me be there with you."

I noticed his shoulder hitch every few seconds and I watched, a breath trapped in my chest. I faded into the sounds of rustling fabric and his ragged exhales as I moved the device between my legs. It was heavy and plush, and the anticipation that'd built in the past few minutes had me shuddering at the slightest touch.

I switched on the vibe and dragged it along my seam. I was already wet and clenching, and the deep, rolling rumbles of the toy hit me like a series of tiny, pinprick orgasms. "Oh my god," I gasped.

Ryan groaned and I heard the light slap of skin. "You have no idea how fucking beautiful you are," he said, each word bitten out.

I held the toy to my clit, but I had to pull back. It was too much, too fast. I tried again with a bit less pressure and a long string of unintelligible swearing spilled from my mouth. I twisted and shook with every wave of vibrations. I knew my neck and cheeks were beet red, my body covered in a fine sheen of sweat. A minute in and I was already working hard for this orgasm.

"What are you doing?" he asked.

"Teasing my clit."

Another gorgeous growl and then, "Show me."

Honestly, I didn't know where I found the audacity. I kicked away the blankets and grabbed the phone, holding it against my inner thigh. I didn't know if the angle was any good and I refused to let myself think about how I looked in this position. There was no way in the world for this to be flattering—or just not awful—but I was in too deep to care about any of that.

"Fuuuuck." I heard him swallow. "You are fucking perfect."

I dragged the head down my seam and held it to my opening. The vibrations made it hard to keep my eyes open, to do anything more than dissolve into the bed as I moaned for more.

"You want it inside you," he said. "Don't you, my love?"

I cried out as the thick head filled me. I liked this kind of pressure, especially with all the nice rumbles, but it did shut down entire portions of my brain as I adjusted to it. A minute passed while I let these sensations turn me into soft, throbby need.

"You're doing so good," he said.

I didn't respond. Couldn't. Not when the head slipped a bit deeper as I positioned the suction element. I should've given myself a second before turning it on, but the only thing I cared about right now was pleasing my husband. Hearing more of those tender, gentle words, the ones that felt like him brushing my hair over my ear and kissing my forehead.

I loved suction toys because I could always count on them to suck all the tension from my body in a minute or two. It was my everyday stress relief valve. But now, with Ryan watching and telling me how hard I was working, how pretty and sweet my cunt was, how amazing it'd feel when I came for him, it felt like a miracle. Like magic I'd conjured just for him.

For my husband. The one I *loved*. The one I wanted to keep for—for always.

"I'm—" I wanted to say more but all I had were cries and moans and the occasional *oh fuck* as my back arched off the bed, my hips rutted against the hand holding the toy in place, and my legs shook uncontrollably.

"That's it," he growled. "That's my fucking girl."

I twitched and panted for a minute, too shattered to turn off the toy. When I could finally command my fingers to press the buttons and pull it from my clenching core, a fresh wave of sensations washed over me and I was pretty sure I watched my soul leave my body.

"Wow," I whispered. I heard Ryan's answering murmur and that was when I realized I still had the phone positioned below deck. I propped it against the pillow and glanced at him, a surge of shyness wiggling through me. "Hi."

I watched as he mopped his balled-up shirt over his torso. He smiled and he seemed so…proud. As if he just couldn't believe me. As if I'd done something remarkable. I hadn't, but I still adored the way he looked at me. It magnified all the aftershocks coursing through my body. "How's my girl feeling now?"

"After review of the play, the ruling on the field stands. *Wow*." I grinned at his bare chest. "How's my husband?"

"Missing you so fucking much." He glanced down at himself, laughing. "Thinking about flying home tonight."

"No, you'll just have to go back for another shoot," I wailed. "Stay and get it over with. You're there now."

"The only place I want to be is between your thighs."

"And you will be," I said, pulling out my most severe teacher voice. "When you finish all of your work."

Heat flared in his eyes. "You're not making this any easier."

I hit him with a stern gaze. "Let's put on our thinking hats. Will it help us to throw away all our hard work just because we want to play? Or will that make more work for us—and our friends who are only trying to do their jobs—later on?"

"Okay, okay, I'll stay." He threw his shirt across the room with a grunt. "But if you keep talking like that, we're going to be setting up at the line of scrimmage real quick."

"Hmm." I reached for the box and held up a waterproof suction toy resembling a rubber ducky. "Any chance your suite has a bathtub?"

"I fucking love your devious mind, wifey." He dragged a hand up his bare chest, settling at the flowers near his shoulder. "Let's go."

chapter twenty-eight

Emme

Today's Learning Objective:
Students will be able to plan ahead.

FIELD DAY EXISTED FOR MANY PURPOSES. ONE LESS DAY OF instruction to plan at the end of the school year when none of us had the stomach for more of that. An opportunity to let kids cut loose when they had the most energy to burn. A chance to spend the day outside while the weather was perfect. Most importantly, it gave us all something to look forward to—the beginning of the end. It was always the last Friday of the school year, the final event before a short week with class picnics and grade-level promotion parties.

If we could make it to field day, we could make it to the end.

Yet field day had never been any remarkable event. When I'd taken over the coordination in my first year at the school in an attempt to impress my principal, I'd thrown myself into research to find the best activities. I came up with a fairy-tale adventure theme and shaped the games, team names, and awards to match. Fun, cute, silly—and all the supplies came from the phys ed closet. Everyone loved it. And I used that exact playbook for the next few years, mixing up the themes and swapping in different activities. It still required a good deal of prep but I knew what I was doing and everyone was happy enough.

But I knew I'd never be able to go back to that playbook after this year's field day. No part of my hula hoop hopscotch would ever compete with the professional obstacle course that filled the school grounds. Or the dozens of college athletes—not to mention all the NFL players—on hand to help. There was a *climbing wall*, for fuck's sake. And a massive blow-up slide that looked like an obscene amount of fun. I wanted a turn.

As promised, I didn't have to do a thing. I walked my class outside in the matching t-shirts that'd arrived earlier in the week and the college kids jumped right in, splitting them into small teams and leading them to different stations where Ryan, McKerry, Hersberler, Wilcox, and Bigelow showed them how to complete the activities. There were a few other players from Ryan's team manning the drills and obstacle courses, including a wide receiver still recovering from knee surgery who'd been appointed the low-impact task of high-fiving kids at the bottom of the slide.

All I had to do was sit on the sidelines and watch very large, very tough men who made a living by being relentlessly aggressive cheer on a bunch of elementary kids. They made accommodations for the kids who needed it and made sure everyone had a chance to succeed. Wilcox followed one anxious kid through an agility course, his hand outstretched and ready the whole time in case the student needed support. Hersberler carried another kid to the top of the blow-up slide after he had a hard time getting the hang of the steps. Bigelow spent half an hour teaching a child with a limb difference how to fall safely —and then taught her a modification of his signature end zone move. McKerry was the loudest, most magnificent cheerleader in the whole world. These kids all walked away from his station with the brightest beaming smiles.

I still didn't know if Ryan chose the climbing wall as his station or if he'd simply ended up there but he spent the entire day going up and down that wall with kids, talking them through every step and toehold. He hung back with the scared kids who screamed when they were no more than six inches off the ground, and he raced the ambitious ones up the wall, always slowing down just enough at the end to let them win.

I hadn't anticipated that he'd take it to this level. I knew what he'd said but I still didn't think it would be this big, this fun, this perfect for *all* kids. I didn't think he'd let me down but this was so far from a letdown that I couldn't even grab hold of my expectations.

And maybe expectations were the problem. Mine didn't make sense. I'd expected a marriage proposal from Teddy despite him critiquing my body and scolding my food choices. I couldn't believe Ryan—my oldest friend and newest husband—would want to help with field day despite his constant willingness to help me with anything in the world. Including getting revenge on my ex.

Every teacher stopped me to say how much they loved this year's event and ask how I pulled it off. All I could do was blame my husband. I sent them to the climbing wall to tell him he'd ruined us all. They thought I was joking but I knew the truth of it.

As I saw it, there were only two options for me. Either I unloaded this event onto an unsuspecting first-year teacher in the fall or I stayed married to Ryan indefinitely.

He was the one who'd insisted we drop the deadlines. I was just doing my part.

Obviously, it was all in good fun. I wasn't using him for his willingness to hire people to entertain the students so my colleagues and I didn't suffer any mid-June emotional breakdowns. If I'd ever mentioned needing help for this in the past, he would've done the same thing. It wasn't about the fake marriage.

Or keeping it going until we forgot about the fake part and it turned into a regular old marriage.

Was that what he'd meant by no deadlines? Probably not.

I joined Jamie, Audrey, and Grace in the shade of the building. I followed their gazes to the climbing wall and the divine way the harness bracketed Ryan's backside.

"You're being rather obvious," I announced.

"No one is paying any attention to us," Grace murmured, a hand shielding the sun from her eyes.

"If you don't marry him," Jamie said, "I will."

"You don't believe in marriage," I reminded her. "Or monogamy."

She tipped her chin toward Ryan as he raced a group of older kids up the wall. "I'd let him change my mind about that."

It was Audrey—*Audrey*—who said, "I'd let him crack me like a glow stick."

We all turned to face the ever demure blonde. It took her a minute to notice since she was eye-fucking my husband.

"Yeah, girl." Jamie held up her hand for a high-five. Audrey reluctantly met her palm. "I didn't think you had it in you."

"It's not like it would ever happen. Obviously," she added. "He's your fiancé."

"Have you seen his friends?" Grace asked. "I'm sure one of them would be up for the challenge."

"They would," I said, leaning my forearms against the fence. "Let's see. We have Jaden Wilcox over there. The one with the huge smile. He's a running back which means he's carrying the ball and getting it downfield with the intent of gaining yards—and he's very good at it. His production was unreal last season. Carries, rush yards, scrimmage yards, all of it. He was on fire."

"You really know football," Jamie said. "Not just the basics because it's your boy's job but you understand the game."

"Yeah." I shrugged and went back to looking for the guys. I didn't want to get into my ancient history. "Colton Squire is the one in the leg brace. He's a wide receiver so he's breaking away from the play to get in position to catch a pass. Last I heard, he has a girlfriend."

"Bummer," Jamie murmured. "I could've nursed him back to health."

"Damon McKerry is the goofball with the locs. He's a left guard. He creates lanes in the play and protects the quarterback from the other team's defense, and he's an absolute force of nature on the field. There's no one else like him in the League. He's also a puppy dog and I've heard he's a big fan of all variety of jerky."

"I don't think I have the fortitude for a puppy. Or jerky," Audrey added. "But he's precious."

"Then we have Crawson Bigelow," I said. "He's an offensive tackle which means he's out there clearing blocks for the running backs and looking after the QB's blind side. Very talented. Also very much in love with his high school sweetheart."

"I don't know what's wrong with me but I like the preppy one," Jamie said, tipping her chin toward Hersberler. He kept looking in this direction and shooting smiles at the group. "His shorts were ironed so hard I'd slice my hand on the crease."

"You are a ride he wouldn't survive." I glanced at her. "You'd grind his bones into dust and turn him into your most famous stalker."

"Figured as much." She looked back to Audrey. "We'll find someone for you to play with, love."

"How do you feel about the defensive line?" I asked.

Audrey scrunched up her nose. "What's the difference?"

"These guys"—I pointed my water bottle toward McKerry and the others—"are on the offensive side. Their whole objective is protecting the quarterback in order to make opportunities for the running game. The defense is all about shutting down that run game and getting in the QB's way. Those boys are the size of a barn and they're *strong*."

Audrey hummed as Bigelow swept Hersberler off his feet and carried the tight end from one side of the field to another. "These guys seem strong enough."

"Mmm. They must be building barns bigger these days because I thought firefighters were brawny," Grace said.

After a minute of watching Bigelow and Hersberler chasing each other the same way eight-year-olds did, Audrey said, "I think I'll stick to window shopping."

"If you change your mind," I said, "I know where to find them."

Jamie leaned over to say to Audrey, "I've already told her I'm going to be on my worst behavior at her wedding. You should just be bad with me."

With a grin, Audrey said, "I like the sound of that."

RYAN STROLLED INTO MY CLASSROOM SHORTLY AFTER DISMISSAL ended. I'd flopped into my desk chair to shovel stale pretzels and peanut M&Ms into my mouth between gulps of water. I hadn't been required to do much of anything today but I was still sweaty and exhausted from it.

On the other hand, Ryan looked fresh as a daisy.

"You know, you've really fucked things up for me," I said, my cheek full of M&Ms.

He held out his hands. "What? What's wrong? I thought everything was okay."

"I'm gonna have to quit my job," I said, as seriously as I could manage. "There's no way for me to even come close to this amazingness next year. The kids will heckle me for trying. The teachers too." I gave a slow shake of my head. "I'm finished here."

His shoulders bounced as he laughed. "I'm sure there's another solution."

"Well. I have thought of one way." I leaned back in my chair, crossed my arms over my chest. "I just have to figure out how to trap you in this marriage a little longer. I'll have to trade sexual favors for field day arrangements but that seems like a small price to pay."

"Not so small." He edged onto the corner of my desk, his long legs stretched out in front of him. "How long would you need to trap me?"

"I'm not sure yet." I bit my lip to hold back a giggle. "Probably not more than five years. Ten at the most."

He reared back. "Shit. Okay. That's like a for-real marriage."

"Yeah, I know," I went on. "That's taxes, probably some kids, maybe a dog. Definitely a joint holiday photo card with us walking on the beach in coordinated looks. It could get pretty involved. There might even be family gatherings in our future."

"And the only alternative is leaving your job?"

"Only one I can find."

"I take it you don't want to do that?" he asked.

"Not especially. I'm aware that I complain about my job a lot and this year has tested me in ways I don't care to repeat. It's left me questioning everything about the education system and wondering if I have what it takes to do this for the long haul. But looking for a new job would suck. Also, I love second grade and everyone at this school, even if Grace is abandoning me for suburbia."

He shrugged. "Then I guess we're stuck in this marriage."

I gave him an exaggerated grimace. "I am so sorry."

Waving me off, he said, "I'm sorry for putting you in this position. Just for my own scheduling purposes, when do the sexual favors start?"

I pointed to the bookshelves lining the side of the room below the windows. "Not until after I've packed up my classroom for the summer."

He leaned back to get a better look. "All those books need to be packed?"

"Yep. They move all the furniture over and deep clean the floors after school lets out so everything has to be empty."

The next few days would be busy. Grace and Ben's couples' shower was tomorrow and her final dress fitting was on Sunday, and we'd planned to make a lunch-and-pedicures afternoon of it with all the bridesmaids. Monday and Tuesday would be wild with the final days of the school year, and then Ryan and I left on Thursday night for a pro sports awards event in Vegas. The news of our secret wedding was scheduled to drop on Friday and my birthday fell on Sunday, and I didn't think we could cram much else into those days even if we'd tried.

Grace's wedding was two weeks away and Ryan reported for training camp not long after that. Based on everything he'd said, it seemed like his franchise deals would go through before the end of July. When we crossed those lines, we wouldn't need to keep this going. We'd only be doing it because we wanted to—and that felt right but also terribly dangerous, like jumping headfirst into water without knowing what hid under the surface.

Ryan had started longer, more intense workouts and spending time studying game tape. He met with coaches and trainers almost every day. I'd pored over his schedule for the season, nearly gnawing straight through my lip when I realized he'd be on the road for five straight weeks to start. He'd come home between them of course but I'd be going back to school at the same time and I already knew it'd be tough for us. I'd be able to travel to some games but not all of them. Probably not most of them.

I'd had to stop myself when I started looking up how long it would take to fly to Baltimore on a Monday afternoon. I hadn't even decided if I wanted to attend his games yet and I was already mapping out flight plans. I required seven to ten business days to recover from any amount of travel and I didn't like putting myself in the spotlight enough to endure a camera panning over me for ten seconds.

It would be tough for me. If we kept this going. But I knew I wouldn't have to figure it out alone. And I knew with every bit of me that my mother was wrong. Ryan wouldn't cheat. He wasn't like any of the men she'd chosen for herself. He wouldn't lie and he wouldn't break me.

I stood, pushing away from my desk to grab the storage bins I used for my books. "There's a system."

With a nod, he said, "Show me how you want it done."

"So, *you* can show *me* how you want it done when we get home?" I teased.

His gaze landed on my mouth and then scraped over the bustline stretching my t-shirt to its limits. "Yes."

Oh, these were dangerous waters and I was getting in way too deep. Any minute now, one of us would break and we'd laugh and blow this off as a joke. Just like the time I'd asked him to be my date to the prom at the last minute. I didn't know why I'd tacked on *as a joke,* but I had. I didn't even know what I'd intended by that. But those had been dangerous waters too. We'd held the friendship line hard in high school and we'd never crossed it. Even at the end when we'd made that pact, it'd been as friends.

But we'd crossed the line now—and I didn't want to go back.

chapter twenty-nine

Ryan

Today's Learning Objective:
Students will go to war—and win.

"Can you explain this to me one more time?" I glanced at Emme as she redid her hair again, her phone propped on her knees and the camera in selfie mode. Since I knew it was a matter of time until we hit a pothole and this all went to hell, I reached across the back seat and held the phone steady. Bowen was off tonight, and as much as I liked Soto, he drove like he was trying to qualify for an F1 race. "I understand the basic concept of a bridal shower but I don't see how it turns into a bar crawl."

"They're not into the traditional stuff but we still wanted to give her something like a shower," she said, a few bobby pins held between her lips. "We came up with some different ideas to involve both of them. Trivia night. Wine tasting. Some really cute stuff that seemed like a lot of fun. But I missed the conversation for a weekend and then it was a shower followed by a bar crawl. I asked Grace if that was what she actually wanted because that sounded like something boys would come up with. But she said it was great and here we are."

I nodded as she plucked all the pins from her hair and started over. "Got it."

"All I know is that I appreciate the hell out of Audrey for doing the actual work of planning this night," she said. "Her compulsive need to organize things came in clutch with this one. She sent out a twelve-page PDF with interior and exterior photos of every venue, an itinerary with scheduled bathroom breaks and the contact info of every bar manager, and dress code suggestions to balance the locations with the wedding's colors."

I hadn't been able to place it until now but I realized her simple blue and white dress was nothing like her usual bright, saturated styles. Not that I'd say it out loud but the soft floral print reminded me of my grandmother's nightgowns.

Still, Emme looked amazing. I loved her summer dresses with flouncy little shoulder straps and long, ruffled skirts that made me want to put her on my lap and see what we could get away with.

"Last chance to back out now," she said around the bobby pins. "I wouldn't blame you if you did. You're going to get mobbed by fans."

"Nothing I can't handle."

She cut a sharp look in my direction. "You realize we're going to a bunch of bars in Boston, right? That's where they recite the Ryan Ralston lore."

"I think I'll be okay." I nodded to the driver's seat. "And we'll bring Soto in with us. He's not bad at crowd control."

"Thanks, boss," he replied.

"I give up. I'm done." She huffed out an impatient breath and waved away the phone. "If you're sure you want to do this, can you just promise to save me from another conversation with Clara?"

"I can commit to that only if you're never more than"—I stretched my arm out across the back seat and brought my hand to her shoulder—"this far away from me."

Emme dropped a hand to my thigh. "Works for me."

THE PARTY STARTED ON THE SECOND FLOOR DECK AT A TAPROOM ON State Street. As far as June evenings went, it didn't get much better than this and everyone knew it. The drinks were flowing and, at first glance, everyone seemed in good spirits.

"Okay," Emme said, almost to herself. "Audrey was right about reserving the deck even if we'll have to sell our eggs to pay for it. This is nice. This works."

"*You're* paying for this?"

She gave me *do you know anything?* eyes. "The bridesmaids throw the shower."

"The whole night?" There was no way in hell I was letting that happen. I wasn't letting any of it happen but first I had to figure out how to settle up here without leaving Emme's side. I could probably fire off a message to Marcie. "You're picking up the tab for this *and* all the bar stops?"

She shook her head as she studied the crowd. "No, Jamie laid down the law with the groomsmen and told them they had to figure out the stops by themselves. She can be terrifying when she wants to. She could command an army."

"I believe that." I looked around for the happy couple but didn't see them. "What do you want to drink? They have one of those weird fruity stouts you like."

"I think I should start with something lighter than a stout," she said. "It's going to be a long night and I don't want to start the *crying in the bathroom* phase until later."

Audrey spotted us then and made a beeline across the deck, a small notebook tucked under her arm and her phone clutched in her hand. She could also command an army.

"You remember the guy?" she asked Emme, ignoring me entirely. I didn't mind. Sometimes it was nice to watch from the bench. "With the truck? The one who agreed to load up all of the gifts and drop them off at Grace's house? He got called into work."

"We have no guy? No truck?" Emme yelped.

"No guy." Audrey shook her head, sending her white-blonde hair swishing over her shoulders.

Her dress was just like Em's. The blue was a little darker, the skirt hit at her knees, but the same grandma-nightgown energy. Grace did *not* strike me as someone who'd choose a wedding with grandma-nightgown energy but what the fuck did I know?

"Can we schedule a car service and request a big family van? Would that work?" Emme asked.

"But then someone needs to go with the family van to Grace's house and unload everything tonight. And then get a ride back here." Audrey crossed her arms over her chest. "I could go but—"

"You've done *everything* for this party," Emme said. "You're not cramming yourself into an Uber with a bunch of kitchen appliances and bath towels too."

"What's the problem?" I asked, glancing between them.

Emme pointed to the gifts piled on a picnic table. "We can't leave the gifts here. We have to pack up everything and drive it to Grace's house outside the city, but the person who had both the truck and the disinterest in drinking all night has to fight fires instead. Now we're fighting over who gets the short end of the stick."

"Does it have to be delivered tonight? Or would tomorrow work?" I asked. "I can make a call and arrange to have everything stored tonight and then delivered when they're home tomorrow."

"Really?" Audrey asked just as Emme said, "You don't have to do that."

"I don't want to watch you two stress over how to solve this and I'm sure as hell not letting either of you do it all by yourself."

Audrey pressed her palms together and exchanged a glance with Emme that I couldn't decipher. Something that had my wife smiling and shaking her head like she disagreed but not enough to put any weight into it.

"Please don't call Jakobi," Emme said. "Ines told me they were going on a midnight harbor cruise to see some special constellation and she was extremely excited."

"Not Jakobi," I said with a laugh. He'd skin me alive if I cut into his plans for the evening. "Marcie always has someone on hand to do odd jobs. It's not a problem."

"It would relieve a massive headache," Audrey said. "And neither of us would have to miss the rest of the party."

I pulled out my phone. "Consider it done."

"Where the hell is Jamie?" Emme asked. "Of all people, she's the one most likely to have a guy with a truck waiting around to help her out."

"You also have a guy with quick access to a truck waiting around to help you out," I murmured as I swiped through some messages on my phone. "Your husband."

"Your—" Audrey's mouth fell open as her eyes damn near popped out of her head. She brought her hands to her cheeks as she swung her gaze between us. *"What?"*

Emme closed her hands around Audrey's wrists, saying, "Listen to me, sweet girl. I am *begging* you to take that little morsel of information and tuck it away. This is Grace's party and I'm not stealing any of her thunder simply because this bull in a china shop boy of mine can't stay quiet."

"How long?" Audrey breathed.

"A few weeks," she said. "And we're going to tell everyone really soon but I want Grace to have her moment first."

"My lips are sealed. Oh my god, I'm so happy for you." Audrey bounced on her toes as tears filled her eyes. "I'm *so* happy, Em. You deserve all these good things."

"And so do you," Emme said, still holding Audrey's wrists.

"I have everything I need," she replied. I knew from the way Emme cocked her head that there was more to that story.

I stepped away to talk to Marcie about getting someone in here to handle the logistics and picking up the check for the girls. She was kind enough to cackle in my ear when I asked if she had enough lead time to coordinate all of this.

When I returned, Jamie had joined the group. Her dress was almost identical to Audrey's but she had a wide navy ribbon tied around her waist. "I've looked everywhere," she said. "Checked all the bathrooms and made a pass through the kitchen too."

"They wouldn't leave," Audrey said.

"Shay would find them in four minutes flat," Jamie said. "I find it outrageous that her school had to schedule a family dance for tonight."

"Isn't the more outrageous part that we didn't check her schedule before booking this place?" Audrey asked.

"Everything about this is outrageous." Jamie made a show of glancing around. "I was promised a minimum of two firefighters carrying me on their massive shoulders the whole night and I see none of that happening."

"Okay, well, we've still lost the bride and groom so how about we fix that problem first and then get you some beefy men?" Audrey asked.

"Maybe they stepped out for a second," Emme said. "Ben and Grace wouldn't ditch this party. Or us! Wherever they are, I'm sure they'll be back soon and we can start on the gifts."

"We're already seventeen minutes behind schedule," Audrey said. "They'll need to unwrap quickly."

"Such a weird tradition," Jamie mused as she chewed on the wooden end of a cocktail umbrella. "Sitting there and opening presents while people watch."

"Yeah, now that you mention it," Emme said. "I'd be so awkward about everything I opened. Like I'd tell a story about what I'd use the pots and pans for, or whatever."

"I told everyone I didn't want bridal showers and they threw them anyway." Audrey grimaced like she was reliving it. I knew that look. It was how I reacted when I saw someone take a bad hit on the field. "But my grandmothers and my great-aunts gave me all these ugly gold necklaces and bracelets. Thick, hideous things I'd never wear. I thought I was doing a good job of being gracious but one of my aunts piped up and said I didn't have to worry about wearing it but I did have to worry about hiding it somewhere my husband would never find. So that I'd have the money to leave him if I needed to." She shrugged. "I didn't need the gold to leave him, but goddammit, I've never gone to a shower since without a bunch of ugly bracelets and telling the bride those exact words."

Emme and Jamie folded Audrey into a hug and I stood there, hating that this thought process had to exist. "Muggsy, you don't have to hide jewelry from me. If you want to leave me, just take all the money. You can have it."

Jamie chuckled. "We'll make sure she does."

Emme grinned at her friend before glancing back to me. "This isn't about you, Wildcat."

"You're one of the good ones," Audrey said. "But yeah, if she ever decides it's time to go, you better believe we'll get her out."

A startled laugh rumbled up from my chest. I grinned at Emme. "An impressive line you have here." I nodded at Audrey and then Jamie. "A strong safety, quick cornerback. And with Grace as your nose tackle? They could fuck up any offense."

"Don't you forget it," Jamie said. To Audrey, she asked, "What do those words mean?"

"I don't know, honey," she said.

Emme started to explain but then pointed to the taproom doors. "Look! There they are!"

I saw Grace and Ben emerge, both glancing off in different directions. He shoved his hands in his pockets and she crossed her arms over her chest. They pulled on stiff smiles when friends greeted them. I didn't know how couples were supposed to look at their pub crawl showers but I didn't think that was it.

"Finally," Audrey said with a sigh. "I'll get them seated to start on the gifts." She hooked her elbow with Jamie's. "You have to keep them moving. Be tough! No time for chatter."

"Believe me, I can be tough," Jamie replied.

Alone again, I rounded on Emme. "That was really fucking intense."

She lifted her shoulders. "Sorry? But also it's real life for some women so maybe just cope with it quietly?"

"Do I need to tell Chloe that she can always come to me if she needs to leave her husband?"

Emme glanced at me before turning her attention back to Grace and Ben, who were not at all interested in keeping to Audrey's schedule. "I'm sure your sister knows that."

I stared off into the distance for a moment, watching cars creep by as the sun sank lower into the horizon. I wanted to say something more about leaving marriages and money—even if I really didn't want to talk about the end of a marriage with the woman I was trying to convince to stay married to me—but then I felt her grow tense.

"*Ryan.* Do not fucking leave me."

Emme balled her hand in the back of my shirt and I found her iron-jawed gaze staring up at me, silently pleading for help. I glanced around and found Teddy and Clara headed straight for us. After a second of flat-out annoyance that this fucking guy thought he deserved a second of my wife's attention, I looped an arm around her waist and smacked a kiss to her temple. I knew what he was doing and I knew I could do it better. "Let me take this one."

Teddy strolled up with Clara's hand clutched in his, all swagger and inch-thick confidence as if he hadn't spent that whole housewarming party avoiding me. He stuck out his hand like we were old pals with, "Good to see you, man. How's it goin'?"

"Not too bad," I said easily. I took his hand but refused to end the shake first.

"That's a really cute dress," Clara said to Emme. "You always look so beautiful and put together."

"Thanks. My stylist gets all the credit." After a moment of both Teddy and Clara blinking at Emme in surprise at that remark, she added, "You look great too."

Teddy skimmed a glance down my wife's body that I didn't appreciate at all. Then, "Seems like you're doing all right, Em."

I hooked my arm around her shoulders and turned her toward me. She reached up and gripped my forearm, tightening my hold and putting her engagement ring on display all at once. "Couldn't be better," she drawled.

A group of fans chose that moment to approach us, and when they asked for photos with me *and* Emme, I said, "Yeah, no problem. I'm sure my friend Teddy here would be thrilled to help."

Clara snatched their phone from his hand with a teasing comment about him taking the worst photos. Over the next ten minutes, half the taproom got in line for a pic and she happily accepted every device they handed her while Teddy's expression grew darker. He repeatedly crossed his arms, braced his legs, worked his jaw. And he never once took his eyes off Emme.

I wasn't sure who the fuck he thought he was, glaring at her like that but I knew it was time to put some permanent distance between us. The audacity that led him to approach us in the first place needed to be drained like the abscess it was.

I played with a lot of guys who made a habit of cheating and I'd always chalked it up to the ego trip of the game. It seemed like a lot of trouble for a short-lived benefit but I knew other guys didn't see it that way. They liked having it all but they also felt like they *deserved* it. That they were entitled to the wife holding it down at home and the women hanging around the hotel bar after an away game.

It hadn't hit me until now but Teddy was no different than any of them. He expected everything and it killed him that Emme was better off now. I could see the screws twisting in him and the hostility rolling off him in waves.

Yeah, we'd put a stop to this tonight.

When the photo line wound down, Clara pointed over her shoulder. "It looks like they're going to open gifts soon. We should find a place to sit."

After a weighty pause where he completely ignored his fiancée, Teddy asked, "How's the backfield looking this year? Any word on Hersberler?"

Emme glanced up at me, lips pulled together into a delicious pout while I debated how much of a shitstorm I'd stir up if I started a fistfight. "We had a good time with those boys on Nantucket, didn't we?"

"We did," I said, grinning down at her adorable face.

"Let's have them over some time this week," she said, her eyes sparkling. I played along because that was the game and I needed to stop fantasizing about throwing this guy off the deck, but I kind of loved the idea of having my guys over and letting Emme verbally slap them around while feeding them her home cooking. It filled something inside me that I didn't know was missing. "Everyone's in town, right? Pick a day that works and I'll cook. Bet they'd love my fried chicken. Like a last supper before they have to get on their training camp diets."

"You don't need to do that," I said, and I wanted her to know I meant that. Even if this entire conversation was a work of fiction to fuck with Teddy, I meant it. She didn't exist to serve me. That wasn't our relationship. I wasn't this shitbag ex of hers, I wasn't the husband Audrey ran from, and I wasn't her father. "You have enough going on with the end of the school year. I'm not adding dinner for half a football team to your list."

"But I want to," she said, and I wanted more than anything to lean down and snag her bottom lip between my teeth.

"All right, I'll make it happen." I settled for a quick kiss. From the corner of my eye, I saw Teddy cross his arms again. "But I'm helping."

"Just as long as you remember I'm the quarterback in the kitchen," she said.

I let myself drown in her dark, endless eyes. "As if I'd forget."

Teddy cleared his throat. "Well, we're gonna get a drink," he said through a forced smile.

"Great." I tipped my chin toward the bar. I knew he heard the indifference in my tone when he blinked away. "Have fun with that."

But this dog didn't know how to die because he added, "Nothing for Clara though. We're not telling everyone yet but we figured it would be obvious by the end of the night since she's not drinking." He rested his hand on her belly and she beamed up at him like the dawning sun. "We're due at the end of November."

What a little bitch.

Under my palm, I felt Emme's back tense but her expression stayed neutral. It reminded me of the way she gave her students instructions while carefully ignoring the kid sitting under his desk where he pretended to be an animal in a zoo enclosure. She knew what was happening but if she stopped to acknowledge it, the situation would get much worse.

Which was why I couldn't punch him in the mouth right now.

Yet I couldn't help the aggravated scoff before saying, "Congratulations," and leading my wife away.

When we reached the deck railing, she said, "I'll take that stout now."

THE NIGHT PROGRESSED MUCH AS I'D EXPECTED IT TO AFTER TEDDY and Clara's announcement. Emme insisted everything was fine despite the ever-present shine of tears in her eyes and no, she didn't need to tell Grace or the others about this news because everyone was having so much fun and she didn't want to start any drama. She did this while gluing herself to my side, barely saying more than "This worked out better than I expected" and "It's just the perfect weather to walk the city" to anyone, and working through two beers.

That was about one hundred percent more beer than I'd ever seen Emme drink in one night.

After the taproom, we hit the old standbys—The Green Dragon and Bell in Hand before crossing into Grace and Emme's old neighborhood, the North End. In retrospect, stopping at Modern Underground for espresso martinis wasn't the best decision but it wasn't the worst of the night.

Emme chugged her martini at the bar while another teacher from the school carried a conversation about the need for more structured play in the school day. I stationed myself behind her, a hand on her lower back and my coldest, most cutting glare burning into Teddy's back while the bartender told me about going to the first home games of the football season at the old Foxboro stadium with his father when he was a kid.

I was a sucker for those kinds of stories—pretty much anything with dads and football traditions with their kids hit me real hard—but watching the sobriety leave my wife and devising a plan to push her ex into oncoming traffic meant I didn't have much attention to spare. But I got his name and sent Marcie a note to get him tickets to the home opener.

The next stop was at Twenty-First Amendment on Beacon Hill. It was also the longest trek between bars and by the time we started up the slope of Somerset Street, Emme and the girls congealed into a grandma-nightgown clump of giggles and screams and swearing. They stumbled and staggered, moving at a pace that made me want to toss two over my shoulders and have Soto grab the other pair, and jog the last half mile. Just to be done with it.

The groom ordered shots of whiskey. I plucked the glass out of Emme's fingers and knocked it back even though I hated hard liquor. I ordered her a soda and sat her at the bar while the boys—and Jamie—went in for another round of shots.

Audrey claimed the spot beside Emme and they leaned into each other with deep, commiserating sighs that confused the hell out of me. I wasn't even going to begin to guess at Audrey's problems but I still didn't get why Teddy wielded so much power over Emme. I knew everything he did was a punch in the gut to her but wasn't this better? Weren't *we* better than whatever the hell she'd had with him?

I wanted to watch him run straight into a brick wall but I didn't see any reason to let him run the board. We were married to get revenge on this guy so why weren't we? Why was my wife sitting at the bar with her head on Audrey's shoulder and tears in her eyes just because that douche got his girlfriend pregnant? Fuck him. He wasn't in control here.

The last stop was Beantown Pub and it was just around the corner. It was also across the street from the Granary Burial Ground where Samuel Adams of Revolutionary War fame was buried. The idea was to drink a cold Sam Adams while looking out at...a cold Sam Adams.

The group—or, what was left of it after losing a few along the way—scattered to the pool tables and high-tops right away but I led Emme to a quiet corner.

"We don't have to stay much longer," she said. "I know you hate this."

"I don't hate it," I said, my hands on her waist as she dropped her head back against the wall. "But I do hate seeing you torn up because of the shit your ex pulled tonight."

"He's not pulling shit, he's having a baby," she drawled. "He's allowed to tell people. It's fine. I'm the problem."

"You're nowhere near the problem. What he did was the biggest dick move I've seen in a long time but that's just it—he's a dick. You know that. I know that. With the exception of his fiancée, I think everyone here knows that. So, I need you to explain why you let it matter so much."

"I don't know, Ryan. Like I said before, it's chewing tree bark.

Everything he did cut me so hard, and now—this? This one cuts even deeper than finding out he's engaged."

"You want a baby? Is that it?" I tipped her chin up and leveled a gaze on her. Gave her ass a rough squeeze. "Because I can give you a baby. We can get to work on that right now."

She choked out a watery laugh. "No." Then, with a sideways glance, "But maybe we can talk more about that later."

"We can definitely talk about that later. Put it on the schedule. Write it down in your planner." I brought my hand to the back of her neck, stroked her soft skin. "If it's not the baby, why are you letting this guy tank your whole night? I need you to explain it to me. I don't get it."

"Because I wanted him to suffer," she said quietly, almost a mumble. "I wanted him to see me and realize he made a huge mistake, that the way he treated me was really wrong and fucked up. I didn't want him to end up marrying the person he cheated with as if they were meant to be together all along. It's awful and I hate that I'm saying it but I wanted him to be lonely and miserable. I wanted him to regret all the terrible things he did and everything he said—"

"Wait. What are you talking about?" My mind was a frozen lake, dead silent and unforgiving. "He cheated on you. That was what happened. Right?"

"I broke up with him because I found out he was cheating on me," she said, her eyes filling with tears all over again. "Which was my mistake because I never asked if we were exclusive." She sniffled, glanced down. "But I should've ended things because he only wanted to see me when I cooked for him and did his laundry, and he'd always forget to tell me when something had shellfish in it."

I felt my heart rate slow down the way it did when I walked onto the field. The cold, silent focus that filled my head when it was time to destroy my opponents. "Excuse me but *what the fuck*?"

"I know, it's so stupid," she continued, seemingly unaware that I was going to put that boy in the ground before the night was over.

"He'd toss a whole bunch of crab into scrambled eggs or broccoli cheddar soup or something else that didn't make any sense. When I'd ask about it because my throat started closing, he'd say I shouldn't be eating those things anyway because I was putting on too much weight."

My knuckles cracked as my hands curled into fists. "How many times? With the shellfish?"

She sniffled. "Three."

"Are you fucking kidding me?" She shook her head and I wanted to press my hand to her chest just to make sure she was breathing right now, to prove that she was okay. The back of my neck prickled. I wanted to kill him—but I also needed to hear the rest of this. "What else, Muggsy?"

"He'd pinch me"—she motioned to her side and reality shifted into the kind of slow motion where I could see plays before they went into effect and my body knew how to respond—"and tell me to go easy on the sweets. Or say my clothes looked too tight when we were going out or slap my hand away if I reached for the bread—"

"I love you and you're perfect and you can have all the bread in the world." I leaned in, pressed a quick kiss to her lips and brushed away her tears. "I'll be back in a minute."

She grabbed my hand as I turned to leave. "Ryan, no. Whatever you're thinking, don't. He's not worth it and—"

The resignation in her eyes almost killed me. "But *you* are."

I made my way through the bar, Emme's hand locked around my wrist, and found her ex near the dart board with a few of the groomsmen. One of the guys elbowed him when I stepped up to their group.

Teddy turned around with that shifty-eyed look of his. He glanced at me and then Emme over my shoulder. "How's it goin', man?"

"I want to thank you," I started, "for being such a phenomenal bottom-feeding parasite. Because if you'd found even an ounce of sense in that empty tuna can you call a brain and kept your dick in your pants, I wouldn't be making this gorgeous, irreplaceable woman my wife. If you hadn't shown her what rock bottom looks like, hadn't made it really fucking clear that knowingly triggering a life-threatening allergy *multiple times* is as low as someone can go, she wouldn't have left your ass and I wouldn't be marrying my best friend. Thank you. You gave me an incredible gift by showing her exactly who the fuck you are, and paving the road she walked right out of your sorry life."

Teddy glanced around but his boys had all taken several large steps back. From the corner of my eye, I noticed Ben closing in. He didn't look happy. I didn't care.

I leaned in, dropped my voice so no one else could hear. "I'd like nothing more than to take you outside and kick your fool ass around until the only thing you can do is piss yourself and cry for a mother who probably doesn't like you very much. But my arm is worth more than seventy million dollars a year and you have proven you are worth nothing." I stared at him for a beat. "If I ever find out that you have so much as breathed in my wife's direction, I will bring my entire offensive line to your door and teach you about what lies beneath rock bottom."

He gulped.

"Do we understand each other yet, Teddy?"

A nod. Sweat glistened on his forehead.

"It's good that you're scared." I tugged Emme to my side. "Now you're going to apologize for not only being the kind of juvenile piss troll who'd break rocks on his own head but also attempting to kill my wife."

He wet his lips and kept his gaze low. "That was an accident."

"Once, maybe." I could make that concession. "But not three times."

"What the fuck, man?" Ben asked.

It was good to see his furious attention trained on Teddy. I wasn't sure which side he was on until now. Ben crossed his arms over his chest and shot Teddy a stare that smacked of disappointment.

"There are no accidents," I said. "Just fools who don't give a fuck about anything but themselves. You know which one you are."

"I'm sorry," he said. "I—I made a mistake. Lots of mistakes. And I am sorry."

"Thanks for saying that, Teddy," Emme replied. Her fingers twisted in the back of my shirt. She gave a little tug. Time for this to be done.

"You're going to be a father in a few months. A husband. Time to grow the fuck up, young man. Find Jesus, go to therapy, whatever the fuck you need to unlearn this toxic shit. Because the last thing the world needs is more of this." I jabbed a finger at him. "Stay the fuck away from my wife. Listen to me when I say I'm keeping score and I never forget."

I turned, wrapped an arm around Emme's shoulders, and led her toward the door. Behind us, I heard Ben echo, "What the *fuck*, man?" We were almost there when Grace stepped into our path, her hands held out and her gaze panicked.

"What just happened?" she asked.

"I'm so sorry, honey, but I can't do this tonight," Emme said. "I've had a lot to drink. Probably too much, but at least I didn't mix it with allergy pills this time. I need to go home. Okay? I'm sorry to leave your party early. You should throw me out as your maid of honor. Put Audrey in first position and knock me down. I'm the worst. We'll talk tomorrow."

Grace pushed her fingers through her dark hair. "Can you at least tell me if you're all right? Because I don't know what's going on and I'm kind of freaking out about it."

Emme dropped her head against my chest. "I think I might be okay. Finally."

Grace spared me a glance, her brows pinched and her lips twisted into a severe line. Then, "You're not the worst. Don't say that shit to me. You're the only maid of honor I'd ever want. Even if you keep getting drunk and leaving my parties early."

Emme folded her into a hug and they said a few things I couldn't hear. When she returned to my side, I scooped her up and carried her out to where Soto waited at the curb.

When he pulled away and it was just the two of us in the darkness of the back seat, I asked, "Why didn't you tell me about all of it?"

"Because I started thinking he was right about some of it." She lifted her shoulders. "I felt foolish. Like I should've known better. Like it was my fault. And I didn't want you to tell me I shouldn't have let that happen to me."

"You didn't let anything happen, Em. And none of it was your fault."

The city lights streaked by as she nestled into my shoulder. "Thank you for not starting a fight. It would've ruined your deals."

"Fuck the deals." Soto turned toward the private garage attached to my building. "I didn't start a fight because he would've milked it for his fifteen minutes of fame and we're finished giving that guy anything."

Emme's breath hitched. "You're a really good husband."

"Good," I whispered into her hair. "It's the only job that matters to me."

WE ENDED UP SPRAWLED ON THE DECK SOFA AFTER ARRIVING HOME, Emme's head pillowed in my lap while I peeled tangerines for her. She didn't say a word as she ate each segment and I didn't push. The city was dark and quiet, and a cool summer breeze blew in off the water.

It was late and we both had places to be in the morning, but it didn't seem like either of us were finished processing this night. I was furious that I hadn't realized how much he'd hurt her. I should've put the pieces together and noticed something was off in her single-minded quest for revenge. She'd had plenty of bad breakups and always took time to lick her wounds after, but she never wanted to make them pay for what they did.

I should've known there was more to the story. Should've read her pained, broken reaction to Clara at the housewarming party as proof I didn't know what was going on—and not that she was just taking it too hard.

And I should've punched that guy in the face.

The last thing I needed right now was that kind of drama in my life, but someone had to do it.

When Emme finished with the tangerines and I had nothing left to do with my hands, I assigned myself the task of rubbing her back and shoulders. Her dress was confusing in many ways and I had to ask, "What's the deal with this dress?"

"What do you mean?"

"I mean"—I ran a hand through the ruffles—"this isn't your usual style."

"Ah. Yes." She laughed as she sat up and snuggled into my side. Her cheek was lined with creases from my jeans. I pulled her in close and ran the backs of my fingers over her face. "Bridal party secret."

"Anything you could share with your husband? Or would I need to wear a nightgown to a pub crawl in order to qualify?"

"Give that a try and tell me how it goes."

"You think I won't," I started, "but you'd be wrong."

She rested her head on my shoulder with a laugh. "Grace is an aggressive planner. There's always a plan and a backup plan and five more plans after that. But when it came to the wedding, she decided she wanted to take an easy, breezy approach and just...do whatever felt right. Let it happen."

"That doesn't sound like a great approach for someone who thrives on control," I said.

"It wasn't. It lasted about a month before Grace had a complete meltdown. They had a hodgepodge of ideas, nothing really went together, and since they have big families, the guest list spiraled overnight."

She shifted again, chasing out every last inch of space between us. When that didn't seem like enough, I hauled her into my lap and lashed my arms around her torso. "Better?" I asked.

She nodded. "From the start, she'd said she wanted the bridesmaids to have looks we liked and could wear again. She'd talked about letting us choose any dress as long as it was in her color palette. Everyone was happy. Jamie already had something picked out. But then Shay offered the tulip farm."

"I know you've said you're not fucking with me on this, but is it really a tulip farm? That just doesn't seem practical."

"Oh my god, Ryan." She sighed. "I swear to you, it's a tulip farm. Shay and her husband have built a gorgeous event space on the farm and the whole place is pure magic. You'll understand when you see it."

"I hope so."

"Grace's mom visited the farm with her and Ben, and fell in love—which is not hard to do at Twin Tulip. But then she decided she was going to make the bridesmaids' dresses. She *insisted*. There would be no way around this. She does a lot of sewing, but she believed deep in her heart that we needed to wear soft, flowery, cottage-core dresses. There was no convincing her otherwise." She laughed, a light, bubbly sound that did my heart good to hear. "Grace spent a full week hyperventilating over that idea until Audrey came up with a compromise. She's an expert negotiator when it comes to complicated families."

I toyed with the ruffles. "I'm not sure I see how this is a compromise."

"Since Jamie already had a dress, we threw her to the wolves and made that the reason we couldn't have flowery dresses for the wedding day. We offered the rehearsal dinner, but Grace's mom thought the shower was a better choice. Don't ask me why." She shrugged. "That's the story."

I ran my hands up her legs, dragging the flowy skirt as I went. "That's a lot of backroom bargaining."

"You don't know the half of it." She watched as I slipped a hand between her thighs, savoring the silky soft skin there. "These dresses are just one of the many, many reasons I couldn't let her call off the wedding."

"Even though holding it all together for her was killing you," I said. She nodded, turning her gaze out toward the sleeping city. "I never want you to feel that way again."

She shifted, dropping her knees on either side of my hips and sinking into my lap with her nightgown-dress settling around us. She looped her arms around my neck as she rolled her lips together. "I didn't realize how bad it was with him until it was over," she whispered. "I thought it was good enough."

I reached under her skirt and gripped her backside, rocking her against me. "And now? Do you see that good enough isn't close to what you deserve?"

She stared at me for a moment, her brows pinched and her eyes dark like she didn't understand the question. Then, she turned her attention to unfastening my belt and shoving her hand into my boxers. She gave my shaft an urgent stroke. "I don't know what I deserve."

I leaned in and captured her lips with mine. "But I do," I said between frenzied kisses. I held her backside hard, my fingers tracing the damp line of her panties. I tugged the fabric aside and urged her closer, to where her small fingers worked me over. "Let me take care of you, wife."

She gasped as I boosted her up and then dragged my cock through her wet heat. Her hands went to my shoulders as I eased inside her, her nails biting into my skin through my shirt.

"Ryan," she cried out.

"Too much?" I forced myself to hold steady as she adjusted to me. We hadn't done much to warm up and I didn't have any lube stashed out here.

She shook her head, her hair falling in front of her face as she rocked against me. "No, I just needed a second."

"Take all the time you need," I said. "There's nowhere in the world I'd rather be."

She found a rhythm, slow but deep, and I let her set the pace for a few minutes. But when her moans increased and her pace faltered, I gathered her close and took charge.

"*Yes*, that's my girl." I fisted a hand in her hair and kissed her neck as I thrust into her. "Look at you taking my cock. Do you see this? Do you see how hard you make me? No one does this to me. Just you. Just my wife."

"Oh my god," she whispered, her mouth hanging open on an endless moan. "I can't—"

"You can," I growled, my fingertips digging into her ass. "Let me give it to you. Let me give you everything."

She dropped her head to my shoulder as I felt her walls clench around me. "Ryan," she gasped.

"I don't know why you think you don't deserve better," I said, thrusting into her with each word, "but that ends now."

A cry broke free from her chest and I felt the great spasm of her release shudder through her. She slumped against me, her chest heaving as I barreled toward my own orgasm and heat pumped through me. I came with a shout, bucking into her for another minute as I poured my entire soul into her.

When I could move my limbs again, I smoothed a hand over her hair. "That's my girl. Don't forget it."

She stared up at me, her eyes wide and shiny with unshed tears, and she said, "I'll try."

I kissed her forehead. "That's all I want."

chapter thirty

Emme

Today's Learning Objective:
Students will take lessons from a badass.

I COULDN'T REMEMBER WHY WE'D DECIDED IT WAS A GOOD IDEA TO schedule Grace's final dress fitting for the day after her pub crawl shower and make an afternoon of it with her side of the bridal party. I had to assume we didn't do it to torture ourselves but as I groaned into my pillow and kicked my feet in the sheets until Ryan slapped my ass and told me to stop with the tantrums, I saw only demonic forces at work.

"I'll go with you," he said.

"No," I groaned, still buried in the pillow. "You have a workout with your trainer this afternoon and I'm sorry but I can only be married to the number one QB in the League. If you start falling behind in your conditioning, I'm out."

He slapped my ass again. It kind of helped dull out the lingering headache from mixing alcohols—such a rookie move—and crying my whole eyes out last night.

He smoothed his palm over my backside. His fingers slipped between my legs. "My conditioning is fine but I love the support."

"You better keep it that way," I said lightly.

"I can reschedule. I don't want you going into this alone."

"No, no, it's going to be okay," I said. "Grace is just going to have a lot of questions and I'm going to have to answer them."

"And that's a bad thing?"

"It's a complicated thing. I wanted Grace to have the whole wonderful engagement season experience but giving her that has meant withholding a few tidbits."

He gave my ass a rough squeeze. "You have to explain this to me because I've never known you to keep anything from Grace but now everything is about her *moment*. You didn't have a *moment* before our wedding."

"Because I wasn't really engaged."

His hand cracked hard against my ass. This one actually stung a bit. "You break my heart every time you say that."

"No, I don't," I yelped, trying to kick him away.

He responded by banding an arm around my hips and holding me down. "It's a wonder I'm still alive with all the times you've broken my heart." He locked a hand around my ankles when I went on flailing. "Would you have wanted the whole moment thing? If it'd been different?"

"I don't know." I shook my hair out of my eyes. "Probably not, but being engaged can be a lot of fun if you do it right. It's like Mardi Gras. Nonstop parties, someone's always pouring champagne, and endless reasons to dress up and look cute. And people basically throw gifts at you the whole time."

"You don't want that?"

I shot him a lopsided grin over my shoulder. "All I've done for the past few months is go to parties with you, drink champagne, and dress up in very cute outfits. And I had a small panic attack over the gifts we received. I've had all the Mardi Gras I need. I'm good."

His hand left my ankles to trail up between my legs. "You don't want the traditional stuff? Like Grace?"

"Really, I'm good. But no one's ever really celebrated Grace before," I said. "Her family is extremely nice but they never had birthday parties or graduation parties or anything special for each kid. Their holidays were *only* about religious services. If one kid in the family had something great happen—winning a soccer tournament or honor roll or whatever—they had to wait until all the other kids had something great to acknowledge them all at once. Doesn't make a lick of sense to me but it's how they did it. And Ben and Grace are paying for this by themselves. He's working a ton of overtime, she's waxing vaginas left and right, all so they can have this dream celebration. And I didn't want to ruin any of that."

"Muggsy, how the hell could you ruin it by telling her that your ex is a sociopath?"

"Because when I tried to, she wanted to cancel her wedding."

"That's a trick play if I've ever seen one." He slapped me again and I had to admit I didn't mind it. His hand was large enough to connect with a wide area and when I spread my legs a tiny bit, the blows landed lower. "You can't just pretend everything is okay and expect it to stay that way. You gotta speak up when things aren't good."

I went back to groaning into my pillow. He continued spanking me. I was probably beet red by now.

"You're sure Clara won't be there?" he asked.

"That would never happen," I said with a rueful laugh. "Grace didn't want a bachelorette party because she didn't like the idea of us spending more money on her, but she did want to have a cute lunch date with her bridesmaids. There's no way in hell Clara would be invited."

"You'd be shocked at what really goes on in hell so give me a call if you need backup."

"I think I'm going to be all right." It felt weird to say that *and* believe it. It felt weird to wake up without the tang of bitterness on my tongue, the gnawing anger in my belly. If I reached for it, I could find the last shards but the rest was gone. It was like Ryan had plucked it out of me and given it all back to Teddy. It was like I was free. "Even if she made an appearance, it would be okay. It doesn't feel like it matters in the same way it did before."

Another rough slap though this one landed squarely between the thighs I'd been inching open. "That's what I like to hear, wifey."

I glanced at him over my shoulder. "Did Ines come home last night?"

He barked out a laugh. "Uh, no, she did not." Grabbing his phone off the side table, he said, "But Jakobi texted me at three in the morning to tell me her phone died but all was well."

I skimmed the messages. "So, she stayed with Jakobi?"

Ryan shrugged. "That's what it sounds like."

I dragged my lower lip between my teeth. "I can't decide if I'm worried about her getting involved with someone so much older and more experienced or happy that she's found someone who plans constellation cruises just because she likes seeing the stars."

"Jakobi doesn't fuck around. When he sees something he wants, he goes for it."

"That's not helping me balance the worry with the happiness."

With a laugh, he said, "I've known Jakobi a long time and Ines is only the second or third woman I've ever seen him pursue. He doesn't go all in for nothing. He likes her. He made some noise about marrying her the night we moved you two in here."

I bolted up from the mattress. I remembered then that I wasn't wearing any pajamas. "And you're just telling me this now?"

His gaze dropped to my bare breasts. He stroked the back of his finger over my nipple until it perked up. "Do you not remember that night? I was a little preoccupied. Coming in my pants at thirty thousand feet does that to me."

I watched as he went to his knees, his shaft long and thick between his legs. "That's the last time you can use that excuse."

"Until you make me come in my pants again," he replied, shoving the blankets and sheets away.

I followed the stretch of his muscles and the way his ink twisted as he reached into the drawer. I still needed to figure out those tattoos. There had to be more to the story. But then he popped open a bottle of lube and drizzled it over his cock and between my legs. The cool liquid met my flesh and I gasped out, "Just promise you'll tell me if he's going to propose."

Ryan pulled me beneath him and settled between my thighs. "I'll do my best. Now, enough about them. Let me put you in a good mood."

I grew up in a lot of different places. Chicago, Miami, Vegas, and then the New Hampshire seacoast—but there were also a bunch of other cities in between those spots. Indianapolis after my parents divorced. Jacksonville after the Feds seized Gary's assets. Los Angeles before Mom ended up with Dell.

I kept parts of all those places with me, though I'd never kept friends. Even if I'd wanted to stay in touch, there'd been no time for that. All we could worry about was getting Mom situated with someone new.

While I knew deep in my bones that Grace was a friend for life, there was still a wobbly part of me that walked into the bridal boutique with a thread of worry tying itself into a knot in my belly. It didn't make any sense, but it was there just the same.

Grace glanced up from a rack of gowns when the door jingled behind me. "Hey," she said, a tentative note in her voice. "How are you?"

I joined her at the rack and pulled out a dress. It wasn't my style—or anyone's in this century—but I studied it carefully. "I shouldn't mix beer and martinis, but otherwise all right. What about you? How late did you guys stay out?"

Her sigh was impatient. She wanted to get to the point. "Everyone left not long after you did."

"Hello there." At my side, I found a cheery-faced saleswoman dressed all in black. She had that in common with Grace. "I'm Mackenzie. What can I help you find today?"

"Oh, no, I don't need anything. I'm here for my friend's final fitting," I said. "We're just waiting for a few more people to join us."

Mackenzie's smile brightened. She dropped a glance to my ring. "I hope this isn't supremely awkward, but I'm a huge fan of your fiancé's and if there's anything I can do—"

"Wow," Grace huffed. "Bold strategy."

"—it would be my complete honor." Mackenzie went on beaming. "If you want to try on some gowns after your friend's fitting, I can start pulling a few. I'm obsessed with your style and I think we have looks that you'd love."

"Thank you so much," I said, hazarding a glance at Grace only to find she'd stalked off to the other side of the store. "But I'm here for my friend today."

"If you change your mind," Mackenzie said as I set out after Grace, "I'll be here!"

I caught up to Grace near the flower girl dresses. "Sorry about that. I didn't think anyone would recognize—"

"Can you stop being sorry for a minute? I don't need any more apologies. I need you to tell me what the hell happened last night and why I had to find out about it from Ryan."

"Miss Kilmeade?" came another sunny voice. Everyone was so damn happy here. "We're ready for you."

"Fuck," she grumbled under her breath. With another impatient sigh, she linked her elbow with mine. "Come on."

"I should wait out here for everyone else," I offered as we crossed to the boutique's alterations department. This was a small place, a free-standing building in a strip mall that looked suspiciously like an old Pizza Hut or Papa Gino's location.

"Audrey and Jamie can handle some unstructured time," she

snapped. "And Shay's already texted me to say she's going to be half an hour late. Some goats went loose or something farm-ish like that."

We followed the seamstress to a large dressing room, but instead of changing out of her clothes and into the satin robe provided, Grace told her we'd need a few minutes.

She pulled the curtain shut and crossed her arms. "Why didn't you tell me?" she asked. "Why didn't you tell me *anything*?"

"Because every time I do, you threaten to throw your whole wedding out the window."

"Because I don't want to have a wedding if you get hurt in the process!"

I blew out a breath as I paced in front of the mirrors. "Do you even want to get married? You've put your wedding on the line so many times now that I'm half convinced you don't want to get married and you're hoping I'll give you a way out."

A stunned expression crossed her face and my breath caught, thinking I'd gone too far. But then her shoulders slumped and she dropped her gaze to the floor. She slid down the wall until her backside hit the carpet and she folded her arms over her knees.

That was when I realized I had gone too far—but it was exactly where I needed to be.

After a minute of heavy silence, she said, "Everything is changing so fast." Her voice wavered and something in my chest cracked. "It's really overwhelming and you know how I hate that feeling."

I nodded. Grace didn't get overwhelmed because she was obsessive about planning and preparing. She didn't let things catch her off guard.

"I do want to marry Ben. I like him even if everything has been really fucking stressful for the past month. I want to keep him around. But I'm afraid I'm losing everything I love in the process." She sucked in a breath as tears filled her eyes. She worked hard at blinking them away before she continued. "I left my job. I left the city. The apartment's gone and now I live so far away that it's basically Maine and no one wants to visit me."

"We'll visit you," I said. "Just ask Audrey to create a dinner party schedule and I promise we'll make the trek to Maine at least once a month."

She leveled a gaze at me. "Will you though? Because it feels like I've lost you most of all."

I swallowed against a lump in my throat. "You didn't lose me."

"Then why does it feel like you're already gone?"

I dropped down to the floor across from her and folded my legs in front of me. "I'm not, but you needed me to be okay and I did what I had to do to make you believe I was." When she gave an incredulous shake of her head, I added, "I knew this would be hard and I wasn't going to make it any harder. You deserve to be happy—and I couldn't let you cancel the wedding. Not for *me*."

"You should've told me." She drew in another breath, fighting hard against those tears. "You should've told me everything that he did."

I stared down at my hands as I said, "He's Ben's friend. I didn't want to make you choose sides." *Especially since you kept threatening to call off the wedding.*

A watery laugh cracked out of her. "Not anymore."

I blinked at her, confused. "What?"

"We got kicked out of Beantown Pub last night," she said with another laugh. "Because Ben lost it on Teddy after you left." She ran a finger over her brow. "Ben yelled at him for at least five straight minutes until Teddy shoved him and then Ben punched him in the mouth. It all went to hell and they threw us out." She gave me an uneven smile. "Bottom line, Ben broke his middle finger and Teddy won't be coming to the wedding."

"What? No! Not from punching Teddy?"

Her shoulders shook as she laughed. "No, he tripped outside of Beantown. Completely unrelated. Didn't even split his knuckles from wailing on Teddy, but he breaks a whole finger walking down the sidewalk." As she sobered, she said, "He feels terrible about everything that happened. He wants you to know he should've kicked Teddy's ass a long time ago."

"Tell him I appreciate that. And I'm sorry about his finger."

"Don't be. He's having the time of his life showing it off." She dropped her head back against the wall. "I should've drawn the line months ago and thrown Teddy out of the wedding. I shouldn't have dumped any of that on you. A part of me thought that if you needed me, I'd just put it all on hold. We could go back to our old apartment and the way things used to be, and the wedding would wait. But I'm not sure we can even do that anymore."

I nodded slowly. "Remember when we finished school and moved down here? And everything was new and magical, even though we had no money and no idea what we were doing? This is just like that—without worrying about having to move back in with our parents. Think of all the amazing things happening for us."

She let out a long breath. "We're getting married."

Time to put it all out there. "You are," I said with a shrug. "I got married last month."

Her eyes rounded. "You fucking what?"

"We eloped. Seemed like the right time but I didn't want to take anything away from you." I shrugged when she flipped me off. "We're thinking we'll have a big wedding next year. Whenever Ines learns enough of the harp to play for us."

She cocked her head to the side as she studied me. "Then this is for real, you and Ryan."

I nodded. Didn't even question it this time. "Yeah. It is."

She scrambled to her knees and caught me in a tight embrace. "I hope he deserves you."

"He does," I said, bringing my arms around her. I was starting to believe that.

"Come on, y'all. We'll find them. They're back here somewhere," came Jamie's voice. "This one's empty. That one's empty. If they aren't in the last one, it's because they took it on the run which is a different issue. Hello? We're coming in. Final warning."

The curtain flung open, revealing Audrey, Jamie, and Shay. They stared down at us, locked in a haphazard hug on the floor.

Jamie dropped her hands to her hips. "I know one thing and it's that there's a boy to blame for this."

"Always a boy to blame," Grace said.

Shay tucked her rose-gold hair over her ear, saying, "I don't know what I missed but I expect you'll catch me up soon enough."

With that, she dropped to her knees and scooped us both into a hug.

"Me too," Audrey said, following her lead.

Eventually, Jamie gathered up her maxi dress and joined us on the floor. Glancing between me and Grace, she asked, "Are we still trying this dress on today? Don't feel like you have to say yes. I'm just covering the exits."

Grace laughed. "Yeah, we're trying on this dress." She smiled at me and gave my hand a squeeze. "When I'm done, Emme's going to try a few too."

"It's your day," I said.

She shook her head. "I'm tired of it being my day. I have to be happy and gracious all the time. It's exhausting. I'm ready for it to be your turn so I can stop playing nice and go back to being a nightmare."

A true, warm smile filled my face. And then Shay said, "Okay so I love you all but half of my ass is asleep and I don't know where Gennie went."

"Everyone up," Grace said. "Find my flower girl."

"One last thing," I said as we climbed out of our pile on the floor. "And it would really help if you didn't tell anyone until next weekend when the media release goes out but...Ryan and I eloped."

Shay let out a shriek as Jamie jabbed a finger in my direction. "I knew it! I knew something was different!"

As they folded me into another hug, I heard the battle cry of, "*Auntie Gracie!* Look at my badass dress!"

Gennie, Shay's husband's niece who lived with them on their farmland in Rhode Island, came barreling down the hall and bounded onto the round platform in front of the mirror. She shimmied her hips, watching as the black and white tulle swished. Officially, Grace's colors were the hydrangea palette: blue, green, and cream. But for Gennie, a pirate at heart, she'd picked a dramatic dress.

"Stunning, my dear," Grace said.

"You're going to knock 'em dead," Jamie said.

"I'm gonna be the best goddamn flower girl you've ever seen," Gennie said.

"That's right." Shay glanced at me and, dropping her voice, she said, "Don't you dare ask her to be your flower girl until a few weeks before the wedding. She wakes up every single day and asks if it's time for the wedding yet. We're going to have to hide the dress so she doesn't wear it to clean out the chicken coops. I love you and I support you but I'm putting you on notice, Ahlborg."

I laughed, holding her closer. "My lips are sealed."

"Yeah," Gennie said, mostly to herself. "I'm a badass fucking flower girl."

chapter thirty-one
Ryan

*Today's Learning Objective:
Students will fly a little too close to the sun.*

"To kick off your birthday weekend," I said, leading Emme onto the plane, "I have a few surprises."

"Is it a soft pillow to sit on? Because I'm still recovering from all the surprises you gave me this morning," she said with a wry laugh.

We'd been a little rowdy. Mostly me, but Emme was no angel. It was just so damn good to wake up with her knowing we had a stretch of time to ourselves that I couldn't help myself.

I motioned to my usual seat. "You don't need a pillow when you can sit on me. Even better"—I held up the oversized blanket draped over the seat back—"I'll keep you cozy. Or we can do whatever you want under the blanket. Your birthday, your choice."

She dropped her bag to the seat across the aisle from mine and shot me an indulgent grin. "Good to know."

I grabbed the gleaming silver bowl and held it out. "We also have thirty oranges."

Her gaze landed on the red box perched atop the mound of fruit. "What is this?"

"Open it up and find out," I said.

She aimed a wary glance at me, like she couldn't figure out why I'd have a birthday gift for her. She'd need to get used to it real fast because the entire weekend was going to be a birthday blowout. I had a full day of spa treatments and massages scheduled. Reservations at the most exclusive restaurants in Vegas. Tickets to every show I could imagine her wanting to see. An adventure day where she could choose from a helicopter tour to the bottom of the Grand Canyon or an off-road dune buggy race through the hills and valleys beyond the Strip. And that was on top of staying in one of the best penthouses in the entire city.

There was a bit of time carved out for a sports industry awards event on Saturday night and I'd promised we'd meet up with a bunch of guys from my team too, but everything else belonged to us. Even better—by this time tomorrow, news of our secret wedding would land.

The last surprise, the one I was saving for her birthday on Sunday, was a trip to the Seychelles. A proper honeymoon right after Grace's wedding and before the start of training camp.

After a moment of hesitation, she pried the box open. Her eyes went wide and she clapped a hand to her mouth. "Oh my god," she whispered.

I considered that proof of a job well done.

"When I saw it," I started, "it reminded me of your tangerines."

"Well, they're basically the same size," she cried.

I set the bowl down and plucked the necklace from the box to put it on her. "I know it's not orange, so it's not exactly the same as a tangerine, but I liked the plump, oval shape of the diamond." I swept her hair over her shoulder while the flight crew closed the aircraft doors. "And the marquise-cut diamonds sitting on top too. Made me think of an orange blossom's leaves." I slipped the chain around her neck, adding, "You can wear it up here"—I held the closure at the shortest point, the pendant sitting at the base of her throat, and then let it slip to the rise of her breasts—"or down here."

She turned around when I clasped the necklace, her hand over the pendant. "Thank you." She wrapped her arms around me and tucked her head under my chin. We fit together like puzzle pieces, and even if we did this for the next thousand years, I didn't think I'd ever find something so right. "It's...incredible."

"Mr. Ralston? If you're ready, we'll be taking off shortly," the pilot called from the cockpit.

"Are you ready for your birthday weekend to commence, Mrs. Ralston?" I asked.

"I think I am." She glanced up at me, laughing. "Let's do this."

I WATCHED WHILE EMME ATE SIX TANGERINES, ONE AFTER THE OTHER without stopping. There was something hypnotic about the way she unraveled the rind and pulled at the pith. It brought me back to the earliest days of our friendship and how I'd ply her with tangerines just for the pleasure of sitting by while she took them apart. I remembered staring at her fingers and feeling a prickle on the back of my neck, and riding that high all day.

"Have you told anyone?" she asked between orange segments.

I stared as she sucked a bit of sweetness from her thumb. We could not get under that blanket fast enough. "Told anyone what?"

"About the news we're dropping tomorrow."

"Who would I tell?" I asked, still locked in this trance. "Jakobi was there. As far as the guys are concerned, we've been married for months. Ines and your friends already know."

"Hmm. Let me think." She licked the rest of her fingers and I might've groaned out loud. "Oh, yeah. What about your *mother*, Ryan? Your sisters? Gramma CeCe? Don't you think they'd like to know?"

A deep, barking laugh burst out of me. "Oh, you have no idea."

"Dare I ask what that means?"

She went for another tangerine and I almost took the bowl away from her, but I knew she'd fight me for it. Some people could drink ten cups of coffee in a day and sleep straight through the night. Emme could eat a bushel of oranges without making herself sick. It was some kind of witchcraft.

"It means my entire family has been gagging over how much they adore you for months." I held up my phone. "I had to stop following the group chat when they started debating when we'd give my mother a grandchild. Gramma CeCe thinks the horse is out of the stable, as she put it."

Her cheeks stuffed with citrus, she pointed at her midsection. "I look pregnant?"

"No, Muggsy." I laughed as I ran a hand over my face. "They came across a photo from some event and decided that was the outcome I wanted based on the look I was giving you."

"Is it? The outcome that you want?"

My chest tightened. We hadn't talked any real specifics about the future. The conversation after field day was too much of an Emme fuck-around to count as tangible plans. All I knew at this moment was that we weren't running up to a deadline anymore. It shouldn't have blindsided me but her question took me to the ground. I was desperate to hold on to her as long as I could. Any little piece I could get, I'd keep.

"If you do, yeah," I said. Giving her the answer she wanted was the only goal. "But I need some time with you first. A few years just for us."

She nodded slowly. "I think about it a lot because I know getting pregnant probably won't be easy for me, but I also know I'm nowhere near ready. I'm barely a functional adult." She pointed toward me with an orange segment. "I like what you said about a few years for us. Tell Gramma CeCe we're not in a hurry. The stable is locked and the horses are secure."

Pressure gathered behind my breastbone. I had to work hard at swallowing down a rock of emotion. "Okay," I said, almost to myself. I had to replay her words a few times because there was no way she'd just decided to wait a couple of years to have kids with me. With *me*. That we'd be together in a couple of years. Me and Emme. No way. "Okay."

"You should call them," she said. "Tell them the news."

"They're obsessed with you. They can't wait for me to bring you home."

"Then why haven't you?"

"Because I don't get enough of you as it is. As I've previously stated, I don't want to share."

"That's not the reason." She gave me a knowing glance before going back to her tangerine.

"It is the reason. My schedule has been packed all fucking spring and I'm lucky if I get three consecutive nights with you a week. Even when I do, we have to go to Nantucket and bridal showers and whatever the fuck else."

"Okay. I'll give you that. But you don't like going home and it has nothing to do with me."

"I don't," I admitted. Emme motioned for me to expand on that. I heaved out a sigh. "Nothing in that house has changed in fifteen years. It's like going back in time and I hate it."

She nodded as if she understood, and I knew she did. She'd been there for me through the worst of it.

"I think—no, I know my mother likes it that way," I said. "There's a comfort in keeping things the same. Her memories are baked into it—but that's the problem. Those memories kill me. They're suffocating." I rubbed a hand over the back of my neck. "Everyone else loves it there. They love stepping inside the memories." I shook my head as the sounds of breathing and heart rate monitors rang through my mind. All these years later, the first thing I still noticed when I went home was the silence. The machines weren't beeping and the oxygen compressor wasn't whirring and I was hit with the truth all over again that he was gone. "I'm the only one who suffocates."

"That doesn't mean it's wrong. There's no right way to experience grief." Emme set aside her tangerines and crossed the aisle to climb into my lap. "Would it help if I was there with you?"

"Maybe. Yeah." I wrapped my arms around her waist and let myself relax. "You really think we should tell them today?"

"Let me put it this way," she said. "If you don't come around to the idea on your own, I'm going back to my seat and staying there for the rest of the flight."

I kissed her forehead. "You're vicious."

After some debate, we settled on dropping one of the photos Ines took during the ceremony in the family chat with our announcement, a note about a big wedding to come next spring or early summer, and a promise to visit soon. I didn't specify a location for that visit.

"Prepare yourself," I murmured as I sent the message.

Emme curled into me, her eyes on the screen. The responses started pouring in immediately.

> Claudia: IT'S HAPPENING
>
> Claudia: and it didn't even require some light breaking and entering
>
> Chloe: holy shit what
>
> Mom: <10 sobbing emojis>
>
> Amber: tell her we feel like she's already part of our family and we love her so much!
>
> Gramma CeCe: Congratulations, my boy. We're so happy for you both. Give that sweet girl our love.
>
> Claudia: is it too soon to ask if I'm going to be a bridesmaid?
>
> Ruthie: yes
>
> Mom: <10 bride and groom emojis>
>
> Ruthie: but I'd also like to know about bridesmaids

> Ruthie: if it helps, I'm very good at organizing and haggling
>
> Amber: really we hadn't noticed
>
> Gramma CeCe: girls, we should let the newlyweds be. They don't need to worry themselves with all of these questions. Not when there are more important things for them right now. Remember to give yourselves plenty of time in the bedroom.
>
> Mom: <10 heart-eyes emojis>
>
> Claudia: This is your one and only warning, Gram
>
> Gramma CeCe: I'm only encouraging them to explore
>
> Gramma CeCe: Between the sheets, that is.
>
> Chloe: we knew what you meant, Gram
>
> Mom: <10 more sobbing emojis>
>
> Mom: When can we see you two? How about Sunday? I'll cook your favorites!

I glanced at Emme, trying to read her reaction to my family's outpouring of love and chaos. "What do you think?"

"We're not back until Monday," she said. "Later in the week is blocked for Grace, but maybe Tuesday? We don't have to go to your mom's house if it's too much for you. We can meet them somewhere or invite them to our place. Whatever you want."

I stared at her for a long moment as a smile pulled at my lips. I couldn't grab hold of all these emotions to figure out what they were, but I knew I'd never felt so many good things at once. "Tuesday, then."

> Ryan: We're in Vegas this weekend for Em's birthday. How about Tuesday?
>
> Mom: <another 10 sobbing emojis>

> Mom: I can't wait!

I put my phone down and turned to Emme. I tapped my finger to her lips, saying, "I hope you know what you've done."

She beamed at me. I could smell the citrus on her. "We'll find out on Tuesday."

I shook the blanket out and tucked it tight around us. "Let's not talk about my family anymore. We have this wonderful blanket to enjoy however we want."

Her whole body shook as she laughed and I nearly blacked out from the bliss of it. At this point, it didn't take much to turn me on. The mere mention of my wife was enough. But having her warm and soft against me while we put one official stamp after another on this relationship? I was fucking done.

"What is it with you and *enjoying the blanket*?" she asked.

"I seem to remember us having a very good time under a blanket," I said. "I don't see any reason why we shouldn't give it another spin. I have a change of clothes in my backpack too."

Still laughing, she pressed a hand to her eyes, but I grabbed it away and sucked the lingering sweetness from her fingertips.

"I barely touched you that time," she said.

"Yeah, that's what made it so incredible. It was completely out of my control."

She shook her head against my chest. "I'm not sure I believe that."

"You're forgetting that the way you feel and the sounds you make when you're aroused get me at least eighty percent of the way there. Throw in a little friction and I'm done."

"Hmm." She ran her fingers down the center of my torso, stopping at my belt. Her hand settled over my shaft and I jolted up to meet her. "Let's see if that math checks out."

"Does it feel different?" I asked, my lips on the back of Emme's neck and my hand splayed across her belly as I moved in her from behind. "Now that the world knows we're married?"

She groaned something into the pillow as morning sunlight streamed into the room and I kept up our slow, lazy rhythm. I loved this. I loved waking up beside her, loved pulling her sleepy body into mine, loved her soft hands reaching for me, asking for me without saying a word.

I loved that she was *mine* in all the ways I'd ever wanted her to belong to me—and now that the handful of photos Ines snapped at our secret wedding were splashed all over the internet, everyone else knew it too.

"That's what I thought," I replied, thrusting deep and holding myself there as her inner walls pulsed around me. I dug my fingertips into the round flare of her hip as a blast of heat shot down my spine. My entire body drew tight before a growl snapped out of me and I lashed my arms around her torso. "I fucking love you."

I felt her head bob against my chest. "Mmm."

She was breathing hard when I rolled her to her side and held her close. I knew she'd scamper away in a second to use the bathroom like she always did and I just wanted to soak up as much of this as I could. I wanted to remember this morning. I wanted to remember all of our mornings but it felt like the energy around us was shifting. It was heavy, but I had to think it was positive. Things were happening. It was real now. Even more than it'd always been.

I leaned to the other side of the bed and grabbed the small box I'd hidden there last night. The plan had been to wake Emme up with this gift, but I wasn't mad about this turn of events.

"Since we're getting married twice," I said, taking her hand, "I decided you need two rings." I slipped the halo-shaped diamond bands on either side of her engagement ring. "Perfect."

Still bleary-eyed and breathless, she twisted in my hold and pressed her lips to mine. "I love them."

"Good, because I want to be married to you," I said. "I want us. Together. For as long as you'll have me. If there are kids or pets or… Ines, it doesn't matter. You're all I need."

She studied me for a long moment and I'd never heard seconds tick by so slowly. But then she said, "I picked out something for you too. Stay right here."

I folded my arms behind my head as she strolled away wearing nothing but the diamonds I'd put on her. There was no finer sight.

When she returned a few minutes later with a small box in hand, she climbed on top of me, her thighs bracketing my hips and the heat between her legs almost exactly where I needed it. A few quick moves and we could see how well she carried this conversation while I was buried inside her.

"Not yet," she said, wagging a finger at me. "I know what that face means."

"What face?"

"The *I'm thinking about fucking you* face. Stop it. I'm doing something and you're not going to interfere."

"Muggsy, you can do anything you want to me and I'll sit here, happy as a fuckin' clam." I cupped her breasts, my thumbs sweeping over her nipples. I needed to spend more time with those beauties. "But you should know I'm never not thinking about fucking you."

Laughing, she held up the box. I grabbed for it and she responded by shooting me a withering glare and holding it over her head. Adorable. As if I couldn't reach that. "Let me do this."

I motioned for her to continue. "Go right ahead, my love."

She inhaled like she needed a breath to steady herself and drummed her fingertips on my chest. "I know you can't wear this on the field or when you're working out, and that's pretty much all the time, but I liked it and thought you would too. Seemed like your style." She opened the box to reveal a platinum band with a simple milgrain detail around the edges. She snared her bottom lip between her teeth and put it on my finger. "I won't be upset if you don't wear it."

"Enough of that." It could've been actual barbed wire and I would've treasured it. "Of course I'm going to wear it."

"It's okay if you don't." Tracing a finger over the ink on my shoulders, she said, "I was thinking you might want something a little more permanent."

It took everything inside me to keep from laughing.

If she only knew how permanent she'd always been to me.

But I'd explain it all later. That story was a series of confessions, and though I'd imagined telling her so many times, I still didn't know where to start.

I'd get it right soon enough. On our honeymoon, maybe. I'd have plenty of time to unravel our history and how I'd fallen in love with her over the years. How I'd waited and how I'd wanted her, and how everything in my life seemed to propel me toward her now—when it was time to make good on our pact.

I swallowed down those emotions, that tension. The lurking panic that it would change things for us. "What did you have in mind, wife?"

"I don't know," she mused, her fingers still stroking my skin. "Something that fits with your other pieces."

She had no idea how well it would fit. "I'm sure it will."

Smiling, she asked, "Will you tell me what we're doing today? Or is that another one of your secrets?"

"We're doing many things today."

"No hints?" I shook my head. "How will I know what to wear?"

I straightened the pendant on her chest. "I'll take care of that for you."

"What if I had plans for the day? Have you considered that?"

"I don't think you'd believe how thoroughly I've considered that." I pushed up to brush my lips over hers. "You can decide if we're trying out the shower this morning or the bathtub."

She glowered at me for a second, but I ran my palm up her torso, the cool metal of my wedding band leaving a trail of goose bumps as I went. "Shower," she said. "There's a bench and a bunch of showerheads."

I gathered her close and swung my legs over the bed. "Fuck yes, let's go."

We flew to the bottom of the Grand Canyon for a picnic lunch, soaked in volcanic mud imported from Colombia before being massaged to a pulp, and then alternated between floating in a private pool and napping on a king-sized lounge chair. It was heaven. I never wanted to leave.

Since everyone was in town for tomorrow night's awards event and Hersberler had finally signed his contract, we reserved the back room at one of the best steakhouses in town to celebrate. Everyone was there, just about the whole team plus a bunch of significant others. The O-line was in a phenomenal mood, everyone busting Hersberler's balls over him milking free agency for all it was worth and fawning over Emme like they always did.

It turned into the kind of night that reminded me of all the things I loved about this game—the tenacious optimism that roared to life in the preseason, the bone-deep trust that grew from sweating and bleeding together week after week, the sense of family—of brotherhood—that propelled us to keep fighting for every inch of turf.

We told stories that prompted us to confirm on multiple occasions that no one had a phone out and was recording anything. We ate like we wouldn't be back on egg whites and kale protein smoothies by the start of training camp. We ordered bottles of wine and whiskey and bourbon that cost more than most used cars, and we let Emme pose us for a series of ridiculous photos, but we were having too much fun to care.

It was late when we left the restaurant, but time had no meaning in

Vegas. Wilcox, McKerry, and Crawson headed to the blackjack tables while Hersberler wandered with me and Emme down the Strip. He was in one of his morose moods despite getting the exact contract terms he'd wanted, though every time someone stopped us to say hi or ask for a photo, his spirits lifted. Nothing if not vain, that one.

"And I thought this guy was a moody motherfucker," Emme said to him as she tipped her head toward me. "Take it one day at a time, okay? And if that's too much, just remember you're the legendary Pumpkin Dick. No one else will ever live up to that."

"They stopped making that formula," he said, dismal as ever as he shot me a frown. "This might be the year it falls apart for me."

"That's no way to go into a preseason," Emme said. "Listen, dude. You're one of the few tight ends who are weapons of mass destruction in both receiving and blocking. You're fast as fuck. You put up outrageous numbers, you know how to work in tight traffic, and you catch everything that comes anywhere near you. You have the most reliable hands in the League, my friend. You're my guy's safety valve and I need you to fortify yourself and be there for him this season." She patted my arm, and even though she was running down Hersberler's stats, her words had me smiling brighter than anything else in this city. "My biggest problem with you as a player is that I can't have you on pass protection and plucking the ball out of the air at the same time."

"Since when do you follow football?" I teased.

"I don't," she replied, fake horror all over her face.

I grabbed her hand, pressed a kiss to her knuckles. It gave me a chance to admire the rings on her finger. "Sure sounds like you do."

"Can you please be quiet? I'm very busy nurturing your tight end because the team's management dicked around on his deal and he doesn't feel special anymore."

Still frowning like someone just stole his ice cream cone, Hersberler stared at his shoes as we stepped through the front doors of our hotel. "I don't need to feel *special*," he grumbled.

I shared an amused glance with my wife as we headed toward the elevators. "Okay, sweetie," she said. "Whatever you say."

"I'm going to try jerking off with a different self-tanner," he said just as I heard a woman shout, "Emme! Ralston! Are you staying here too?"

And then I found myself staring at Charles Ahlborg and his wife Danielle, the woman he left Emme's mom for.

"Oh, fuck me," Hersberler said as he ran a hand down his face.

I took half a step forward, putting myself slightly in front of Emme as I reached for her hand. She grabbed hold, squeezing hard. Charles stared at his daughter, his lips parted and his brow wrinkled, and though it seemed completely out of character for him, it appeared he had no idea what to say.

His wife noticed this too, and she jumped in with, "Congratulations! Oh my god, sweetheart, you're *married*! I loved the photos so much." She clasped her hands under her chin and wiggled a bit where she stood. "They were the sweetest. You were stunning, my darling. Absolutely gorgeous." She reached out and skimmed a finger over Emme's cheek before glancing back at her husband. "Wasn't she beautiful, honey? Didn't you say that this morning?"

Charles cleared his throat. "You looked lovely. I-I'm happy for you." He shot a glance at me and I tipped my chin up in challenge. I didn't care who the fuck he was. He'd need to go through me if he wanted to get to Emme. "Could we sit down somewhere private? For a few minutes?" He waved to the people streaming through the lobby. We drew a fair amount of attention to ourselves. "To celebrate your news?"

"I am late for my, um, my"—Hersberler tapped his watch no less than fifteen times—"my hour of meditation. Yes. That's what I need to do. Tonight. Right now, actually. I'll be going. To meditate and balance my…quadrants. Great seeing all of you. Really great. Princess, Ralston. The pleasure's been all mine." He bowed his head toward us before glancing at Emme's father. "Sir. Ma'am. Until we meet again."

"Don't forget the self-tanner," Danielle called as he sprinted away.

I felt the shocked huff of Emme's laugh over my shoulder, and if I hadn't been so busy making sure Charles didn't step out of line, I would've appreciated the fuck out of that comment. But my job right now was putting up an impenetrable defense around my girl and nothing was getting in my way.

"I noticed the cutest bakery café on our way in," Danielle said, pointing across the lobby. "They have a whole menu of hot chocolate. You're a big fan of hot chocolate, aren't you, Emme? Remember that time we got those truffle cocoas in Vail? Argh, so good!" She shimmied at the thought and I realized this lady was breaking her back to carry the conversation. "I think they have frozen hot chocolates too since it's a little toasty-roasty out there tonight. We could just pop on over and check it out." She gave her husband a not-so-subtle jab in the side. "Wouldn't that be spectacular, honey?"

Charles seemed to struggle with finding the words. For my part, I struggled with not hauling off and laying this fucking guy out for the shit he put his daughter through. But then he said, "It would be wonderful, if it's not too much trouble." He shot a quick, plaintive glance in my direction. "But I don't mean to intrude and I would understand if this isn't the right time for you."

Emme gave my hand a squeeze and I interpreted that as the signal to get us out of there—and do a much better job of it than Hersberler—but she said, "Yeah, okay."

And that was how the four of us ended up crowded around a small table in a mostly empty café with mugs the size of soup tureens in front of us while Danielle chatted endlessly about the weather, the flight from Chicago, the new construction in Vegas.

I kept an arm around the back of Emme's chair and my free hand laced with hers, my thumb stroking the inside of her wrist while her pulse hammered away. As far as I knew, this was the first time she'd seen her father since that horrible Christmas in the islands.

Danielle paused the monologue to reach for her mug and stabbed

Charles with a meaningful glance in the process. "Oh, this is delicious," she cooed. "Honey, you should try yours."

Instead of touching his drink, Charles leaned forward, his hands clasped and his shoulders hunched. Not his usual look. The last I'd checked, the guy double-fisted arrogance and entitlement.

But then he said, "I checked myself into a treatment facility for alcohol abuse about five years ago. I didn't go with the right mindset and it didn't stick once I was out. I wasn't ready to face myself and the person I'd become. It took another year for me to hit the bottom, and when I went back, I did better. I worked harder. There were relapses"—he exhaled heavily and his shoulders slumped even more—"but I didn't let that pull me under. I got help. Therapy, medication. My diet is mostly plant-based now."

His brows lifted like he wasn't totally convinced about that one.

"I've been sober for two years, six months, and seven days. It's the hardest thing I've ever done, but it was long overdue." He looked up, meeting Emme's gaze. "What I did to you was inexcusable and I won't ask for your forgiveness. But I want you to hear me say that I was wrong. I wasn't the father you deserved. I've earned all the distance between us. My behaviors are the reason you are not in my life and I regret it everyday, but I understand it was the only choice you could make. I don't blame you for a minute of it." He knuckled a tear from the corner of his eye. "I do love you—very much—and I'm so proud of you."

Emme stared at him, nearly motionless, before picking up her mug with shaky hands and downing half the drink. I watched her gazing into the overlarge cup for a moment like she wanted to climb inside and disappear.

When she set it on the saucer, she glanced between Charles and Danielle. "That's a lot of information," she said softly, a finger tracing the small plate.

"I don't expect you to respond to all of this," he said. "I just want you to know I'm deeply sorry and I hope that someday you'll be willing to allow me into your life again."

"I'll think about that," Emme said.

Charles nodded. "Thank you for giving me the chance to speak to you—and to extend my congratulations."

"We're so happy for you," Danielle added. "Can you send me the originals of those photos? I need to get them framed."

Emme made a vague noise of agreement, nodding. As far as I was concerned, we were done here. We'd heard everything Charles had to say and he'd indicated he wasn't waiting on her forgiveness, and that was enough family time for us tonight. It was great that he'd put in the work, but my wife didn't have to give him another second.

A beat passed while I considered the cleanest exit strategy, and Charles seized that moment to turn to me with a glimmer of the cocky smile he was known for. "I imagine you heard that I pulled my offer last month. Once I realized I was up against my future son-in-law for those teams, I knew it was time to back out."

I felt the breath go out of me like I had three hundred pounds of linebacker on top of me. From the corner of my eye, I saw Emme slowly turn toward me. Her grip on my hand went slack as his words—those wrong fucking words—played on a loop in my head.

"I'll come up with something else to keep my hands busy, but if you ever want to talk shop, you know how to find me," Charles went on. "Though it did cross my mind to outbid you and offer them as a wedding gift." He grinned at Danielle. "I was told I was doing too much."

Emme pushed to her feet, shaking out of my hold in the process. She took a very intentional step away from me and then another when I tried to follow. Everything inside me turned upside down, revolting against the gulf of wrong forming between us.

"Thank you for telling me all of this," Emme said. "I don't know—I need some time. Okay? I'd like some time." She clasped her hands and stared at her father for a long, heavy moment. "I'm glad you're doing better."

She strode out of the café, her arms crossed over her chest and I knew—*I knew*—this was how I'd fuck it all up.

How I'd ruin all the best things in my life.

chapter thirty-two

Emme

Today's Learning Objective:
Students will go to confession.

I DIDN'T LIKE ELEVATORS. IT WASN'T SOMETHING I FUSSED ABOUT, BUT I hated the way my belly flipped over when the car started moving and then again when jerking to a stop. I'd heard that some people liked those moments of near-weightlessness, but I'd never understood that.

And now, pressing myself deep into the corner of an elevator and doing everything in my power to avoid making eye contact with Ryan, I could add *too damn small* and *not fucking fast enough* to the list of things I didn't care for.

"Say something," he rasped.

I held my arms across my chest and glared down at the floor. My toenails were red with a swipe of green and some black dots. Like a watermelon. A few days ago, things were going well enough for me that I cared about a cute pedicure design.

And look how that worked out for me.

When the doors opened, I cut in front of him and stormed down the short hall to our suite. I had to wait for him to open the door because I hadn't bothered myself with something as silly as a room key when we'd left for the night.

And why would I? Ryan took care of things like that. He handled the plans, the private jets, the stylists who put me in all the right clothes to be perfectly presentable as his stupid fake wife. He put all the pieces together and he pulled all the strings, and I was nothing more than the right doll for this play.

I felt him staring at me as he held the door open, but I didn't let that slow me down. I marched into the spacious suite, crossing the wide living space to the wall of windows overlooking the Strip. I focused on all the people down there, crowding the sidewalks and stumbling out of clubs while I struggled to wrap my hands around any of the events of the past hour.

"Emme, please," Ryan said. "Talk to me."

"You want me to talk to you?" I cried, jolting away from the window. "Okay, let's talk. I finally understand why you needed to marry me. Makes a lot more sense now that I realize your story was a bunch of fucking bullshit and fifteen years of friendship is worth approximately eight soccer teams to you."

He shook his head like I'd lost the crux of it in translation. "No, that's not what happened at all."

I dropped my hands to my hips. "Then you're saying it was a surprise to you that my dad was going after the same teams? You just discovered that tonight?"

He clenched his hands into fists at his sides before shaking them out. His lips parted, but he didn't say anything for a second. Then, "No."

"Yeah, that was obvious, but thanks for only lying to me about the entire basis of our relationship."

"I didn't lie to you," he said, taking a step closer.

I ducked around a potted tree and out of his reach. "You didn't tell me the truth," I yelled. "You kept the important stuff to yourself and you used me to provoke my father."

"That's not how it went," he said, following me across the room.

"Do you know how hard it is for me to trust people?" I asked. "How hard it is to let anyone in? I basically have five people in the entire world that I trust. I thought you'd always be one of them, but I realized tonight you're not. Maybe you never were."

"Em, no, listen to me."

"How long have you been planning this?" I asked, putting the dining table between us. "Just trying to get a sense of how far back the manipulation goes."

"The only plan was to clean up my reputation," he said.

"Bonus points for using my fucked-up relationship with my father to turn up the heat." I shook my head. "Did you know he'd decided to deal with his demons and wanted to make amends? Were you hoping to cash in on his guilt?"

He pushed his fingers through his hair, hanging his head. "I knew about him going to rehab." After a moment, he added, "Both times."

I took a step back, those words hitting me like a gust. "Would you say you're entirely full of shit? Or just mostly?"

He shook his head but didn't meet my gaze. I felt my blood rushing through my veins, quick and bubbly. My hands shook the way they did when my mother went off on one of her rants. My head didn't feel like it was truly attached to my body and I wanted more than anything to fall to the floor and curl into a ball.

"I didn't mean for this to happen," he said, his gaze still lowered.

"But you did it anyway. You lied to me and used me. And for what? Some soccer teams? That's all I'm worth to you?"

I hated that I had to ask. That I was back in this tired, old place where I was forced to stare down the truth that once again I'd let someone become my universe only for it to slip away like a sandcastle at the shore.

"You're worth *everything*."

Because I was good at accepting crumbs, I almost believed him. *Almost.* Then I remembered his deals hadn't been inked yet.

"It wasn't for the teams."

"Then what the hell was it for?"

He looked up then, his eyes heavy and full. "We had a deal. Thirty and single."

"Oh, fuck you," I cried. "We also had a friendship based on being the only people in the world we could trust, and years of sharing all the horrible things we had to go through, and you took the worst of those things and used it as leverage."

"Your father had nothing to do with this," he said.

"There is no way in the world I'll ever believe that," I said. "Just admit I was a pawn in your chess game. Give me that much."

He sliced a hand through the air. "No."

I gripped the dining chair in front of me. "Then get the hell out."

"I'm not leaving you."

The look he gave me was one of pure agony and I appreciated that. I hoped he was in as much pain as I was. I hoped he felt like his bones were breaking and his organs were being ripped out because I certainly did. "Okay. Great. I'll leave."

I stormed through the bedroom and into the closet to grab my suitcase. I tossed it on the bed and started throwing clothes and shoes and cell phone chargers inside.

"Emme. Slow down. Please. You're not going anywhere," he said from the doorway.

"You don't seem to understand that I just sat through the first conversation I've had with my father in eight years and that it also was another one of the many emotionally grueling experiences I've had this year. And at the end of it, I had the pleasure of discovering that my best friend manipulated me into *marrying* him as a maneuver to push that emotionally overwhelming father out of the way of your business deals. You're not the one deciding what I do or where I go but I can promise I'm not staying here with you." I stomped into the bathroom and swept all my makeup into a bag. I'd regret it later, but I wasn't about to slow down and pack everything carefully now. "Either you go snuggle up with Hersberler tonight or you watch me walk out the door."

"Just give me a minute to explain," he said.

I tossed a few more things into my luggage before zipping it up. "Don't you think you've asked enough of me yet? If there was an innocent explanation, you would've coughed it up by now. You don't have one and I'm finished being a prop in this little production."

He followed me through the suite and stopped near the door, his arms crossed and his legs braced like he was thinking of blocking my way. "I've made a mess of this. I'm sorry. But please don't go."

"Think of it like this," I said, checking my shoulder bag for my wallet and phone. It wasn't a good look to storm out only to knock on the door five minutes later. Not doing that. "You won't have to lie about loving me anymore."

His eyes flashed. "I never lied about that."

I yanked the door open and pulled my luggage into the hall. "I used to think the worst thing that could happen to me would be losing you. But now I see it's not losing you that hurts. It's losing everything we had. It's losing the past fifteen years of my life."

"Emmeline." He reached for me as I started down the hall. "Wait. *Please.*"

It was good that I'd turned away from him. He didn't deserve my tears.

THE FIRST FLIGHT BACK TO BOSTON DEPARTED FROM LAS VEGAS shortly after midnight. I spent the entire flight trying to trace back the roots of my newest disaster, desperate to find the place where it'd all gone wrong.

The answer, obviously, was that it'd gone wrong way back when we'd made that pact. Those sorts of things never worked out for anyone. But I'd thought I was losing Ryan to football, to Arizona, to the distance that would rush in when I didn't have him in my life everyday. I'd wanted a reason to pull him back to me even after the years passed. Wanted to hold on as long as I could. I'd loved him—though I'd had no idea what that really meant until now.

I landed in Boston with the sunrise and hid from the fresh, new optimism of the day behind huge sunglasses and a floppy hat when I waved down a cab. I went straight to the condo and gathered only the basics. I'd come back another time for everything else. Or Ryan would make a call and have a crew of movers dispatched to pack and deliver the rest of it.

I was just about to the door when it swung open and my heart lurched, thinking Ryan had followed me back here. That he wasn't letting me go without a fight. That there was a perfectly acceptable explanation that would make me feel a lot less like an object to be picked up and moved around whenever it suited people. That he'd never, ever do that to me.

But it was Ines.

She yelped, I dropped all fifteen of the tote bags I'd crammed my life into, and then we stared at each other for a minute.

"Why aren't you in Las Vegas?" she asked.

"Why are you coming home at seven in the morning?"

She pushed her glasses up her nose with a look that said *Must I explain everything?* "I spent the night with Jakobi, but I forgot to bring my weekend sneakers." She motioned to me when I didn't respond. "And what about you?"

I busied myself with gathering my totes again. That bought me a minute or two to decide how to explain this. It wasn't complicated—he'd used me to get my dad to back off from a business deal—but it was massively complicated. We had fifteen years of friendship behind us and we knew each other in ways that no one else ever could. And if he'd just told me about my father's role in this, I would've helped. I wouldn't have liked it, but I would've helped because that's what friends did for each other.

"We had a fight," was what I landed on.

"The kind of fight that ends with you flying home early and packing your bags?"

I glanced at my things. "Um. Yeah. I'll find a new place for us since the old apartment is transitioning into a bog and the landlord is in no hurry to prevent that. But you don't have to worry. I'm sure Ryan won't care if you're here for a few weeks or even the rest of the summer."

"Actually, I need to talk to you about that." She slipped her hands into her pockets and rocked back on her heels. "Jakobi asked me to move in with him. I said yes, but I wanted to talk to you about it first."

"But-but you hardly know him," I cried, leaning fully into screeching parent mode. "You have your grad program starting in the fall and—and you know he's a lot older than you, right?"

"I do know that," she said easily. "I think it helps. It's better. He's not as"—she wiggled her fingers together as she reached for the right word—"disappointing as most of the guys my age. He's settled and he knows who he is, and I can be who I am without constantly needing to adjust myself for him."

"Okay," I managed.

"And he's very supportive of my grad work," she went on. "He brought up the idea of selling his place and finding somewhere closer to campus. We're going to some open houses this morning." She pointed to her shoes. "That's why I needed my weekend sneakers. I tried going with the work week sneaks but I couldn't do it."

"That's...that's great news, Ines." I needed to get myself together. I knew I sounded like I was announcing a tragedy and not celebrating this new beginning with her. "I'm happy for you."

"Thanks." She scooped up a hoodie that'd slipped from one of my bags and shoved it back in. "I don't want to say that I'm sure things will work out with you and Ryan because I have no factual knowledge to support that. However, I can't comprehend a world where you two don't end up together because you're like a law of nature. Maybe you need to give nature time to sort itself out."

"I'll try that," I said. "Thanks."

We rode the elevator in silence, though Ines ended up shouldering half the totes since I couldn't keep anything together this morning. Jakobi was waiting by the entrance and he almost fumbled his iced coffee when he spotted me.

"Emme," he said, alarmed. "What brings you back to the city so soon?"

"We're not discussing that," Ines said to him.

"Hey, Jakobi," I replied with a smile that must've been a fright because his brows pitched high above the rims of his sunglasses. "I hear you're stealing my roommate. You better be good to my girl."

Still staring at me like I was the walking dead, he said, "My greatest joy in life is taking care of my lady." He clasped Ines's hand and gave her an adoring look. "Can we give you a ride somewhere? You're always welcome at our place. How about that? Come over and we'll order brunch. Ines can show you her harp."

"You have open houses to see." I waved him off. "I'm all right. I swear. Even if this whole picture is a little terrifying."

He shared a glance with Ines. "Then let me call your driver. Ralston would kill me if I left you here to"—he motioned to my hat and bags, and shook his head in disbelief—"handle this by yourself."

"You really don't need to worry," I said, turning toward the garage entrance. Ryan had more than enough cars for one person. He wouldn't miss this one. "Good luck with the house hunt." I shot Ines a glance as she handed back the other half of my bags. "We'll talk later. I don't want you forgetting about me."

"You're my sister," she replied. "I couldn't forget you even if I tried."

Tears welled in my eyes as I descended the stairs to the underground garage. I dumped everything in the back and then climbed into the driver's seat. I knew the right thing to do would be calling ahead, but I hadn't turned my phone on yet and I didn't have the stomach for it now.

So, I hit the road with my bleary eyes and heavy heart, and hoped for the best—even if I didn't have a great track record with that sort of thing.

BEN ANSWERED THE DOOR, HIS MIDDLE FINGER STILL IMMOBILIZED IN A hard, metal splint, and he crowed, "Emster! Get in here, girl!"

I interpreted this as an invitation to burst into loud, hysterical tears.

"Shit. Fuck. Jesus. Dammit. What did I do wrong?" He pulled me inside as he called out, "Grace. I need you out here. *Grace!*" He shuffled me toward the sofa and pushed a box of tissues into my hands, all while yelling for Grace with increasing panic as I cried harder. He dropped down to kneel in front of me, tipping my chin up as he looked me over. "Just try to breathe."

I was halfway through the tissues and blowing my nose like a squawking goose when Grace strolled in from the patio. She stopped in her tracks when she spotted me on the sofa and her future husband watching me like I might combust at any moment.

She pulled out a pair of earbuds and dropped them on the countertop, saying, "Ben, I need you to go get some pineapple juice. A jar of cherries too. And the biggest bottle of vodka you can find."

I TOLD GRACE EVERYTHING. THE *REAL* EVERYTHING, NOT THE smoothed down version Ryan and I had sold everyone over the past few months. The revenge husband, the business deals, all of it.

I told her how I'd allowed myself to believe it was all true and how I realized this weekend that nothing had been true.

"I don't think that's accurate," she said as I loudly slurped up the last of my drink.

Ben appeared a moment later with a refill. Ben was a keeper. Ben wouldn't orchestrate a marriage to his competitor's daughter just to buy some soccer teams.

"What's not accurate?" I asked.

"That none of it was real," she said from her lounge chair. She held a hand up to block out the sun. "I know you, and I know when you're faking it. Like the first time he came to school. You were shocked when he kissed you. Could not have been less convincing."

"I was *not* shocked." I barely recognized my voice. It was rough and slow, like I'd been choking on pebbles all day. Though I wasn't even sure what day it was. Or the last time I'd slept. And these cherries were just about the only solid food I'd consumed in—hours? Days? Couldn't be sure. Flying overnight was the worst.

"But then it changed," she said. "It happened so fast and it was so strong that I convinced myself you weren't faking it that day, but now I know I was right all along."

"You always are, sweetheart."

She swatted my arm. "What I'm trying to say is that whatever you two started out doing isn't what you ended up doing."

"Except he manipulated me for months and missed every opportunity to tell me what was really up," I mumbled around my straw. "So, he did exactly what he started out to do."

Grace was quiet for several minutes while I struggled to spear my cherries with the straw. It was harder than it sounded. Ben stopped by with a bunch of takeout menus, pointing out his favorites with the use of his splinted finger.

When her fiancé left to order the food, Grace said, "I don't think it's a secret that I was jealous of your relationship with him."

"I just thought you didn't like him." I'd never understood why, but Grace was prickly in that way. She didn't like a lot of people and her reasoning wasn't something I'd describe as logical. Most of the time, it didn't bother me. Until recently, there wasn't much overlap between Ryan and Grace in my life.

"I didn't go to college knowing how to have more than one close friend," she said. "For a long time, I worried that it would be me or Ryan. I didn't see how it could be both."

I rolled my head against the cushion to stare at her. "Why didn't you ever tell me that?"

"Because it's shameful even for a villain," she said with a cackle. "You always described him as your best friend and that made me jealous. But I got to know Ryan over the years and I realized—slowly, since villains never come to their realizations lightly—that I didn't have to be jealous because he might've been your best friend at one time but that wasn't who he was meant to be to you for all time."

"It sounds to me like you're on his side right now." Another slurp. "I don't think I like that."

"No one works as hard as Hades, so it shouldn't come as a surprise that I'm gonna tell you things you don't want to hear." She folded her legs in front of her. "But I'm always on your side. Nothing will change that."

I linked my fingers together and let myself sink into the chair. After a minute, I asked, "Is it okay if I stay here for a few days?"

"Baby, you can stay as long as you want. But our spare room is full of wedding stuff, so I'm going to need to clear a path first." She pointed to the phone on the table between us, still dark. "Do you want me to turn this thing on? I can manage your correspondence if you'd like. You know I'm an excellent secretary."

I didn't want to deal with anything waiting for me there. Not this weekend, not after the wedding announcement. And my dad and Danielle. God, I hadn't even started unpacking all of that. I shook my head. "Not yet."

"Does he know where you are?"

"No," I said evenly, "and I'd like to keep it that way. It's only fair that I get to keep a few things to myself since he kept the true motive behind our marriage secret."

"You're not going to give him a chance to grovel?"

I glanced at her. "Would you?"

She seemed to consider this for a moment as she tapped a finger to her lip. "If it was me and I'd fake-married my best friend from high school to get back at my ex? If that husband did everything in his power to make my life comfortable and happy, even giving my semi-half-sister a place to live and helping her find a job? If he came to parties with me where he was mobbed by his fans for hours? And put on an unbelievable field day just so I didn't have to worry about it? If I'd developed some very serious pants-feelings for him along the way? If he handed my dickhead ex the verbal beatdown of the century and did it in front of enough people that the beatdown turns into a thing of legends? Then yeah, I would give him a chance to explain his enormous error in judgment and expect one hell of a grovel. I'd probably hold out for a trip to Paris and some grapefruit-sized earrings and maybe a beagle too."

"A beagle?"

"Yeah, one of my neighbors growing up had a beagle named Martha Washington and that girl would hunt anything that came into her yard. Quite the body count she put up." Grace shrugged. "I always wanted a cute dog with the heart of a savage. Ask him to buy you a beagle."

I went back to spearing the cherries as I realized Grace would take him back. Grace, the cutthroat villain that she was, the one who wouldn't even *speak* to Ben until he worked through some of his personal issues, would take back the husband who'd engineered our whole relationship. I couldn't believe it. "How is it you're more forgiving than I am?"

"I'm not," she said. "I want to barbecue his balls."

"But you also want him to grovel and buy me a dog."

She tipped up her sunglasses and stared at me for a moment. "You might not believe this, but relationships don't have to end when someone makes a mistake. Ben and I are constantly figuring out how to peacefully coexist. We both make mistakes all the time. Some of them are important and we have to work through them. Others are ridiculous. We had a big, stupid fight right before our couples' shower over—and I can't overstate how stupid this is—him keeping ceiling fans on when he leaves a room. I hate it, he loves it, and it turned into a symbol of all the other adjustments we'd made since moving in together. Then he went and beat up your ex and broke his finger, and I decided there was no point in getting pissed about ceiling fans. It's a choice."

I stared into my cup rather than meeting her gaze. I knew what she was saying. That I'd lived through one divorce after another. That most of those divorces were ugly—and the fights still raged on all these years later. That my mother hammered iron spikes into my heart about cheating, lying men. That I'd been cheated on and lied to so much that I was a tragedy in multiple parts.

And that it didn't have to be like that.

I shook my head. "The problem is that he got caught."

"The problem, I am convinced," she said, as if she had a grand proclamation coming, "is that he hasn't told you the whole story yet."

I slurped a cherry into my mouth. "That doesn't make me feel any better."

chapter thirty-three

Ryan

Today's Learning Objective:
Students will wallow in regret.

I WENT HOME TO BOSTON AND SAT ON THE FLOOR IN EMME'S ROOM FOR hours while her absence wrapped itself around me. I was late in getting back here because—well, because I was a fucking idiot. There really wasn't much more to say about it than that.

Jakobi told me she'd left with a bunch of bags, but I had to see it for myself. Had to stand in her closet and stare at all the empty hangers, had to open all of her drawers and see the blank spaces, had to run my hand over the surface of the bathroom counter where she used to store her makeup and creams.

When the sun dropped from the sky, I climbed onto the bed and pressed my face into her pillows. I could smell her there—her shampoo, her lotions, her tangerines—and it cracked something open inside me.

I felt it right behind my breastbone. Heavy, aching pain that made it hard to breathe or think of anything beyond the inescapable throb.

I knew from the start it would end this way, but I'd never accounted for everything in the middle. I'd thought I knew what it meant to love

Emme, but that was like a pantomime of love. These past few months with her changed me in ways I could barely explain and I just couldn't go back, knowing what I did now. I couldn't carry on with my life without her.

I'd continue existing, but not well. Not with any amount of joy or contentment. Not after I'd fucked it all to hell and back. I was a fool, plain and simple, and I'd convinced myself I wasn't. I thought I'd be able to get everything I wanted and keep it all too.

I was wrong.

My phone buzzed while I buried myself deeper into Emme's bed. I ignored it for a minute, but then twisted and flailed in the blankets in the hope she wanted to talk. Or scream at me. I didn't care. Anything would be better than the cold, quiet disappointment she'd aimed at me last night or the finality with which I let her walk away.

I never should've let her go. I knew that now. I knew she'd drawn a line—just like all the lines I'd watched her draw before, the lines I knew better than anyone else—and she was *done*.

But I should've followed. Should've tailed her to the airport, hopped on the same flight, kept close when she landed in Boston. Should've come home with her and told her everything, all the things I'd been holding back for the right time. We should've had the fight and put everything on the table here.

> Grace: hey, asshole

> Grace: in case you were wondering, your wife is with me. Do not take that as an invitation to show up at my door. I thirst for your blood and if that isn't enough of a warning, Ben will turn the hoses on you and he has 5 different stun guns.

> Ryan: Is she all right?

> Grace: no, you fucking armpit, she's not all right. you manipulated her and betrayed her trust for a goddamn business deal.

> Ryan: I know
>
> Ryan: Thank you for taking care of her
>
> Ryan: Please tell me if there's anything she needs

I stared at the screen for five minutes, but Grace didn't respond. With a grunt, I turned back to Emme's pillows and blankets, and fell into a sad, empty sleep.

I didn't drag myself out of Emme's bed until the next afternoon. It was her birthday, and I didn't get to be with her, and I hated that.

I ignored all of my calls and texts though I still checked my phone compulsively for anything from Emme or Grace. After locking myself in the home gym, I jogged for a solid hour. When that didn't help anything, I hit the weights and only stopped when my shoulder felt like rust.

I staggered out of the gym on overworked legs and a hip that made an awful lot of noise with each step, and wandered through the empty rooms of my condo. The whole place felt hollow, like I'd scooped out the best parts and saved the dried-out rind for myself.

The worst part was finding all the little pieces of Emme that she'd left behind. A pair of shoes by the door, a new blanket on the sofa, hair ties all over the place. Proof that she'd been here—and I'd been too much of a fool to keep her.

I forced myself to shower in my room, but when that was done I went back to pacing the floors and trying to find a way to fix this. There weren't many answers, and I was the only one to blame for that.

Gifts wouldn't work. If anything, inundating her with presents would only backfire. She didn't want to be bought. Couldn't be bought.

Jakobi wouldn't let me anywhere near Ines. I knew that without asking, but I also knew there was no situation in which I could use Emme's family to get to her. That wasn't the move.

It was too soon to go to Grace's house. If Ben didn't hit me with the stun gun, she would, and no part of that worked out well for me. Even if Grace gave me the green light, I was too fucked up to fix anything right now. There were so many things I wanted to say to Emme that I knew I'd get it all wrong if I tried.

Which left me with only two options, each equally difficult. Since I couldn't stay here, stewing in my misery and overexertion, I knew what I had to do.

chapter thirty-four

Emme

Today's Learning Objective:
Students will be able to fake-smile and smuggle jewels.

I DROVE TO SHAY AND NOAH'S FARM IN RHODE ISLAND WITH BEN AND Grace, anchored down in the back seat of his truck with a pile of garment bags over my lap. I tuned out their conversation from the start and stared out the window as the city gave way to endless stretches of green and trees.

We'd start setting up when we arrived. If we stuck to Audrey's schedule, we'd have the reception space finished well before tonight's rehearsal kicked off. I was counting on the work to distract me. I didn't need another minute alone with my thoughts.

When we turned down the lane to Twin Tulip and the grand old Victorian home that'd been renovated and expanded to house commercial kitchens and a ballroom looking out over acres of lush gardens and a small cove, a leaden ball of disappointment settled in my gut.

I'd hoped Ryan would fall in love with this weird, magical place the same way I had when I first visited. I'd never said it out loud because I wanted him to feel how special it was and insist we host our big wedding celebration here. I hadn't been able to stop thinking about it since the day Grace mentioned all of us getting married at the farm.

Just one more thing that won't be happening.

Ben pulled around back to the service entrance—another addition since my last visit—and ordered us to wait while he unloaded the boxes in the back.

Grace leaned on the center console to shoot a smile at me. "Claustrophobic yet?"

I glanced at the heavy bags from the bridal boutique. "Surprisingly, no, but I haven't been able to feel my toes for the last half hour."

"They're not all necessary." She studied me for a second. "You're sure you're okay?"

I wanted to put on a good face for Grace. I wanted to sink into maid of honor mode and block and defend for my girl, so she didn't have to worry about a single thing. Most of all, me. "I'm actually okay," I said, and I believed some part of that. I looked around outside the vehicle for Ben. "Since we're alone, how are *you*?"

She motioned to her chest. "I feel like I could throw up at any moment, but I'm also too excited to sit still. It's good, I'm all right, but I won't be drinking tonight."

"Smart," I said. "Do you want me to go to the oyster place just to check that everything is the way you want it?"

"You're not going to the oyster bar," she cried. "I have two goals for this weekend. Number one, get married. Number two, no shellfish incidents."

We had a quick rehearsal scheduled tonight with the wedding party, and then Ben's family was hosting a bigger event at the local oyster bar since many of their guests were arriving in this quirky, coastal town today. Since they'd reserved the entire roof deck for our party and open-air situations were always more manageable for me, I figured I'd be fine. I just wouldn't eat much.

"Would you rather we send Audrey?" I asked.

"No, the in-laws have it under control," she said with a laugh. "I decided a long time ago it's their thing and it wasn't for me to worry about."

"Also smart," I said. "We'll start upstairs and organize the bridal suite and then move into the reception area to work on table setup, but I'm kicking you out at four."

She laughed. "I do *not* need two hours to get ready."

"Maybe not, but I'm still kicking you out."

I heard Ben slam the truck's rear gate before he opened my door. "We're gonna do this nice and easy." To Grace, he said, "Killer, you take the lead. Open the doors for me, tell me where to go, keep me from face-planting on the sidewalk, et cetera and so forth."

"I'll do my best," she said with a laugh.

"Emster, you're the caboose," he said, reaching for the hangers. "Keep the end moving. Let me know if you need me to slow down or if we're making a tight turn. I'm on strict orders to get these dresses to their destination without wrinkles."

We made our way inside the Victorian that'd once belonged to Shay's step-grandmother and up the wide, sweeping staircase to the sunny room that overlooked the best corner of the gardens. All while Ben belted out "Chapel of Love."

Once the dresses were secured in the closet, he dropped his hands to his hips and surveyed the room. "Am I allowed to be in here?" he asked, eyeing an antique sofa that practically begged for a bride to sit there with her long veil draped over the back.

"That depends on how superstitious we want to be," Grace mused.

He held up his hand, the one with the metal splint on his middle finger. "I think we could use a little superstition, honey."

We finished hauling in the last of the wedding goods and our bags, and Ben and a few of his friends who'd recently arrived went to work moving tables and chairs into place.

Before joining everyone else, I dropped my things in a room down the hall from the bridal suite. This one had a view of the trees that marked the property line between Shay's family farm and her husband's. I loved how the lazy, wandering fields that burst with tulips in the spring and hydrangeas in the summer ran headfirst into those precise rows of apple trees, each one marching up and over the rolling hills without an inch of deviation. It reminded me of Shay and Noah.

Jamie, Audrey, and I would sleep here tonight with Grace. Months ago, I'd told Ryan there was room for him to stay here too. Not long ago, that shifted into him staying with me in my room. And now I'd be alone.

I stared down at my rings. I'd wanted to take them off. Told myself I would every day. But then I put them back on the second I emerged from the shower and decided I'd wait for the next day to deal with that problem.

Same with the necklace.

I hated myself for wearing it and that I wore it low, hidden inside my shirt. Of all the things I couldn't let go of, it was the jewels? I didn't know what was wrong with me. I just knew I felt better when I pressed a hand to my chest and felt the pendant warm against my skin.

I'd take it off tomorrow. The rings too. I just needed another day.

THE BALLROOM CAME TOGETHER QUICKLY, ALTHOUGH THAT DIDN'T shock me. Leave it to firefighters and teachers to knock out an organization project in no time at all. Grace still wanted to fuss over the exact position of every place setting and Audrey went a little nuts hunting down wrinkles with her portable steamer, but the room was gorgeous and it didn't require a lot of work.

Unfortunately for me, I was counting on that work. I needed to wrestle with some string lights and hunt down missing candelabras and tie big, satiny ribbons until my fingers bled. There was a moment when I noticed the guys racing each other to move the furniture into place and I had to stop myself from lapsing into my teacher voice and saying, "We use our walking feet when we're inside, boys."

I went to the wide wall of windows when there was nothing left for me to do and I stared out at the flowers, the fields, the cove. The ballroom opened up into a series of large patios. One, deeper in the gardens, for the ceremony. A tall archway wrapped in thick, flowering vines stood at the far end and it was like a storybook. I couldn't imagine a more beautiful place in the world to get married.

Except for the botanical garden Ryan had thrown together in his condo.

As I dragged in a breath meant to chase those thoughts away, Audrey came up beside me, steamer in hand. She didn't say anything and just stayed there with me, taking in the gardens.

After a few minutes—and Shay sending the guys out on an errand when they started playing red rover between the tables—Audrey said, "There was a boy in high school and I loved him."

I glanced at her, my lips parted, but no words making their way out. I'd told the girls that Ryan and I were taking a break and I'd explain everything later—when the wedding was over and Grace and Ben were off on their honeymoon.

I asked, "Not your ex-husband, right? Someone else?"

"No, not the ex," she said with a strained laugh.

"Before him, then," I said, pointlessly. Audrey didn't talk much about her family or her life before teaching at our school. I was pretty sure she had a sibling and possibly grew up in the New England area, but it was hazy—and she preferred it that way.

"Our families didn't approve," she went on. "Mine most of all. It ended badly. I thought I was making the right choice for everyone and I believed that as deeply as I believed anything. But I was wrong, and I handled things poorly."

"I'm sure it wasn't that bad," I said.

"Oh, it was." She gave a quick shake of her head. "Sometimes I let myself wonder what it would be like if we put everything behind us and started over."

"Can you?" I asked. "Start over? Could you reach out to him or—"

"No, that's not—he isn't—we can't— No," she said quickly. "I don't know what happened with you and your boy from high school, and I don't know where the blame lies. But I know what it feels like to be eaten alive by regret and I don't want that for you because I see how much you love him. I watched you bloom these past few months and maybe that had nothing to do with him, maybe that was you finding yourself again—but I don't want you to lose it. I don't want you to give up everything if there's any chance to fix this."

Audrey gave me a side hug and left me to stare at the gardens.

When I blinked away, I realized I was clutching the pendant through my shirt.

I WAS CONVINCED THE SMALL POINT OYSTER COMPANY HAD THE BEST roof deck in Rhode Island. I hadn't been to any other roof decks in the state, but with the breeze blowing off the ocean, a vibrant sunset as the backdrop, and a server readily able to explain their shellfish allergy protocols to me, I didn't see how it could get any better.

At least as far as my current circumstances went.

"I'm impressed," Grace whispered when she made her way over to me after she and Ben greeted their guests. "This place is really nice."

"What were you expecting?" I asked.

She let out a weary laugh and her ice-blue sequined romper shimmered from the force of it. "At this stage, all I want is to survive." She watched as Ben and Noah talked near the buffet, Gennie busy dancing between them. "Is that wrong? Am I a bad bride?"

"You're a *perfect* bride," I said. "This stuff is exhausting. That's why you get a vacation when it's over."

"You had the right idea eloping," she said with a pointed glance.

I groaned into my wineglass. "I haven't had a good idea once this year."

"That's not true and you know it." She rubbed my arm. "That's why I'm hoping you'll forgive me."

"Forgive you for what?" I asked. She smiled and glanced across the deck. When she didn't respond, I followed her gaze to—Ryan. Standing at the top of the stairs in a crisp navy suit, his white shirt open at the throat. I was too far away to know if it was the shirt with the tiny flowers like the one he'd worn the night we got married, but I raked a stare down his chest just the same. His hands were loose at his sides and his scruff thicker than I remembered. Like he hadn't trimmed it in a few days. Maybe not since Vegas. Since we'd been together. Since—

"*Grace*. What did you do?"

She took a step away, saying, "I'm sorry but you'll thank me later."

I glared after her, growly, raspy noises rolling up my throat as she went. Then, as if I was experiencing life underwater, the breeze stopped, the noise faded away, and my gaze bobbled back toward Ryan. My husband.

He crossed the deck in a few quick strides and then he was here, standing before me with his palms open as he reached for me. "Muggsy," he breathed.

I crossed my arms over my chest and glanced away. We couldn't do this in front of Ben and Grace's families. "What are you doing here?" I asked.

"I promised I'd be here," he said, "and I never break my promises to you."

For a second, he was mine once again. He was my friend and my partner and the person who knew me best. Who loved me best. For a second, I believed him.

But that second ended and I remembered I was a very convenient pawn. The truth of it sliced through me all over again and I stepped back, putting a hand between us.

"You won't break a promise, but you'll use me to drive away your competition," I said, trying my damnedest to keep my voice down. "Got it. Glad we cleared that up."

He pushed a hand through his hair and his wedding band glinted in the evening light. A burst of hope flared inside me, but it burned out as quickly as it came. It meant nothing. It couldn't. And I wasn't going to be a fool again. I wasn't going to build castles from these crumbs.

"Emme, please. We need to talk. I just want—"

"There's nothing to talk about. We got what we wanted out of this and now it's over."

"No, it's fucking not, Emmeline. If you'd just give me a minute to explain and—"

"Even if I was inclined to let you manipulate me with another story, don't you think you should stop and look around first?" I asked, surprising myself with the cold venom in my voice. "Do you have any idea where we are right now? Do you understand that this isn't the time or place? It's nice that you came all this way and that you're trying to make a sappy statement about your promises, but I'm here with my friends tonight. I'm sorry if Grace led you to believe I wanted to see you, but I don't and I'm not doing this with you."

I walked away without a backward glance.

chapter thirty-five

Ryan

Today's Learning Objective:
Students will be the life of the party.

WELL, I REALLY WAS FUCKED.

I knew that coming in here—and Grace had held nothing back as far as death threats went. But the detached way Emme looked at me drove that fact home hard. Watching her walk across the deck hit like a dagger to the gut.

That didn't mean this was over yet. I wouldn't let it be over. Not until she gave me a minute to explain and many more minutes to apologize, to throw myself at her mercy. Not until she took off those rings and told me we were done.

It was obvious I'd have to wait for that minute. She was busy flitting around the deck, never far from Grace or another one of her friends. The smile plastered on her face was entirely fake, and the way she threw herself into one conversation after another with various members of the bride or groom's extended family reminded me of the way she listened intently when her students told her extremely random, disjointed stories. She never stopped messing with the flower centerpieces on each table or straightening the place settings or tapping a finger in the air to count chairs, of all things.

As if I didn't know it already, she was avoiding the fuck out of me.

"We should start a group chat," Ben said. He'd positioned himself beside me at some point and only stopped with the rambling comments long enough to inhale another mountain of shrimp cocktail. "The three of us. Since our wives are all best friends."

I dragged my gaze away from Emme—an older woman had her cornered near the bar while my wife nodded along—to eye Ben and the burly guy on his left. Didn't know when he'd joined us. The jam farmer, then.

The burly guy came through with the save, asking, "Are there things we need to discuss?"

"We could help each other out," Ben replied.

The other man speared Ben with a glance as he leaned over to me, his hand out. "I'm Shay's husband. Noah Barden."

"Ryan Ralston," I said, shaking his hand. "Emme's"—I swallowed hard as the word *husband* stuck in my throat—"mine."

"Congratulations on that," Noah said. "Not a bad year for you, huh?"

I blinked at him as I slipped my hands into my pockets. Nothing existed outside my catastrophic fuck-ups. Then, in a distant corner of my mind, I remembered I'd won another Super Bowl and, as of yesterday morning, I was the co-owner of eight undeveloped pro soccer teams. "Yeah. Thanks," I managed. "I've heard a lot about you. The jam farmer."

"Emme would say that. That girl's a hoot." He gave a rough, rumbling laugh as he shook his head. "You've got your hands full there. I hope you know what you're doing."

I felt my face warm into something like a smile for the first time in days. It was like trying to speak a foreign language I barely knew. "I have no idea what I'm doing."

"And that's why we should start a group chat," Ben said.

"I see where you're going with this," Noah said to him, "but I don't spend much time on my phone."

"That's all right. Ralston and I can hold it down." Ben clapped me on the shoulder and held his plate out to me. "Try the oysters. They'll change your life."

"I'm not touching anything here," I said, nudging the plate away. "Emme's severely allergic to shellfish."

I sensed both men staring at me. I didn't care. I was too busy trying to find my wife in the crowd. After a minute, I caught sight of her glossy hair as she squatted down to talk to a little girl.

"This is the last place she should be," Noah said.

"Trust me," I said with a brittle laugh, "I know."

"Why?" he asked, motioning to a table covered with raw seafood. "Just…why?"

"Because she's the best friend anyone could ever ask for," I said. "Loyal beyond logic."

"My aunt Linda is an impulse shopper," Ben said. "She booked this place and plunked down a nonrefundable deposit and then surprised us with it a few months ago." He rolled his neck from side to side, loud cracks punctuating each movement. "We tried to say no, but when we found out how much she'd already paid, there was nothing we could do except move the party up here and make sure they'd have something the Emster could eat." He shot us a pair of pointed glances. "Getting married is supposed to be the happiest day of your life, but we sure as shit put a lot of time—and fuckin' money—into keeping everyone else happy."

"That's why some of us elope," Noah said, tapping his beer bottle to mine.

I nodded. "It has its merits."

"This is the kind of advice that belongs in a group chat," Ben said.

"You're fucking relentless, man." I rattled off my number. "Don't make me regret this."

Ben swung his expectant gaze at Noah. With an enormous eye roll,

Noah followed suit. A second later, my phone buzzed with a new message.

"That's from me," Ben said, grinning. "You should see what I named our group."

"Let's save that surprise for later," Noah said.

I nodded in agreement and went back to watching Emme. A woman around my mom's age held Emme's fingers, turning her hand this way and that to study her rings. I watched a soft, real smile spread across her face as she spoke and I felt a bit of the tightness in my shoulders flag.

"You gotta try these." Ben slapped my back as a server stopped beside us with a tray of appetizers that looked like mini muffins. "Grace loves artichokes and they made this special for her. No fish," he added.

I tried to remember the last time I'd eaten real food, but when all I could come up with was protein shakes, I reached for an artichoke muffin. It wasn't bad, so I grabbed another two before the server left.

A little girl—the one Emme was with earlier—skipped over to Noah's side. She handed him a loaded plate and hoisted a small cocktail skewer in the shape of a sword, saying, "You promised there'd be carrots but there's not and this shit is gross, Noah."

I swallowed a laugh at that, but I seemed to be the only one reacting to the mouth on this child. Ben leaned in, saying under his breath, "You'll get used to it."

Noah scowled down at the plate. Everything had one bite taken out of it. "Sorry about that. I assumed there would be veggies," he said. "Want me to see if they can make some chicken fingers?"

"Fuck yeah," she replied, jabbing her cocktail sword in the air before turning her attention to me. "Who are you?"

"Gennie, come on." Noah shook his head. "We talked about using our manners tonight, didn't we?"

The look she gave him seemed to say *These are my manners*.

"Gennie, this is Ryan," Noah said. "He's Aunt Emme's husband."

"Hi." I shifted the napkin filled with artichoke bites to my other hand with my beer, and went in for the shake, but then thought better of it and waved. Kids didn't want to shake hands. "Nice to meet you, Gennie."

"Am I supposed to call you Uncle Ryan?" she asked.

"Um"—I shot a glance at Noah, but his only assistance was a shrug—"if you want?"

She eyed me up and down, her tiny sword pinched between two fingers and aimed at me. I felt like I was back at the scouting combine before draft day. "Nah, I don't think so."

"Okay, then," I called as she trotted away.

"She must like you," Ben said, bumping me with his elbow. "She usually tells me to prepare to walk the plank."

Since I didn't have the mental capacity to explore any of that, I went back to the artichoke bites. I figured we had another hour or two here and then Emme would probably keep herself busy with Grace for a bit. I'd wait all night to talk to her. All weekend, if that was what it took because—

"What's in this?" I asked, my mouth full.

"It's artichoke and something else. Leeks, maybe," Ben said. "Grace loves them. She makes this hot dip and—"

"It's oyster. There's oyster mixed in with the artichoke," I said as I scanned the deck for the server. My stomach dropped as I saw him a few paces from Emme and an artichoke bite sitting on a napkin in her palm. *"Shit."*

"Fuuuuuuck. Grace is gonna kill me. Goddammit, Linda." Ben plucked the beer bottle from my hand and issued another hard slap to my back. This guy was a high school football coach waiting to happen. "Go!"

The world condensed down to a series of routes across the deck to get to Emme. I took off, twisting between guests, leaping from a chair to a tabletop to another table, and then hitting the floor at a sprint. Everyone around me seemed to move in slow motion. The only sound was the rush of my heartbeat in my ears.

I watched Emme pick up the artichoke bite as I charged toward her. My only goal was getting it away from her. I had no plan for how I'd accomplish that or what I'd do with all the speed I'd built up as I bolted across the deck. I knew all of these things would become serious problems in a matter of seconds, but all I could do was bellow, "No!"

I slapped her hand away from her face and wrapped my arms around her torso as we collided. Tumbling to the deck floor, I held her tight, my back taking the brunt of the impact. No QB liked getting sacked, but at least we did it on turf. This was murder.

"Oysters," I gasped out, "in the artichoke bite."

"Now that's how they do it in the pros!" Ben shouted.

Emme pushed off my chest and I saw blood streaking down her face. *Oh, fuck.* Everyone else saw it too because the stunned quiet that'd surrounded us now burst into panicked cries and the rumble of people pressing in around us.

"Let's give them some room to breathe," Ben called, pushing the crowd back. "No reason for concern. Everything's in order. My good buddy Ryan was just making sure Emme didn't have an allergic reaction. Nothing to see here, folks. Back it up."

"Oh, god. I'm so sorry, Muggsy. Come here, baby, let me see." I cupped her chin and tipped her head back. Yep, that was one hell of a bloody nose. "Awww fuck, I'm sorry. Does it hurt?"

She stared at me, her eyes wide, a little shocked. "What—what the hell was that?"

I gathered her close to me, skimming my hands over her head, her arms, everywhere. "There were oysters in the artichoke muffins," I said again, yanking my shirt free and mopping up her face. It was clotting quickly, which meant it only took five full years off my life instead of ten. "You almost ate one. I'm sorry. I didn't mean to bust your nose or whatever the fuck else I did."

Emme went on staring. "You're a terrible outside linebacker."

I shook my head because, yeah, this wasn't my finest hour and it came at a time when I needed all the halfway decent hours I could get. Bloodying my wife's nose was no way to make up for my mistakes. "Believe me, I know it."

I accepted a wad of napkins from someone, a bag of ice from someone else, a bottle of hand sanitizer from another. I squirted the liquid into my palm and scrubbed my hands before moving to Emme's. She watched, her lips parted and her brow creased. I didn't know which reaction to expect after tackling her at a dinner party, but I couldn't help feeling like none of this was good.

"Stick to the backfield. Fewer casualties."

"This wouldn't have happened"—I motioned to the blood staining the front of her dress, and the shoulder strap I'd ripped at some point—"if you'd just worn the appropriate protective gear tonight. I'm sure we could've found a helmet to match this dress."

"This isn't the time for a fuck-around," she seethed.

"I'm sorry. I'm so fucking sorry. Please let me fix it."

She didn't respond to that and it concerned me more than anything else. She lived to jab at me, to tease, to fuck around. I didn't know what to do with her silence. All I could do was hook an arm around her waist and bring her to her feet.

Jamie and Shay pushed through the crowd to flank Emme. "Daddy Football is a rowdy beast," Jamie said.

I glanced over my shoulder and found Grace there, her lips pressed into a tight line and her eyes worried. She stepped between us and worked on fixing Emme's strap. "Are you okay, babe?"

Emme gave her friend a grimace. "I'm so sorry," she said under her breath. "I can't believe I screwed up another party for you."

"You don't get to apologize," Grace replied. "I was the one who swore they were vegetarian and basically shoved one in your mouth." She hooked a thumb in my direction. "But do you want me to take this guy out back and beat him up for you? I will—and I'll delight in his torture—but keep in mind, he did save you a trip to the ER tonight."

Shay curled an arm around Emme's shoulders. "Let me take you back to my place," she said softly. "We'll soak your dress in some cold water and get you changed into something clean and, if you want, we can come back. Good as new."

Before I could weigh the risks of Emme's reaction, I said, "No. I'll do it."

Her cool gaze hardened. She tipped her chin up. "Fine."

A ripple of icy awareness moved down the back of my neck. My stomach twisted. This was it. No more time on the scoreboard. Either I made this play happen—or I didn't.

chapter thirty-six

Emme

Today's Learning Objective:
Students will evaluate symbolism in works of art.

I HELD THE ICE TO MY FACE AS I STARED OUT THE CAR WINDOW, though I didn't see the gentle hills and glittering waters of Friendship, Rhode Island as we passed. It was a blur of blue and green, all melding together as the silence between us grew heavier by the minute.

My fingers throbbed from the ice, but it felt like my grip on that bag was the only thing holding me together right now. If I put it down, even for a minute, I'd end up walking in circles around the fact that Ryan came here for me tonight. This wasn't the right time for us to hash out our issues and he should've known that, but he showed up—and he blitzed his way through the party to spare me an allergic reaction.

Unfortunately for me and the silence I was clinging to, it wasn't a long ride back to the tulip farm. The old Victorian was lit with warm, welcoming light, and I directed him to park near the barn off to the side.

Though it was completely unnecessary, Ryan jogged around the front of his car to help me out. I was fine, but he scooped me off the seat and kept his hands on my waist for a moment after setting me on the ground all the same.

He plucked a bag from the back seat and surveyed the fields. With a laugh, he said, "It really is a tulip farm."

"Yeah, that's what I told you," I said, forgetting for a second that I was trying to maintain some distance here. That I'd told him where I stood, and even if I really appreciated the save tonight, I couldn't do this with him.

His gaze settled on me and I saw a breath sagging his shoulders. "I know," he said, and he sounded exhausted. I realized then that dark shadows circled his eyes. "But sometimes I don't understand until I see it." He frowned at the blood on my dress. It was pretty awful. "I spend so much time thinking about something that I can't always make sense of it until it's right there in front of me."

I didn't know what point he was trying to make, so I headed toward the Victorian. It was quiet and empty, and my heels snapped against the hardwood as I climbed the stairs. Ryan was right behind me, his hand on my hip as if I needed the support. I didn't, but I couldn't bring myself to brush him off either.

Once in my room, I went straight for the adjoining bathroom to wash away the blood and ruined makeup. Ryan followed, looming in the doorway as I twisted the taps. I shot him a scowl before leaning over the sink. He was quiet for several minutes, watching as I rinsed the dried blood from around my nose and then lathered a facial wash into my skin. There was a low throb across my cheeks from the artichoke-oyster incident. It wasn't too bad. Better than the swelling and observation in the ER that came with my allergic reactions.

"I'm sorry," he said when I patted my face dry.

While his words seemed to spring from deep inside him and they sounded more sincere than any other he'd ever spoken to me, a bitter laugh cracked out of me as I turned around. "That's the last thing I want to hear."

"Then let me explain," he said, his hands braced on the doorframe. "It's not what you think."

"I don't want an explanation. I don't care what happened or why or what you thought you were doing. None of it matters. I just want to know..." I leaned back against the sink, closing my eyes and pressing my fingers to my temples. "Was it just about the business deals? Because every time I trace it back to the beginning and go looking for the signs that the only thing you cared about was using me as a tool against my father—"

"No, Emme, no," he whispered.

"—I wonder whether *any* of it was real." I stared at him with his overgrown scruff and tired eyes, and a twist of pain cut through me for our friendship, for everything I thought we'd found together, for a future we wouldn't share. "Was any of it real?"

He heaved out a breath and stared at the floor for a long minute as everything inside me slowly sank.

"Right," I said, hating the tears filling my eyes. "Well. You should go and I'll—"

"Real? You want to know about *real*, Emmeline? You have no fucking idea how real it is." He grabbed the loose ends of his bloodied shirt and pulled them apart, tearing the fabric and sending buttons flying. "How real it's always been for me." He yanked the shirt from his arms and threw it aside, revealing his bare chest—and a large bandage over his ribs. Before I could ask about that, he pointed to a design near his shoulders. "Your corsage from senior prom. These are the flowers I picked out for you."

I stared at him but I still didn't understand. "What?"

He gestured to another cluster of flowers, this one on the inside of his biceps. "These are the ones I gave you for Homecoming. Tenth grade."

I swallowed hard and pressed my fingers to my lips.

"Clouds, because you liked to complain about New Hampshire being gray and overcast all the time," he said, tapping a few spots on his chest before moving to the wave design on his arm. "The field trip to the Isle of Shoals? You fell asleep on my shoulder during the boat ride back and that hour was the happiest fucking moment of my entire year."

I made a noise then, something like a cough and a choked sigh, and *All this time?*

"These are the stamps from the postcards you sent the semester you studied in Paris. Lines from your favorite movies. Lyrics from your favorite songs." He pointed to the tall trees climbing up his arm. "Remember the botany project in biology? When we had to observe changes in the ecosystem once a week for the whole semester? And you picked those woods about a mile behind my house?" He laughed as he shook his head. "I didn't give a shit about biology, but I fucking loved that project."

My head swam. I stumbled back a step.

Ryan followed me, crowding me against the sink. He took my hand and pressed it to his chest. "When I was in Arizona, I realized there're orange trees all over Tucson. There used to be hundreds of acres of orange groves around the city, but not as many now." He tapped our joined hands to a cluster of small, five-petaled flowers over his heart. "Every spring, those trees would bloom and the whole city would smell like orange blossoms and it was like you were there with me. I would go running early in the morning because it was strongest then, and you know what I'd do while I was out there? I'd listen to the goddamn *Les Mis* soundtrack. I'd think about all the hoodies you stole from me and never gave back. And I'd do the math. I'd count the days and months and years until I turned thirty and I could come and get you."

A glimmer of understanding prickled over my skin. All I could say was, *"Oh."*

He dragged our hands across his collarbones, down his arms, up his sides, and though it took me a minute, I realized those flowers were everywhere. Tucked into every design, filling every space. *Everywhere.*

Tears rolled down my cheeks as I asked, "Why?"

"Because it's always been real for us. Because I fucking love you."

"Even then?"

"Always." With his free hand, he ripped the bandage off his ribs. "National championships," he said, motioning to the dates of his biggest college and pro wins tattooed there. And then to another date, a fresh one. "The day I married you."

"But—but—" I dashed the tears from my cheeks, shaking my head. There were too many things happening at once here. "But it was a fake marriage—"

"It was never fake," he said, gathering both of my hands in his. "Not a single minute of it, and you know that. I *know* you know it."

"But my father," I said, my voice breaking over the words. "You used me to get him to back down."

Ryan squeezed his eyes shut and his shoulders drew tight as he sucked in a breath. "Emmeline. You own every inch of my soul," he said, his eyes still closed. "That's not how it happened. I swear it on my life. I'd swear it on *your* life."

"Then tell me," I whispered. "From the start."

chapter thirty-seven

Ryan

Today's Learning Objective:
Students will revise history.

EMME SAT ON THE FOUR-POSTER BED IN A T-SHIRT AND SHORTS, HER legs folded in front of her and a small pillow clutched to her chest as I paced the room. I hadn't bothered to put on a clean shirt. I figured it would be easier for her to gut me without clothes getting in the way.

The sound of crickets blew in through the open windows and the floorboards creaked beneath my feet. Neither of us mentioned returning to the party, and I appreciated the hell out of that.

But it meant I had to confess everything else. Even with all this time on my side, I still didn't know the right way to do it.

"That night when we met up for dinner, back in March," I started, "I was going to tell you everything about the franchise deals and the Wallaces and how your father was involved. The plan was—"

"I do enjoy being the subject of everyone's plans," she said.

"—to ask you to come to some of my events and make it look like we were together." I shrugged as I added, "I was going to wait until it was all over to bring up the pact."

She pushed her fingers through her hair, grumbling, "Why, pray tell, did you not?"

I stopped pacing and shifted to face her. "Because you were breaking, Em, and I had to do something. Everything was going wrong for you and I couldn't leave you like that. You had this terrible ex—and fuck, I didn't even know the half of it—and I couldn't let you go on hurting like that."

"Then you didn't plan on proposing?"

I laughed, dipping my hands into my trouser pockets. "No, that was a game-time decision."

"Why?"

I stared at the quilt for a second before saying, "You were talking about how the only thing you wanted was to be with someone, how you just wanted to be loved and—and I was right there, Em, just fucking waiting to give you that. The words were out before I even thought about them."

"I don't recall you trying to take them back."

"Why would I? You said yes." I shrugged. "It was all I'd ever wanted."

She tilted her head to the side, her eyes narrowed. "And my dad? Why did that have to be a secret? I would've been okay with it if I'd known. I would've been on your side. I would've helped. Why couldn't you clue me in that you were using me for leverage there?"

"Except you weren't the leverage." I curled my hands around the footboard. "Charles was never a serious contender for the soccer clubs. He might've thought he was, but that's not how it went down." When her brows pinched, I continued. "There were a lot of bidders. He was one of them—and I should've told you that, but I knew how it was going to shake out for him and I didn't want to add to your stress. You already had enough with that fucking ex and the headaches with your class, and Ines and then your apartment. I wanted things to be good for you, for once."

"I can hear his name without freaking out," she said.

"I know, baby, but I just didn't want to add to your worries. Especially not with the issues he's dealing with. It's a well-known secret in the industry that he's had problems with alcohol and spent some time in rehab. I hate that you were the last to know." She turned her attention to the window and kept it there, her jaw clenched. "The Wallaces are high off their own hypocrisy and they didn't want to be anywhere near those issues. They kept him engaged to jack up the price and I suspect he realized that toward the end, which was why it was so easy for him to bow out."

"You've known this? The whole time?" she asked, the words barely audible.

I nodded. "They strung him along up until the final days, but they never intended to sell to him. They're dicks so they made a lot of noise about me being a feral bachelor or something—"

"Like a wildcat?"

There was a laugh in her words, and it took me a minute to realize she was teasing me. A grin lit my face as I said, "Yeah, like a wildcat." I watched as she absently zipped her pendant along the chain. "When I met you that night, I told you I needed to make it look believable. That you were the only one who could help me clean up my image. I told you I had to get married. It had to be you. None of it was true."

Her fingers froze on the necklace. "What?"

"I could've asked anyone," I said. "Hired someone, even."

"Why didn't you?"

I spread my hands out in front of her. "I waited all these years and —and I didn't want anyone else. I've *never* wanted anyone else. So, if I had to pretend, I was going to do it with you. And I was going to pray to all the gods I don't believe in that you liked pretending with me enough to make it real."

"Why didn't you just…tell me?" she asked.

I motioned to the championship wins on my torso. "You hate football."

"You know that's not the case." She tossed the pillow aside. "That's just something I say because I'm disgustingly dramatic and I'm still patching up my childhood traumas."

"I spent all of high school listening to you tell me you'd never date a player."

She chucked the pillow at my head. I caught it and threw it back. "You never asked if that included you."

"Emmeline. Listen to me." I leveled her with a gaze because we just couldn't fuck around right now. "I have wanted you for half my life. I don't remember what it's like to wake up in the morning without thinking about you. Everything good in my life has your fingerprints on it and you've been there for me to lean on through all the bad times." I grabbed my discarded shirt off the floor and held it out for her. "I buy shirts with little orange blossoms on them because I want all the reminders of you I can get. I don't know who I am without you, and I don't want to find out." I rested my hands on the footboard again and leaned toward her as she swept her thumb over the delicate stitching on my shirt. "But I knew if I dropped all of this on you from the start, it would change things between us. I couldn't risk scaring you off. I couldn't risk losing you."

"Were you ever going to share any of"—she skimmed a hand down my arm and that single gesture stitched my soul back together—"*this* with me?"

I nodded. "Yes."

She laughed. "Any time soon?"

Another nod. When she rolled her eyes, clearly not buying it, I added, "I was going to take you to the Seychelles for a honeymoon next week. I figured a remote archipelago in the Indian Ocean was the safest place to confess fifteen years of secrets."

"Because I wouldn't be able to leave? Or no one would care if I strangled you?"

"Pick whichever answer you like best."

She laughed then, loud and deep, and it reverberated like a crack cleaving through ice. I rounded the bed and sat in front of her, pushing aside my shirt and taking her hand in mine. "I went about this all wrong."

"You did," she agreed.

"I overthought and overcomplicated everything."

"All of it."

"I put you in a terrible position with your dad last weekend and I basically assaulted you tonight, and I swear to god, those are the last two things I ever wanted to do to you."

She gave me an unimpressed glare. "I hope no one caught that tackle on camera because you'll be laughed out of the League." She ran a hand over my shirt again. "But it's nice that I'm not coming down from an epinephrine injection right now."

"Muggsy, what were you doing at an *oyster bar*?"

"I'll have you know I had the entire situation in hand," she said. "You were the one who caused a scene. Did you see yourself? *You jumped over a table.* Have you been working on your vertical conditioning? Because that was impressive. Insane, but impressive."

We shared a laugh and I brushed my thumb over her rings. Quiet settled between us, and for a moment the only sound was the cry of crickets in the fields outside. "Will you let me have another chance?"

"A chance at what?"

A rush of emotion and exhaustion and blinding need welled up inside me, and instinct ordered me to wrap my arms around my wife and rest my head in her lap. "At being yours."

An excruciating minute passed and then another before Emme moved so much as an inch. But then she huffed out a breath and her fingers speared through my hair, and it was like my parachute finally popped open. "I was specifically instructed to request a beagle in these negotiations."

I turned my head to catch her eye. "A...beagle? You want a dog?"

"I was also told to ask for a trip to Paris, but I think the Seychelles checks that box pretty hard," she went on as she traced the ink on my shoulder. "What's this?"

Glancing back, I said, "Gemini, for my June baby."

I watched as her teeth sank into her bottom lip. As she understood it was just another piece of her that I kept with me. Orange blossoms on my heart and stars on my shoulder. "I can't believe I never noticed."

"I've spent a long time making sure you didn't."

She swept her hand down my spine as she asked, "What are you going to do with all that time now that I know your secrets?"

"The beagle will keep me busy."

She brushed her fingers through my hair again, up the back of my neck. It brought a shiver out of me, a blessed relief to my frayed nerves. I held her tighter as she said, "You're on the road too much. We'll get a dog when you retire. I'm not ready to be a single dog mom. Not in a high-rise condo."

"Does that mean you're coming home?"

Shrugging, she said, "Someone told me it's legally mine so…"

I growled against her torso. "Emmeline."

She stopped stroking to grip my hair. "Don't put me in the dark ever again. Promise me you'll tell the truth—even if it's ugly, even if you think it's going to hurt."

"I promise. I've loved you for a long, long time and in a lot of different ways. I'm going to love you in new ways tomorrow and ten years from now. The only life I want is one where I get to do that." I sat up and reached for the bag I'd abandoned on a nearby chair when we came in. "It's not a beagle," I said, taking out the heavy box, "but I hope you like it."

She stared at the box for a second before pressing both hands to her cheeks. Her smile lit the whole room. "You remembered," she whispered.

"I tried to find the best one," I said, scratching the back of my neck. "I might've overcomplicated that too because there're eight more waffle irons back at home."

Her eyes went wide with delight. "I guess I'll have to test them all out." She ran a hand over the box, smiling. "I can't believe you brought a waffle iron to Rhode Island."

"I brought the waffle iron to Vegas," I said. "It was the last of your birthday surprises."

She closed her eyes for a moment and pulled in a long breath. Then, "I've loved you for a long, long time and in a lot of different ways too. And I think"—she ran her hands up my arms, over my shoulders, and clasped her fingers at the back of my neck as she gave me a small, devious smile—"I think it's a fantastic thing that I had the foresight to make you promise to marry me."

I dropped a kiss on her lips. "And I had the foresight to convince you to go through with it."

Downstairs, a door banged open and raucous laughter and shouts filled the house. There was a stampede to the second floor and then Grace, Shay, Jamie, and Audrey appeared in the open doorway. Their cheeks were rosy and their eyes bright, and Jamie had one hell of a hiccup going.

That party must've gotten a lot more interesting after we left.

Grace pointed at me as she ran an assessing glance over Emme. "Do I need to beat him up?" she asked.

With a laugh, my wife said, "No, please don't. There's been enough bloodshed for one night."

"If you say so," Grace said, a slur loosening her words. "But I am going to make him sleep in the barn."

"No, you're not," Shay said.

"You have a worse place in mind?" Grace asked her. "With the goats? You have chickens. What about the chickens? I enjoy punishment and suffering. There must be both."

I shared a glance with Emme. She smothered a laugh behind her hand.

"Where are the dudes?" Jamie asked. "Can't we just send him off with them?"

"They're at my place and we're not doing that unless he wants to bunk with Gennie," Shay said. "That's as rough a punishment as any."

"Let him stay here," Audrey said, the words soft and squished together. "Listening to us cackle for the next few hours will take care of the suffering."

"And we'll be stealing his gal away, so that's plenty of punishment," Jamie added.

"I could be convinced of this," Grace said, stroking her chin.

"Here's a better idea," Emme said, holding up the box. "Ryan's going to help me whip up some waffles while you change into comfy clothes and fix your faces."

"Oh, let me go find some blueberry jam. Must have jam for waffles," Shay said, already darting down the stairs.

Emme nodded after her. "If that's what's important to you, sure."

"It *is* a jam farm," I said.

She smiled at me, wide and soft and wonderful, and it jump-started my heart. "Excellent point." Swinging her attention back to her friends, she said, "After waffles, everyone's getting a very big glass of water and some under-eye patches because I'm not letting a single one of you walk down the aisle tomorrow looking like old newspaper. Got it?"

"Yes, Mom," Audrey said, heading down the hall.

"She's a tough maid of honor," Jamie called as she stepped into the room next door.

"The best there is," Grace said, still watching us from the doorway. She pointed to me and then made a throat-cutting gesture. "I can dig a deep hole and I don't believe in second chances."

When we were alone again, I said, "I should file that under Grace being Grace rather than a serious death threat, right?"

"Grace *is* a serious death threat," she said. "But tell her you're thinking about getting me a beagle. That might change things."

I gathered her in my arms and pulled us down to the mattress. She held on tight and it didn't matter that we were in an awkward position or that her friends were on the other side of the walls and they would claim most of her attention tonight. I had everything I needed.

Though one thought pushed its way to the front of my mind.

With my lips on her neck, I said, "There's something else I should tell you."

"Is it crazier than your postcard stamp tattoos?"

"No," I said quickly, but then doubted myself. "I was going to buy your building. In the North End."

She was quiet for a second. "To evict me? And force me to move in with you?"

"No, I wanted to get the fucking roof fixed," I said.

"Oh, no, that's fine. That's entry-level crazy." She traced the orange blossoms on my chest, her eyes bright. "Wait, were you going to tell me that you bought the building?"

"Probably not."

"You were just going to buy the building, fix it up, and never mention it to me? And then what? You're a landlord on the side? How does that make sense?"

"I'd figure it out when the time came," I said. "Just had to get a read on the situation."

"Such a quarterback." Her shoulders shook as she laughed. "My god. I really fucking love you."

I pressed a kiss to her forehead. "I love you. Always have. Always will."

I WOKE TO DAPPLED SUN STREAMING IN THROUGH THE LARGE, OLD windows and my wife tucked up against me, her backside nestled in my lap. A mild breeze billowed the diaphanous curtains, carrying with it the scents of green and saltwater. I ran a hand over her hip, across the soft of her belly, and then lower, into her sleep shorts.

I just didn't see how life could get any better for me. There wasn't a single thing I'd change.

When Emme stirred, she shot a glance at me over her shoulder, eyes bleary. There was a white cast on her face from some kind of skin product and hot pink half-moon stickers under her eyes. The gods must've smiled down on us because I didn't see any bruising from last night's incident.

"Are you petting me?" she asked, nodding down the length of her body to where I gently stroked between her thighs.

I kissed her shoulder. "Is that a problem?"

She shook her head. "No, but waking me up this way seems like a hobby of yours."

"And what a fine hobby it is." I slipped a finger along her seam and back up to circle her clit. "What time did you come to bed?"

"A little after two." She stretched, the movement pushing her ass right against my shaft and forcing a groan from me. "Shhhh." She turned her face to moan into the pillow. "The walls are thin."

I knew all about that. I also knew Audrey talked in her sleep and that Jamie's phone had three different notification sounds. Didn't care. "Then be quiet, wife."

I worked her shorts down to her knees, kicked off my boxers, and pushed into her just like this, with my mouth on her shoulder, her plush, gorgeous ass cradled in my lap, and my rings on her finger.

She reached back, her arm twisted around my waist and her other hand layered over mine as I went on tracing her clit. We moved in slow, lazy thrusts like we had all day, all weekend to get lost in each other.

We didn't and that became increasingly apparent as doors banged open, showers turned on, vehicles rolled up outside—but we did have the rest of our lives and that was good enough for me.

A STRING QUARTET PLAYED A SONG BY THE SMITHS AS I TOOK IN THE lush grounds of Twin Tulip. It wasn't the dusty, fallow field I'd expected. Quite the opposite. Trees and flowers burst from every corner in a scheme that I could only describe as cultivated chaos. Gentle hills rolled down toward the sparkling blue of Friendship Cove. It was like a secret garden with a wickedly wild side.

I understood now—and I kinda loved it.

I followed a rough-hewn stone path to the outdoor ceremony site. More than two hundred white chairs sat in a semicircle before a vine-draped arch. I spotted Shay's husband off to the side and headed in that direction.

"This is your place, right?" I asked him, motioning to the grounds. "It's incredible."

"This is my wife's place," he said with a decisive nod. "I help her with it." He pointed to a line of trees at the far side of the gardens. "Our farms and pastures start over there and extend around the cove and back over Windmill Hill."

"I take it you do more than jam."

He laughed. "Yeah, you could say that. I like having new projects on my plate."

I slipped my hands into my pockets and rocked back on my heels. "Yeah, I know something about that."

"We've been kicking around the idea of opening a tavern on a piece of land a little closer to town," he went on. "A comfortable, local place. But those things take a ton of time and planning. And money."

I glanced over at him. McKerry owned a pub in his hometown. Hersberler was a partner in a restaurant group in Baltimore. Since those two never shut up, I knew what these things cost. "Let me know if you want a silent partner."

"How silent?"

"I just got married, bought eight soccer teams, and have a national title to defend. Really fuckin' silent."

"But you'd make time to show your face once in a while?"

"If it made my wife happy, I'd move here."

He gazed at me for a second. "Then I'll keep that in mind."

I murmured in understanding and we stood in easy silence for several minutes. I didn't get the impression this guy cared much for small talk. I couldn't have been happier.

"Did the girls stay up all night?" he asked.

I shook my head. "No, they had waffles, watched a movie, and did something with face masks. They were out by two."

"Waffles? Okay." Noah pointed to the mobile phone in his hand, saying, "This group chat might kill me. He wants to know if we have fire blankets at home and if either of us have opinions on smoker grills. Did you see what he named the group?"

"No, I must've missed that. I've had my hands full since giving my wife a bloody nose last night in front of forty people," I said.

Noah held up his screen for me. "He started with The Real Househusbands of Rhode Island, but changed it to Wife Guys this morning."

I choked out a laugh. "Maybe he realized you're the only one living in Rhode Island."

"He's going to change the name every day. I can feel it coming." With a shake of his head, he added, "I don't know how anyone has the time for all this."

"You should see my family chat." I opened my messages and scrolled through the new ones in the past day. Claudia was still busy posting headlines and pics from our wedding announcement last weekend. "My four sisters, my mother, and my grandmother are nonstop with it. I miss ninety percent of the conversation. More during the season. They don't seem to mind."

He ran a finger under his collar, nodding. "Then it's not just me."

I clapped him on the shoulder as the music changed and the guests started filing into their seats. "Nope."

I GRABBED TWO CHAMPAGNE FLUTES FROM A PASSING SERVER AND ducked away from the cocktail hour to find my wife. Grace and Ben posed for photos in the garden while Shay and Emme lingered nearby, occasionally stepping in to fix the bride's dress or hair between shots.

"For you," I said, handing Emme a glass. She all but snatched it from my grasp.

When I offered the other to Shay, she waved it off, saying, "No, but thank you. I need water first." She dropped a hand to Emme's arm. "I've got this. They're almost done."

Emme frowned. "You're sure?"

She laughed. "This is the twenty-ninth wedding we've had here this year. I know the drill." Pointing to the opposite side of the farm, near the barn, she added, "Take the long way around. We planted a load of sunflowers and hollyhocks over there."

After a moment of discussion where Grace confirmed several times that she'd survive without her maid of honor for a few minutes, we took off toward the sunflowers. We passed a pair of tire swings hanging from a tree that had to be older than everything in this town and a cluster of rosebushes twined around the weathered frame of an old brass bed.

When we reached a high point on the hill where the early evening sun bathed the cove in warm, golden light, I wrapped an arm around her waist and pulled her close. She touched her glass to mine with a smile.

"I like this place," I said.

"Me too."

"Would you want to have our big party here?"

She tipped her glass back and drained the champagne. "I have a secret of my own, you know."

Now this caught my attention. "Oh, do you?"

Nodding—and so pleased with herself—she said, "I've been thinking about having our next wedding here since the day you visited my school."

"Why didn't you say anything?"

"Do you see now? How annoying it is when someone has an important thought but keeps it to themselves?"

"All right. Fine. I'll take that penalty."

"I didn't bring it up because I knew if I suggested it, you'd go along without question. I wanted you to come here and see how dreamy this place is and then realize that we should have it here."

I brushed my lips over her temple. "You wanted both of us to choose it."

"Mmm. Yeah. Seems only fair to reach this decision together, since I was the one who roped us into this pact, and you're the one who held us to it."

"With that in mind..." I cleared my throat and pulled a folded paper from inside my breast pocket. She eyed me warily as she opened it. I shrugged. "What's mine is yours," I said easily. "Just drawing a line under it."

She shook the paper at me. "Why does this say I'm the co-owner of your soccer clubs?"

"Because you are."

"But *why*?"

"You made this deal happen just as much as Jakobi and I did," I said. "And I wanted to make it clear that you're not leverage, you're not a chess piece to move around the board. You're my best friend and my partner, and as long as I live, I'll never again make you feel like you're anything less than my equal."

She swallowed hard as she scanned the page. "You didn't mention this last night."

"This stake was yours regardless of whether you gave me another chance or sent me packing. I wasn't going to let it get in the way of that decision."

She arched a brow. "I'm not that easily bought."

I traced the pendant around her neck. "Believe me, Muggsy, I know."

She threw her arms around my torso, squealing a little as she held me close. "I don't deserve you."

"You deserve everything," I said into her hair. "Get used to believing that."

"Should we go back to the party?" she asked, her head resting on my chest.

I motioned to the wall of sunflowers behind us. "Let's take a pic."

Emme set our champagne glasses on the stone path and tucked herself against me as I held up my phone. I held her waist tight and pressed my lips to her neck, and she giggled and squirmed when I nipped at her skin.

She picked out the photo, one where we were both laughing and the breeze hit the sunflowers in a way that they seemed to sway toward us. I loaded it to my social accounts and she helped me find Twin Tulip's account to tag the farm. She buried her face in my arm with a giggle when I typed out the caption.

Wifey.

epilogue

Ryan

Today's Learning Objective:
Students will make it last.

One year later
Friendship, Rhode Island

"Listen, Ralston. Listen. What if I walk down the aisle like a bear? Claws out, growling? I could bite the ring pillow like it was a fish I just caught in a stream. I'll be the ring *bear*."

I glanced up from my phone and dropped a hand to McKerry's shoulder, giving him a good shake. "You promised you wouldn't make me regret this."

"How could you regret it?" he asked, his tuxedo shirt open and his bow tie hanging out of his pocket. "It's going to be the tightest fuckin' thing that happens all day."

I blew out a breath. Somewhere in the past year, plans for our wedding had shifted from *big party at Twin Tulip* to *three-ring circus taking over the entire town of Friendship*. Though it didn't bother me and Emme much. Between our kickass wedding coordinator and Grace's whip-cracking, very little landed on our plates. We sampled the food, listened to auditions from bands, and compared notes on tequila options. We left the rest—which included lodging for roughly three hundred people, conflict mediators to manage Emme's parents, and pyrotechnics permits—to everyone else.

Except for McKerry. He was always on my plate.

"You can't be a bear, man," I said. "I'm sorry."

"Cool, cool," he said to himself. "I'll go with my original plan, then."

I scrubbed a hand down my face. I really didn't have time for this right now. The show started in less than an hour and I needed to check on a few things before sneaking into the bridal suite.

"Can I ask what the original plan was?"

"Just some backflips," McKerry replied, as if end zone dances were a common occurrence at weddings.

"Allow me to take this one for you." Hersberler came to my side, a cocktail in hand. "Time to play it straight. No shenanigans out there."

McKerry glanced between us, utterly baffled. "But…why?"

"Because that's what Ralston wants," Hersberler said. "The princess too."

With a great heave of his shoulders, he asked, "Why didn't you say so? Is the princess cool with some breakdancing?"

Hersberler dropped his voice, saying to me, "That's the best offer you're gonna get. Take it before he circles back around to the bear idea."

I patted my breast pocket, confirming for the twentieth time today the rings were safe in there and McKerry's role in this was purely symbolic. "Sounds great," I said to him, accepting his high-five.

"Still recovering from the party last night?" McKerry pointed to Hersberler's drink. "What kind of trouble did you get into?"

Since most of our guests were traveling in for this event, we'd started the festivities last night at the new Little Star Bar and Tavern, my venture with Noah Barden. We didn't officially open until next month, but we figured there was nothing like a rowdy rehearsal dinner party to shake out the issues. Best of all, there was no shellfish to be found at the tavern. Noah and I decided we'd leave that to the oyster boys.

Redness creeped up Hersberler's neck and he tugged at his collar. "What are you talking about, man? I didn't get into any trouble."

"Looked like you were starting some trouble with Ralston's sister."

My gaze snapped to the tight end. "Excuse me?"

Hersberler cringed. The guy was bigger, stronger, and faster than me—and he looked *terrified* right now. Which was a bad fucking sign. "Nothing." He shook his head. "I didn't say anything."

McKerry doubled over laughing. "Boy, you better run."

I stared at Hersberler, my eyes narrowed. "Which sister?"

He took a step back, a hand held out like he was trying to calm me down. "I would never—"

I growled. "Which. Sister."

"Ruth," he said, "but I swear—"

A laugh cracked out of me. "Ruthie? You're fine. She doesn't need me to kill you for her. She'll do it herself."

"Oh, I know," he said quietly.

"I have things to do." I pointed at McKerry. "Keep an eye on Pumpkin Dick. And put yourself together. You're not going out there with your shirt open. It's not that kind of party."

I jogged from the newly converted barn toward the old Victorian where Emme and her girls were getting ready. I found Claudia out on the porch in her navy blue bridesmaid dress, leaning against the railing as she aimed her phone at the surrounding gardens.

"You're not supposed to be here," she called.

"And you think that's going to stop me?" I asked as I climbed the steps. I heard the smooth strains of harp music in the distance. Surprising no one, Ines was a baller harp player.

"I know it won't."

I paused at the door, listening for a second as Ines started a familiar

Smashing Pumpkins song. "Did something happen with Ruthie last night?"

She snorted. "Define *happen*."

"On second thought, I don't want to know." I had to shove everything I knew about Hersberler into a steel trap and out of my head. "Where's Mom?"

"She's attached herself to Emme's mother like moss on a rock and keeping her far away from the stepmother."

Thank god. Heather had been a headache from the start. Lots of opinions, lots of noise. Nonstop drama. The truly unfathomable part was that Heather believed she was helping. She thought it was necessary to stake claims on Emme like she was a territory to be won. I didn't understand it and it was tough on my wife, but we managed.

Charles continued to surprise me. Emme had spoken with him a few times since that weekend in Vegas. I appreciated that he'd gone out of his way to put her at ease in their conversations and bit the bullet when it came to awkward topics—like whether he was even invited to this wedding. He'd made it clear he had no expectation of an invite and certainly no hope of walking her down the aisle, but that he'd like to share in our day. I gave him credit for immediately signing over her trust fund and admitting he should've done it years ago—because he fucking should've. They weren't close and I didn't see a route through this mess where they would be, but Emme had started talking to Danielle more in the last year. It was easier now that Danielle wasn't trying to rebuild the bridge between father and daughter. I liked that Emme had her in her corner. She needed more people she could count on.

Though the obstacle for this weekend was keeping Heather far, far away from Charles, Danielle, and Emme's half brothers. They could coexist as long as they didn't have to make eye contact or cross paths. Ships in the night.

Between my mother and Gramma CeCe, my sisters, Emme's friends, and all of the O-line boys—and the private security firm running things behind the scenes—we were playing some intense zone defense this weekend.

I glanced back at Claudia. "Do me a favor and stay away from the guys."

"Are we referring to specific guys? Or all guys?"

That was an excellent question. "You'd be smart to be wary of all of them as a general rule, but for right now, definitely stay away from the players."

"I'll take it under advisement." She flicked a glance toward the Victorian. "Good luck getting past the drill sergeant."

"Grace?" I laughed when Claudia gave a wary, wide-eyed nod. "I know how to handle Grace."

"Thoughts and prayers," she muttered.

I made my way inside, ducking past the hairstylists and makeup artists working on my sisters in the left parlor and one of the photographer's many assistants moving furniture in the right parlor. I shot a glance at my phone and darted up the stairs, and found Jamie seated on the top step.

"How are we doing?" I asked.

She jerked a shoulder up, but she seemed quiet, not like her usual over-the-top self. "No complaints." She smoothed a hand down her dress, the same one she'd worn almost a year ago for Grace's wedding. Again, I didn't understand anything about these dresses, but I knew better than to get involved. "Grace is in there with her. Audrey went to find some coconut water. She thinks Emme's dehydrated. Apparently, that's the best remedy." Jamie motioned to her cheeks. "She's a little flushed, but it's probably just the heat getting to her."

I swallowed a laugh at that. I didn't think it was the heat.

"What about you?" I cocked my head and peered at Jamie. She really didn't seem like herself today. Over the past year, I'd come to know Emme's friends well. They were extended family to me now. And I knew something was off with Jamie. "Are you doing okay?"

She bobbed her head as she pushed to her feet. "Just tired. I went hard last night."

I studied her as she smoothed her dark hair over her ears. I would've accepted this explanation if not for the fact I knew Jamie had spent the evening dancing with the little kids and sipping club soda with my sister Chloe, who was a few months pregnant and having a tough time of it.

"You want a few minutes with the missus?" she asked, pointing toward the bridal suite.

"More than anything."

She dropped her hand to the doorknob. "Whatever you do, don't wrinkle the dress."

I slipped my hands into my pockets. "I'll try."

Jamie opened the door a crack, saying, "Mistress Terror? We need you for a moment."

When Grace came into the hall, she gave me an unimpressed up-and-down glance. "We're not steaming that dress again. No wrinkles."

"I've already explained the rules," Jamie said.

"I'm giving you ten minutes," Grace said. "Not a second more."

"You run a tight ship," I called as she and Jamie descended the stairs.

I found my wife gazing out the wide bay windows overlooking the gardens and the cove, her hands on her hips. She wore a pale yellow gown with a full skirt that came outfitted with pockets, which seemed to be a very big deal. I was told it was also perfect for twirling.

To me, it was perfect because it was Emme. She could be in one of the oversized hoodies she wore to death and I'd be happy. I didn't want for much. Not when I had my wife.

"I don't need any coconut water," Emme snapped. With her back to me, she thought I was Grace. "I love you all so much, but I really just need a minute alone."

"Can I be alone with you?"

She whirled around, her eyes blazing. "I don't like this."

It took everything inside me to calmly shrug out of my jacket and drape it on a chair before strolling across the room. "Really? Because I'm having a lot of fun."

"You've been having fun for hours and I've—I've—" She wagged her fists at me, her teeth clenched and eyes shimmering with need. "I've been *dying*. This isn't fair and it's not very nice." She stabbed a finger toward the window, pointing to the ceremony area below. "I can't walk down the aisle like this."

"Then isn't it a good thing I'm here to take care of you?" Her gaze burned into me and I had to bite back a laugh. Perhaps I'd taken this a little too far. I cast a quick glance around the room and settled on a small, ornate sofa. "I'm going to be very nice to you now."

I helped her perch on the edge of the sofa, the skirt fanned out around her and over the back to minimize the wrinkles. As I dropped to my knees, she gave me a pouty face that made me want to devour her.

"Everyone keeps asking if I'm nervous because my face is red and I'm *sweating*." She crossed her arms over her chest and arched a brow. "Or better yet, they ask if I'm pregnant."

I brought my hands to her knees, my fingertips gliding over the smooth skin of her inner thighs. "What did you tell them, my love?"

"That I'm not pregnant, of course," she cried. "But it's not like I can tell them my husband left a remote-controlled vibrator inside me this morning and that he's been torturing me with it ever since."

I pushed her thighs apart and found myself staring at a completely soaked pair of lacy blue panties. I could *hear* the toy buzzing inside her and feel the pull of her leg muscles against my palm. And the scent of her arousal, my god.

"You said you needed a distraction." I edged the panties down and folded them into a crisp square. "I gave you a distraction."

"And it's almost killed me." Her eyes widened as I tucked her panties into my front pocket.

"You're not using my underwear as a pocket square."

"But I am," I said, rolling up my cuffs. I brushed my knuckles down her swollen seam. She hissed out a violent curse that made me chuckle. "It's my something borrowed. And blue." I leaned in and gave the toy's cord a gentle tug that sent her hips bowing off the sofa. "Quiet, wife. I'm busy here."

"Be quick about it," she said, gasping when my tongue met her clit. "I might actually die if you don't—"

Those were the last coherent words she spoke for several minutes.

Since there was no time for teasing, I sucked her clit hard and kept the pressure right there. She was unbelievably wet and every inch of her pulsed with aching need. The way she lifted her hips and strained toward me, it was like she was feeding me her sweet cunt and the thought alone was enough to turn me to hot, throbbing stone.

When I groaned into her, she said, "Do not come in your pants. No time to change."

I grabbed the cord, pushing the toy a little deeper and then pulling it back to watch her stretch around it. "I have an extra tux in the barn."

"Wha-why?"

"Because I come prepared now," I said, circling my tongue around her clit again.

"I love you," she whispered, dropping her head against the sofa's back. "I really fucking love you."

I was too busy between her legs to respond and I didn't have to. Emme knew.

She loosed a broken, gasping cry and her legs started shaking. Her whole body bucked against me and I had to bring both hands to her backside to hold her steady. She twisted her fingers in my hair as she pulsed and shattered under my tongue, her moans and cries rough, almost primal.

I pulled at the cord again, slowly drawing the egg-shaped toy out and slipping it into the black satin pouch I'd kept in my pocket as she panted. "Get up here." She beckoned to me with her eyes closed and her breath coming hard.

As I stood, she immediately pawed at my trousers, unlatching my belt, yanking at the zip, and pushing my clothes down until my cock sprang free. There wasn't even a second before her mouth was on me.

"Fuck, Em, slow down."

I cupped her jaw, my thumb stroking her cheek as she sucked me. But she didn't slow down. She went on working me hard and I just didn't have it in me to hold off.

"Baby," I gasped, my hands flexing. I couldn't mess up her hair or makeup. "I'm close."

She nodded, taking me all the way to the back of her throat and holding me there with her hands on my ass. I lasted about fifteen seconds and I was proud to admit it. My wife was *amazing*. Nothing she couldn't do.

"Really fucking love you too," I choked out as she pulled away. I skimmed a thumb over her plump lips. "Want to marry me?"

She faked a cringe. "Again?"

"They say practice makes perfect," I said as I straightened my clothes.

"I don't know." She lifted her smooth, bare shoulders and let them drop. "The past year's been pretty good."

I smiled at her. It'd been a *great* year. I had my beautiful wife, another championship win, and our soccer clubs were in development. There was much more work to be done on getting those clubs operational, at least a year or two, but it was all coming together. We'd decided to locate our flagship teams here in Rhode Island and we were talking about making Friendship home after I retired from the League. We hadn't finalized anything yet but this place and these people had grown on me. "Let's make the next one even better."

An urgent knock sounded at the door. "Time's up, you two."

"Not yet," Emme hollered.

"I'm afraid so," Grace called back. "The photographer's ready for you and I'm guessing we're going to need to touch-up your face. Probably the dress too."

Emme pushed to her feet and stepped into my arms. She ran a

finger over the lace peeking out of my pocket. "You can't keep my underwear."

"Why not?"

"Someone will notice," she whisper-shrieked.

"Every pair of eyes in this place will be on you," I said. "No one's gonna pay attention to this little souvenir."

Another knock. "Save it for the honeymoon."

"One more minute," my sweet, delicate wife bellowed. She held out her hand. "Will you come with me?"

I laced our fingers together. "Always."

---

*Thank you for reading! I hope you loved Emme and Ryan! If you're not ready to let go yet and need a little more from these two, get the bonus chapter here! (*https://geni.us/IAREE)

If you want more from Audrey, Jamie, and a few other of our favorite friends, join my mailing list
*(*https://geni.us/officememos)

also by kate canterbary

Friendship, RI

In a Jam — Shay and Noah

In a Rush — Emme and Ryan

Shucked — Sunny and Beckett

The Good Girl's Guide to Crashing Weddings

Change of Heart — Whitney and Henry

Vital Signs

Before Girl — Cal and Stella

The Worst Guy — Sebastian Stremmel and Sara Shapiro

The Walsh Series

Underneath It All – Matt and Lauren

The Space Between – Patrick and Andy

Necessary Restorations – Sam and Tiel

The Cornerstone – Shannon and Will

Restored — Sam and Tiel

The Spire — Erin and Nick

Preservation — Riley and Alexandra

Thresholds — The Walsh Family

Foundations — Matt and Lauren

The Santillian Triplets

The Magnolia Chronicles — Magnolia

Boss in the Bedsheets — Ash and Zelda

The Belle and the Beard — Linden and Jasper-Anne

Talbott's Cove

Fresh Catch — Owen and Cole

Hard Pressed — Jackson and Annette

Far Cry — Brooke and JJ

Rough Sketch — Gus and Neera

Benchmarks Series

Professional Development — Drew and Tara

Orientation — Jory and Max

Brothers In Arms

Missing In Action — Wes and Tom

Coastal Elite — Jordan and April

Get exclusive sneak previews of upcoming releases through Kate's newsletter and private reader group, The Canterbary Tales, on Facebook.

about kate

USA Today Bestseller Kate Canterbary writes smart, steamy contemporary romances loaded with heat, heart, and happy ever afters. Kate lives on the New England coast with her husband and daughter.

You can find Kate at www.katecanterbary.com

- facebook.com/kcanterbary
- instagram.com/katecanterbary
- amazon.com/Kate-Canterbary
- bookbub.com/authors/kate-canterbary
- goodreads.com/Kate_Canterbary
- pinterest.com/katecanterbary
- tiktok.com/@katecanterbary